D1458462

RANDALL AND THE RIVER OF TIME

RANDALL AND THE RIVER OF TIME

By

C. S. FORESTER

THE BOOK CLUB
121 CHARING CROSS ROAD
LONDON, W.C.2

MADE AND PRINTED IN GREAT BRITAIN BY
MORRISON AND GIBB LIMITED, LONDON AND EDINBURGH

ONE

RANDALL WAS ASLEEP on his chicken-wire bed in the company headquarters dugout. He was sleeping dreamlessly and without any jerky movements, for he was young and had not as yet been worn down by war. In sleep he could forget his peril and his fatigue, live unconscious through some hours of his stay in the line, so that when he should awake he would be by that much nearer to the time of his relief. Compared with hundreds of thousands of men in the line he was at this moment supremely fortunate; sleep was more to be desired than gold or diamonds, for its own sake as well as for the oblivion it brought, because in the line it was never possible to sleep enough, and as the days wore by men were more and more beset by lack of sleep, growing more harassed and more weary, yearning for uninterrupted rest as a man cast away in an open boat might yearn for a drink of water. Randall had been on duty until midnight, and now he was permitted to sleep until an hour before dawn. The shell-bursts were far enough away to make the earth of the dugout tremble only faintly; the machine-gun fire was hardly audible, so that he could lie there and renew himself in his nineteen-year-old innocence.

An invisible river was bearing him along, an immense flow of events to which he hardly gave a thought even when awake; the microscopic life carried in a river does not think about being swept along by the water around it. But rivers do not run at the same speed all the way from source to mouth; there are long tranquil reaches where the current is hardly perceptible, and yet, inevitably, the river reaches a cataract and tumbles wildly down the slope, roaring against the rocks, and whirling in apparently unpredictable eddies. In August 1914 the river had tumbled over just such a cataract, and now in August 1917 Randall was being dashed down it, conscious of the insane confusion about him, conscious of the quickened current, yet far more acutely aware of the tiny minor eddies in which he himself was involved; in which he was whirled about, eddies which meant life or death, danger or discomfort, or momentary tranquillity. All mankind was hurtling over that cataract, hundreds of millions of struggling protozoa, distributed all across the stream, some flung with the foam against the rocks, some hurried on in quieter, deeper channels. Randall was one single protozoon among those hundreds of millions; the river might continue in its tumultuous course until it emerged again into a placid pool, but whether Randall was still with it would depend on the coincidences of the individual course along which he was being directed.

The orderly woke him and the blessed unconsciousness came to an end. Randall struggled up, breathing the foul air of the dugout; even before he was fully conscious he was automatically checking the items of his equipment: revolver, helmet, gasmask, notebook. The other subaltern off duty up to now appeared in the gloomy candlelit shadows —Cross, his name was. Among the other shadows the shadow of the chinstrap of his helmet gave a queer distortion to his face, and his scrubby little black moustache made him slightly comic. He made a sound which might possibly have been interpreted as ' Good morning ', and Randall echoed it no more understandably. This was no time for frivolity.

" Captain's at post 12, sir," said the orderly, putting the mugs of tea on the table. " 'E went out 'alf an hour ago."

Nobody answered him. Cross picked up his mug of tea and drank from it noisily. They had to sip slowly, as the liquid was steaming hot—marvellously grateful at that hour, after that night. It was strong, it was thick with condensed milk and sugar, and its heat was in pleasant contrast to the feel of Randall's damp clothes against his body. Cross held his wrist-watch in the light of the candle.

" My God ! " he said, and slammed down his mug on the table and started for the dugout steps.

Randall followed him; it was black night outside still, raining heavily, and after the stuffy dugout the air struck chill. It was the gloomiest moment of the day, this period just before stand-to. Cross growled something unintelligible again and started off along the trench to the right, the duck-boards sloshing under his feet. Randall was mildly piqued. He was senior to Cross; in fact at the moment, with one officer away on a course and another recently a casualty, he was second in command of the company. Cross might have shown him a little deference, might even have waited to hear which way he intended to go. The headquarters dugout was beside the junction of three communication trenches, and Cross had gone off along the trench that led to No. 11 post, and only to there. Battalion orders laid it down that at stand-to an officer should be on duty at No. 11; company orders did not name the officer, and it was Randall's responsibility as second in command to see, in the absence of the captain, that there was an officer at the post, allotting for the duty any one of the officers available. This morning the choice lay only between Cross and himself, and he might well have chosen to go there, sending Cross to No. 9. No. 11 was desirable, because the communication trench that led there was dry and easy and because it was out of the usual route of inspecting officers. Cross always had his eye on No. 11, and this morning he could easily plead that he was justified in taking it for granted that he would be detailed to No. 11 as the only officer available besides the second in command. It was just like Cross to take advantage of a loophole like that, and Randall, standing at the junction and hearing Cross's footsteps dying away, toyed for an instant with the notion of calling him back and saying what he thought of such behaviour, but he was easygoing enough to let it pass. Cross might as well go up into the comfortable isolation of No. 11, since he wanted to so badly; Randall philosophically set himself to pick his way along to No. 9.

It was still dark, and the rain was falling briskly. A duck-board reared up under his foot so that he slipped into the detestable mud; he recovered himself with a curse and stumbled on to identify himself when challenged as he entered the bay. And then it happened—the appalling noise, the vivid flashes, shouts in the darkness, the sharp crashing explosions of grenades—subsequent ones muffled, indicating that bombs were going off after being pitched into a dugout. Rifle shots; machine-guns raving; flares going up all along the line. It was only a matter of seconds before the artillery caught the alarm as the gunners ran to their guns; up and down the line could be heard the din as if a thousand doors were being slammed, and shells were flying overhead and bursting in volcanoes of mud. The Germans had raided No. 11 post. That much was evident instantly. No one could tell at the moment whether it was the beginning of a general attack or not, which was why the flares were going up, and why nervous machine-gunners were traversing their fire back and forth along the line. Before the question could be decided Randall and the company commander were gathering men for a counter-attack, Randall shaking off his sleepy stupidity as he listened to his captain's orders bellowed through the din; his heart was pounding with excitement as he looked round him in the light of the flares at the mud-daubed men crowding into the bay. Then he started off down the trench, revolver in hand, bayonet man and bomber preceding him, back to the junction, up the other communication trench. The din was still going on up and down the line, shaking the earth, but ahead of them, as they went round one traverse and another, there was silence. Not silence round the next bend; groans. Dead men and wounded men, lying in the bottom of the trench, and fainter groans, a chorus of faint groans, coming up from the mouth of the dugout beyond. A flare which went up near enough to light their path—paler than usual in the growing light—showed them a dead German lying with his face on the firing step, and the raindrops glistened in the flare as they fell. There were only dead and wounded in the post; the garrison had been wiped out.

It had been a well-planned raid. Randall, standing on the firing step and peering through a muddy periscope, could see the path which had been cut through the wire, and with his mind's eye could see the attack in the darkness —the stealthy approach, the cutting of the wire under cover of the rain, the final crawl through the mud, and then the rush, the scaling of the parapet, the bombs hurled from traverse to traverse, the bombs flung into the dugout, the seizure of half a dozen dazed prisoners, and the instant retreat, all neatly carried out in that hour before stand-to when vitality is at its lowest and the senses least alert. Randall had taken part in more than one such raid himself. Jerry knew his business, he told himself, as he busied himself with sending back a runner with the news, and posting fresh sentries, and then seeing what could be done for the wounded.

There was enough light now to see clearly, while the rain still fell remorselessly, and with the coming of light men's fears were stilled so that the firing along the line died away. And there was light, too, to see Cross, lying diagonally across the trench with his arms spread out and his head propped up against the revetment. The position meant that his helmet was rakishly tilted awry; there was abandon in the spread of his arms, as if Cross had been frozen in an attitude of drunken mirth; the idea of drunken merriment was accentuated by the gleam of Cross's teeth. But the teeth were in the side of Cross's face, where his cheek had been torn away, making a large mouth that caused his real mouth to look ridiculously small and out of place, especially with the ridiculous little bristling moustache on the upper lip. Cross's trench coat was dark with mud and rain, but it was darker still in patches over the thighs and belly where the blood had poured from his wounds.

So Cross was dead; he had to be buried, his possessions packed up and a letter written to his mother. But it might not have been Temporary Second Lieutenant Albert Cross's name which appeared in the casualty list. It might have been Temporary First Lieutenant Charles Randall's. It might easily have been, as Randall well understood. The result of a dozen chances had sent Cross up to No. 11 post and to sudden death. Randall had the resilience and the carelessness of youth. It was a long time before the incident, and a hundred, a thousand other incidents began to show evident effect. But in time he began to wonder what would be the result of anything he decided to do, before he did it—that was the point, he began to worry before he did it. Before he turned to the right or to the left there was a moment of wondering whether he should be killed if he made the wrong choice. In certain situations there was some element of calculation in such wonderings; when in a dugout making up his mind whether he should go out to the latrine now or later he could make a guess as to the possibility of a sudden German strafe, and as to the moment for such a strafe, but there were also times when he would debate about changing his shirt or his boots—there were pros and cons, but none of them connected with German shells and bullets. And once or twice there were times when he had to force himself to decide which puttee to put on first, when he had to bully himself into admitting that whether he put on the right before the left or the left before the right it would not affect the aim of a German artilleryman three miles away.

TWO

HE CAME HOME ON LEAVE, arriving in the darkened station along with a thousand other battle-worn young men who in happier times might have been coming home from the university on vacation or returning from a Bank Holiday outing to the seaside. But those were men who had seen dead men lying in the battlefield by the hundred, by the thousand; they were soldiers who had gone for days and weeks in the most imminent deadly peril when their comfortable fathers in all their lives had known nothing more dangerous than a slippery pavement. The surprising thing was not that the soldiers were different creatures from their fathers, but that they were so little different.

There were no taxis available at the station by the time Randall had made his way to the cab rank from the leave train. That was not surprising, nor did it unduly annoy him. In the station in life in which he had been born there was no tradition of making use of taxis—until he had received His Majesty's commission they were awesome, expensive things, to be engaged only in some extreme emergency and then to be sat in uncomfortably, watching the twopences click up on the clock, and even now the thought of using a taxi was so alien to him that there was no particular hardship about having to carry his baggage out of the station and look for a tram or a bus to take him home. He had been a school-boy until he had become a soldier, and until then it was one of the rarest of treats to travel up to London north of the river from the South London suburb in which he lived; this afternoon, as he climbed on to the tram which would take him back there, there was still some of the thrill of those days, mingling oddly but pleasantly with the pleasure of being on leave, out of danger, away from the sleeplessness and the discomfort and the inflexibility of discipline.

He was looking forward to seeing his mother and his father, and Jimmy and Harriet and Doris, his brother and his sisters. With a bubbling feeling of excitement he went up the iron steps of the tram along with the rest of the people who had been waiting for it. By the time he reached the upper deck there was at least one person in every seat, so that he sat carelessly down beside a woman in the third seat from the rear on the left. He was going home, to the familiar Harbord Road, where to the unsympathetic eye every house looked like every other house but where a child could see such great and inexplicable differences. Harbord Road, between Medford Road and Bushy Park Road—he knew every flagstone there, and he yearned to see it all again, to comfort his eyes with its familiar details. His anticipation was so keen and so pleasant that he paid no attention to the woman beside whom he sat; he might have some vague thoughts about women at the back of his mind, but until he should be home they had no chance of asserting themselves.

But the woman was fully conscious that there was a man beside her. She braced herself a little more tensely than she would have done if it had been a woman who had come to share the seat; she looked sideways at him with a different kind of curiosity than she would have displayed towards a woman. The shoulder-flash on the sleeve of Randall's tunic, marking his division, caught her attention, and she looked at it twice before turning to him.

" My husband's in your division in France," she said.

" Really ? " said Randall politely.

But he stirred uneasily in his seat. To speak to a stranger was uncomfortable; to speak to a strange woman was doubly so. And he had been warned so often about discussing military affairs with unauthorised persons. This might be one of those cunning German spies he had heard about.

" He's in the Kenningtons," went on the woman. " He's a captain now. Are you on leave ? "

" Yes," said Randall. With his kit resting on the floor between his feet, and with his generally grubby appearance, he felt he could not be revealing any military secrets. " Just got in."

" That's fine," said the woman. " Didn't your wife come to meet you ? The leave train must have been late."

" Yes, it was," said Randall. It had never crossed his mind that he might have a wife, and it may have been surprise at the suggestion that made him volunteer the next statement. " I'm going home."

" To your mother and father ? "

" Yes," said Randall; that was what he had meant to imply by the word ' home '.

The tram was lurching along the twilit streets, and on this upper deck the air was thick with tobacco smoke. The conductress was pushing her way between the seats, piping out: " Fares, please. All fares, please." Randall felt in his pocket for the English money he had obtained at Folkestone in exchange for French notes; the woman reached across him and slid some coppers into the conductress's hand, and it was only after she had done so that Randall realised he was relieved of the trouble of guessing whether he should offer to pay her fare.

" Lower Oak station," she said, and accepted the ticket that the conductress punched.

Randall offered a shilling and asked for Upper Oak Library.

" You don't live far from me," said the woman, watching.

" A penny fare," replied Randall.

This was happiness, this was reality again, to sit on the upper deck of a lurching tram buying a ticket to Upper Oak Library. What he had come from was not reality— taking out a wiring party on a dark night, hearing the cry of ' stretcher bearers ! ' being passed down the trench, crouching amid the horrors of a bombardment, waiting dry-mouthed to go over the top. That was a nightmare, unavoidable as any nightmare. But to feel again under his boot soles the iron ridges of a tramcar deck, to ask for a ticket, visualising as he did so the corner of Medford Road where he would get down to walk the hundred yards along to Harbord Road, the gas-lit tea table with the bread and butter and jam, his mother at one end and father at the other; this was life. His happiness and his excitement neutralised his fatigue.

" I live just beyond the Fire Station," said the woman. " Calmady Road—do you know it ? "

" Yes," said Randall. Calmady Road had a sudden dip in it which he could remember times without number shooting down into and out of on his bicycle, before emerging on to the main road at the Fire Station. It was comforting to think about; he stretched his legs and relaxed.

" Vauxhall already," announced the woman, looking out through the window, and then, apropos of nothing, " What

about the Kenningtons ? My husband's regiment. Do you
see anything of them in France ? "

" A little," said Randall. The Kenningtons were in another
brigade, but his own battalion had relieved them on more
than one occasion. " What's your husband's name ? "

" Speake," said the woman, " Captain Henry Speake. I'm
Muriel Speake."

" I don't remember him," said Randall.

" He was adjutant for a time, but now he's commanding
a company. It's—oh, it must be six months since he was
home on leave last. This your first leave ? "

" Second," said Randall. He had been fortunate in the
matter of leave.

" You don't look very old," commented Mrs. Speake.

" I'm nineteen."

" Joined up straight from school ? "

" Yes."

" My husband's thirty. He was in the Terriers before
the war. He worked in a bank—we got married as soon as
the war started. We were going to soon, anyway. I'm working
in the bank myself now. Carrying on. Harry—that's my
husband—says everyone should do their bit."

Randall vaguely—for he had never spent much time in
analysis of the subject—divided the female sex into categories.
Leaving out of consideration those who might as well be
neuters as far as he was concerned—girls behind counters,
tram-conductresses, and so on—the remainder fell into three,
or perhaps four, age groups. One was composed of kids,
younger than himself, his sisters' friends, nuisances, unin-
teresting; one group was composed of girls, in the neighbour-
hood of his own age, to whom he felt drawn, although when
he was with them he never thought of them in connection
with the stories told about women by his young brother
officers; and the third group was composed of women,
which meant everyone more than a year or so older than
himself, adults—maybe he did not actually describe them to
himself as ' grown-ups ' but he might well have done—who
had entered into the world and dealt familiarly with problems
of house purchase and earning a living and managing a family
and all the other mysteries with which he was unacquainted.
Mrs. Speake was one of this group, of which the typical

representative was his mother; every woman on earth from
twenty-three to seventy (with the possible exception of the
oldest ones, who might be included in a fourth category as
' old ladies ') was one of this group. They might be agreeable
or disagreeable, somewhat older or somewhat younger than
the average, dark or fair or grey, but they were only women.
Mrs. Speake, married, with a husband of thirty, and presumably almost the same age herself, was no more to him
than any of the others, which meant nothing, sexually; and
' sexually ' was not a word which readily occurred to Randall,
in any case.

"Have you lived in Upper Oak long ? " asked Mrs. Speake.

"All my life," said Randall, smiling in happy reminiscence.

That was his ' life '; his service as a soldier, with its dangers
and its compulsory close contacts with the world, was not
living, but a nightmare to be endured. The memories of
boyhood, even of childhood, were more important.

"It's a nice district," said Mrs. Speake. "I wouldn't live
in Bayswater or anywhere like that, not for anything."

There is a bond of sympathy between all those who live
in London south of the Thames; everyone there disclaims
all desire to live north of it. Randall was conscious of the
bond. Before he joined the army his visits to London north
of the river had been few—pantomimes and theatres, and not
many of either; and some visits to the Science Museum in
South Kensington. He had no affection at all for the almost
unexplored areas of the West End.

"Neither would I," he said stoutly.

"Our shops are just as good," said Mrs. Speake. "Not
that there's anything worth having in any of the shops now.
You ought to see the prices ! "

"So I hear," replied Randall.

His mother wrote to him regularly while he was in France,
snatching time with difficulty from her never-ending domestic
labours, and she could only write about her own little world
because she saw no other.

"But I mustn't talk to you about our troubles here," said
Mrs. Speake, "not after what you've been through."

She smiled at him with understanding, and Randall began
to warm towards her. It was a grievance with soldiers in
France that when they emerged for a moment from their

unspeakable hell they were greeted with stories of the hard-
ships of having to stand in queues for potatoes and of having
to go short of margarine. Randall himself, thanks to his
mother's letters, could understand the mental attitude that
made this possible, and he knew, too, that no civilian could
even imagine the horrors of the Salient; but it was pleasant
to meet someone and not have to make allowances for her
lack of sympathy.

" But I was saying about living in Upper Oak," went on
Mrs. Speake. " You went to the school, I suppose ? "

" Yes. My father is a master there."

" Oh, really ? What's your name, may I ask ? "

" Randall."

" Oh, of course I've heard of your father."

That was not quite so tactful, at first sight. A boy whose
father had been known to generations of schoolboys as
'Toffee Randall' was likely to be sensitive about it, even
though his father was distinguished by no remarkable
eccentricity, despite the nickname which clung to him. Mrs.
Speake had enough perspicacity to realise this; maybe she
saw the change of expression in Randall's face.

" I've a lot of friends who went to the school," she said.
" George Pocock, Bunny James—no, you wouldn't know
them, of course, they're before your time. Bunny was
wounded—he's in hospital somewhere in the west of England.
But I can remember their speaking about your father.
But I can't remember anything particular that they said."

That was better, to have a father about whom nothing
particular was said. And it was possible that Mrs. Speake
knew it to be better.

" Camberwell Green," she said, looking out of the window
again and changing the subject. " You'll soon be home now."

She settled herself back in her seat, making the faintest of
contacts with him by doing so. Randall was not actively
aware of the slight warmth that was being transferred from
her to him, but it worked on him without his knowing it.
He was relaxed enough and free enough from excitement
now for his fatigue to assert itself. He could not fight down
the yawn that overmastered him.

" You poor child," said Mrs. Speake. " You're tired."

Her sympathy was quite genuine.

" Only sleepy," said Randall stoutly.

" You'll be able to sleep as much as you want to on this leave. But I expect you'll be out enjoying yourself every evening. Is that what you want to do ? "

" Not exactly," said Randall.

He might go out with his father and mother up West. If Harriet were any more grown up he might even take her out. But he was really looking forward to mere freedom, to the old life, to little brick houses with slate roofs and iron garden railings.

" You just want to feel human again ? " asked Mrs. Speake.

" That's exactly right," said Randall, in pleased surprise at having his wishes neatly defined and not knowing that Mrs. Speake was quoting what her husband had said on his last leave.

" I understand," said Mrs. Speake, smiling into his eyes the way his mother did.

The genuine emotion she felt towards this boy helped her to understand, or at least to convince herself that she did. There was an actual feeling of unity between them as they sat side by side while the tram ground up the hill and Randall yawned without concealment in his fatigue.

" We're over the hill now," said Mrs. Speake suddenly. " Why don't you get out with me at the station ? If you cut along the path at the end of Calmady Road you'll come out on Bushey Park Road just near where you live. Or is your kit too heavy for that ? "

" Not a bit too heavy," said Randall.

He was nineteen and as hard as nails; even when sleepy a half-mile walk with a heavy bag meant nothing to him, literally. And—as a glance at his wrist-watch informed him —he would be too late for tea. And he would like a few minutes more of this woman's company.

" Here we are, then," said Mrs. Speake.

Randall picked up his bag and clattered down the iron-ribbed stairs. Five or six people were leaving the tram here and he waited for them to dismount before he stepped down and stood by the step as his mother had taught him, to put his hand under Mrs. Speake's elbow as she stepped lightly down beside him. Here was Calmady Road, just as he remembered it, even in the faint gas-light; the half-dozen people who had arrived in the tram had already scattered, and they were alone as they walked along.

" It's only a little house that I have," said Mrs. Speake. " Generally my mother-in-law lives with me, but she's away at present. Those last air raids were too much for her. Hope we don't have one while you're home on leave."

She put her hand protectively on his arm as she spoke.

" Cross over here," she added. " It's just over beyond the next lamp."

It was at the crest above the dip in the road; it was just at the point where he could cease pedalling his bicycle, knowing that his momentum would carry him down, up the other side, and all the way out to the main road without further pedalling. He must have passed this gate hundreds of times.

" I'd like to offer you a cup of tea," said Mrs. Speake, opening the gate and walking up to the darkened house without offering to say good-bye, so that Randall, after a moment's doubt, had to walk up with her. " But I expect you'd like something stronger, and I haven't got anything in. Only tea, and I was going to have a cup myself. But I don't expect you'd like that."

She had put her key in the door as they stood in the dark porch, and now the door was open. Randall wanted his tea ; despite a year's service as an infantry officer he had not yet acquired a taste for spirits. Mrs. Speake had worded her last sentences so that it would appear, if he left her now, that he was doing so because of the meagre hospitality she was offering him, and that would be churlish. There were many reasons why he should leave her now and go home. He wanted to see his family. It was certainly six o'clock by now and they had been expecting him all day if his telegram had been delivered. And there was something not quite respectable about being alone in a house with a woman, even a married woman as old as Mrs. Speake. But only not quite respectable ; that was hardly a factor that mattered and not nearly as important as the danger of allowing Mrs. Speake to think that he was leaving (if he did leave) just because she had no whisky to offer him. And he really did not want to part from her yet. All these factors except the last influenced Randall to his knowledge, in that single second as he stood on the doorstep with the dark hall open before him. He was not consciously aware of the last factor, which was the most important.

"I have to shut the door before I turn the light on," said Mrs. Speake. "The police are very strict nowadays."

Randall stepped into the hall, felt a fibre mat under his feet, heard the door shut behind him, and then the light suddenly came on and she stood there smiling warmly at him while he blinked at her. This house was newer than his own home, for it had electric light instead of gas. Of course he could remember when this row was built, not so long before the war.

"You can put your bag down there," said Mrs. Speake, "and come in here."

A little conventional sitting-room was revealed as she opened a door and switched on the light.

"You can sit down here while I put the kettle on. I'll make the tea in a jiffy. The lav's upstairs—I expect you can find it."

That was a somewhat unconventional thing to say; it was not at all usual for someone to volunteer information about lavatories to someone of the opposite sex—such information could be given if necessary, but even then with a certain amount of constriction. But Mrs. Speake said it so lightly, and whisked away so quickly after saying it that this time constriction was not at all apparent. Randall was left standing in the sitting-room. A silver frame held a photograph of an officer in uniform; the regimental badge and three stars told him that this was the husband. Nothing remarkable about him—a rather heavy jaw and the eternal clipped moustache, and possibly a hint of melancholy in the eyes. An officer like a hundred thousand other officers, going through the same horrors, with as precarious a hold upon life; in a year of active service Randall had already seen many officers come and go, and have their place in the mess for a few days or weeks and then be carried off by wounds or death. They were fleeting wraiths who drifted into and out of the battalion without making any substantial contact with it. This man in the silver frame was not one of these wraiths, all the same. He was a pre-war Territorial, who must have survived the Somme, and Loos before that, and Ypres and countless periods in the line besides these. But veteran officers were as vulnerable to shell fragments or machine-gun bullets as were newcomers. This captain had lived this long because death had not yet needed him—some of Randall's thinking was coloured by the dark superstition, noticeable in many soldiers after three years of slaughter, that the war would go on until every fighting man was dead and rotting in the slime. Randall looked at the captain's photograph with a vague sense of brotherhood; infantry men who had served long in France were sharers of a deep secret, initiates into dark mysteries that the rest of the world knew nothing about.

From the kitchen came a cheerful clattering of crockery and a cheerful voice.

" Do you take sugar, Mr. Randall ? "

" Yes," said Randall, " I'm afraid I do."

He went out into the hall to the kitchen.

" I've brought some sugar with me," he said " I'll get it out. I brought it for my mother, but there's lots to spare."

Mrs. Speake was moving quickly and efficiently round the kitchen.

" Thank you. That's very kind of you," she said. " You needn't worry, though. I've got plenty—don't use it myself."

Randall stood on the threshold of the kitchen looking in at her.

" Let's have tea out here," she said. " It'll save carrying it in."

" Whatever you like, of course," said Randall.

Mrs. Speake laid a neat cloth on the scrubbed deal table.

" Only a minute now, Mr. Randall," she said, and then " It's silly to call you Mr. Randall like this, isn't it ? What's your other name ? "

" Charles."

" Charles, and not Charlie ? "

" That's right."

Mrs. Speake was clairvoyant, it seemed—she knew without being told that Randall disliked being called ' Charlie '.

" Do you mind if I call you Charles ? "

" Of course not."

" My name's Muriel—I told you that in the tram."

" Yes," said Randall.

It seemed unlikely to him that he would ever call an older woman Muriel, all the same.

Mrs. Speake turned out the gas under the kettle and poured the water into the teapot.

" There," she said. " Now we're ready."

Before she picked up the pot she turned and looked at him, her eyes meeting his eyes, her shoulders braced back a little, her bosom thrust forward a little, a smile on her lips. But Randall made no move towards her—it did not even dawn upon him that he might do so—and she took up the teapot and turned towards the table. Randall held her chair for her as she sat down, and took the other chair.

" Not much for tea nowadays," said Mrs. Speake.

But there was bread and butter, and a glass dish of jam, and a jar of potted meat, and two-thirds of a cake.

" It's very nice," said Randall.

" It's very nice for me," said Mrs. Speake. " I was going to have a lonely tea to-day. I was hoping one of the girls at the bank would come out with me to-day, but they were all busy. Saturday night, of course."

" Oh yes, it's Saturday," said Randall.

He had come from a world where the war went on even on Saturday afternoons, and the confusion of his journey had left him vague about the day of the week. He was eating bread and jam with the lusty appetite of a young soldier of nineteen whose meals for the last twenty-four hours had been decidedly irregular.

" Is your family expecting you ? "

" Oh yes, I sent them a telegram from Folkestone. We were late getting in and then the train didn't start at once. But they won't worry as they know I'm in England."

" Any brothers or sisters ? "

" Yes. Two sisters and a brother."

" That's quite a family," said Mrs. Speake.

Whatever her motives in asking this young man in to have tea with her (and they defy analysis) she was aware by now that Randall's feelings in the matter were similar at present to what his feelings would be if he were having tea with a nice and not too elderly aunt. But she still smiled, and she poured his cups of tea as he drank with thirst, and she made no attempt to direct the conversation along more intimate lines; she may have realised that any such attempt would be unavailing. She found a yellow packet of cigarettes and pushed them across to him.

" I'd better smoke my own," said Randall, taking out the big flat case from his breast pocket. He was sensitive about civilian feelings regarding shortages.

Mrs. Speake pulled on her cigarette, looking closely at him, her elbows on the table.

" You don't mind women smoking ? " she said.

It was still possible to ask that question despite the spread of the habit among women during recent years.

" Of course not," said Randall.

He was self-contained and introverted, and it never occurred to him to worry about what the rest of the world did as long as it had no bearing on his own fate. But he was a little flattered at having his possible prejudices consulted, and he showed it in his smile. He had a pretty mouth, Mrs. Speake thought— not girlish, but appealing, firm enough and yet sweet. She shifted her elbow on the table and moved her forearm so that her left hand as it lay there was easily within his reach. Randall drew on his cigarette. He was pleasantly full of tea, pleasantly sleepy, and yet not mortally fatigued. There lingered with him the flattering feeling of occupying the centre of the stage. Mrs. Speake put out her cigarette in the ashtray; she had smoked it fast and conversation was not flowing freely now. The fingers of her hand on the table drummed for a moment.

" Well ? " she said, her eyebrows raised in the faintest of inquiries.

Randall was aware that the question was being asked as to what should be done next, but his modesty and inexperience directed his thoughts along the wrong lines.

" Let me help you wash these things up," he said, rising from the table. He was making it clear that although he was home on leave, a first lieutenant, whose prejudices had just been consulted, he was aware that in this changing world it was possible for him to do domestic, women's work.

" Goodness me, no," said Mrs. Speake, rising from the table while Randall, of course, rose with her.

He was in a peaceful little eddy of the great river at the moment. A floating fragment circling in an eddy may come out at some point of the circumference and be hurried down the rapids, to emerge in the pool below at a point quite different, and having followed a course quite different, from what would be the case if it emerged from the eddy at another place only an inch or two away. The whole subsequent course of that fragment may be profoundly affected by that small difference—by what appears to be the mere chance that dictates where it shall escape from the eddy. Naturally it is not mere chance. A mind possessed of enough knowledge and calculating ability could predict where the fragment would emerge from the eddy at the moment it entered. In the same way it was not mere chance that dictated Randall's future. That future hinged on whether, as he rose from the table, he should take Mrs. Speake in his arms or not, and that, in the same way, depended upon the sort of man Randall was, on what sort of upbringing he had had, what his previous experience had been, what tradition lay behind him.

If Randall had taken Mrs. Speake into his arms at that moment he would not have gone home that evening, probably not that night, and he would not have met Graham at his father's house, and his whole life would have been very different, so different that it is hard to imagine what would have happened to him. But the chances that had left Randall inexperienced, the chances that had made him that particular kind of man at that particular moment—and those chances are frightening in their complexity, even when no account is taken of those chances which had made Mrs. Speake just the woman she was at just that moment—all those chances dictated the present one.

"Well," said Randall, doubtfully, as he stood by the kitchen table while Mrs. Speake told him she would not hear of his giving her any help with the tea things.

He looked at his wrist-watch, and Mrs. Speake looked at him. Saturday evening; and Saturday evening supper awaited him at home, his mother, and his father, and the house in Harbord Road. Muriel Speake had pride; for that matter she was not quite certain as to what it was she wanted, although Randall could have made her certain quickly enough. She watched him as he stood debating with himself, and she had sympathy enough to realise that what he was really debating was whether it would be polite to leave now, the moment he had finished his tea. He was not conscious at

that conjuncture that women might be approachable, and the
tradition behind him was quite the opposite of that other
tradition by which failure to make advances when advances
were possible might be construed as discourtesy.

Randall looked suddenly up from his wrist-watch and
met Mrs. Speake's eyes. For a fleeting second the decision
of his expression made her expect that he was going to do
what she considered the obvious thing, but the expectation
died as soon as it was conceived.

" I think I'd better get home now, I'm afraid," he said.
He lapsed into the mumbled politeness of the shy young
Englishman. " My people—telegram—very kind of you—
But I ought to be going——"

" I hope I'll see you again sometime," said Mrs. Speake,
holding out her hand.

Randall took it, and Mrs. Speake did not allow his arm to
escape at once.

" If you have any time to spare on this leave please come
in," she went on. " Any evening, that is. You can ring me
up at the bank—I'll give you the number—during the day."

" That's very kind of you," said Randall.

That was the moment when it was most possible that
Randall would not encounter Graham that evening, when
Mrs. Speake put back her head to look up at him. If he
had kissed her then her mouth would have told him much
that he did not know, would have called his attention to
things that his schoolboy training had taught him to ignore.
But he did not kiss her—to offer to kiss a woman on short
acquaintance was disrespectful, insulting, showing a low
estimate of her morals or her modesty, and it no more occurred
to Randall to try to kiss her than it would have occurred to
him to slap her face. And she was a married woman, too;
in the absence of any personal knowledge to the contrary
Randall was chivalrous enough to class stories of unfaithful
wives as fantasies like the fairy stories of princes and dragons
of his childhood.

Out in the hall he picked up his hat and stuffed into his
pocket the scrap of paper with the telephone number written
on it. He opened the door and said good-bye again, and then
he stepped out into the brisk evening air. The garden gate
clanged behind him.

THREE

THEY ALL CAME HASTENING to the door when he knocked; it was his mother who opened it, but he had heard, as he waited, the sound of many feet along the passage, and behind his mother were Harriet and Doris, with Jimmy pushing them aside, and his father behind them.

"Charles!" was all his mother said as she opened her arms to him.

"We've been waiting for you!" said Harriet. "We got your telegram."

"Mother thought it was——" began Doris, and Harriet hushed her with a dig of her elbow; but Randall knew what a mother with a son in the trenches would think when a telegram arrived.

"Welcome home, son," said his father.

"Did you bring anything from France?" asked Jimmy. "I got some shrapnel after the last air raid. Dug it out of the street at the corner."

"What about something to eat? I expect you're hungry," said his mother, as they moved out of the hall into the well-remembered dining-room.

"I'm not very hungry," said Randall. "I got something to eat on the way."

It was only at that moment that he had considered at all the question of telling his family about meeting Mrs. Speake, and it was at that moment that he decided to say nothing.

There was a fire in the dining-room grate, as he expected, and a cloth on the dining-room table. The familiar arm-chairs were on either side of the fire, and two or three other chairs in a semi-circle showed that he had arrived to join a united family. Standing by the fire, evidently just risen from one of the armchairs, was a man unknown to Randall. A largish man, inclined to fat, with a double chin and a big dark moustache dividing his pink face. The eyebrows were black and very noticeable, too, but the hair on the top of the head was scanty and practically grey. Two very keen grey eyes met Randall's as he entered.

"This is an old friend of mine. I don't expect you remember him," said his father, "Mr. Graham. We were at school together. The last time you met him you were five, Charles."

"Good evening," said Mr. Graham, proffering a large square hand. "I'm intruding, I know. But there seemed no certainty of your arrival to-night, and I thought I'd stay until you came. It was a long journey over here, and it was only after I got here that I heard that you were coming on leave."

"Don't go, Victor," said Mr. Randall. "Sit down again. We'll be having supper soon."

"Don't go, Mr. Graham," said Harriet.

"Of course you're not intruding, sir," said Randall.

Mr. Graham reseated himself in his armchair, and Randall was led to the other one and put down in it. Doris sat on the arm, and Jimmy proceeded to climb up and down the back of it, looking at him over the top.

"The bath water's hot," said Harriet.

"Good," said Randall, "I got a bath at the base. But I want another one."

"And I'm sure you want some supper," said Mrs. Randall.

"I suppose I do," said Randall, yielding to the inevitable.

His mother would not be satisfied until she had fed him; her instincts told her to feed the man returning from the war, and she had no imagination regarding his other needs. For the moment the preparation of supper was postponed while Randall's kit was dragged in and opened. He took out the two tins of bully beef, the two pounds of sugar which he had brought. He gave Jimmy the nosecap of a shell and Jimmy squealed with delight, handling its impressive weight and of course letting it slip from his fingers with a thump on the linoleum-covered floor. Randall had lain prone upon the ground sweating with fear, fingers and toes moving as if to dig himself in with them, when that shell had arrived, and the earth heaved under him as he lay, like the waves of the sea, and that nosecap had screamed towards him with the most vicious noise that even a tortured lunatic could imagine. It had struck the earth five feet from his head, flinging earth over him in a light shower which immediately presaged the heavy rain of the other earth flung up by the shell. That shell had not killed him—it was hard to guess why not—and now Harriet was taking the nosecap from

Jimmy's grubby hands after he had picked it up again, and setting it on the mantelpiece out of harm's way.

It was better not to think about that; it was better to discuss the question of the extra rations they would be able to draw on account of having a soldier home from the front with them.

" Come on, girls," said Mrs. Randall, rising from the uncomfortable chair on which she had been perched so far with all the appearance of transience. " Let's get supper and leave the men to talk."

Mrs. Randall's world was one where the men naturally had the best of everything without any protest from her. It was absolutely in the course of nature that she should have to tear her gaze away from her son, and leave the comfort of his voice, and go out into the kitchen while her husband and Mr. Graham could still enjoy him; yet the only necessity for her to do this lay in her own mind. Uncomplaining, she sought out paths to self-martyrdom.

She shepherded her daughters out of the room—if her training should have any effect they, too, were destined victims to the domination of the male—and the men resettled themselves in comfort by the fire.

" Any more noise and I'll remember about your bedtime, Jimmy," said Mr. Randall.

Mr. Graham's big square hands were at work filling a pipe; he took a spill from the mantelpiece and lit the tobacco in the bowl, his sharp eyes squinting at the flame while his raised black eyebrows gave him a mildly devilish appearance in the shifting light.

" Have you killed anybody yet ? " asked Jimmy. " Last time you came home you hadn't."

" Remember what I said," interposed his father fortunately. It was not a question Randall wanted to answer.

There was a pause while the three men debated what to say next.

" I don't have to ask after your bodily health, son," began Mr. Randall. " I can see you are well."

" Oh yes, I'm absolutely fit," said Randall.

" And how are things going out there ? "

The eternal question, and it received the eternal answer, given by a man who felt a growing certainty that he was doomed.

chute's all right, I suppose, if it's given a chance. Those tests of yours proved that, anyway. So's the illuminant. It's the design that's wrong."

" You seem to have put it right now, for all that," said Mr. Graham, taking the page of the notebook in his fingers (Randall noticed the well-manicured nails). " Do you mind if I tear this out and keep it ? "

" Of course not."

" Have you invented something, Charles ? " asked Jimmy.

" Oh, I don't think so," said Randall.

" Mathematical talent is nearly always inherited," commented Mr. Randall. " It runs in families. I'm glad to see it showing up in you, Charles, despite your recent experiences. And it says something for my teaching, after all."

" Mathematical ability doesn't have much to do with inventive talent," said Mr. Graham a trifle brutally. " You'd be surprised to find what a poor inventor the average scientist makes. And some of my most successful clients are comparatively uneducated men. It's the other qualities which are important. Of course the first thing is ingenuity, inventiveness, but there's realism needed, too, and it's equally important, or pretty nearly. The brutal ability to admit that something's wrong and needs remedying—you've no idea how rare it is in this world of easy optimism."

" I thought we were all prone to complain," said Mr. Randall.

" Not in certain ways. Primitive man dealt with nuts first by cracking them with his fingers. Any nuts that were too hard he'd throw aside, with a possible lament that the gods had been so unkind as to make some nuts too hard for human fingers. The man who decided to circumvent the gods and lay the nuts on one stone and hit them with another was an inventor of the first order. He saw the need, guessed at the possibility of a remedy, and provided one."

" What about the man who invented nutcrackers ? " asked Jimmy.

" He was an inventor, too, but only of the second order. He improved on a process already in use. He made things easier but he didn't make available something that wasn't already so."

" I gather that Charles is an inventor of the second order," said Mr. Randall, pointing at the notebook leaf still held in Mr. Graham's hand.

" This ? Yes; it's an improvement on an old design. But, as I said, there's the realism that admits the possibility of improvement—I've no doubt there are plenty of officers resigned to the fact that a large percentage of flares should be duds—and there's also the ingenuity to suggest the means."

Mr. Graham folded the sheet across and put it in his breast pocket. He was actually breathing a little hard at having talked so much; but Randall guessed two things—firstly that Mr. Graham had often before discussed inventors in exactly the same terms, using the same example of primitive man cracking nuts, and, secondly, that Mr. Graham would not be nearly as eloquent on any other subject.

The door opened and Harriet and Doris came clattering in with trays and set about the task of laying the table.

" Charles has invented something," said Jimmy.

" That's good," said Harriet absently.

" He has *really*. He's invented a—a flare."

" And you've invented your bedtime," said Mr. Randall.

" Oh," said Jimmy, " can't I stay up to supper ? "

Mr. Graham kept aloof from the bustle and the wailing.

" Do you think you might spare enough time during this leave to come and see me at my office about this ? " he asked of Randall and made a gesture towards the paper in his breast pocket.

" I suppose I might," said Randall; his withholding of an unqualified affirmative was due merely to surprise at being taken seriously.

" Well, why don't you ? We could have lunch together, perhaps. If you were to give me authority to act for you I might be able to get a money grant for you from the Inventions Board."

" Oh," said Randall, genuinely surprised again. " I hadn't thought of that."

" No ? Well, I won't make any promises in any case. But here's my card. Telephone me when you have time. Make it soon, though."

" Supper's ready," said Mrs. Randall.

Now was this, or was this not, the reality ? And was life in the Salient the dream, or was it not ? Here was the dining-room table with the white cloth, as he had always thought of it, and he was sitting at it with his father and his mother and his sisters; Mr. Graham's presence opposite him was not a disturbing note, for visitors were not unusual at Harbord Road. The gas-light from the shaded burner over the table shone down on the china and cutlery. Harriet and Doris talked their usual trivialities. These were the solid things he had tried to remember in France, telling himself that they still existed, although he was in a world of mud, and rotting corpses, where cornered rats screamed as soldiers beat them to death with entrenching tool handles, where cornered Germans fell writhing with bullets in their stomachs.

" You look tired, dear," said Mrs. Randall.

" Yes. I suppose I am," he said.

This was the dream now, and that other was the reality. It was like a dream to sit through supper, to say good night, to go up to the well-remembered room where the wallpaper showed a hundred identical pictures of the cottage with creeper on the walls and the well beside it. Here was the bathroom with the naked gas flame, and the bathtub with its chipped enamel. The warm water soothed him; the sheets struck chill as he crawled between them, but in his weariness he soon forgot the chill. But there was a lonely feeling about waking in the night, in the darkness, clutching the bedclothes to him as he struggled away from the fears that had assailed him in his sleep; there was a temptation to call out to his family, to reassure himself that they were there, to find company for himself. That was a temptation which he could combat, of course; he could tell himself in the darkness that his nightmare fears were only nightmare fears, and he could close his eyes, and force his hands to let go of the sheets, and compose himself for sleep again like a brave man.

FOUR

SUNDAY WAS BETTER, all the same. To walk in the autumn sunshine and see the Sunday-morning churchgoers in their best clothes; to hear Harriet bewail a hole in her best pair of gloves; to listen to his father talk about the state of the world; to half-listen to Doris talking about the new Domestic Science mistress at school—that was all good. The iron railings of the front gardens were reassuring. His father and he looked down at the school from the hill.

" I walk there every day," said his father. " And I suppose you have no illusions about my enjoying my drudgery there."

" No, I haven't," said Randall.

" But I'll come with you if you want to walk down," went on his father with unusual insight. " If you want to remind yourself of the scenes of your youth."

" We might as well," said Randall.

There were the playing fields over which he had wandered during happy hours, the railings where he had fallen and broken his collarbone; up there were the windows of Science VI where he had spent his last year at school—an incredibly happy year, when even his father's teaching of mathematics was pleasant, when the drills and instruction of the Officers' Training Corps could be lived through as unimportant compared with the business of working for the Intermediate Science examination; when the freedom and prestige of being a Sixth Former were so delightful that there was never more than a second thought to spare for the fact that at the end of the school year he would be old enough for the army. Sometimes he had thought then about the possibility of being killed, and he had been philosophic about that; but he had never realised for one moment the degrading fear, the stinks, the dirt, the sleeplessness and the fatigue. No healthy boy would have imagined one-tenth, one-hundredth, of the reality.

Over there were the windows of the Lower First—not quite such happy memories there; a new boy, finding his way about unexplored corridors, and having to explain to incredulous classmates that he was the son of Toffee Randall, the forbidding mathematics master; many were the jokes

which he had had to endure about discussing the Binomial
Theorem at breakfast. Cardwell had been prominent in that
kind of teasing—Cardwell of the red hair and freckles, who
had gone up through the school with him, always in a parallel
form and always with something faintly hostile about him.
Cardwell had been shot down in flames at Arras six months
ago. Randall felt at that moment that he would gladly endure
another nine years of Cardwell's irritating humour to bring
him back again.

" They'll be waiting for us at home," said his father.

" Yes," said Randall, and then, after a glance at his watch,
" We've still got a few minutes. I'd like to call in somewhere
first."

" On your own ? "

" Yes," replied Randall, a little hesitantly.

" Well, I'll go straight home, then," said his father. " You
can come along when you're free. So long."

Randall watched him go, walking with the springless and
positive tread of late middle-age. It had been tactful of him
to accept Randall's hint so readily—almost painfully tactful.
But at least Randall was free now, able to walk round to
Carter Crescent and see if Helen was at home. It was late
enough by this time for a Sunday call to be socially possible,
and the door was promptly opened when Randall rang the
bell. Barrel-chested and walrus-moustached, Helen's father,
Mr. Dawe, looked out at him, and recognised him after only
a moment's hesitation.

" Why, it's young Randall," he said. " How are you,
Charles ? "

" Very well, thank you," answered Randall.

The smell of Sunday cooking came wafting through the
open door, telling Randall that his call was only just reasonably
timed and explaining Mr. Dawe's hesitation about asking
him in.

" I was wondering if Helen was at home ? " said Randall
inquiringly.

" No," answered Mr. Dawe, shaking his ponderous head.
" I'm sorry. She's away from home, doing war work down
at Faversham. Her mother and I didn't want her to go, but
she was so keen on it we had to let her. Would you like her
address ? "

" Well——" said Randall, shifting his weight from one foot to the other. What was the use of the address of a girl at Faversham when he was home on a week's leave ?

" We're expecting her home next week-end," said Mr. Dawe helpfully.

Next week-end ? Randall would be elsewhere then. He shook his head.

" You're on leave from France, of course," said Mr. Dawe, beginning to appreciate the circumstances. " How are things over there ? "

" All right," answered Randall; for the hundredth time the inevitable reply to that idiotic question, and he added, to keep the conversation from straying into such undesirable channels, " I'm sorry to have missed Helen, Mr. Dawe."

" She'll be sorry, too."

Mr. Dawe was only beginning to adjust himself to the new circumstances arising out of his daughter's having attained the age of nineteen, so that young men calling at the house were potential suitors.

" Well, remember me to her, will you, please, Mr. Dawe ? I'll be getting along."

" I will," said Mr. Dawe.

" Good-bye, then," said Randall.

" Good-bye, and good luck."

So Helen was away from home; Randall tried to forget his disappointment by walking as briskly as he could over the flagged pavements. Helen was a girl he had kissed at parties. He might have kissed her again during this leave. Both worlds seemed unreal now; the past was given its quality of unreality by the fact that Helen Dawe, the pig-tailed girl whom he had kissed at parties, was doing war work in Faversham; as for the other world—could it be really true that his friends were struggling through the mud in duck-boarded trenches while he was walking along paved suburban roads ?

There was a moment at home when reality burst upon him again; his mother was mending the lining of his tunic.

" You untidy boy, you ! " she said. She had her hand in one of the big side pockets, and her fingertip stuck out through a hole. " Just look at this ! It looks like a cigarette burn to me. Did you put a lighted cigarette in your pocket ? "

" I shouldn't think so, Mother," he said.

" Perhaps it was a spark from a fire," said his father.

" I expect that's what did it," agreed Randall; but it was a bullet hole, he knew. Whistling past him, it had just nicked his bulging pocket; torture and death not more than five inches away.

" These were in your pockets," went on his mother with two scraps of paper in her hand. " I don't expect you want to lose them. One's Mr. Graham's card with his business address on it. And the other—I'm not sure. It's the name of a bank, and what looks like a telephone number to me, but I don't know the writing."

" Yes, I'll keep that," said Randall.

" Are you going to see Graham ? " asked his father.

" I think I might as well," he answered.

He had actually forgotten about that telephone number until his mother called his attention to it. Strangely, the bit of paper seemed to be sending inspiration into his hand and arm as he held it, even while he sat and talked about Mr. Graham with his father. He put it in his pocketbook as if it was of no account; nor was it, in certain ways. If he told his mother and father about Mrs. Speake they might be hurt that he had stopped to have tea with her instead of coming straight home to them; and in his relationship with them he had always retained for himself a certain amount of private life. There were excuses in plenty for him not to mention the incident.

He played a game of chess with Jimmy, who played remarkably good chess for a boy of eleven. Doris sat on his knee and he teased her about her pigtails; Harriet retired upstairs and reappeared with her hair precariously ' up '—she would be doing it that way and ' going into long skirts ' next year, and she wanted his opinion on the result. It was all very pleasant and domestic, and Randall slept the better for it that night, without quite as much of the tension that had disturbed him the night before. But when he woke next morning and lay in bed listening to the trampling on the stairs, and his mother's warnings about the time, and Jimmy's protests, and his father's complaints, he realised that with them all going to school it would be an empty day for him save that he might perhaps go and see Mr. Graham. His mother came bouncing into the room, flushed with the exertion of getting her family off to school, and carrying the tray of breakfast that she had promised him the night before.

" I still can't get used to seeing you smoking, sonny," she said.

She had said that the last time he had come home on leave, and the time before, on his passing-out leave from the Officers' Cadet Battalion, and the time before that.

" Shall I pour out the tea for you ? "

" If you don't mind," said Randall.

" And you're smoking in bed, too," she said, at work with the teapot. " That seems a very wild thing to do."

" I *am* very wild," said Randall. He had made the same reply to the same remark last year.

" And you've smoked all those cigarettes before breakfast," went on his mother, looking at the ashtray wherein Randall was extinguishing the current one.

" I'm a bad boy," said Randall, tackling the difficult problem of cracking a boiled egg while sitting up in bed.

He took a sip of tea and glanced up at his mother still standing at the bedside. There was a hungry, distressed look about her, and when he met her eyes her face crumbled— like a brick wall blown down by a demolition charge. Tears ran from her eyes and her mouth was lopsided.

" Oh, sonny, sonny," she said, and she dropped to her knees at the bedside to put her face on his shoulder.

Her shoulders heaved with her sobs, and the sounds she uttered were pathetic.

" Hush, Mother," said Randall.

He had to move cautiously to put his arm round her, with the loaded breakfast tray across his knees. He patted her shoulder and her sobs worked up into a paroxysm, her hands clutching at him. On his left breast he felt the dampness of her tears soaking through his pyjama jacket, and the sensation shocked him.

" Mother, Mother," he said, " you mustn't let yourself go like this."

On the tray on his knees there was an opened soft-boiled egg and a brimming cup of tea; it was not easy to move. She lifted her streaming face to him.

" You're right, sonny," she said. " I mustn't."

Then she weakened again.

" Oh, sonny," she said, with the tears running afresh, " you're my first little boy. You were my baby. I remember how I used to bath you. And powder you. You used to go to sleep while I fed you, so that I had to pinch your nose— just a little tiny pinch, darling—to wake you up so that you'd go on with your supper. And now——"

She put her face back on his shoulder with a helpless gesture; her baby now (as Randall understood, quite un- certain as to how to deal with the situation) smoked in bed and was shot at by Germans.

" Gosh !   Mind the tray ! " he said involuntarily, as the tea spilled into the saucer and the cosied teapot slid precariously.

The clatter steadied his mother as nothing else could have done. She straightened herself up and took hold of the tray.

" There ! " she said. " Now I've spilled your tea."

" Hold it a minute while I get myself straight," said Randall; by leaning over to comfort his mother he had disturbed his balance.

" I hate a sloppy saucer," said Mrs. Randall. " Lucky the egg didn't fall over. I'll pour this out and bring it back. And you mustn't let your egg get cold."

" No, Mother," said Randall. He had seen in France shaken men—even once a man with a tear-stained distorted face like his mother's—come back to precarious sanity at the call of routine.

When his mother came back with the emptied saucer and cup he was eating his egg with every appearance of appetite.

" I'll pour you another cup," she said; her voice had almost no expression in it.

" That's fine," said Randall, spreading marmalade on a piece of toast.

" You've everything you want ? " said his mother.

" Oh yes, thank you."

"Well, I'll leave you to it, dear. Call out to me if you want more hot water or anything."

"Right-o, old thing."

"I'm sorry, dear," said his mother, and marched square-shouldered out of the room; even Randall could appreciate the sacrifice his mother had made in making that apology, not because it was so hard to say she was sorry, but because by saying it she admitted that there had been an emotional scene, and she and her son both knew that it was bad manners to be visibly emotional.

Randall sighed and poured himself more tea. This was the breakfast in bed he had promised himself a week ago, when he was sitting wet to the skin on a muddy firing step under a streaming breastwork, his feet ankle-deep in mud, sleepless and weary and cold. It was disappointing, but a man who had served for a year in France was inured to disappointment; on the other hand, he could lean back against the pillow with the pleasant feel of the sheets round him and fill his lungs with cigarette smoke, comfortable in the knowledge that he was free; that there was nothing he need do, that there were no Daily Orders to study, no reports to make, no forms to sign. It was at times like these that one most became conscious of the discipline of the army, the orders that must be obeyed—the lurking shadow, far back in one's consciousness, of the death penalty on which ultimately (in the last analysis) obedience rested. For he was now conscious of other compulsions, enforced by no death penalty and yet just as compelling; the need to be patient with his mother, the need to pretend to the civilian world that service up the line was nothing worse than unpleasant—these were things he did because he was made that way, and at least until something should alter his make-up he would have to go on doing them.

He thought vaguely about this as he shaved and dressed; he looked himself over carefully, because he had heard that the Assistant Provost-Marshals in London enforced the uniform regulations very strictly, and he went downstairs still not quite certain about what he was going to do for the rest of the day. But his mother herself dispelled any doubts he may have had about leaving her.

"You're all ready to go out, are you, dear?" she said. "I hope you have a nice time."

No one looking at her could have guessed that half an hour ago she had been a weeping wreck of a woman; now she was composed and apparently engrossed in her house-work. She was ashamed of her recent outburst, and bent on making amends for it, on being the opposite of a possessive mother.

"You can telephone from Little's, on the corner," she went on. "But of course you remember that. Have you got enough pennies?"

It was his mother who was making up his mind for him to telephone, who in fact was putting ideas into his head.

"I don't expect you'll be in this evening," she said.

"Well——" he said doubtfully.

"You needn't make up your mind now," said Mrs. Randall briskly. "There'll be some supper for you if you come home and it won't matter if you don't. Here's a latchkey. Turn the light out when you come up to bed."

There were areas of high colour over her cheekbones, and her eyes were bright.

"Uniform suits you," she said, looking him over. "Of course, I said that to you long ago. And I don't expect I'm the only one. Hat? Gloves? Stick? Good-bye, dear."

She kissed him lightly and ushered him out through the door; some part of Randall's later life was decided by his mother's determined unselfishness.

In the telephone booth at Little's he found Mr. Graham's card and a couple of pennies. It took an interminable time to make the connection, but at last he heard a sharp female voice at the other end. He said who he was and tried to state his business, and then he heard Mr. Graham's voice.

"Are you free this morning? Then why don't you come up now? We can get a lot settled before lunch, then. You're speaking from home? Oh yes, of course. Well, I'll see you in an hour's time or so. Good-bye."

Randall hung up the earpiece on its hook and stood un-decided for a moment before he found the other scrap of paper and addressed himself to making his second call. It was a little strange to say, "May I speak to Mrs. Speake?" and there was a further long delay before Mrs. Speake was found and came to the telephone. But he knew her voice at once although he had wondered if he would.

" Of *course* I remember you," she said in reply to his self-conscious apology. " I hope you're enjoying your leave."

" Yes, very much," he said, as he would have said even if it had been untrue. " I was wondering if you were free this evening ? "

" Ye-es," she said.

" Would you come to a show with me if I can get tickets ? "

" I think that would be nice."

" And dinner first ? "

" If you would like to."

" Where shall we go ? "

He heard her laugh at the other end of the wire.

" That's for you to say."

" But I don't know what's on," he hedged. " I don't know——"

His voice trailed off in his embarrassment; he was a very inexperienced young man, and he had almost no personal knowledge of where to take a young woman for an evening's food and entertainment.

" The theatres all start at eight now," said Mrs. Speake. " And dinner'll take a long time, I expect. I won't want to come home after I leave here. Could you meet me outside the bank at half-past five ? "

" Yes, I suppose I could," said Randall.

" That would be nice. There's a pillar-box on the corner. I'll see you there—you can't miss it."

" All right."

" Good-bye, then."

" Good-bye."

Everybody seemed to be making up Randall's mind for him to-day. He felt a little dazed as he hung up the receiver again and came out into the chill air. Mechanically he walked out to the corner and waited for a tram, and mechanically he climbed to the top when it came and paid his fare. He had no very clear idea in his mind about how to get to Holborn, where Mr. Graham's office was, and he made a tentative inquiry of the conductress.

" Change at Camberwell Green," she said, reeling off a series of route numbers.

Later he found himself on the Embankment, still vague. A taxi-driver slowed down while passing and looked at him inquiringly, and Randall made a sudden tremendous resolution. Never before in his life had he taken a taxi when a bus would serve, but this time he waved his stick at the taxi-driver and stepped in and gave the address. It was pleasant to sink back on the cold black cushions and be taken to his destination without further trouble. There was a moment's doubt while he wondered how large a tip he should give, but it was worth it, all the same.

A sharp-featured woman received him in the outer room at Graham's office, which he found up three flights of stairs, and took him through to an inner room. Here was Mr. Graham, behind a large desk in a comfortable room furnished with leather chairs; Randall was vaguely conscious of various models mounted on stands—one in a glass case immediately behind Mr. Graham, Randall thought might perhaps be a carburettor. Mr. Graham himself appeared supremely comfortable, leaning back in his office chair with his feet on another chair, his pipe in his mouth, while he studied a sheaf of papers held in his big hands. He swung his feet down and took his pipe from his mouth to welcome Randall.

" I'm glad you've come," he said. " Pity to break into your leave like this, but you may find it a profitable investment of your time in the end."

" That's all right," said Randall.

To be received thus in a City office was as unreal an experience as the Somme, but not nearly as unpleasant.

" Won't you sit down ? " said Graham. " Cigarette ? "

" Thank you."

" One of my assistants," said Graham, punctuating his words with occasional pulls at his pipe " is over the way going through pre-war specifications regarding flares. It's possible that the principle you suggested has been anticipated. But I'll be surprised if it has. In fact I'm quite certain it hasn't. I went through every pyrotechnic patent myself when I first began to handle the Phillips flare."

" I suppose so," said Randall.

" The position with regard to wartime inventions is quite different, as of course you'll understand."

" I don't know that I do," said Randall.

" Inventions of military importance can hardly be patented in the ordinary way," explained Graham. " It would never do to have them open to the inspection of any Tom, Dick or Harry, would it ? "

" I suppose not," said Randall.

" It only took about a year for the government to appreciate the point and to set up new machinery by which the inventor's rights might be protected at the same time as secrecy was preserved. But in this case I'm familiar with all the developments, naturally."

" Naturally," echoed Randall.

" And you'll understand that the question of remuneration for the inventor is a difficult one, especially when the inventor is a member of the armed forces."

" I suppose so," said Randall, conscious that nothing he had said so far had been at all original.

" But the Inventions Board has been fair enough so far, even generous within limits—it's the taxpayers' money, of course, that they're giving away. In any case payments made during the war are strictly in the nature of an advance made *ex gratia* in contemplation of a final settlement after the war, when recourse to the courts will be possible, if necessary."

" Yes," said Randall, not entirely sure of the meaning of what Graham was saying.

" How old are you ? " asked Graham, with a sudden change of subject.

His grey eyes were in odd contrast with his dark moustache, even though half the latter was hidden by the hand holding his pipe.

" Nineteen," said Randall.

" Just nineteen ? "

" Well, nineteen and a half."

" Nineteen and a half," said Graham.

To Randall there was nothing either odd or pathetic about a war-worn soldier saying he was nineteen and a half. In his world men of nineteen and a half commanded companies in desperate actions, made decisions that sent men to their deaths, and encountered misery and death themselves as a matter of course. He did not seem young to himself, in that respect, although the second lieutenants hardly younger who came out with the drafts—the ' fleeting wraiths ' who came and died—seemed irresponsibly young to him. The softening in Graham's expression seemed quite unnecessary. He was unaware that he had any claim on other people's sympathy.

Graham shook off the passing mood.

" The fact that you're a minor as well as a member of the armed forces is only one more complication," he said. " I expect I'll be able to deal with it. Maybe by the time court action is necessary—if ever it is, and I don't expect so—you'll be of age."

" Yes," said Randall.

" Anyway, let's get down to business. I've been assuming you were willing that I should act on your behalf regarding this improvement in the Phillips flare ? "

" Oh yes, I suppose so."

Randall felt as if he was playing some make-believe nursery game, and he made the responses without which the game could not go on.

" I have here," went on Graham, " a form of contract between principal and agent. It is the usual form, one which I ask my clients to sign before I undertake any business on their behalf. Will you read it ? "

Randall took the sheet in his hand and tried to read it as the next move in the nursery game. But none of the printed words made any sense to him, except ' Victor Percival Graham, barrister-at-law ', which appeared in the opening paragraph. But the second paragraph was typewritten in a space between printed paragraphs, and there he saw the words ' called, for the purpose of this agreement, the Phillips-Randall flare '.

" I'm calling it that," said Graham, " because the thing's got to have a name. But I wouldn't be surprised if it stuck."

" Yes," said Randall, quite unable to make himself read.

" And I don't know your full name. There's a space left for it. Anything besides Charles Randall ? "

" Charles Lewis Randall."

" I'll get Miss Ebbisham to type it in. L-e-w or L-o-u ? "

" L-e-w."

" Your grandfather was Lewis Randall, of course. You see that the agreement's confined solely to the flare. It's not a general agency agreement."

" Yes," said Randall, who had seen nothing of the kind.

" If you should come to form a habit of inventing we

might consider a general agreement. But it can wait at present. And you might prefer another agent when that time comes."

" If it ever does," said Randall. " I doubt if it will."

" It's perfectly possible," said Graham, pushing a bell-push on his desk.

Miss Ebbisham came in; her thin nose had a red tip, and she had the appearance of disapproving of everything. Graham handed the agreement over to her with instructions about the name.

" Here's the draft specification," said Graham, and Randall turned to study such a thing for the first time in his life. It seemed much more real to him than anything else in this strange morning, and he was impressed by Graham's easy manner of explaining it. There was something which Randall thought of as ' artistic ' about the big hand holding the pencil and pointing out the main features in the diagram and the argument. Miss Ebbisham came tiptoeing into the room and laid the agreement on the table at Randall's elbow.

" Where do I sign ? " he asked.

" You haven't read it yet," said Graham. " That's a habit you had better not form—signing agreements without reading them."

Randall remembered hearing stories about men being cheated out of their rights by being lured into signing documents they did not understand. But he could not imagine for a moment that Mr. Graham would attempt to cheat him; he was sure about that, and all his instincts reassured him. And he could not bring himself to believe that he was worth cheating, in any case; he could not believe that there was enough at stake to make it worth while—all these agreements and specifications and so on were so many trivialities, successive acts in a nursery game. If he were to lose a nursery game he would not feel any regrets; and if someone else were desperately anxious to win Randall would be glad to let him. One more point; this was the third day of his leave, and there were only three days left. The prospect of returning to the Salient was beginning to colour all his thoughts; it lay like a dark shadow across his present happiness. The future made the present unimportant.

" I've read enough to understand it," said Randall. " I sign here, I suppose ? "

Miss Ebbisham had a fountain-pen handy for Randall. He signed. Miss Ebbisham blotted, whisked the sheet away, and put the duplicate before him. Graham had pen in hand and was signing, too. Miss Ebbisham, when Randall gave her her pen back, signed both copies as a witness. She produced a stout manila envelope and put one copy into it.

" That's your copy," she said, handing it to him. " Put it in a safe place when you get home."

" Good ! " said Mr. Graham. " Now let's have lunch."

In Holborn Mr. Graham put out a huge hand that stopped a taxi in full career; he bundled Randall into it and gave the name of his club to the driver while heaving himself through the door.

" Lucky to catch a taxi as easily as that," he said.

Randall was interested in the fact that Mr. Graham had merely given the name of the club and no address. It must be a famous club, and Randall had never been in one.

" That's where the bomb fell in Long Acre," said Graham. " London's changing—I don't mean because of the bombing. But the people are changing, aren't they ? "

" I suppose they are," said Randall.

He had almost no memories of London in peacetime; to him there was nothing new about the uniformed men in the streets, the patriotic posters, the unnatural crowds.

" Can't get used to women servants in the club," said Mr. Graham, ushering Randall up the steps and into a huge Victorian hall. " Here's where we wash."

There were men who nodded to Graham; men who said " Good morning " to him; men who said, " Hullo, Graham ". There was the biggest nail brush he had ever seen on the side of the washbasin.

" A drink before lunch ? " asked Graham, leading the way again.

Randall wondered what to say. For a considerable part of his time in the army he had done without alcohol, but during the last few months he had learned to drink whisky in the company mess. He did not like it very much, and he did not drink at all up the line, and yet there were times in the trenches when added to the longing for relief there was the longing for that first evening in billets when he could pour the stuff into him and feel the relaxation and ease that it brought, the definite ending of the tension. Here he felt none of that need.

" A gin and French ? " suggested Mr. Graham.

" Well——" said Randall; and then, brightly, " What about you ? "

" I'm one of those curious people," said Graham, " who don't drink. Call me a teetotaller and you'll make me angry, but that's what I am, all the same, I suppose. But don't let that stop you, unless you want to hurt my feelings. I'll drink a ginger ale gladly."

" I don't think I want a drink," said Randall.

" Let's have lunch, then," said Graham, after running a considering eye over him for a moment.

FIVE

AT LUNCH MR. GRAHAM had talked about inventions and inventors, about systems of royalty payments as compared with the licensing of machines, about the difficulty of keeping a new process secret as compared with occasional difficulty of securing complete protection under the patent laws. He had touched lightly on the war, and, looking round at the many uniforms visible in the vast dining-room, he had talked about leaves and what to do on leave.

" I'm going to the theatre myself this evening," said Randall.

" Which one ? "

" I don't know yet," said Randall.

" You haven't booked seats yet ? "

" No."

" That's bad," said Graham looking at him from under his eyebrows. " Seats are hard to get at the good shows nowadays."

" So I understand," answered Randall—he understood it now even if he had not understood it before.

" Can I be any help ? " asked Graham. " It would be a pleasure."

" Well——" said Randall. It was not easy to explain, sitting here in this solemn club, amid grey hair and generals, that he had never taken a woman to the theatre before.

" You're going with a girl, of course ? "

" Yes." The ' of course ' made it easy to reply.

" Any particular show ? Comedy ? Serious ? Revue ? If it isn't any particular show it might as well be a revue—there's nothing in particular about *them*."

" I suppose so."

" Well, why don't you let me see what I can find for you ? I'd like to."

" But I don't want to be a nuisance."

" No nuisance to me. Miss Ebbisham's used to it. She'll arrange it."

" It's very good of you, sir."

" There's no need for that ' sir '. And I suppose you'll be dining first ? Have you booked a table ? "

" No," said Randall.

"No chance of a decent meal before the theatre if you haven't. I'll get Miss Ebbisham to see to that, too. What are you doing after lunch?"

"Well——" said Randall again. He had thought more than once about how to fill the gap between lunch and five-thirty, and he had reached no satisfactory conclusion.

"If you haven't another appointment you could stay here. I could leave you in charge of George, the smoking-room waiter. You could read the magazines until the tickets come —Miss Ebbisham will send them along to you here. It'd be convenient for her."

"I don't know how to thank you," said Randall.

He felt inexpressibly relieved. He could revet a trench or post a machine-gun so as to obtain a good field of fire; he could even, when necessary, give a shirking sergeant the rough side of his tongue, but he had worried about making the arrangements for an evening with a woman.

So the afternoon found him comfortable in a vast leather chair in the club smoking-room; all round him grey heads were beginning to nod as his elders took their afternoon naps. Mr. Graham had collected up a mass of illustrated papers for him—one of them, indeed, he had dexterously lifted from the lap of one of the sleepers without awakening him—and had then left him with a smile and a shake of the hand and a wag of the head at George. And in that soporific atmosphere Randall felt sleepy himself. He had the example of the nodding heads around him; he had eaten a large lunch, but the real explanation of his sleepiness lay in his experiences of the preceding weeks. Even two nights at home and in bed had not enabled him to catch up on the hours of sleep he had missed for so long. The illustrated paper slipped from his hand to the floor; his chin sank down on his breast. Tumultuous dreams roused him now and then, but each time he slept again without regaining complete consciousness.

The pleasant clatter of china at his elbow awoke him in the end. George was putting a tray of tea-things on the side table there.

"I thought I'd let you 'ave your sleep right out, sir," said George. "There was a note came for you 'alf an hour ago by a special messenger, but I wouldn't wake you then. I know 'ow you young gentlemen from France needs your sleep. But it's three-thirty now, sir, and I thought perhaps you'd like your tea, the way Mr. Graham said."

"Thank you," said Randall, returning to the world with the rapidity to be expected of a nineteen-year-old.

"Tea, sir. 'Ot water. Toast, sir. An' a piece of cake. An' 'ere's the note, sir."

Randall took the envelope from the salver and opened it. A smaller envelope inside contained two theatre tickets. Then there was a typewritten note on a piece of office paper headed 'V. P. Graham, Patent Agent'. It was signed 'Florence Ebbisham, secretary' and was as coldly informative as divisional orders. He was told please to find enclosed two tickets for that evening's performance at Carpenter's Theatre of the revue *Miss Muffet*, for which the curtain was due to rise at eight o'clock P.M. A table for two had also been reserved for him in the grill-room of the Savoy Hotel, and he was warned that on no account would it be kept for him after seven o'clock P.M. There was another sheet of office paper with a few words scrawled in a bold hand—" Have a good time. Good luck. V.P.G."

This was very pleasant. In the world there were few young men with less experience of it than Randall. A schoolboy—and a sheltered one at that—until he became a soldier, he knew nothing about the people for whom he was fighting. Clubs with vast leather chairs; secretaries who obtained theatre tickets at a word, these were things he was learning about during what might well be the last few days of his life—and seeing how inevitable it seemed to him that he should imperil his life, and how naturally modest he was after an upbringing where necessaries were only barely plentiful, he had no thought that he was in any way entitled to luxuries, which made them all the more delightful when they came his way. There were some slight misgivings about the technicalities of dining at the Savoy, only partially relieved by touching his breast pocket and reassuring himself as to the presence of a thick wad of Treasury notes—in France he never spent more than half his pay.

He drank his tea with pleasure and ate his toast with the appetite of a nineteen-year-old in good physical condition. There was a decided sensuous pleasure about waking up from a sound sleep and being immediately supplied with tea. And the doubts about how to deal with waiters at the Savoy could be ignored in the absence of any physical fear.

When he had finished his tea he nodded to George—it was miraculous that almost the only thing he knew about men's clubs was that one did not tip in them—and walked downstairs. He was helped into his trench coat and handed his cap and stick and gloves. As he emerged upon the pavement a taxicab approached him hopefully; taxicabs expected to pick up fares outside that club. He gave the address to the driver and they plunged into the traffic towards the City. He could have gone by bus for a penny, but already he was sufficiently initiated into a life of luxury to face the expenditure of half a crown without a qualm.

Of course he was too early for his appointment; he would have been too early even if he had gone by bus. He found the pillar-box which was the place of rendezvous without difficulty, and he stood by it in the dying evening light while the office-workers released from their labours swarmed past him. Middle-aged men, mature women, and pert young girls—more pert young girls than either of the other classes, girls with clicking heels, and something staccato about their gait as they tried to hurry in their skimpy skirts. Naturally Randall had heard about this history-making invasion of the City by young women, but as he had had no experience of the pre-war City he was not struck by the contrast. But he was impressed by something else; many of these girls looked him in the face as they passed him; some of them with a softening of their expression, some of them with a smile, some of them even with something of an invitation. Even Randall, wrapped in the clouds of his withdrawal into himself, could not but be conscious of it. He stood by the pillar-box, a pleasant-faced young subaltern in a trim trench coat, so obviously waiting to keep an appointment with a woman that other women simply had to smile at him. Randall felt an increase of emotion within him, strange temptations which momentarily and oddly reminded him of those other temptations of thought which had assailed him when he was a little boy sitting trying to concentrate upon doing his homework.

Then these unusual feelings were overlaid by misgivings as the time drew nearer for his appointment. He wondered if he would recognise Mrs. Speake when she arrived—he felt dangerously vague about her features, even about her general appearance. He scanned the women walking past him, and more than once he felt a quickening of his pulse-beat as he thought he saw someone who might be Mrs. Speake. Perhaps she had forgotten about the appointment. Perhaps he had come to the wrong place. That could hardly be—there was the name of the bank in gold letters right in front of him—unless this was the wrong branch, and a hurried glance at the scrap of paper which he took out of his pocket reassured him. Or there might be another pillar-box; Randall made hasty excursions in three directions to make certain about it. He returned to the pillar-box a little breathless. An office messenger with an armful of letters made him stand aside while he thrust them into the slit. And then, as he watched the process, he felt a touch on his arm and he looked round and there was Mrs. Speake. How could he have doubted whether he would know her again? There she was, with her smile and her warm brown eyes; she wore a neat coat and skirt and an unobtrusive hat, and the hand she had laid on his arm was trimly gloved. She smiled more warmly as he saluted her.

" I'm four minutes late," she said. " And it's my fault. I shouldn't have said half-past, because I have to start getting ready after that. Please forgive me."

" It's nothing at all," said Randall, looking down at her from his advantage of an inch in height. Her smile was infectious; no one could help smiling in return on meeting her eyes.

" At any rate, I'm here," she said.

" Yes."

Randall could say no more than that at the moment, and they stood smiling at each other beside the pillar-box while the crowds went by them, until Randall made himself speak.

" I've got tickets for *Miss Muffet*," he said; and then, as an appalling chasm seemed to open unexpectedly at his feet, " I hope you haven't seen it."

Randall belonged—or had belonged until now—to a stratum of society that went to the theatre so rarely that to go to the same show twice would be an unheard-of misfortune, and not merely a misfortune, but a freak so outlandish as to be beyond contemplation except at terrified moments like the present.

" Oh no," said Mrs. Speake. After one look at Randall's face she would have said that even if she had. " That's lovely."

" And I've booked a table at the Savoy for dinner," he went on, trying not to sound self-conscious as he said it. It was like saying, " I'm the King of the Castle " or " London Bridge is falling down " except with the paralysing qualification that it was true.

" That's lovely, too," said Mrs. Speake, with the inevitable glance down at her clothes; in London in 1917 it was possible to dine anywhere in any clothes, practically speaking.

" Let's get a taxi," said Randall, utterly reckless.

Mrs. Speake thought for a moment.

" We've a lot of time," she said. " We don't want to get there too early. What about walking some of the way ? Or don't you like walking ? "

" I'd like to," said Randall quite truthfully.

They set off along the crowded pavements in the gathering night, Randall striding along, with the free step of the man who had tramped hundreds of kilometres of French pavé in the confinement of the ranks and now was gloriously rid of pack and the necessity of keeping step, while Mrs. Speake hastened beside him. There was something very pleasant about walking like this, about having found Mrs. Speake, about the prospect of an adventurous evening. Randall grinned as he walked, exchanging platitudes about his enjoyment of his leave so far. He clove his way through the crowds like a ship through the sea, Mrs. Speake bobbing along beside him like a trim little yacht. Here and there soldiers in uniform saluted him—if every private they passed had done so he would never have stopped saluting. Burly undisciplined Australians grinned at the sight of the subaltern and the girl, passing shopgirls eyed them enviously, grey-haired men with something keener than envy.

" We can turn down here and get on the Embankment if you want to go on walking," said Mrs. Speake.

" Let's," said Randall; and with a sudden recollection of his good manners, added hastily, " What about you ? Shall we get that taxi ? "

" Oh no. I like walking."

This bubbling boy had said " Let's ", and that was enough
for her. Her husband on his leaves had been morose and
moody, and these high spirits were infectious. They made
her feel much younger than her elderly twenty-six.

" I've been here once before to-day," volunteered Randall
as they turned on to the Embankment at Blackfriars.

" Really ? What for ? "

The walk along the Embankment was enlivened by Randall's
description of his visit to Mr. Graham's office. With a
sudden access of discretion he modified what he was about
to say regarding the flare to a vague sentence about ' a wartime invention ', but that made it sound all the more impressive.

" That sounds wonderful," said Mrs. Speake. " I'm sure
something will come of it. Perhaps they'll make you a
colonel."

" Some hopes," said Randall—the peculiar expression
implying that it was most unlikely.

" Well, here we are," said Mrs. Speake.

Randall looked round him and felt nervousness conflicting
with his well-being.

" Have you been here before ? " he asked, his hand first to
his cap and then to his tie.

" Oh yes," said Mrs. Speake.

She had the tact not to say, " It's this way ", and any
guidance she gave him was quite unnoticeable. They passed
into the roaring centre of London's wartime social life.

" I've got to make myself tidy after that walk," said Mrs.
Speake and left him.

All about him there were uniforms and pretty women.
Subalterns, captains, field officers, generals, naval officers,
Flying Corps officers, gunners, sappers, Canadians, South
Africans, Americans (the minor differences in cut and style
of their uniforms were quite startling to an eye grown
completely accustomed to Service dress), Frenchmen,
Belgians, and one officer at whom Randall had to look
twice before identifying him as Portuguese—they were all
here to enjoy the legendary delights of dinner at the Savoy,
and among them Randall was just one more subaltern and
satisfactorily inconspicuous. Quick observation showed
him how to get rid of his trench coat and cap and stick;

further observation prepared him to be ready with the right speech when Mrs. Speake reappeared.

" A drink before dinner ? " he was able to ask, and when Mrs. Speake accepted he could go on " A gin-and-French ? "

His first sip of gin-and-French made him cough a little; it brought a warm glow into his interior which spread mightily through him as he finished the drink. Noisy subalterns were talking all about him, and now they did not seem quite so puerile to him.

" Let's have another," he said; Mrs. Speake had momentarily raised an eyebrow at sight of that drink disappearing so fast, and she had wondered whether she had been mistaken in thinking of her escort as a mere boy until she decided that it was through pure inexperience that he had poured it down himself like that.

" We've got to think about dinner," she said. " Look at the time. We might have wine with our dinner, perhaps, if you wanted to."

So they might; so they did.

" Oh yes, Mr. Randall," said the headwaiter when he identified himself. " I had a message from Mr. Graham about you. This way, please."

Clearly a message from Mr. Graham was of importance. They were seated; they struggled with the menu—despite Mr. Graham's sponsorship it was so clear that Randall was just one more subaltern from the suburbs or the provinces. But they decided on dinner by simply agreeing to the waiter's suggestions, and when the wine waiter came to him Randall found himself ordering champagne in the same way. He was a subaltern in the army; he was one subaltern in an army of subalterns whose primary tenet of belief was that leave was incomplete without dinner at the Savoy, and champagne. He ate the food that was put before him, without paying much attention to it, for most of his attention was taken up by Mrs. Speake opposite him. He was conscious of her warmth and friendliness, and he talked freely in answer to the questions which she used to draw him out. She asked him what he intended to do when the war was over, and he told her that he had no plans beyond taking his degree in science in London University—an honours degree, he hoped. After that—he did not know. His father cried down teaching as a profession.

He would like to be a research physicist, but there were not many jobs available for physicists.

She listened to him; she had asked the question in much the same spirit as she would have asked a younger child what he would be when he grew up. She had been ready to pay a pretence of polite attention to his answers, but as it was she found herself actually interested, even though she was vague about the difference between physics and chemistry. It was news to her that mathematics was a vitally important adjunct to science, for to her mathematics was a rather dreary memory of school days, where A did a piece of work in four days and B did it in five days, and where, to satisfy her teacher, she had to discover what x amounted to in a string of arbitrary symbols about which she knew almost nothing and cared not at all. She might have classed an interest in mathematics with an interest in postage stamps or white mice (two other subjects which did not stir her emotions in the least) if it had not been for the fact that this nice-looking young man before her showed such undoubted keenness about it and at the same time was obviously no crank.

And the conversation was specially pleasant to Randall, because somehow he could discuss the future with her as if there was a chance of its becoming a reality; he was not a soldier destined in three days' time to return to the Salient, but a budding science student, with a vague yet attractive future before him—not a future of rotting away to a skeleton hanging on the barbed wire in no-man's-land. He drank again from his champagne glass.

Here came the waiter.

"Excuse me, sir," he murmured, bending towards him. "The air-raid warning's just gone."

Mrs. Speake heard what the waiter said; her eyes met Randall's across the table, without fear—without any ascertainable change of expression. She was waiting on his decision, and he knew no more about the etiquette of London air raids than he knew about dining at the Savoy—no more than hearsay would teach him, in other words.

"What do we do about it?" he asked.

"There's the basement if you would care to go down into it, sir," said the waiter.

The zeppelin raids he had seen while he was a schoolboy

had been dangerous nuisances. Quite a number of people
were filing out of the dining-room. There was champagne
and gin-and-French in his inside to make his judgment not
quite keen; but there was one ruling motive still in the
ascendant and that was a passionate desire not to make
himself conspicuous, the deeply ingrained result of his training
and his environment. In France he would fling himself to
the ground without shame at the sound of a shell, but everyone
else did that, too, and it was a clearly sensible procedure. As a
man who had been through a German bombardment he could
not bring himself to believe that there was any danger worth
troubling about in an air raid on London, but if the civilians
saw fit to take precautions he was willing to do so, too.

" What would you like to do ? " he asked of Mrs. Speake.

" I don't care," she said, and then she shrugged her
shoulders. " Let's finish our dinner."

" Very good, madam," said the waiter.

He removed the remains of the main course; the dining-
room was not nearly as crowded or as noisy now. And then,
very faint in the distance, the flat thud-thud of distant gunfire
made itself heard.

" That's the barrage starting," said Mrs. Speake.

It was a sound which, despite Randall's previous calculation of chances, made his pulse beat a little quicker and
brought a slight feeling of constriction into his chest which
he had to relieve by swallowing. Guns much nearer began
to bellow now, full-throatedly. Randall was surprised at his
tenseness. He did not realise that he had been shaken by
so many bombardments, he had been through so much
peril and misery to the accompaniment of that din, that the
noise brought its customary physical reactions despite his
intellectual analysis of the situation. It was beyond his
power to keep from the back of his mind the memory of the
times when he had escaped death by moving to the right
instead of to the left, times when shell fragments had howled
close beside him; and along with that memory was the germ
of the doubt as to whether by sitting here he was, in effect,
moving to the left instead of to the right, as to whether the
wanton fate that had, in his sight, flung fragments of men high
into the air with the debris of a shellburst, had perhaps
decided this evening, in its grimly humorous way, to write

his name on a bomb about to be released by a German aviator
five thousand feet above him.

The war was a *danse macabre*, where the skeleton figure
of death came and summoned away the soldier squatting in
the latrine, the hero leading the attack, the unwarned crossing
the line of fire of a fixed rifle, the frightened man cowering
in the trench; it would be an artistic and neat addition to the
series if the next victim should be a subaltern home on leave
and wallowing in the fleshpots of the Savoy. If Randall did
not think about it as clearly as this—if he had been able to
do so his tension would have disappeared—but he had seen
enough of blind chance, and he had crouched under too many
barrages, not to experience physiological and psychological
results.

The waiter returned with compote of fruit.

" Would you be down in the basement if we weren't keeping
you up here ? " asked Randall.

" No, sir. I'd still be on duty," he answered.

The speech in itself served to quiet Randall. He smiled a
genuine smile at Mrs. Speake and addressed himself to his
dinner again. There was quite a respectable barrage thun-
dering through the City—London's defences must have
been considerably strengthened since he had heard them
last. Then through the echoing barrage came a series of
more solid thumps. Those were bombs. He raised an eyebrow at Mrs. Speake and received a nod in return.

" They're a long way off," she said, and took another
spoonful of compote of fruit.

" I wonder how my people are," said Randall.

" They'll be all right. There's only been one bomb in
Lower Oak so far—a zepp dropped one at Nile Road, just
by the Wellington."

" Yes, I heard about that," said Randall.

" There's nothing for them to aim at there—no gas works,
no factories. We don't have to worry. I told my mother-in-
law that, but she wouldn't listen to me. She went off to her
sister in the country when we had that last lot of raids—the
last time it was full moon. It was the noise that frightened
her, of course."

" Of course," said Randall.

The sound of the barrage was dying away now, quite

obviously. The waiter came to clear away the dessert dishes.

" I could bring you a savoury, sir," he murmured. " It's against regulations, but some people didn't finish their dinners."

" Top-hole," said Randall.

They each ate a sardine on a strip of toast, and Randall passed his big cigarette case across. It was delightful to swallow down a lungful of cigarette smoke; the waiter made sure the champagne bottle in its ice bucket was empty, and suggested liqueurs. Randall had finished off the last glass of champagne without being really aware that he had done so. He looked up at the waiter's face through the cigarette smoke and suddenly realised that he was a little light-headed.

" Cherry brandy ? Crème de menthe ? " said the waiter.

Randall had drunk such things when dining with brother officers while out of the line in France. To youths who had been schoolboys a year before they were more palatable things to get drunk on than whisky.

" What do *you* say ? " he asked, addressing himself to Mrs. Speake.

Mrs. Speake had a husband who had been drunk four nights out of five on his last leave; she thought about him but she did not mention him.

" Let's just have coffee," she said. " The champagne was so good."

" Nothing more than coffee," grinned Randall to the waiter; the latter was used to alcoholic grins from subalterns on leave.

" The all-clear has just gone, sir," he said, when he brought the coffee.

" Top-hole," said Randall again.

He suddenly remembered the next item in the day's proceedings.

" We've got to get to the show," he said, looking at his wrist-watch and in a sudden panic feeling in his pockets to make sure that he still had the theatre tickets.

" We've plenty of time," said Mrs. Speake. " We can walk there in less than five minutes."

Randall looked at the folded bill that the waiter laid on

the table for a moment or two before he realised what it was. He brought out his notecase while he goggled at the total. It was an amount that would have paid, before the war, his mother's housekeeping bills for a fortnight, but Randall's mind did not record that fact. He was too much exercised over the problem of how much to tip, conscious of the hovering figure of the waiter in the background—the waiter, on his part, was anxious as to what would be the fruits of his evening's labours; waiting upon celebrating subalterns was a gamble, for few of them knew what was expected of them at the Savoy. Some of them tipped wildly, some of them (without any intention of being miserly) meanly. He watched while Randall slid a layer of notes from his case and came forward at the strategic moment.

" Thank you, sir," he said, taking up bill and notes. He had seen to it that the tip was handsome without being extravagant, and Randall was relieved that the ceremony had gone off so well. In his present mood money meant little to him, even though he had been brought up in a household where every penny had to be counted. This stuff in his hand was not money at the moment, not the stuff that brought bread and shoes; it was one of the accessories in a children's game, a ritual wherein one side gave him food and he in return, to complete the formality, handed over these pieces of paper.

" Good night, sir," said the waiter.

Out in the streets there were crowds again by now; the streets were dark, but they did not look like streets that had been battered with high explosives.

" I don't know where Carpenter's Theatre is," said Randall; he did not mind now admitting ignorance of the West End— and related to that freedom was the loudness with which he spoke.

" Carpenter's Theatre, sir ? Just up the Strand on the left. You can't miss it, sir," said an obliging Cockney.

" Thank you," said Randall, somewhat sobered at finding his conversation overheard by a stranger.

It was only in the vestibule of the theatre that he realised that he did not know what seats had been reserved for him by Miss Ebbisham, but they were already in the line of people filing in and there was nothing to worry about.

3

"This way, please," said the programme girl, and for the first time in his life Randall found himself in the stalls of a theatre—he had never before been lower than the Upper Circle.

A theatre looked very different from down there—it had never occurred to him how close to the stage were the fortunate people who sat in the stalls. Randall found the money for his programme and sat down beside Mrs. Speake. This was exciting. Before he sat down he noticed the crown and crossed swords and baton of a lieutenant-general on the shoulder-straps of the officer in the row in front, and the lady with the general was in an evening gown with an ermine wrap. At least he guessed that it was ermine, as he had never seen ermine before to his knowledge. He had sat in audiences with generals before this, at dreary concerts behind the lines, but he had never until now sat with a lady in ermine. And it was thrilling to be in a theatre at all, just as it had been when he was taken to a pantomime. The fact that he was in charge, taking and not being taken, gave added gratification— he ungratefully spared no thought for Mr. Graham and Miss Ebbisham, who were really responsible for his being here. The lights were going down, the orchestra was beginning to play, and life was bubbling inside him—it could hardly have been champagne, which by now must have largely evaporated.

The curtains opened on a fairy world of colour and light and grace. The music had a shallow brilliance that satisfied Randall's unformed musical taste, the girls were the prettiest in England. Many of the jokes dealt with rationing and civilian difficulties in England and so were often above Randall's head, but it was enjoyable to have the audience laughing all round him, nevertheless. A quarter way through the performance Randall came to the realisation that the girls' legs were bare; the secret was made clear to him by the sight of a bruise on one of the waving thighs—he looked for that bruise and found it after every change of costume. He had always believed that girls on the stage wore tights; he did not know that bare skin was being displayed now as a result of a combination of a shortage of material for tights and a relaxation of English prudery. Randall thought that he was aware of the bare skin because he was in the fifth row of the stalls, just as he was able from here to see the expressions

on the actors' faces. A good deal of the music he had already
heard times without number played by gramophones in
dugouts in France, but that did not detract from his present
enjoyment; it may even have added to it—everything was so
different here. He could overlook the deplorable bad taste
of the patriotic jokes, the cheap crying down of an enemy who
fought to the limit of discipline and human endurance. At
the interval he came back to an excellent world from an
enchanted one, to smoke cigarettes and exchange appreciative
comments with Mrs. Speake. But at the first hint of the turning
out of the lights in the auditorium he abruptly ended the
conversation so as to address his whole attention to the stage.

Towards the end a new number was introduced, the climax
of the evening, worked up to by every device of showmanship.
It was 'The Poppies of Wipers', sung by a woman star of
the cast. She made the most of the sentiment in the words;
the orchestra wrung every possible drop of sentiment out of
the music.

> ' Poppies grow in Wipers
> And ever will they grow
> In the garden of my memory
> Because I love you so.'

Randall stirred a little uneasily in his seat; the singer
came down to the footlights with her arms extended to the
audience; the lights shifted and changed about her.

> ' Poppies grow in Wipers
> And tears are in my eyes
> The while I think about you,
> About your sacrifice.'

The voiced patriotism of the earlier part of the programme
had hardly jarred on Randall at all, but this was excruciating.
Ypres was not a place to sing songs about—not for civilians
to sing songs about. Randall remembered the heroic columns
he had seen tramping up towards La Bassée. They could sing
' A Long Long Trail ' as well as ' Who Were You With Last
Night ? ' But this woman had no right to sing about Wipers.
Randall felt a moment's rage; he wished he could condemn

every civilian in the world to a week's stay in Ypres. No
civilian would sing about ' sacrifice ' then—not if he knew
that sacrifice meant that the stubborn, resolute hero changed
into a mass of flesh whose stink poisoned the air and roused
his fellow heroes to bitter jests.

> ' Poppies grow in Wipers
> And where each poppy grows
> Fond memory is planting
> A red, red, English rose.'

The lights faded, the timpani gave a last roll, the curtain
fell, and the audience broke into crashing applause. Up
went the curtain again, and once more, twice more, Randall
had to hear about the Wipers poppies. The singer stood
smiling with her hands outstretched, and Randall with a
new cynical insight could see that she was elated about this
triumph. Glamour and illusion were gone and in their
absence Randall's imagination was at work; despite his
ignorance of the stage he could suddenly picture the singer
at supper after the show receiving the congratulations of
her friends, the composer and the lyricist rubbing their
hands with glee, the members of the orchestra, even the
programme girls, pleased with the new success—vampires,
ghouls, feasting on the dead bones of his friends. The
curtain had gone up again, but Randall hardly saw the
finale. He was in this new black mood, and it was not allevi-
ated when he stood at attention while the orchestra played
' God Save the King ' and the civilians groped furtively
about for hats and coats. Mrs. Speake turned a smiling
face to him when the lights came on and was quick to notice
his lowering brow.

" He's in a mood," she said to herself—her husband on his
last leave had these moods, too.

" I hope you liked it," she said aloud.

" It was all right," said Randall curtly—he could not trust
himself to speak further.

They were filing out of the theatre now; in the aisle
Randall encountered the lieutenant-general, who ran a cold
eye over Randall's uniform, noting the two stars and the
absence of medal ribbons, and somehow that glance accen-

tuated Randall's feeling of friendlessness in this civilian world. Outside many people were waiting for taxis.

" I suppose we'd better have a taxi," said Randall; in this mad world he might as well suggest the uttermost absurdity.

" What, all the way home ? " said Mrs. Speake. " That would be nice—but, of course, it would be fearfully extravagant."

" Who cares ! " said Randall. In his bitter mood he welcomed the possibility of one more grievance.

He elbowed his way to a strategic position in the waiting group, and with beginner's luck he secured the next taxi but one. The driver demurred on being asked to drive out to Lower Oak. Randall self-consciously felt the driver's eye take note of his lieutenant's stars, and of Mrs. Speake's hat and coat and skirt—suburban people who had no business intruding upon a taxi-driver at the moment when he could reap his richest harvest.

" What'll you give me ? " he asked in surly fashion.

" He'll give you your legal fare, driver, if you're not careful," interposed a sharp-featured civilian in the group.

The taxi-driver surveyed him with every appearance of indignation, opened his mouth, and then shut it again.

" He's bound to take you wherever you order in the London area," explained the sharp-featured civilian to Randall. " And you could report him to the police for trying to bargain. Then he'd lose his licence."

He held open the door for Mrs. Speake, and after she had got in he ushered Randall after her.

" Thank you," said Randall, a little bewildered, hesitating with his foot on the step.

" Don't mention it. Always glad to be of service to you fellows. These taxi-drivers are getting impossible. But don't be too hard on this one, though. He has his living to earn. Five bob besides the meter reading would be fair. Ten if you're feeling specially generous. Good night. Drive on, driver."

The taxi swung into the Strand with a clashing of gears, and Randall sat beside Mrs. Speake in the darkness; the light from the occasional shaded street lamps hardly penetrated into the taxi. Randall was more bewildered than ever. The civilian's aid in dealing with the taxi-driver, freely proffered, had been of enormous value, and his tactful advice on tipping a relief to Randall's mind. He was freed from some of his sense of grievance, but there was still a vast complication of emotions within him.

"I think it's been a lovely evening," said Mrs. Speake at his side. "I haven't enjoyed myself so much for a long time."

"Neither have I," said Randall, as politeness dictated.

"Is that true?" asked Mrs. Speake. "I didn't know—I wondered—I thought perhaps—perhaps you weren't happy."

"I? Oh, I'm all right," said Randall, with that in his tone that left the matter in doubt all the same.

"Something's upset you, Charles," said Mrs. Speake, turning towards him; Randall felt her hand on his arm. "What is it? What's the matter, dear?"

He felt her touch; a faint breath of scent reached his nostrils. The woman who had smiled at him while he was waiting outside the bank, the half-naked women who had danced before him on the stage, the champagne at dinner, the numerous excitements of the day—his physical fitness as well for that matter—made him sensitive to her touch, to the scent she wore, to the little endearment which had escaped her. To-morrow he might be able to look back at himself and to say cynically what it was he needed; to-night he was quite ignorant of it, extraordinarily enough. He only knew he felt friendless, that Death was lurking in ambush awaiting him at the end of his leave, that he wanted something and did not know what it was.

His gloved hands had been resting on the top of his walking-stick between his knees; he turned and reached for her clumsily. In the darkness the regimental badge on the front of his service cap caught in the trimmings of her hat and there was a moment's deadlock, a moment's lack of co-operation. When his cap came off and tugged her hat over her ear his lips brushed her cheek, cool and smooth and delightful. But no woman could kiss with her hat dangling; pure instinct made her take her hands from him and raise them to her head, leaning back from him. He misinterpreted the movement; he felt himself rebuffed, groped for his cap, and allowed his walking-stick to fall with a clatter on the taxi floor. By the time he had recovered cap and stick, and she had reskewered her hat to her hair, the crisis was momentarily over.

" I'm sorry," he said in the darkness; he had kissed more than one girl in his life since adolescence, but all his past training led him to apologise for the attempt.

" It doesn't matter," she said.

She waited beside him for something she would not name to herself. To be kissed in a taxicab after an evening's entertainment was almost part of a ritual, according to contemporary thought. But Muriel Speake had never yet been unfaithful to her husband; she had twice been kissed in secluded parts of the bank by clerks over military age, and had only found enough enjoyment in it to be tactfully cool. She had a young woman's ardour, but she was by no means conscious of it as yet. She was attracted to Randall, but at the same time she was aware that she was nearly seven years his senior, and it appeared to her a little unnatural that a woman of twenty-six should be drawn to a boy of nineteen, even though he was a veteran soldier—even though he could provide dinner at the Savoy, and stalls in a theatre, and a taxicab all the way home. She was shallow as well as ardent—contrariwise she was tactful and sympathetic as well as shallow. She was perfectly well aware of the possibility that she might be unfaithful to her husband; but she was restrained by the conventional upbringing of a woman of her time and circumstances—much more was she restrained by the fear of appearing ' cheap ', of demanding too brief a wooing, too low a price.

And Randall sat with a fast-beating heart and a troubled mind. His lips were still aware of the smooth cheek they had brushed. He had little objection to sin, considered just as sin; he had hardly the vaguest thought of Captain Henry Speake, somewhere up the line with the division. His concern was really about Mrs. Speake; he had probably hurt her feelings. She had been very kind about it; she had said " It doesn't matter " in a cool and level tone, disguising the offence she felt. Of course, she was a woman of the world and must think of him as a clumsy schoolboy. There had been a nice relationship between them up to that moment, and now it was all spoilt. A clumsy subaltern, grabbing at a woman at the first possible opportunity, was how she must think of him. She had been kind enough to give him her company for the evening, and this was how he had repaid her. She must be hurt and disappointed.

" Can I apologise ? " he said in the darkness, trying to find the correct phrases. " I—I——"

" Don't let's discuss it any more," she said, and there was only the muttering and complaining of the wheezy old taxi-cab to be heard as they ground along.

She was going to ignore the whole affair, thought Randall, as a lady should, as she would have closed her eyes to some revolting spectacle if they had happened upon one together. It was necessary then that he should play his part manfully, too.

" I suppose the driver knows his way," he said stiltedly, leaning forward and peering out of the window at the dark streets.

" He'd ask us if he didn't," said Mrs. Speake almost as stiltedly, arriving by slow degrees at an appreciation of Randall's feelings.

" Oh, I can see where we are," went on Randall, his interest caught. " Fancy his knowing about this route."

The taxi-driver was taking a succession of back streets which cut across the angles made by the main roads ; Randall had found that way out with map and bicycle as a boy, and he did not know about the microscopic knowledge of London demanded of taxi-drivers by the police licensing authority.

" Yes," added Randall. " We're crossing Clinton Road now. He's good, this fellow is."

" Yes," said Mrs. Speake, puzzled by his change of mood. She was piqued as well ; whereas previously she had allowed her instincts to carry her along and dictate her actions, she now deliberately settled herself closer to him. Randall felt the warmth of her.

At that moment the driver opened his little window.

" Which way after we get to the station, sir ? " he asked.

" First on the right and then straight on," answered Randall.

So now the journey was fast ending. Now they were in familiar streets ; they were going past the park where he had played as a child. Things looked different through a motor-car window, even allowing for the wartime darkness. The taxi bumped over the tram lines and swung round to the right, low gear protesting as the driver drove slowly along a road unknown to him.

"Here we are," said Randall.

He got out and held the door for her, and then dragged out his pocketbook to pay the fare. Five shillings would be a just tip, his kindly informant had told him, and ten shillings generous; it was convenient that with the silver in his pocket he was able to pay the fare and seven and sixpence more, drawing a neat line between conspicuous expenditure and conspicuous meanness.

"Good night, sir," said the taxi-driver, grinding away.

Mrs. Speake had walked up the garden path of the front door—partly because she was wondering how many of her neighbours, roused by the unusual sound of a taxicab at midnight, were peeping through their bedroom blinds, and partly because now she was determined that Randall should follow her in. Randall stood hesitating at the gate; the last thing he wished to do was to thrust his undesirable society upon her uninvited. He heard the key in the lock—was she going in without even saying good night? Was his offence as unforgivable as that?

"Aren't you coming in?" said Mrs. Speake, speaking as softly as she possibly could for fear of her neighbours, and Randall went up the path in five quick strides.

"Let me shut the door," said Mrs. Speake.

Randall heard it shut behind him, and then there was the click of the switch and she was revealed to him in the light. There was a smile on her lips; there was a look on her face which Randall could not possibly believe was expectancy. From force of habit, after meeting his eyes, she glanced next at the mirror in the hatstand and then down at the doormat under the letter-box.

"Letters," she said. "*There's a telegram.*"

An orange envelope lay there, between two white ones, and she stooped for it while Randall stood aside. She tried to open it, impeded by her gloves; she tore the envelope almost in half and took out the form inside and opened it.

"Harry," she said.

She looked up at Randall, down at the telegram again,

and then up at him once more. In those few seconds she had
turned pale.

"What is it?" asked Randall.

"Wounded."

She thrust the form at him, and he took it and read it, the
meaning leaping up at him before a second reading imprinted
the wording on his mind.

"Regret to inform you," he read, "Captain Henry Speake
seriously wounded."

"What shall I do?" she said. "What shall I *do*?"

Mechanically he looked at his wrist-watch; midnight. There
was nothing that could be done at that hour. He knew what
that telegram meant; he could hear the cry of ' Stretcher
bearers!' being passed down the line; he could see the
stretcher being coaxed round the traverses, with a moaning
burden on it, or something very still, the face chalk-white
under the dirt and the sunburn, white against the red flowers
of blood splashes.

"I'm sorry," he said idiotically.

"What shall I *do*?" she said again.

Randall applied his mind to thinking about that.

SIX

MRS. RANDALL WAS LYING awake in bed worrying about her elder son. She could not picture the perils of service in France at all, but she could vaguely picture the perils of a young subaltern on leave in London. She knew that there were wicked women there; she knew that there were diseases that could be caught (that was all she knew about them); but really she was worrying merely about his losing his virtue. And there had been an air raid that night. Perhaps the West End had been bombed—but Mrs. Randall knew more about air raids than she did about loose women, and consequently did not worry about that possibility so much. But it must be twelve o'clock by now, time for the last tram to pass Upper Oak—it would be just terrible if her son were out all night. She lay wakeful in bed, resentful of her husband sleeping lightly beside her.

Then her tenseness increased. She could hear footsteps in the silent street outside. That must be Charles. But there were two people walking, there was a murmur of voices—it could not be Charles. But the steps were coming along the road—they were pausing at the gate—they were approaching the front door, and she sat up. The silent house echoed the sound of the key in the door, she heard the door open, heard the voices again. A feminine voice ! She had thrown back the bedclothes when she heard Charles speaking to her quietly through the bedroom door.

" Mother."

" I'm coming," she said.

As she came down the stairs in her nightgown her eyes met Mrs. Speake's in the gas-lit hall, and some relief and some perplexity mingled with her apprehension as she sized the woman up. She was much older than Charles and respectably dressed. Mrs. Randall heard her son's explanation, and for the moment her sympathy went out to the stranger, and she willingly offered her hospitality. But doubts beset her almost at once. Who was this married woman who had been out with her son ? And undoubtedly on the tobacco-laden breaths of both Charles and Mrs. Speake there was the reek of alcohol. The whole business seemed very unpleasant to Mrs. Randall, and the unpleasantness was intensified when it became clear that Charles would have to sleep on the couch in the icy unlived-in sitting-room while Mrs. Speake slept in Charles's bed. It was the only possible arrangement, but Mrs. Randall (who had never seen the water-logged trenches of Passchendaele) was hurt at the idea of Charles sleeping on a couch.

" Please don't trouble," said Mrs. Speake when Mrs. Randall made a move to change the sheets on Charles's bed. " I shall be all right for to-night."

Very obliging of her, but there was a sinister significance about a woman being willing to sleep between sheets in which Charles had already slept—it is to be feared that whatever Mrs. Speake had agreed to in the matter would have been held against her by Mrs. Randall. But, after all, the woman had just heard that her husband had been wounded, and Mrs. Randall could not but be sorry for her. She offered to make tea, and when that was refused she took Mrs. Speake upstairs and showed her the room, and tiptoed into her bedroom to get a nightgown for her, and did what she could to see that she was comfortable before going down again to find Charles philosophically laying blankets on the couch in the sitting-room.

She herself, of course, was shuddering with cold by the time she went back to bed and to the hopeless task of trying to tell her somnolent husband about it all. She lay awake almost until morning thinking about all the implications of the affair; in fact she had hardly fallen asleep again when the alarm clock woke her and she had to hurry out of bed to dress and set about getting breakfast and sending her family off to school. Her husband and children did not seem to attach the deep significance to the incident that she did; when Mrs. Speake's presence was hurriedly explained to them at the breakfast table they did not spare her more than a glance, not even Harriet, who at sixteen might be expected to take an interest in her brother's women friends—but Harriet was preoccupied that morning with qualms about her French homework. The old cat who taught French at school did not accept even air raids as an excuse for bad homework.

Randall watched them all go; he looked at Mrs. Speake across the table while his mother hovered in the background.

"I must let them know at the bank if I'm not going this morning," said Mrs. Speake. "I'm late already."

"I can do that," said Randall.

"And I must find out about Harry," she went on. "How he is, and what hospital he's in. Do you think if I went up to the War Office——? Or I suppose the Red Cross——?"

"I'll see what I can do about that, too," said Randall. "I'll try on the telephone. Better find out what we can before you go up there."

"Do you think you could?" asked Mrs. Speake. "Wouldn't it be better if I tried?"

She was dry-eyed; she spoke objectively, as became a patriotic woman with her background.

"No. Let me go," said Randall. "I'll walk down to the telephone."

Casualities were something he knew about, something with which he was more familiar than these grown-ups. And that was the cheek his lips had touched last night— of course this news had driven from Mrs. Speake's mind all thought of his appalling offence. He was anxious to do all he could by way of atonement.

"If you're going I'll help with these things," said Mrs. Speake. "I can, can't I, Mrs. Randall?"

Randall left the women together and walked out into the streets where a few tardy children were still hurrying to school, and so he found himself once more in the telephone booth at Little's—so much had happened since he was in there twenty-four hours before. The bank received with sympathy the news that Mrs. Speake would not be coming to-day on account of her husband being wounded—it was a masculine voice which replied to Randall and told him that the manager was not there yet, it being too early for the bank to open, but that he would be informed as soon as he arrived. Then Randall addressed himself to the task of trying to get news of Captain Speake; despite the confident way in which he had spoken he knew little about government offices and he had to expend no less than three twopences before he succeeded in making contact with the right depart- ment; there were interminable waits for connections, difficulties in hearing what was said, difficulties in making himself understood. But at last some female at the other end paid attention to him.

" What was the name again ? " she asked.

" Speake," said Randall patiently. " S-p-e-a-k-e. Captain Henry Speake, First Kenningtons—Thirty-second London Regiment."

" Hold on a minute," said the girl.

Randall waited again until clicks and rumbles in the receiver told him that she was picking up the telephone again.

" Did you say Captain Speake ? " asked the girl.

" Yes," said Randall, swallowing his exasperation.

" I don't understand why you are asking. You say you are speaking on behalf of his wife. We sent her a telegram some hours ago."

" Yes, I know. We've had that. But I want to find out where he is and how he is now."

" I mean we sent a second telegram. You haven't received it ? "

" No," said Randall—he realised it must be lying on the doormat of the house in Calmady Road as the other had lain. " What did it say ? "

" Here is the wording," said the girl. " Regret to inform you Captain Henry Speake died of wounds received in action."

" Thank you," said Randall and hung up the receiver.

Outside in the street the last children had long ago gone into school. A housewife or two, some wheeling perambulators and some with shopping bags in hand, were setting out to do their morning's shopping, but long sections of the streets were deserted and bare and bleak. Randall walked back to Harbord Road, his mind as bare and bleak as the roads. He had tried to make himself think how he would break the news, but his mental processes would not function. He turned in at the gate; his mother heard him coming and ran to the door, opening it, with Mrs. Speake looking over her shoulder. Mrs. Randall saw his face and did not need to be told, although she half-asked a question.

" Is it——? Is it——? " And then she turned to Mrs. Speake, her jealousy momentarily forgotten in face of tragedy. " You poor child."

So Randall found the rest of his leave occupied with matters he had never dreamed of when he had started from France. Coincidence thrust on him the duty of informing Captain Speake's relatives, signing the telegrams ' Muriel ' and ' Muriel Speake ' more as his judgment dictated rather than as she told him to. He sat downstairs in the little house in Calmady Road while she packed her clothes in her bedroom upstairs. He heard things about insurance policies; he discussed pension problems. Mrs. Speake wept at times, but she did not speak much about her dead husband; Randall thought he understood that she was concealing her grief behind a façade of preoccupation with the details of widowhood, and he appreciated her stoicism and self-control. She slept two more nights at Harbord Road, in Randall's room, while Randall slept in Jimmy's bed with Jimmy in a made-up bed beside him. There were air raids both those evenings—this was the time of the October full moon—and Mrs. Speake sat with the Randall family in the dining-room while the barrage echoed around them, and was accepted as one of that family. She heard some of the family's traditional jokes and smiled politely at them.

She was unfeignedly glad of Randall's society, and made free use of his time: he escorted her at her request (sitting beside her in the tram just as he had done on that first evening) to the shops when she bought her mourning, waiting for endless hours in the street outside. That was a monotonous occupation probably as good as any other to enable him to recover from the nervous exhaustion resulting from active service, and he endured it without the thought occurring to him that he could do anything else. He met her relations and her old friends, shaking hands with the women and quite unconscious of the searching glances which were sometimes directed at him by inquisitive females who wondered just what his position was and would be in relation to the widow. Finally he took her and her baggage up to Paddington and put her in the train for Gloucester, where she was to recuperate without the added strain of air raids, staying with cousins. When she put her black-gloved hand in his to say good-bye she thanked him prettily for all he had done for her.

" Don't mention it," he said.

" Will you do me one more favour ? " she asked, the words

coming out hurriedly as if she had given some thought
beforehand to this speech. " Will you call me ' Muriel ' after
this ? Don't think of me as ' Mrs. Speake '. Think of me as
' Muriel '. Will you ? "

" I'll try," said Randall.

" I've always called you ' Charles '," she said. " I'll always
think of you as ' Charles '. I'll call you ' Charles ' when I
write to you."

" Thank you," said Randall.

She was an understanding, admirable woman, keeping a
stiff upper lip in adversity, tactful and considerate in her
forgetting that deplorable business in the taxicab, pleasing
in the way she addressed him as one adult to another. He
felt, as he went out of Paddington Station, that he would
miss her during these last twenty-four hours of his leave.
He even thought that some of the horrors of France would
be mitigated if he should get himself to remember her during
the worst of them.

But there was a distraction when he reached home again.

" Here's a telegram for you, Charles," said his mother. " I
opened it, just in case——"

Randall saw nothing at which to take offence in her opening
it, even though presumably she could do nothing about the
contents until he should get back from Paddington; it was
the conventional thing to do with telegrams.

" I wonder what Mr. Graham wants ? " went on his mother.

" It's from Mr. Graham, is it ? "

He read the few words. " Kindly telephone me when
convenient—Graham."

" I suppose I'd better go and phone him," he said.

Truth to tell, as a result of recent events he had almost
forgotten about Mr. Graham's existence, about the agreement
he had signed, even about the Arden Club. Back he went to
Little's shop to go through the now utterly familiar motions
of getting his two pennies ready and taking up the telephone
receiver.

" Oh, good morning, Mr. Randall," he heard Miss Ebbisham
say as soon as he told her who he was. " Just a minute,
please. I'll see if Mr. Graham's free."

Then came various clicks and murmurs, and finally Graham's
voice.

" Glad to hear from you, young man," said Graham. " I didn't know when your leave was up and I was afraid in case I'd missed you. How much longer are you here ? "

" Until to-morrow."

" Oh ! I could have wished it was longer—so could you, I daresay. But I wanted to tell you that the flare's going on all right."

" Yes ? " Randall tried without avail to work up an interest in the flare.

" I've been in touch with Phillips and he's in agreement about the necessity for improvement. I've an appointment with the Inventions Board for next Monday."

" Yes ? "

" I don't want you to build too much on it, but there's a definite chance that your improvements will be adopted."

" That sounds top-hole," said Randall politely, without really thinking it top-hole at all, and with no intention whatever of building anything on it.

" I'll keep you informed," went on Mr. Graham. " And— the very best of luck. The very best of luck."

" Thank you," said Randall ; he was going to add " I'll need it," but he resisted the impulse towards bitterness, for there was something too genuine about Graham's good wishes.

" Good-bye, then," said Graham. " You'll hear from me."

" Good-bye," said Randall.

So this was the end of his leave, he thought as he walked home again, feeling no excitement about what Graham had said. The black shadow of having to return to France over-cast all other thoughts. There were a good many things he had left undone during this leave that he had planned to do—even Randall was not yet cynical enough to know that that was the epitaph carved over the majority of leaves. He had intended to go round to the homes of his friends and call on their mothers ; it was significant that he did not have a single friend who was not in the armed services. In that dread year of 1917 every English youth was summoned to pass through the fires of Moloch. There had been a girl or two—sisters of his friends whom he had intended to look up, too. That had proved impossible because of Mrs. Speake's—Muriel's—troubles, but Randall felt no regret on this account. He was glad, he was almost proud, of being able to help her. Muriel had borne her loss so heroically, and she had been so considerate and tactful. Randall actually walked past the front gate of his house without noticing it, so deep was he in thoughts about Muriel, and with the breaking of the thread as he had to turn back the black shadows grew deeper.

Heretics had been tortured by the Inquisition; red men had devised methods of making their captives scream in agony. In the years to come the Nazis were to try to outdo these achievements in the cruelties of their prison camps. A furious and desperate war was to open twenty-one years after the close of its predecessor, with slaughter and heroism and misery. But at no time in the history of misery was there such suffering as a purely fortuitous combination of circumstances brought to a million human beings in 1917. The Marquis de Sade might dream of tortures, but not his insane imagination could compass the torments which chance dealt out to the devoted infantry of the nations at war. For a special reason the freezing dungeons of the Inquisition, the iron cages of Louis XI, were not to be compared with the wet and the cold and the slime of the water-logged trenches in Flanders, where men stood night and day knee-deep in icy mud, or took their rest, head bowed, sitting on a firing step hardly more solid. There was a reason why the degradation of Buchenwald was not as deep as the degradation of the brutish filth of the Salient.

For the men who fought in those trenches had the additional torment of the suspicion that the remedy lay in their own hands, that if only they could think of the right way to deal with the problem they could nullify the stupidity of the peoples and the generals who were driving them to hideous death. It was not by the easy method of self-murder, and it would be something less obvious than mass mutiny although allied to it. They were in the grip of something implacable and yet not necessarily inevitable; in the disillusionment of 1917 they feared that they were giving up their lives, their sanity, and their dignity for something which later on, when they were all mad, crippled, or dead, would be found to be nothing; it was this feeling that doubled their regrets and halved their infantile pleasures.

The Inquisition had its 'continuances' of torture, periods when the victim was left to recover and to meditate on the certainty that his torment would be renewed; service in France had its reliefs, its times out of the line when there was a chance to sleep, a chance to be dry, a chance to deal with vermin. And each relief ended, as had been foreseen all the time, in the midday parade and the night march back into misery and hell. The Chinese killed by a thousand cuts, taking care that the victim should live as long as possible; in France the wounded were nursed back to health again to be sent back into the line.

From the quiet sectors went back a constant dribble of casualties; when there was a 'show', an attack, a counter-attack, or an assault by German troops, the casualty list rose to proportions utterly unexpected by the military experts of the nineteen hundreds. Half the battalion, three-quarters of the battalion, would be wiped out; it would be with-drawn from the line, filled up with drafts, rested and retrained, and sent in again, to lose another three-quarters of its estab-lishment, until it became the rarest thing to meet a man who could say 'I came out with the division in 1915'. Every man in the ranks recognised the chances he faced, and knew that the odds were against his surviving another few months of a war which seemed destined to last for decades. Yet in the heat of battle the battalions fought on with three-quarters of their numbers dead; when the orders came the reconstituted divisions marched up into the line to take their chances again. In that incomparable army courage never faltered and discipline never relaxed, not even in the face of disheartenment more insidious than any treachery could have been. Those men smiled wryly at the catchword phrases which expressed the ideals they felt should be left undescribed, and did their duty in accordance with the tradition and training of their generation; and they left their blood and their bones to enrich the fields of Flanders. And a misguided cynic might say that that enrichment was all the profit their sacrifice brought.

So Randall found himself in the train winding its way across the Kentish fields, wedged in a compartment with nine other silent officers, going back to France, to the hell of the Salient. When he rejoined the battalion he could tell his envious brother officers about dinner at the Savoy, and about the performance of *Miss Muffet* which he had seen; not many days after he rejoined, the company mess secured a gramophone record of ' Poppies of Wipers ', and the saccharine sentiment of its music and words filled the heavy air of the headquarters dugout. There was something different about hearing it out here. The fact that he had assisted at the first public singing of a song which swept into instant popularity distracted attention from the facts that he had been to no other theatre, and had led a celibate life while in London. When he was asked about women, he was able to make a casual reference to ' a girl who got the news that her husband had gone West while I was with her ', and he never referred to his interview with Mr. Graham at all.

SEVEN

THE BATTALION ADJUTANT SHOWED Randall the orders which had just come through, to the effect that First Lieutenant C. L. Randall was to report immediately at the headquarters of an engineer company at Tidworth Pennings, to be under the orders of Major-General Sir John Dunne, K.C.B., for the purpose of completing the trials of the Phillips–Randall flare.

"What the hell's the Phillips–Randall flare, Randall?" asked the colonel.

"Well, sir——" said Randall, and tried to tell him.

"You attended to this on your leave?" went on the colonel, to whom the technical terms clearly meant little or nothing.

"Yes, sir," said Randall. "You see——"

He pointed out that by a fortunate coincidence a friend of his guv'nor's was a patent agent, working with the Inventions Board.

"But that's all to your credit, all the same," said the colonel, fortunately not seeing that he might have cause for complaint. Randall might have called the colonel's attention to the defects of the Phillips flare, and might have made his recommendations through him, thereby bringing credit to the colonel. But the colonel was an unimaginative man of his own generation, a good infantry soldier of a vanishing school, and it did not occur to him that he might have displayed an interest in pyrotechnics; nor, being a gentleman, did it occur to him to doubt Randall's simple explanation of the circumstances which had called the attention of the Inventions Board to the possible improvements in the flare. Randall's own transparent surprise at the news was unnecessary confirmation.

"Good luck to you, Randall," said the colonel.

"It's not three months since you had your last leave!" said the company commander in envious astonishment when Randall reported to him.

"A bit more than that, sir," protested Randall mildly—actually it was more than four.

"I'll bet you anything you like you'll miss the next show, you lucky bargee," said the senior subaltern.

Even the rank and file of the army, emerging from the most

hideous winter in history, knew that this coming spring would bring a furious and immediate German offensive.

" Perhaps I will," said Randall. In his own mind he had progressed only as far as to deduce that he would escape the battalion's next period in the line.

" You'll be able to wangle a couple of nights in London at least," said another subaltern, looking at the man with this incredible luck in a new light.

" I hope so," said Randall.

He thought of Muriel; since his last leave he had received friendly gossipy letters from her once a week at least, telling of her return to her duties in the bank, of the simple details of her life, and it was pleasant to think he had a friend waiting for him there. Now when he thought of London he did not think of the realities of suburban streets and brick houses, but simply of Muriel.

" I wish I was one of these scientific blokes," said the company commander.

" I'm not a scientific bloke," said Randall, startled.

Knowing, as he did, how simple the whole thing was, it was hard for him to believe that it was possible that anyone could credit him with knowledge or ability not possessed by everyone.

" Brains will tell," said the senior subaltern, wagging his head sagely.

This reception of his news almost took from Randall his pleasure at leaving France; if he were expected to be a scientist he was going to have a difficult time with the experts in England. He felt actual qualms when his mind dwelt upon the future as the train crawled across France, but those qualms were temporarily forgotten in the pleasure of arriving in London, and especially when he found that there would be every justification for missing the next train from Paddington—he could only just have caught it with good luck—and that it would be four hours before there was another to take him to his destination. There was a telephone number on a scrap of paper in his pocketbook; he waited restlessly in line to get to a telephone booth, and then he asked for the number.

" Can I speak to Mrs. Speake, please ? " he asked, remembering that he had said the same absurd thing last leave.

" Hold on a minute," said the woman at the other end.

Then—after a long minute—came the voice.

" Hullo."

" Muriel," said Randall—he had never said that name to her before.

" Who is that ? "

" Charles."

" Who ? Oh, it can't be ! Charles ! "

" How are you, Muriel ? "

" Oh, it is ! I didn't know—— Where are you ? What are you doing ? "

Randall explained as well as a few words would permit.

" How lovely ! How long are you going to be here ? "

" I have to catch a train at two," said Randall. " I have to report on Salisbury Plain."

" Oh ! "

" But I want to see you before I go. Can I come down to the bank ? I thought we might have lunch or something. Will they let you out ? "

" I don't know. I could see——"

" I'm coming now," said Randall. " Look out for me in a few minutes."

" Oh, Charles ! "

" Two minutes is up," said a new female voice entering into the conversation. " If——"

" Good-bye ! I'm coming ! " said Charles loudly through the interruption.

"Oh, Charles!" was the last Randall heard of Muriel's voice.

Or was it (he asked himself in the taxicab he eventually secured) " Charles dear " that she said ? He could not be sure, but he sat on the edge of the seat in the rattletrap taxi-cab, urging it on its way as it ground through the traffic to the City. He walked into the bank and looked round, some-what at a loss, at the counters and at the numerous customers. But here she was, eyes shining, colour in her cheeks to counter-balance her sober mourning. And that hand was laid on his arm again—he had often thought of it when he was in France, and the touch stirred strange feelings within him. But she was hatless.

" Are we coming out together ? " he asked her.

" I've got to ask Mr. Jennings. He's been busy with a cus-

tomer all this time," she said. " He'll be free in a minute. Oh,
Charles, it's so lovely to see you. You're looking older,
though."

So did any man who had survived the Third Battle of
Ypres, but Randall neither said it nor thought it.

" I *am* older," was what he said—he had reached his
twentieth birthday a week before.

He stood grinning at her, sublimely unconscious of the
smiles of the onlookers; it was so extraordinarily pleasant
to be made welcome in this way by a woman to whom he
was an individual. She was not so unconscious; her eyes
left his face to look round the bank.

" You could sit down over there," she said. " Oh, Mr.
Jennings is free. Just a minute."

She hurried through a gap in the counter to where a bald-
headed man was shaking hands with a departing visitor at the
door through a frosted-glass partition. He saw her waiting
respectfully at one side for the farewells to be completed, and
the sight brought her in his estimation a little further out of
her Olympian inaccessibility. She was going to ask a favour,
and a woman who had to do that was more closely akin to a
man who had been nothing except a schoolboy and a soldier,
even though it was a shame that she had to ask favours.
Muriel went through the glass partition with Mr. Jennings,
and a minute later Randall was uneasily conscious that Mr.
Jennings's bald head was rising up above the frosted glass to
scrutinise him. He tried to appear languidly unconcerned,
casting his gaze up at the ceiling; and when he next ventured
to look, Mr. Jennings had bobbed down again and Muriel
was coming through the door, through the gap in the counter.

" I can come," she said. " I won't be a minute."

It was somewhat longer than that when she appeared,
with her black hat on and her black coat concealing her
white blouse. Her hands held her umbrella, her black gloves,
and her handbag.

" I'm ready," she said; she looked up at him with big
brown eyes from under arching brows. Randall saw the full
lips and not the weak chin.

Out in the street she looked at him again.

" Well ? " she said, and it was not until that moment that
Randall realised that he had come down to the City and

taken her out of the bank without forming any real plans as
to what he was to do with her.

"I was thinking we could have lunch," he said lamely.

"We can't have lunch at eleven o'clock," she replied.
"Let's come and have a coffee and then we can talk about it."

So they sat one each side of a marble-topped table and
stirred their coffee while he stared at her. The teashop was
full of people come in for eleven-o'clock coffee, including
several of the bank staff. Muriel nodded to one or two of
them, with something of self-consciousness in her manner.
Men, real live men with some pretence at eligibility, neither
bald-headed nor crippled, were exceedingly scarce in London
in the spring of 1918, and to be seen with one was like being
seen in a new hat. Randall had his back to the girl who
favoured Muriel with a conspiratorial wink.

"I'm still wearing black, you see," said Muriel with a
gesture towards herself.

"Yes. Oh yes, of course," said Randall.

The fact had made no impression on him until then.

"Poor Harry," went on Muriel. "The colonel sent me
such a nice letter."

"That was good," said Randall, who knew a good deal
about the letters that had to be written to widows. But it
was hard to think of Muriel as a widow.

"It doesn't really seem as if we were ever married," said
Muriel. "It wasn't until the first Christmas of the war, and
then we only spent his leaves together."

"I suppose that was so," said Randall, magnificently banal.

"Of course, we were engaged before the war. We were
engaged nearly two years, so you couldn't call it a war wedding
really."

"Of course not," said Randall. If Muriel thought a peacetime wedding superior to a war wedding he was pefectly ready
to agree with her even though he could not see her point of
view.

"I've got two girls living with me now," said Muriel.
"I was lonely. And of course I couldn't afford to keep that
house up by myself, and my mother-in-law won't stay in
London because of the raids."

"That must be nice for you," said Randall, referring to the
two girls and not to the absence of the mother-in-law.

" But it's you we ought to talk about," said Muriel, putting down her coffee cup. " How is it you're on leave like this ? I didn't understand what you said on the phone."

" It's because of the flare," said Randall.

" The flare ? "

" The Phillips flare. Don't you remember my telling you about it the night we went to the Savoy ? "

" Oh yes, of course. How silly of me. I hadn't forgotten it—I just didn't think. And what about the flare ? "

Randall told her all he could.

" How exciting ! " said Muriel. " Do you think they'll make you a colonel ? "

" Not a hope," said Randall. " Even to get this spot of leave is more than I expected."

" Oh," said Muriel. " And what about your mother ? Does she know you're in England ? I've seen her a few times, you know."

" Yes, I heard. You wrote to me," said Randall. His mother had not written with enthusiasm about Muriel. " She doesn't know yet. I wouldn't send her a telegram because—you know."

It was embarrassing to talk about telegrams to Muriel.

" I know," she said and nodded.

" I was wondering if you'd mind going round there to-night," said Randall. " Then you can tell them where I am. Then they won't worry for a bit. Tell mother that I'll come home if I can wangle it after this Salisbury Plain business."

" Yes, I'll tell her," said Muriel. For a moment her mouth set hard. There would be a certain pleasure in telling Mrs. Randall that her son had been in London, had spent half a day there, in fact, without going to see his mother although he had seen her, Muriel. That would teach her.

" Thank you very much," said Randall.

He picked up the bill and they walked to the cash desk for him to pay it. Out in the street they paused again.

" The Savoy, I think," said Randall.

" Oh yes," said Muriel.

" And a taxi."

In certain ways this was more wonderful even than regular leave. It was so utterly unforeseen; twenty-four hours before he had been in billets with the prospect of going up

into the line shortly, and here he was now in a taxi heading
for the Savoy. Gin-and-French at the Savoy, and another
gin-and-French. A table for two—he had the sense to
engage it before they had their drinks—and a lunch with
china and glass and a tablecloth. A bottle of champagne.
Everything as merry and as dreamlike as possible. Was it
he who only last week had been working desperately along
with his platoon filling sandbags for dear life to close the
gap in the breastwork which the German mine-throwers had
blown in it ? He felt the healed blisters on his hands and
laughed aloud at the contrast, too loud, so that faces were
turned towards them in the restaurant. His own laugh
abruptly recalled him to himself, to remember what he had
to do next, to look at his watch and to realise, appalled,
that he was likely to miss his train.

" Wait for the next, darling," said Muriel, leaning back in
her chair. Two gin-and-Frenches and her share of the
champagne had made her sleepy.

" I can't, I can't," said Randall. The endearment registered
itself on his memory, for he thought of it later, but seemingly
he did not hear it now.

The bill—the hurried departure—the fortunate taxi—the
wild dash through the streets to Paddington. Months ago
he had seen her off there; now the situation was reversed.
He said a hurried farewell at the barrier, shaking with his
right hand her left hand which came easiest to his grip, and
then dashed through as the guard was looking at his watch
for the last time preparatory to waving the green flag. He
found himself in a compartment full of forbidding-looking
field officers, and perched himself unobtrusively in the midst
of them. There was just room for him to sit back, and he
had no sooner done so than alcohol and fatigue sent him
into a jerky sleep, in which he struggled not to fall against
the shoulder of the major beside him, and struggled also not
to shake with fright as he dreamed about the Salient. And,
of course, after all his hurry he was greeted with the news
(when at last he had found somebody to report to and had
explained who he was) that the general was not expected for
another twenty-four hours.

So next morning he came into the mess with the deference
to be expected of a visiting subaltern, ate his breakfast,

and read a newspaper magnificently unhurried. There was nothing for him to do at all until after lunch, when the committee would arrive, presumably by road. This was a perfect holiday; he could be solitary and lazy without a care for anyone, and yet at the same time his idleness was tinged with happy memories of Muriel. He finished his newspaper and sauntered out to see if he could borrow a bicycle. Although it was still March, it was a magnificent spring day, with perceptible warmth in the sun. He found a bicycle and cycled off. Even Salisbury Plain, where he had tramped so many dreary miles as an officer cadet, was beautiful on this spring morning. Larks were singing ecstatically in the blue above him, the grass was green, and he could think of the battalion on parade and smile, with the bicycle wheels whirring under him. Yesterday he was drinking champagne at the Savoy with Muriel ; to-day he was churning along over Salisbury Plain on a bicycle with worn sprocket wheels, and, to a man of twenty, home from France, both experiences were delightful. It was with real regret that Randall looked at his wrist-watch and turned his handlebars back towards Tidworth Pennings.

That afternoon there was something of a commotion outside the mess. Randall was first conscious of the red tabs of the staff, and rows of medal ribbons—more than one row of ribbons on a tunic was a fairly certain indication that the wearer was a general officer. Here were more red tabs, with single rows of ribbon, and here was a figure in civilian clothes; a second glance told him that it was Mr. Graham, and the civilian clothes were tweeds of an expensive unobtrusiveness.

" Hullo, young fellow. I thought we'd find you here. Glad to see you. Fit and well ? That's fine. General, this is young Randall whom I told you about—General Sir John Dunne."

Randall came to attention and was backward about taking the proffered hand—he was not used to meeting generals in the flesh. Then he met Major This and Captain That.

" Here's the man that started all the trouble," went on Mr. Graham, " Mr. Leonard Phillips—Mr. Charles Randall."

Phillips was in uniform with a first lieutenant's stars, but that was the only thing that was military about him.

He was tall—taller than Randall—and inordinately thin;
it seemed indeed as if he was too thin to maintain himself
upright, for his body drooped in a curve like the stalk of a
flower. He wore large round spectacles through which a pair
of melting brown eyes met Randall's. He was a man not
yet thirty, with a pleasant smile and a firm handshake.

The commandant of the depot was on hand, and the
group spread out with his offer of tea; there was the awkward-
ness to be expected while the general chose his chair and was
supplied with tea, and then Randall found himself with
Graham and Phillips.

" It's a great pleasure to meet you," said Phillips.

" Er—thank you," said Randall. No one had ever told
him before that it was a pleasure to meet him.

" I've some papers in my pocket I'd like you to sign,"
said Graham. " It isn't absolutely necessary, because as
your agent I can bind you in any matter within our agreement,
but it may be better this way if there's any hitch."

" Shall I sign 'em ? " asked Randall.

" What, now ? "

" Isn't that what you meant ? "

Graham looked at him with a curious pity before he produced a couple of typewritten documents and a fountain-pen.

" You'll see a cross where you have to sign," he said, and
then, turning to Phillips, " He's as bad as you are, you see.
Signs without reading. After all the lectures I've given you
I don't think this is a good example for you."

" God bless my soul. I tried to read one of your agreements
once," said Phillips, " and when I'd finished I was no wiser
than when I started."

Randall handed the agreements back.

" Thanks," said Graham. " Since you haven't read 'em I
may as well tell you that with the new design any royalties
or other proceeds are divided between you in the proportion
of one-third to you and two-thirds to Leonard here, after
the deduction of my commission. Any comments ? "

" Sounds funny to me," said Randall. " I haven't done
anything at all."

" Other people think differently," said Graham.

" I don't think I'd ever have hit on that fuse idea," said
Phillips.

The general was speaking authoritatively, and everyone fell silent so that his words should meet with the attention a general's words deserved.

"We'd better make a start soon," he said. "Then we can make the first tests while there's still light. After that it'll be dark enough for the other tests."

"It's the same illuminant, General," said Graham. "It passed all the last tests."

"No harm in making sure," said the general. "Will you see about the cars, Clarence? We'll make a move in five minutes."

They got into the motor-cars in descending order of military rank, the general and his staff in the first one, Randall and Graham and Phillips in the second one. A lorry with an engineer working party brought up the rear.

"I thought you'd like a spot of leave," said Graham to Randall as they jolted along. "That's why I told the general last week it was essential to have you present at these tests."

"Oh, it was you who did that," said Randall. "I was wondering about it."

"And I don't expect I was wrong, either."

"You were absolutely right," said Randall.

At this moment the battalion was probably plodding along a *pavé* road to take its place in the line again, and he was here, with a night between sheets ahead of him, and no fear. This was not like putting his left puttee on before his right; not like going out to the latrine in five minutes' time instead of now. Here, with no chance of a shell falling on him. Randall could be sure that those rituals were only rituals, of no efficacy at all in assisting him to draw a blank in the lottery of death. This was the certain way of preserving his life. Perhaps even now some shell was bursting on the twilit crossroads just where his place would have been in the column.

The motor-cars lurched to a stop on the artillery range, and they all got out while the sappers under direction of Captain Clarence set about getting the materials out of the lorry.

"This is just a revolving clamp on a stand," explained Phillips to Randall. "I had it made so that we can vary the elevation of the pistol in the clamp. The committee wants twenty shots at thirty, forty-five, and sixty degrees, as well as vertical. I don't doubt at all that it'll be all right."

" I hope so," said Randall, wishing that he felt more interest.

" Look at this," said Graham. " The first time you've seen your name in print, perhaps."

In the fading light Randall read the label on the package : ' 10 Phillips–Randall Flares '.

" Highly inflammable," read Graham, and then with a chuckle, " Let's hope they are."

Already the pistol was clamped on the stand and loaded. A sapper pulled the trigger, and the flare shot out at thirty degrees, shooting along in a surprisingly flat trajectory. Randall saw it dip and then burst; the parachute opened smoothly and the blazing flare hung in the evening air low over the ground.

" One," said the sapper sergeant.

" I don't know that that's the hardest test," said Phillips. " A slightly higher elevation—even up to sixty degrees, perhaps—should make it more difficult. But those ballistic problems are tricky."

" I expect so," said Randall.

" Two," said the sapper sergeant—the second flare had behaved satisfactorily.

" There's not a lot of wind," said the general, approaching them. " I'd like a bit more wind for these tests."

" Wind can't really affect the point under investigation," said Phillips, and then, suddenly remembering that he was a lieutenant speaking to a general and not an experimenter speaking to an intrusive ignaramus, he added " sir ".

" That fuse has done the trick," said Graham, shifting his weight from one leg to the other.

" That's what we're here to see," said the general.

They stood in silence while the rest of the first batch of flares was discharged.

" That's twenty at thirty degrees, sir," said the sergeant.

" And not one dud ? " said the general.

" No, sir. Not one dud, sir."

" Very good. Carry on."

The sergeant reset the pistol in the clamp, and the next flare rose in a higher trajectory; with the growing darkness its brilliant light, as it hung in the air after bursting, was more visible.

"That was a good idea of yours, Randall," said the general. "It should have been realised earlier that flares should illuminate the enemy and not ourselves. You were right to call attention to it."

"Thank you, sir," said Randall.

"He not only called attention to it, General, but he came forward with the suggestion as to how to make it possible," said Graham. "A revolutionary device."

"Yes, yes, of course," said the general, quite clearly of the opinion that Randall had received from him personally all the praise that would be good for a subaltern.

Flare after flare soared up, lit, and sank slowly down.

"That's twenty at forty-five degrees, sir," reported the sergeant.

"Very good. Carry on," replied the general; and then, apparently to himself. "No duds. Quite remarkable."

At sixty degrees the first flare rose in its graceful arc, burst, and hung high above the plain.

"That's all right," said Graham, with a trace of relief in his voice.

Flare followed flare, each one giving a satisfactory performance.

"We needn't worry now," said Graham.

"A most satisfactory test," said the general.

"It looks as if it's going to be a hundred per cent, sir," said the staff captain.

"All fired, sir," said the sergeant.

"A hundred per cent," said Graham.

"Now we must repeat the earlier tests made for the illuminating power and time of flight," said the general.

"It's hardly necessary, you know, Sir John," said Graham. "It's the same parachute, the same illuminant."

"No doubt. But the changes in design may have reduced its efficiency in other directions. That's been my usual experience with these inventions."

Graham gave the smallest possible shrug of his shoulders and forebore to reply.

"Clamp the pistol vertically, sergeant," said the general. "Clarence, see about the stopwatch. And what's that other thing they have to use ? Photometer or something. See about that, too."

"We're here for another hour," said Phillips under his breath to Randall.

As was only to be expected, the Phillips–Randall flare passed all its further tests without difficulty.

"Excellent," said the general. "I think we can say we've earned our dinners. I hope you'll join us, Mr. Graham. And your young protégé here, and Mr.—er—er—Phillips, of course."

It was at dinner that Mr. Graham interfered with the course of nature again.

"By the way, General," he said. "I hope you're not going to send young Randall away again immediately."

The general turned a slightly uncomprehending eye first upon Graham and then upon Randall.

"I can't spare him for a day or two," went on Graham. "There's the final specifications before the contracts are put out for quantity production. He must see those."

Mr. Graham turned his head so that his right eye was invisible to the general and yet plainly visible to Randall. His right eyelid flickered momentarily.

"I suppose that's necessary," said the general.

"Absolutely," said Mr. Graham. "There's no time to lose, in fact. We don't want anything to go wrong at this stage. Can you give him orders to that effect ?"

The general turned to Randall.

"Your orders were to report to me ?" he asked.

"Yes, sir."

"How were they worded ?"

"To complete the tests of the Phillips–Randall flare, sir," interposed the staff captain.

"We can't call the tests complete until the specifications are passed," said the general. "How long will you need ?"

"Until the 25th at least," said Graham.

"Very well. Have you anywhere to go until then, Mr. Randall ?"

"My family lives in London, sir. In Upper Oak."

The general shot a quick glance at Randall as though satisfying a long-felt curiosity regarding the strange people who lived in places like Upper Oak.

" Then I'll give you orders to return to London forthwith and report to me by telephone at the War Office daily until the 25th."

" Yes, sir," said Randall.

" See to it, Clarence," said the general.

" Yes, sir," said Clarence.

EIGHT

THERE WERE ADVANTAGES ABOUT moving in the lofty circles of the staff and in hobnobbing with generals. It was long after midnight before the party, with Randall now attached to them, arrived back in London, but a single order put one of the motor-cars and its driver at Randall's disposal to take him home. Mr. Graham was the last of the party to be dropped before Randall.

"Well, you've a week at home," said Mr. Graham, "and nothing to do."

"It was very kind of you to say that to the general," said Randall.

"Oh, it was nothing. I was only afraid in case you'd say something to give me away."

"But thank you all the same."

"Thank me by giving me a ring some time this next few days. I'll have some news for you, with luck. I'll get an interim grant out of the Board or my name's not Graham. I'll be seeing 'em to-morrow—I mean to-day. Ring me the next day."

"Right-o," said Randall.

The car left Graham standing there (except for Piccadilly and the Strand one West End Street was like any other to Randall) and headed for Westminster Bridge and the suburbs south of the river. Randall had to give directions to the driver until they turned into Harbord Road, and Randall walked up to the front door, to ply the knocker and to bring his father and mother down to let him in, while the children slept through the commotion as children will.

Being at home this time should have been just like being at home on his last leave; but it was not. There were differences of one sort and another which combined together to change everything. Harriet had taken over Randall's bedroom. She wanted a room to herself, she had announced, having shared one with Doris ever since Jimmy had been born eleven years ago; she had moved into Charles's bedroom as soon as he had gone back to France last October, and not only did she appear slightly reluctant to vacate it again for him but it seemed—even though it might be unbelievable—that her mother sympathised with her in the

matter. Discussed in the uncongenial atmosphere of breakfast, after Randall had spent the night on the sitting-room
sofa, the matter was definitely thorny. Randall had a
momentarily feeling that his mother's attitude was due to
the fact that she had been told of his presence in England
by Muriel and not by himself, but he dismissed the thought
as too ridiculous for consideration—in making that arrangement he had been actuated by the best of motives, and the
convenience of it was obvious. But both Harriet and his
mother spoke about ' your friend Mrs. Speake ' with a certain
incomprehensible significance.

Jimmy and Doris quarrelled ceaselessly all through
breakfast-time, continuing a feud that apparently had
originated some time back, and had small attention for
their brother. His father had a smile for him across the
breakfast table, but relapsed into his usual morning bleak-
ness; schoolday mornings were always dreary in his father's
view—they had grown drearier with the years and with the
ceaseless and unavailing struggle to maintain discipline, and
now, with his classes unrulier than ever in wartime conditions,
and his vitality drained by his extra work as special constable,
mornings were only the hideous preliminaries to dreadful days.

That was an important difference between this leave and
the last for Randall; he had arrived on a Saturday last
time and to-day was a weekday. And last time he had come
home looking forward to home life, and this time he was
looking forward to seeing Muriel. And the mere fact that he
would have to telephone for orders every morning was
unsettling. And there was this business of the Phillips–
Randall flare, which had snatched him out of France, had
whisked him up from Salisbury Plain in a motor-car, and
would seemingly put his name into the mouth of the whole
British Expeditionary Force. There could be no denying
that the Phillips–Randall flare was a reality. There might
even be money in it, and although his pay and allowances
had always been ample for his simple needs there was an
unsettling thrill about the thought that he might receive
money in other ways. And there was another difference
between last leave and this—he had been nineteen last time
and was now twenty, he was five months older, and those
five months had been spent in the Salient.

The turmoil ended with everyone hurrying off to school, with his settling down with the newspaper and a cigarette, and his mother coming in to him wearing her hat and coat.

"I've simply got to go out shopping, dear," she said. "You'll be all right, won't you?"

"Of course I will, Mother. Don't worry about me. I'll be going out to telephone the War Office later on."

"And what about lunch? There'll be plenty for you if you're here."

"Well——"

Randall looked inevitably at his wrist-watch; it was too early to telephone Muriel at the bank.

"I expect you'll be going out. I was wondering if perhaps you'd like to invite your friend Mrs. Speake to supper this evening?"

"That's a good idea. I'll ask her."

That was all that had to be said; possibly Mrs. Randall up to that time had been hoping against hope that her son would receive the suggestion with surprise, even—wild hope—with a negative. She could still force a smile before she hurried off, leaving Randall to finish the newspaper and then to wander, unsettled, about the empty house before it was time to walk down to Little's and telephone.

"No orders for you to-day. Report again to-morrow," said a voice which may have been Captain Clarence's over the telephone when Randall at last succeeded in making his connection. He hung up the receiver and felt in his pocket for another twopence.

But Muriel after the first words of greeting was somewhat dubious about his suggestion for lunch.

"I can't ask Mr. Jennings for more time off so soon," she said.

"Oh, nonsense," said Randall, trying to speak stoutly with his world freezing around him.

"I can't, dear. Really I can't. You don't know what he's like. I really have to work for my living now, you know."

Even the 'dear' could not soften that speech to Randall's mind.

"But——" was all he was able to say.

"I'll have lunch with you," said Muriel. "I'd love to. But we can't go far. I'll have to be quick."

"Oh, all right," said Randall.

Lunch in a crowded City restaurant, with no intimacies of speech, amid the clatter of crockery, was unsatisfactory. So was the hurried farewell at the entrance to the bank. So was the journey home again in the tram. Tea with the family was better; Randall did not take conscious note of the darted glances exchanged between his mother and Harriet when the former told the latter that Mrs. Speake was coming to supper. After tea he sat at the dining-room table between Jimmy and Doris and helped the one with his Latin and the other with her French, until it was time to hurry down to the tram stop to meet Muriel, who had consented, at his pleading, to come straight from the office, ' just as she was '. He was too early, naturally. He waited at the corner of Harbord Road while two trams came grinding up and went on without Muriel descending from them. But she was in the third, stepping neatly down into the roadway along with a dozen other people, greeting him with a smile. She slipped her hand under his arm as they walked along.

" It's nice to have you come and meet me," she said. " I hope your mother doesn't mind my coming to supper."

" Of course she doesn't," said Randall; he could not imagine anyone not being pleased at the prospect of Muriel's society.

Supper was, for Randall, a pleasant function. He sat and basked in Muriel's presence, contributing little to the polite chit-chat that the women exchanged, while his mother suffered in silence as her family made vast inroads upon the food she had provided; naturally she had done her best to provide an impressive meal at whatever strain it might put on her rationed supplies in the future. She thought of the queues in which she would have to stand, and she made herself smile while Muriel and Harriet discussed hats and dresses. And after supper, while Mr. Randall settled himself wearily at the cleared dining-room table to mark a pile of mathematical exercises, they all withdrew into the sitting-room where Mrs. Randall had lighted an unwonted fire. Harriet, in duty bound as hostess, played the piano and then, with a little persuasion from her mother, sang 'Because' in her small contralto. Then Doris, after some rather more urgent prodding, stumbled through Rachmaninoff's Prelude without too many mistakes, and then naturally they turned to Muriel.

" Oh, I couldn't," said Muriel.

" Oh, please do," said Mrs. Randall.

" I haven't my music here," said Muriel.

" I'm sure we've something you can sing," said Mrs. Randall. " Harriet, go through your songs with Mrs. Speake."

" I might be able to sing this," said Muriel, when they were half-way through the pile, holding up the Serenade Berceuse, " but it isn't my key."

" Harriet can transpose, can't you, Harriet ? " said Mrs. Randall.

" M'm," said Harriet without too much assurance.

After one or two tentative false starts Harriet plunged into the accompaniment while Muriel hurried after her in a breathless soprano. Randall sat by the fire with a cigarette between his fingers looking at her. The gas-light lit up the curve of her cheek and neck; Randall thought how graceful and—and—artless she seemed standing there. She was trim and slender in her white blouse and black skirt, and the hand that rested on the chair back beside her was white and small. Randall felt a great wave of emotion inside him. He had come from filth and misery and fear; soon he would be going back into the midst of them again. He might—he knew the chances so well—be going into oblivion. He wanted to reach out for that small white hand, take it and clasp it, feel its smoothness and coolness, press it against his cheek. He wanted something undefinable, and he wanted it with terrible urgency. He wanted to forget the dreadful world in which he was engulfed, his fear and apprehensions. While he lived he wanted something, maybe a moment of peace and understanding. Perhaps—being in no way self-analytical he had not even the relief of knowing it—he wanted to assert himself in the face of the inevitable destiny that was hurrying him along. He was profoundly stirred, without even realising that he was stirred.

At least all this frantic emotion kept him from criticising the pathetic little soprano voice, the untrained, almost childish efforts to deal with the intricacies of the song. And Harriet hit a wrong note in the final chord, which prevented him from noticing that Muriel did not finish on quite the right note herself.

" Thank you," said Mrs. Randall.

Muriel turned to face them again, flushed a little with her exertions and with her eyes shining, so that she appeared to Randall as if surrounded by an aura of light and beauty.

" Won't you sing us another ? " said Mrs. Randall.

" Oh no," said Muriel, " I simply couldn't."

" Oh, please," said Mrs. Randall, as politeness dictated; and her duties as hostess also dictated that something should be going on all the time, and if Mrs. Speake did not sing someone else would have to do something.

" No, really," said Muriel, and with a glance at the clock, " I ought to be going home. I've had *such* a lovely time."

It was some minutes later, after Harriet had escorted Muriel upstairs to get her hat and coat, that Muriel said good-bye at the door, with Randall waiting to take her home.

" You *have* your key, haven't you, dear ? " were Mrs. Randall's last words, addressed to her son, just before she shut the door, and Randall heard no significant tone in the words although Muriel did and caught her breath a little as she walked down the path.

She put her hand inside Randall's elbow again, delightfully, as they walked along Harbord Road; maybe she was determined to show Mrs. Randall that she was someone to be reckoned with. The night was calm, with a hint of fog. Into Randall's mind as they walked along crept the beginning of the thought that the trenches would be drying out and the battalion able to move about in more comfort, but he checked himself and would not let the thought complete itself.

" Ooh, it's cold after being indoors," said Muriel, with an increased pressure on his arm; she was snuggling up to him as much as it was possible for a woman to snuggle up to a man while walking along the street with him. Randall instinctively returned the pressure, with his emotions somersaulting within him.

" You'll soon be home," he said reassuringly, although he had no desire at all for her to reach home.

" And then I'll be in bed, all warm and cosy with my hot-water bottle," said Muriel, snuggling again.

Into Randall's mind leaped an uninvited picture of Muriel in bed, with her hair unbound and lace at her throat; it stirred him so that he pressed her arm again.

" But it's nice walking along with you like this," bleated

Muriel, although if any man had described Muriel's voice as a bleat in Randall's hearing he would have had to defend himself against personal assault.

Here they were at the gate—the well-remembered gate—with Muriel glancing up at the windows.

"I think Grace and Marjorie are going to bed," she said. "I'd better not ask you to come in."

"No," said Randall.

By the standards in which he had been brought up it was unthinkable that he should penetrate into a house where women were going to bed.

"Oh," said Muriel looking up at him; he could only just see her face, pale in the darkness.

The hand that Muriel had automatically raised to shake his raised itself and rested on his chest. It was like pulling a trigger. Randall stooped to her, and her arms went up about his neck. He felt her soft lips against his, so that his head swam at the touch. He managed to bump noses with her, clumsily, but she contrived to evade that difficulty and next moment her lips were clinging to his again. She was frantic at the touch of him, and he was light-headed at the touch of her. They pressed and clung and kissed; how many times they kissed it would be hard to estimate. Randall was shaking with passion; for he had never known anything like this before.

"My darling! My sweetheart!" she whispered to him as he strove to get his breath, and the whisper started a fresh paroxysm. As it died away, as he stood with her unbelievably in his arms, almost sobbing with passion, she thought of the neighbours—the street was dark with wartime darkness, but they still might be visible to someone peeping from a window, and certainly they would be visible to anyone walking down the street. She drew him up the garden path to the darkness of the little porch; and there she melted into his arms again.

"Darling!" he said hoarsely—he had never said that word before, unless possibly in his childhood.

"Sh," she whispered, and he felt her soft hand on his mouth, the soft palm, which he had not dreamed about before. And within his arms was her relaxed body. It was he who drew back first from the renewed embrace, unable

to bear this sweet agony, and as his grip relaxed she withdrew from it entirely, opening her handbag to seek her
latchkey. Marjorie and Grace might not hear them, or if
they did they might be discreet and not come down or call
to her. But he misinterpreted the gesture.

"To-morrow?" he said to her, and she looked up at him
quickly and keenly, trying to read his face in the darkness
of the porch.

"To-morrow?" he whispered again. "I'll see you to-
morrow, darling?"

She was quick of wit in matters like this, sensitive to
mood, appreciative of motive. Her instincts told her that
what she had been about to suggest would be too crude
for this inexperienced boy—the silent entry into the house,
the cautious footsteps in the hall, the slow opening of the
sitting-room door while she led him to the couch. She had
learned a great deal about Randall in those few seconds.
And there would be other nights than this one; hot with
passion though she was, her emotions were shallow enough
and her feelings of self-interest were strong enough for her
to control herself with ease. She would not spoil things
to-night; she would not shock him, she would not let him
think her cheap.

"Yes, to-morrow, darling," she said, and she added, using
a phrase that would not be too self-revelatory and yet would
test her conclusions regarding his attitude, " I don't know
how I'll wait till then."

"What time do you leave home for the bank?" asked the
simpleton.   "Can I call for you and go up with you?"

"Yes—oh yes," she said. "A quarter-past eight. Call for
me then."

"I will," said Randall, and paused, and then said, "Good
night, darling."

When they kissed again passion almost swept Randall
away, but he would not allow himself to do anything or
suggest anything that he thought she would rightly resent.

"Good night, darling," he said again, and pulled himself
free and left her there in the porch and made his way home.

Perhaps it was not such a good idea to take Muriel to the
office next morning. Muriel actually looked a little surprised when she opened the door in response to his ring.

She had on her hat, but her feet were in pink slippers, and over her shoulder Randall caught a glimpse of another female—Grace or Marjorie, presumably—heading for the stairs in stockinged feet, but also with her hat on and a piece of toast in her hand.

" Oh, just a minute," said Muriel.

She did not ask him in; she left him standing on the doorstep, pushed the front door nearly to, and fled away. Randall stood and waited, looking at his watch, until at twenty-one minutes past the hour Muriel came hurrying out of the door with gloves and handbag.

" We've *got* to catch that tram," said Muriel, and she went running down Calmady Road, with Randall striding beside her.

They heard the tram coming, and a final burst of speed just enabled them to catch it. It was already almost full, and when they climbed to the smoky upper deck they could not share a seat, but had to sit with the aisle between them and conversation in consequence was limited to dreary formalities—not that Muriel seemed in a conversational mood in any case. But when they got out of the tram on the Embankment and Randall hailed a miraculous taxi Muriel allowed herself to smile at last.

" This is the nicest way of going to the office," she said.

Randall caught her gloved hand, and she gave his hand a little squeeze in return.

" Darling," said Randall.

He was not of the type that could be distracted from the path on which he had set his feet, not even by a forty minutes' journey in a swaying tram at the beginning of a morning. Muriel gave him a look into which all meanings could be read.

" I'll be early for once," said Muriel, while the City roared round them.

" What about lunch ? " asked Randall.

" All right, call for me. I'll be ready at half-past twelve," said Muriel.

She smiled even more brightly up at him when they got out of the cab, and then she turned and scuttled into the bank, while Randall made his way across the road to the well-remembered teashop, intent on having a cup of coffee to supplement the scanty breakfast he had eaten while his family got ready for school. Then he found a telephone, asked Clarence for orders and was told there were none for him, and remembered this was the day he had to telephone Graham.

At the news that he was north of the river and close at hand Graham was cordial.

" Come along here, then," he said. " I've got some news for you."

Miss Ebbisham ushered him in to where Graham lounged back in his comfortable chair with the carburettor model in its case behind him.

" I talked to the Committee yesterday," said Graham. " And here's their letter confirming what we settled then."

He waved an official-looking sheet airily as he spoke.

" What do they say ? " asked Randall.

" They're making an interim grant, *ex gratia*, of a thousand pounds," said Graham.

" A thousand pounds ! "

If Randall had been asked to name the sum they would pay he would have guessed twenty or twenty-five.

" It's nothing like that as far as you're concerned, young man," said Graham. " Don't start getting magnificent ideas. Here are the figures. My commission—twenty per cent of a thousand is two hundred, leaving eight hundred. Your share is one-third—two-sixty-six, thirteen and fourpence."

" Oh," said Randall.

" It's enough to give you some pennies to spend during this leave, anyway," said Graham.

" I should think so."

Randall was vague about his exact balance at that moment at Cox's but he thought it was fifty pounds or so, larger than it had ever been, and this sum that Graham mentioned was five times as great; five times as much money as he had ever had in his life.

" They haven't paid up yet," went on Graham, " but they will, some time next week, I expect. I'll advance you your share now, if you like—I suppose you'd like the money ? "

" I suppose so."

Mr. Graham rang for Miss Ebbisham.

"Make out a cheque to Mr. Randall for two-sixty-six thirteen four," he said, and then turned to Randall again.

"If they go on using the flare and it isn't superseded—and you're a better judge than I am of that possibility—I'll get another payment out of them later on. It'll be settled eventually on a royalty basis, of course."

"Yes," said Randall, without much knowledge of what a royalty basis was—the fact that this was a payment by the government confused him.

"My guess—and mark you, this is only a guess—is that it'll work out at about five thousand pounds in the end. Then your share will be thirteen hundred odd."

"Yes," said Randall again; he felt he had to say something and this was the best he could do.

Miss Ebbisham came in with the cheque, and Mr. Graham signed it and slid it across to him.

"Put it in your pocket," he said. "Miss Ebbisham will send you a statement of account by post."

"Thank you," said Randall.

"I don't know about the other allied Governments," went on Mr. Graham. "The French have their own flare, probably not as good as this—once again that's something you know more about than I do—and I expect they'll stick to it. But I've got hopes of the Americans. Very likely they'll adopt it. Their military mission is in touch with the Inventions Board."

"Yes," said Randall.

"That'll mean additional payments, of course."

"I suppose so," said Randall.

It did not seem very sensible to talk about additions to a payment of thirteen hundred pounds.

"Anyway, I'll let you know how things develop," said Mr. Graham.

"Thank you," said Randall, rising to his feet; and then, a fuller realisation of all that Graham had done for him breaking upon him, "Thank you. Thank you very much, Mr. Graham."

"Don't mention it," said Mr. Graham, waving away him and his thanks with a single gesture. "Make the most of this leave."

Out in the street Randall had to stop and consider his next move; even though he had a cheque for two hundred and sixty-six pounds in his pocket, even though he was on leave from France, it was not easy to think of how to fill up two hours of a windy March morning in the City. It was like him to feel no sense of grievance on this account, all the same. It had not happened often enough so far, and he had never in his life had things his own way, so that mechanical difficulties of this sort were to his mind a necessary part of life, like breathing. And there was still a decided minor pleasure after years of army life about being able to fritter time away. He took a bus to the Strand and paid in his cheque at Cox's; he had another cup of coffee; he took a walk which led him through Leicester Square and Green Street and the Charing Cross Road, and finally he rode back again on another bus, sitting on the upper deck with the wind blowing round him, thoughts of Muriel mingling with the air of freedom to make a mixture as intoxicating as gin-and-French.

At lunch-time he had a stroke of good fortune; the crowded restaurant was furnished mainly with tables for four, but there were two tables for two and he and Muriel were able to secure one of them so that they could eat their lunch without having strangers listen to their conversation. It was as well, even though Randall, remembering the morning's journey to town, did not plunge at once into the endearments that trembled on his tongue. It was not hard to find an alternative topic; within three minutes of their ordering lunch he was telling Muriel about his interview with Graham and the cheque he had received.

" *How* much did you say ? " asked Muriel, opening her wide eyes wider.

Randall told her again.

" Have you still got the cheque ? "

" No. I paid it in at Cox's."

" So you'll know soon if it's good or not."

" Oh, I'm sure it's good," said Randall. He did not reach this decision by way of the obvious deduction that in the circumstances Graham had nothing to gain and something to lose by giving a worthless cheque; his conviction was based solely on the impression Graham had made on him.

" You never know," said Muriel. " But I can find out about him through the bank this afternoon."

" I shouldn't trouble, dear," said Randall, uncomfortable at the thought of Muriel exerting herself on his behalf, and to divert her thoughts he went on, " That's only an interim payment. Graham said I might easily get a thousand pounds in the end."

" A thousand pounds ! " said Muriel.

" He said he didn't think I'd get anything from the French Government, but he thought I might easily get something from the Americans, too."

" Besides the thousand pounds ? "

" Yes."

Muriel turned her gaze on Randall in a closer examination. Until this moment he had been just a young man, someone she had been drawn to, someone who would pay for her lunches, someone who could provide an evening or two about which she could boast to her friends, but after all only a callow boy who knew nothing of the technique of kissing, who looked forward to taking examinations, who might easily be a bore, and who had a family which was undoubtedly boring. But now he had changed; besides being the son of a schoolmaster, with a dowdy mother and little cats for sisters, he was someone with prospects, someone who would have a thousand pounds—maybe two thousand pounds. And— although this next thought was so wild as almost not to deserve consideration at all—he might even do this again, and again. Besides being a man with a thousand pounds, he might even be a man with a future.

" Harry and I paid much less than a thousand pounds for our house and all the furniture in it," she said. " Of course, I mean that's what it cost. It isn't all paid for even yet. Harry used to say everyone should own his own house—he wouldn't pay rent."

" Yes," said Randall.

" Why did this Mr. Graham give you this money ? " she asked suddenly. " Did you sign anything ? "

" Of course I've signed an agreement. Two agreements."

" I'm sure he's cheated you. I'm sure you shouldn't have signed anything at all without asking someone about it first."

" But it was all right," protested Randall.

" People just don't give money away like that for nothing,"

she persisted. " He must think he'll get more out of you that way."

" But, dear——" said Randall.

Muriel was quick to notice his expression, and her instincts warned her she was on dangerous ground. His trust in this Graham was utterly unreasonable, of course, but men had these silly prejudices, and it was always a ticklish business to oppose them openly. But once she could get proper control of him she'd see to it that things were different. She did not listen to what he said—she could guess what sort of nonsense it was by the look on his face.

" Yes, of course, dear," she said. " I hadn't thought about it that way. I see what you mean now."

The open gratification with which Randall received this speech reassured her—she had been almost afraid when she uttered it that it might be too fulsome. Randall lived in a world where his fellow men tried to tear him apart with high explosive, poison him with gas, stab him through with bayonets, but he did not believe that his fellow men—or women either—would cheat him over money.

" After all," said Randall, " I did hardly anything. Just sketched out an improvement so as to make sure the parachute would open."

" But you said yourself the flare wasn't any good until you did that, didn't you, dear ? You deserve more credit than anyone else, I think."

Randall congratulated himself on his wisdom (he was pleasantly surprised at being so wise) in not arguing with her. She had this lofty opinion of him, and he need not exert himself to disillusion her, especially as she was willing to bow to his superior judgment in business matters. He changed the subject.

" I think we ought to start deciding on what we're going to do to-night," he said. " We haven't much time."

When Muriel responded to this suggestion by looking him over with a considering eye he thought she was trying to make up her mind as to whether she wanted to go to the Savoy or not; actually she was thinking about a dozen other projects as well, and about the Savoy only in part.

NINE

MURIEL HAD HAD FIVE months' experience now of being a war widow, and she had decided that she did not like being one. Widows of her age were no rare phenomena in England at that date, so she did not even have the gratification of being extraordinary. The sympathy that had been extended to her when her loss was new was not now so evident. A captain's widow's pension was a desirable amount of pocket money with which to supplement her earnings, but she could not live on it, and she had no desire at all to go on working for the rest of her life. And she had no desire at all to live the rest of her life without a husband. She wanted to remarry, and whenever Muriel wanted something she wanted it badly and felt a sense of personal grievance at being denied it.

But husbands were not so easy to obtain. Even at twenty-one, in those carefree years before 1914, she had had trouble in bringing Harry to the point of definitely proposing to her, and Harry, being a provident soul, had insisted on a long engagement until his salary and savings justified marriage. They might even, Muriel sometimes thought, have remained engaged until now if 1914 had not come along to shake him out of his prudence and lead him into marriage on his first leave, and into sinking his savings on the first payment on the house in Calmady Road and on the furniture. That had proved the best investment he had ever made; by 1918 the increasing shortage of housing had doubled the value of that house; rising prices had halved the value of the money that had to be paid for it under the 1914 contract with the building society; and the two hundred pounds for which Harry's life was insured had gone a long way towards paying off the mortgage in any case.

Yet even though she practically owned a house and furniture Muriel did not think highly of her chances of obtaining a husband for herself; there was a shortage of men as well as of houses, and competition was intense with demand far out-running supply. And the more desirable the man—the richer, the handsomer, the more influential—the fiercer was the competition. Muriel frankly admitted to herself that at twenty-six—almost twenty-seven—with nothing much in the way of good looks, she did not have a great chance of winning a prize. And she wanted a husband.

Now here was this Randall boy, deplorably young, deplorably innocent, with a deplorable family, and yet attractive in his youth and his innocence although not in his family. Muriel had known the lusts of the flesh in his arms; her hard little heart was almost soft when she thought about him, so that it was almost difficult to consider him objectively. If the telegram about Harry's death had not been waiting for her on that night; if last night he had not treated her with such absurd respect (and if the presence of Grace and Marjorie in her house had not been a hindrance), she would probably have lost her virtue to him, and gladly. She had begun by thinking of flirtation, of sensuous gratification. Now she knew he was no penniless subaltern. He might also be thought to have prospects; if he had once earned a thousand pounds with an invention he might easily do so again, and a thousand pounds was six times Harry's salary in 1914. There was an absurd difference between their ages, but he was a possible husband, a man (Muriel felt warm and weak at the thought of his embraces), and it did not seem as if the war would ever end and make a mere student of him again. And if he did not survive the war she could be no worse off than she was at present, and what he left would pay off the mortgage and leave a substantial balance over. It was too much to hope for that his life was insured.

" We needn't go out this evening," she said to Randall, putting aside the thought of life insurance. " We could have a quiet evening together. You might even try my cooking, if you come to supper."

" That sounds top-hole," said the innocent. As he looked at her across the table the warmest passions surged up in him; his head even swam a little as he met her warm brown eyes. So that afternoon he met her as she left the bank and endured the smoky swaying discomfort of the tram in which they went home together, and he stood by while she opened the door of the house to let them in.

" The girls aren't home yet," she said as they stood in the hall—the hall where she had picked up that telegram from the floor, but neither of them thought of that—and smiled at him, and came into his arms and shared eager kisses with him for a space before she disengaged herself with, " The girls will be home any minute now."

He had no eyes for Marjorie and Grace; to him they were just women to whom it was necessary to be polite, and even their broad friendly smiles did not make any impression on him. He had only thoughts for Muriel's kisses now; he was hot with desire, dizzy with lust, for Muriel's kisses had loosened all the restraints imposed upon him by twenty years of conventional training. He hardly knew what he was doing— stranger still, he hardly knew what he wanted to do. As he sat dumbly at one end of the table with the three women chattering over their meal strange images came and went in the depths of his mind, like the shifting shapes of smoke and fire visible on the floor of an active crater to a spectator looking over from the lip. With supper over and Marjorie and Grace clattering china in the kitchen, he found Muriel in his arms again, but only for a moment; those soft lips had hardly pressed against his before she was holding back from him, pressing herself out of his arms with her hands against his chest.

" Charles ! " she said. " What are we doing ? We mustn't, we mustn't ! "

" Kiss me," he said, straining towards her.

" No, darling. It's not right. We're not married. We're not—oh, please don't, dear."

The pathetic appeal had its effect, and Randall checked himself, his conscience troubling him. He had thrust his attentions on this virtuous woman with insensitive frequency.

" I love you," he said in pleading excuse; convention still dictated that he should word his passion in that form.

" And I love you, too, darling—at least I think I do— but—but——"

Muriel's tact was sufficient to guide her into maintaining the discussion on a moral plane and to keep her from making any practical reference to the presence of the girls in the kitchen.

" Oh, my darling," he said, moved inexpressibly by this declaration of love; he now held both her outstretched hands, but he was kept at arm's length.

" We mustn't—we mustn't be wicked," she said, and the strange word fanned his passion. " I shouldn't have kissed you—I shouldn't have let myself. Oh, what can we do ? "

Her hands pressed his.

" Do ? " he asked, looking at her clearly for a moment. " Why—why—we could——"

" Oh, Charles ! "

She was nearly back in his arms, only resisting faintly. And the thought of marriage was in his mind now, having penetrated at last; the thought of obtaining for himself the only desirable woman in the world. Until this moment he had never contemplated the possibility of his being married, at least as far into the future as he could see.

" Do you really mean that, darling ? " she said.

" Of course I do."

Now she was back in his arms, now she was yielding up her lips to him, now she was whispering endearments to him, and the world was an enchanted place and his passion was no longer something convulsive to be struggled against. It was liable to become more violent at any moment, but Muriel stirred in his arms and stood listening and then drew away from him at the sound of steps in the passage outside. Marjorie came in and stopped short at the sight of them standing together.

" Marjorie——" said Muriel.

" Well ! " said Marjorie, looking at their two faces. " Don't tell me you two are engaged ? "

Muriel looked sideways up at Randall, too shy to speak for herself.

" Yes, we are," said Randall, and Muriel felt the warm glow of achievement. He had said it, he had made the public announcement, and he could not possibly think in the future that the initiative had come from her.

" Good Lord ! " said Marjorie, and, as Grace came in after her, " These two are going to get married."

" And why shouldn't they ? " said Grace.

Strange how passion could be canalised into activity, how it could be diverted into dealing with practical considerations to achieve its own consummation. Ten minutes earlier Randall had not thought about marriage; now he was discussing the marriage laws of Great Britain, facing the fact that he was a minor, remembering with cold horror that he had not many days' leave left (and forcing a smile as he spoke about it), wondering about what his father and mother would say, and even wondering momentarily what it would be like to be a married man.

Passion was indeed canalised into activity.

" Let's come and tell my people," he said, suddenly and unexpectedly weary already of Grace's and Marjorie's felicitations. " That is, if you don't mind, dear ? "

And odd how easy it was to say ' dear ' like that in public now that his passion had been legitimatised—it was the way his father spoke to his mother.

Muriel clung to his arm as they walked up Calmady Road, and when they entered the dark passage through to Harbord Road she turned to him and threw herself into his arms again.

" Darling ! " she said.   " Sweetheart ! "

She pressed herself against him with abandon, and Randall kissed her with equal passion, but he thought of his family and soon relaxed his grip. He was a methodical person; when his family had been informed and all the business settled kisses and embraces would be more legal and more simply come by, so that it was the sensible and logical thing to do to put first things first and attend to business before pleasure.

He opened the door with his latchkey and ushered Muriel into the hall.

" Mother ! " he called.   His mother emerged from the kitchen into the gas-light.   " Muriel and I are going to get married."

" Oh ! " said his mother.

The children in the sitting-room heard the words and came scurrying into the hall, Harriet and Doris all a-flutter at the news of a coming marriage, Jimmy a little puzzled at their excitement.

" I hope you'll be happy," said his mother then, and not until then.

" How exciting ! " said Harriet.

" Are you going to have a real wedding with bridesmaids ? " asked Doris.

" I doubt it," said Randall.   " Where's Father ? In here ? "

His father was in the dining-room correcting exercises on

the big table. His eyes were on the door as they entered, and he rose with a smile.

" My best wishes and congratulations," he said; and then to his wife, " Don't you think this is good news, dear ? "

" Yes," said Mrs. Randall.

Randall turned to the children.

" Get out of here for a minute," he said. " I want to talk to Father."

They went reluctantly.

" Shall I go, too ? " asked his mother.

" Of course not. It's something to do with you, too. You can guess what I want to say, Father ? "

" Yes," said his father, still smiling bravely.

He looked across the gas-lit room at his son, flushed and handsome in his uniform. Of all the civilians in that house Mr. Randall had the clearest idea of the sort of hell from which Randall had emerged and into which he was doomed to return. He could form the best estimate of what were the chances of his ever seeing his son again. No one in the house—no one in the world—knew the torments of apprehension and despair that Mr. Randall had suffered during the endless months that his son was in France. Nobody knew about them—he concealed them from his wife so as not to add to her worries, and nobody else was friendly enough with him to receive his confidences. But if Mr. Randall could have gone and suffered for his son he would have done so gladly.

Now he thought of the boy's tenuous hold on life; he thought of pain and misery, and of a crude wooden cross that might some day be put up in some desolate French field. He could not deny the boy what he was going to ask; he could deny him nothing that was in his power to give him. A few days' pleasure now, cost what it might in the future—how could he withhold it from him ? He stole a glance at Muriel's expressionless face, the petulant lips, the absence of any sign of intellectuality. Should his son survive the war he would probably come to regret this night's work, but now was no time to say so.

" You want my consent to your marriage ? " he said. " You want to get married immediately ? "

" Yes, Father. There's not much time left, you see."

" Of course I see. I'll give my consent gladly—my only regret is that with the law as it stands it was necessary to ask me at all. And I have no doubts that your mother is in complete agreement with me. Aren't you, dear ? "

" Oh yes, of course," said Mrs. Randall with a gulp.

" That's settled then," said Mr. Randall. " Do I give you my blessing, children ? I've never had a child of mine get married before. But you have my blessing, my consent, every good wish of mine is yours."

" Thank you, Father," said Randall.

" Thank you," said Muriel.

" Now for practical details. Do you know how you set about this, son ? In what form do I have to give my consent ? "

The question started an interesting discussion regarding special marriage licences, and register offices; the children, returning into the discussion, were eager to know about what plan had been made regarding an engagement ring and a wedding ring. Jimmy, with the uninhibitedness of childhood, asked about honeymoons—it was the question most of the people present had wanted to ask and had refrained from asking. Randall had not thought about rings; inconceivable as it might seem, he had not really thought about a honeymoon. He laughed self-consciously and said, " You will have to ask Muriel about that," and Muriel giggled modestly as he turned to her. Despite the giggle, she had already formed her notions both about engagement rings and honeymoons, but she did not say so.

Then Mrs. Randall struck a jarring note with a fresh question.

" How long is it since your last husband died, Mrs.— Muriel ? "

" Five months," said Muriel.

She managed to keep her face expressionless, she managed to look straight in her mother-in-law-to-be's eyes and to keep the hostility out of her own, but she knew it was going to be war to the knife between them. Mr. Randall knew it, too, and interposed to change the subject.

" I believe under the terms of my agreement with the school I can claim a day's leave with pay on the occasion of my son's wedding," he said.

" That'll be to-morrow, I hope," said Randall.

" To-morrow ! " said Mrs. Randall in a different tone.

" It sounds as if you're going to have a busy day," said his father.

It was the prospect of that busy day which distracted Randall from the joys of the present evening. When he took Muriel home he kissed her; he experienced the eager pressure of her bosom against him, but nothing more passed between them than the sternest moralist would permit between an affianced couple on the eve of their wedding, even though the sitting-room at Calmady Road was in modest darkness and Grace and Marjorie were discreetly in bed. To-morrow he was going to be married, and to-morrow's delights could wait until to-morrow.

Especially as Muriel was discreet as well as eager. She looked back over the past and took lessons from her good fortune and she applied them to the present. That first evening when she had been with Charles she had invited him into her house with at least the thought that he might make advances to her—there would have been a thrill about declining them even if she had not accepted them. And that second evening, the night they went to the theatre, the night she heard about Harry, she would have kissed him in the taxicab, she would have permitted him more liberty than that, if his cap badge had not caught in her hat so that he was led to believe she was unwilling. While she had been a married woman chance had seen to it that she had not permitted the smallest intimacy. Her second husband would never know that she had been capable of being unfaithful to her first; on the contrary, he would think of her as someone who had behaved with strict propriety. So to-night she determined to comport herself with reserve as well as with passion, so that he would be sure that she was someone to whom marriage was all-important, and in the future (should there be a future) he would be a trusting and unsuspicious husband. So she saw him out through the door with eager speeches about the morrow yet having made no suggestions about to-night. She was full of desire, but she was provident.

Randall had not the slightest idea about how one set about getting married in a hurry, and his father at the breakfast table reluctantly confessed himself equally ignorant, and his mother had no suggestion to make. Randall felt a momentary alarm; it would never do to belittle himself in his bride's eyes by not dealing with this business quickly and efficiently — and, besides, there was the question of reserving an hotel room in a London which was notoriously overcrowded, besides the simple questions of whether to buy an engagement ring and a wedding ring.

"I'm going to telephone Mr. Graham after I've telephoned the general," he said with sudden decision.

Mr. Graham received agreeably Randall's apologies for troubling him.

"Always glad to hear from you," he said. "What can I do?"

Randall told him he was going to get married.

"Congratulations," said Mr. Graham's voice into his ear. "I suppose I don't know the lady?"

Randall explained that it was the lady with whom he had gone to the theatre last leave.

"Have you been faithful to her for five months?" laughed Graham. "Anyway, how can I help?"

Randall told him.

"Good Lord!" said Graham. "You'll need a special licence. Hold on a minute. I'll put you on to Miss Ebbisham again. She knows everything. I'll tell her to get to work on it."

Miss Ebbisham was as omniscient as her employer said —with *Whitaker's Almanack* and *A Layman's Handbook of Law* on her desk and an unbelievable rapidity in looking up references. She told Randall all about marriage licences and special licences; it was from Miss Ebbisham that he first heard about Doctors' Commons, and he was quickly primed with all the necessary information.

"Are you sure you can manage it all right now, Mr. Randall?"

"Yes, thank you, Miss Ebbisham."

"One minute, then. Mr. Graham would like to speak to you again."

There was a click and a rattle, and then Graham's voice issued out of the receiver.

"Where's the honeymoon to be?"

"I haven't decided yet. As a matter of fact——"

" Well ? "

" As a matter of fact I was going to ask if Miss Ebbisham would mind helping me get an hotel room."

" Of course. Anything else ? Theatre tickets ? Flowers ? "

" Flowers, of course," said Randall, realising—another thing he had never thought about before—that flowers were almost a necessary part of a marriage ceremony.

" I'll get it all fixed," said Graham. " Telephone at lunch-time and we'll be able to tell you what we've arranged. Telephone before that if there's any difficulty."

There was no difficulty; only a busy and exciting day. Making an appointment to meet his parents in London at lunch-time; calling for Muriel, to find her dressed in her best and waiting for him; patiently enduring the tram journey up to town until at the Elephant and Castle they sighted a taxicab and, precipitating themselves downstairs, secured it and told the taxi-driver he was theirs for the day and that they were going to get married.

" I'll do it for you as it's your wedding day, sir," said the taxi-driver. " Lucky I've got an extra two gallons of petrol."

Then to the bank, where Muriel slipped in, with Randall waiting in the taxi, to tell them that she was remarrying and they would not see her again until the honeymoon was over.

" You could have knocked Mr. Jennings over with a feather," exulted Muriel when she got back into the taxicab.

Then to Cox's to cash a large cheque.

" Dear, how much money have you besides the cheque you got from Mr. Graham ? " asked Muriel, and then, when he told her, " Oh, that's good."

And then to Doctors' Commons to obtain a marriage licence, being led from one office to another by grinning messenger girls until they secured the precious document.

A jeweller's next; Muriel suggested which one to go to. Her taste ran to diamond half-hoops, and the one she selected cost nearly two hundred pounds—in fact, when the cost of the plain gold wedding ring was added the total was over two hundred pounds.

" It looks nice," said Muriel, contemplating her finger with her hand held far out. " Thank you, darling."

Her left hand when they went into the shop was bare of rings, but there was a smaller diamond ring on her right hand to which Randall paid no special attention. He was merely glad that he had received that cheque from Mr. Graham, for if he had not he would not have had the money to buy this essential to married life. It was even as well that he had not been in the habit of spending all his pay and allowances; if they were going to spend the next four days living expensively in London he would be making inroads upon his accumulated balance. To take a taxi round London for a single morning, as Randall found, cost more than a whole day's pay for a first lieutenant. But none of this was worth consideration; the happiest man in the world would not waste a moment of his happiness thinking about money.

He telephoned Miss Ebbisham.

" I've got a room for you, Mr. Randall," she said in her prosaic tones as if she was not speaking of the most exciting thing in the world. " It's at the Oldcastle. You know where that is ? It's at the corner of Bruton Street—any taxi-driver will know it. And my best wishes, Mr. Randall. Good luck."

Lunch with his parents and Muriel at the Holborn was a rather awkward affair. His mother was silent and inclined to be over-particular about her table manners. His father tried to make conversation in the face of the obvious difficulties, but somehow it might have been a gloomy function if Muriel had not at one moment found Randall's hand under the tablecloth and given it a warm little squeeze. That ended the gloom entirely.

Now the register office. Business clearly was brisk here; they had to wait while one couple was married, and while they were waiting two more parties arrived. The brides-to-be favoured Muriel with inquisitive stares, while the bride-grooms, one a second lieutenant and one a sergeant, were ready with broad grins when they exchanged glances with Randall. Mrs. Randall fussed with her hat and coat—the second lieutenant's mother was smartly dressed and made her feel shabby in the clothes that had been new in 1913. Now they were in the inner office; now they were declaring that there was no legal impediment to their marriage; now his father was declaring that he had no objection; now he was putting the wedding ring on Muriel's finger, and his mother was crying.

" May I wish you good luck, Mrs. Randall ? " asked the
registrar, and Randall felt a moment's surprise at his mother
being wished good luck until he realised that Muriel was Mrs.
Randall now, now and for ever.

A taxi took the four of them back to Upper Oak together,
to collect Muriel's bags and Randall's kit.

" Good-bye, old man," said his father, shaking hands.
" Let's hear from you."

" Good-bye, darling," said his mother, dry-eyed.

" My goodness, I'm tired," said Muriel, sitting back on the
taxicab seat and stretching her legs. With one toe she
furtively eased her heel out of the other shoe.

" Darling ! " said Randall, as if that was an intelligent
contribution to the conversation.

The Oldcastle Hotel had retained some of its pre-war
magnificence and ceremonial. Two pompous individuals with
foreign accents escorted them up to their room. One of them
had side-whiskers and wore a frock coat with silk lapels;
the younger one was immensely dignified in a braided morning
coat. The outlandish clothes, the foreign accents, the servant
carrying the baggage, the gilt and the magnificence all combined to accentuate in Randall's mind the feeling of being in a
different world. Was he the subaltern who last week was
inspecting his platoon for trench feet ? Was he the schoolboy
who used to walk to school swinging his books on the end of
a strap ?

" I expect Madam would like some tea," said the gentleman
in the braided morning coat.

" Oh yes, please," said Muriel.

Here they stood, alone in the room. There was an immense
double bed, but the room was large enough to dwarf it
entirely.

" Darling ! " said Muriel. " Aren't you going to kiss me ? "

He had been wondering where to put his stick and gloves;
now he dropped them on the bed as Muriel flew into his
arms. She kissed him eagerly, with all the passion she
possessed. She had used restraint up to that moment;
restraint had been necessary to the ends she had had in
view, and she had endured it without complaining. But as
with any self-indulgent and selfish person, restraint was
irksome, and she cast it off. Her hot shallow passion—fire

in the straw—roused convulsive feelings in Randall. His
head swam; he swayed on his feet as he stood there with her
in his arms.

Someone tapped on the door and Randall heard the sound
twice without its conveying any meaning to his seething brain.
Muriel eased herself out of his arms and walked coolly over
to the mirror, looking at herself and her hat before she called
out ' Come in '.

" Tea, sare," announced a waiter, bustling in with a tray.
He put it on a table; he drew up chairs.

" The evening paper, sare," he said and then withdrew.

" Isn't this nice ? " said Muriel, sitting down to tea.

Later on, long after tea, Muriel announced, " I'm going to
have a bath and change my clothes. You're lucky. You
haven't much to unpack."

The bathroom was like a minor room in a museum, with
the huge marble fittings as exhibits. Randall stared at it all
a little uncomprehending—actually he had not realised that
there was a bathroom opening out of the bedroom. The
idea seemed as colossal as the fittings—and the latter, in-
cidentally (although Randalls unsophisticated eye regarded
them with respect), were almost old enough to be museum
exhibits in real earnest.

Muriel turned a considering eye on Randall again. That
tact of hers told her that Randall was not ready for all the
intimacies of married life. She did not want to shock him,
and she could feel in her bones that the possibility existed.
On this honeymoon it was the bride who had to be tactful,
not the groom.

" Now sit down and smoke a cigarette or something," she
said. " I've got to unpack and do a lot of other things."

It was pleasant to sit there while Muriel moved about the
room, opening and shutting drawers, laying things out on
the dressing-table, and finally retiring into the bathroom
with an armful of clothing; soon a thunderous roar of water
into the bath told of her activities in there. Randall picked
up the newspaper which had been neglected ever since the
waiter had brought it in. There had been so much to think
about that he had not even seen the morning paper. Here
was the headline. " Hun Offensive Opens." So it had come,
that German attack which every man in the ranks had been

expecting. Randall began to read the British communiqué.
War was something he knew about—reading the communiqué
he was not at a loss as he had been in going to the Savoy, or
being received at the Oldcastle, or finding out about the
marriage laws. Randall had the special advantage of having
fought in battles and of having read the communiqués about
them later. Along those lines his critical sense was fully
developed.

But this was something different from usual, much different.
Half-way down the communiqué Randall actually broke off
his reading and returned to the beginning again. This was a
tale of disaster, and he could not believe he had read it
correctly. No, there was no mistake about it. The break-
through had come, that break-through for which two million
men had died unavailingly during the three preceding years;
and it was Ludendorff and not Haig who had achieved it.
The newspaper was aware of the gravity of the situation; it
showed a map beside the communiqué, but Randall did not
have to refer to it. Those names were familiar to him.
Gouzeaucourt—bloody Gouzeaucourt—was lost, and St.
Leger and Croisilles. In a day the Germans had made the
sort of advance for which the British army had poured out its
blood in month-long agonies. He could not understand it
at all.

In the next column was the German communiqué, issued
by wireless for circulation in neutral countries. It roared of
overwhelming victory, of triumphant advance. Five thousand
guns and thirty thousand prisoners taken—*five thousand
guns*? That could only mean a frightful disaster, with many
divisions overrun, and German troops pushing through far
into the back areas. Even with the wildest German exaggeration, even with tenfold exaggeration, the losses must be
severe, and Randall did not think the Germans exaggerated
their gains tenfold—and there was the sombre British communiqué to give tacit confirmation to the German claims.

Randall looked unseeing at the paper while in his mind's
eye he tried to call up a picture of that sort of defeat—broken
troops streaming to the rear, confusion and panic and disorder.
It was not an easy picture to conjure up, for the victories in
which Randall had participated had ended in the gain of a few
yards of battered trench, in the hasty building of a parapet,

and in the withdrawal of a dozen exhausted divisions. This other was something new—or something old-fashioned; it might be a Waterloo or a Blenheim, and this time with the British army on the losing side. He got up out of his chair; when he had left the battalion only those few days ago the division had been behind the line in support—it had been designated as a 'counter-attack' division in the new jargon which was gaining circulation lately. What had happened to it? What had happened to the battalion? It might have been already overwhelmed in the advancing German tide, or it might have flung itself in red ruin on the machine guns, or perhaps at this minute they might be digging-in, frantically constructing a new line, filling sandbags, stringing wire, slaving and toiling all through the night in readiness for the next attack. The platoon—the company—the colonel—the captain—Sergeant Macclesfield; while he was here in this hotel room they might be taking up their positions to stand and fall to the last man to-morrow—without him.

The bathroom door opened and Muriel looked roguishly round it. She was allowing only her face to show, for her body was dressed in her rose-coloured dressing-gown, and under her dressing-gown she wore her shoulder-strapped corset cover over her petticoat, and she was coyly thinking of the moment when the removal of the dressing-gown would reveal her bare arms and shoulders. She peered round the door, ready for anything except the blank stony stare which met her eyes.

"He's in a mood again," she said to herself; the newspaper was still in his hand, but she had not the sense, despite her tact, to connect his mood with the newspaper. She could not really believe that anyone could be upset over the possible fate of his friends—certainly not someone with a new wife in a rose-pink dressing-gown. She felt a momentary irritation that this uncertain husband of hers should be going through an attack of temperament at this time of all times; it was certainly not fair that it should be she who made the allowances and he who had to be allowed for. But there it was. Her husband was upset over something, and her quick brain could easily calculate that at this present juncture the only thing to do was to be sympathetic about it. He might easily be the sort of fellow who would remember all these

things far in the future. Harry had been drunken as well as
moody.

She mastered her petulance and came towards him.

" Darling ! " she said, and put her hands on his shoulders,
her fingers twining under the shoulder-strap of his tunic,
her face raised to his. The newspaper dropped from his
fingers, and his hands came out to her automatically; through
the dressing-gown he felt the warm softness of her body.

" I love you, darling," she said. " Be kind to me."

It was the appeal which above all others could influence
him, could call him out of his sombre mood; in a sense it
was an appeal reminding him of his other duty. The deep
wells within him gushed with tenderness. This fragile, gentle
creature had entrusted herself to him and, miraculously, was
dependent on him for love. He put his lips on hers and then
it did not take very long for tenderness to grow into passion,
into surging waves of the most intense feeling. She knew
how to channel that passion, how to guide him and direct
him, even while he was so blinded with love that he did not
know he was being guided. And she did not have to remain
mistress of the situation for long; soon she could abandon
herself to the wild passion that swept her, too, away. She
could give herself up to those lusts of her body which caution
and convention had kept so long suppressed.

" Darling, darling," she sobbed, her arms straining about
him. " Darling ! "

And then peace descended on them both, oblivion falling
swiftly at the climax of passion, like night coming down upon
a tropical sunset.

TEN

" WE CAN TELEPHONE DOWN for breakfast," pointed out Muriel. Randall was not accustomed to the idea of bedroom telephones or of a kitchen awaiting his orders. Having gone supperless to bed, he was immensely hungry. He was also extremely thirsty; for much more than a year now he had been accustomed to being given a mug of strong tea almost before he was awake, and habit was strong. For a few seconds he merely felt thirsty, and then he thought of tea, mugs of strong sweet tea poured down without a thought for his stomach wall. The instant that mental picture formed in his mind his desire was almost uncontrollable; he had Muriel's scented naked body in the bend of his arm, and just before this he had been fascinatedly exploring it, with passion ready to assert itself; but now the thought first of tea and then of breakfast led him to turn away from those firm breasts and silken flanks, and apply himself to the task of informing the unseen powers of his needs. His thirst even overcame his modesty; not until he had crossed the room and addressed himself to the telephone where it stuck out from the wall did it occur to him that he too was naked and that all the back of him was exposed to Muriel's gaze, but he took it for granted that she would avert her eyes. Without a great deal of trouble he succeeded in getting someone at the other end of the wire to take note of his desires, and then he turned away from the telephone to find, as he expected, that Muriel was lying with her eyes closed so that he could plunge hurriedly into shirt and trousers so as not to offend against her delicacy.

It was all very happy, now that it was certain that tea would be arriving soon. Muriel could snatch up various garments and flee into the bathroom (Randall could actually make himself steal a glance at her, registering thereby a picture on his memory's retina that was to abide with him for months to come) and she could smile at him as she emerged again in her dressing-gown and stood aside for him to go in after her. He put his trench coat about him when he came out, having been improvident enough to come away on a honeymoon without a dressing-gown, and then the waiter came tapping at the door with breakfast.

It was hardly after seven o'clock in the morning (although even so it meant that the newly married couple had had a long night) and the waiter was acutely aggrieved that in the Oldcastle Hotel, of all places, he should have to serve breakfast at such an unholy time. He put the tray down with a bump.

" Bad news from the Front, sare," he said, with a wave of his hand towards the morning paper.

There it was. There was the dread news. Here were all those forgotten emotions surging up again. Randall drank the tea which Muriel poured for him and read what *The Times* had to say about the German offensive. *The Times* was grave; while he read he even forgot that he was in a bedroom with Muriel in a rose-coloured dressing-gown.

" Darling, what's the bad news ? " asked Muriel.

" It's about Jerry's offensive," said Randall, tearing his eyes from the paper and turning to encounter hers.

" Oh," said Muriel.

She had heard so much about offensives; she had even been interested in them once.

" Jerry's broken through," went on Randall.

" Has he ? "

" Yes. God knows how he did it."

" Oh well," said Muriel.

The child's toy was broken, and she had to appear sympathetic.

" The division must be right in it."

" Isn't it lucky you aren't there, then," said Muriel.

Randall felt no shock, no offence, at her attitude about that. There was a subtle point which no civilian, no woman, not even Muriel, could be expected to appreciate. Ordinarily a ' wangle ' was something to exult over. The string deftly pulled by which a tedious bit of duty was evaded, the blind chance which took one out of a temporary danger, were things to smile about, and there was no need to feel shame over them at all. All soldiers boasted about wangling, and all civilians must know about it. But there was a limit to wangling. Until now Mr. Graham's wangle which had brought him back from France had been a good wangle but it ceased to be good now that Jerry had broken through. Yet the distinction was too subtle for Muriel to be expected to appreciate it without explanation.

"I mustn't stop here any longer," said Randall.

"What?"

"Of course I mustn't, darling. They'll be cancelling all leaves, in any case."

"But you're not on leave. You said so yourself. You're under orders until the 25th. Doing what you're told."

"I know, darling. But they'll send me back if I ask to go. When I telephone this morning I'll say that I've finished my work on the specifications—you know I never had any to do."

"You want to leave me *now*? We've got up to the 25th, and even that's such a little time."

"I don't want to leave you, darling. Oh, I hate to leave you. But you see how it is."

"I think——" began Muriel, and then checked herself. She had been going to say she thought Randall was a fool, and a heartless fool, and from that she had intended to go on to say that she did not think she was being treated with the consideration to which she was entitled. But a further look at Randall's expression told her that such tactics might be unavailing and even dangerous. Men were likely to be obstinate and moody, actuated by motives as infantile as those of children. There was another method which might be more efficacious.

"I think you're sweet," she said, and she held out her arms to him so that her dressing-gown sleeves slid up them. "Come and kiss me, darling. I can't wait."

Randall came and kissed her gladly enough, sinking into the clasp of her arms. Against her smooth cheek she felt his unshaven one, not nearly as bristly as Harry's had been at that time in the morning.

"This old trench coat feels just horrible," she said.

"I'll take it off."

As Muriel abandoned herself to her body one last thought went through her mind, that men were just like children and just as easily diverted. Yet later on she heard Randall swearing mildly and opened her eyes to see him peering at his wrist-watch.

"What's the matter, darling?" she asked.

"I forgot to wind this up last night. I haven't the foggiest notion what time it is."

" Whatever does it matter, darling ? "

" I've got to telephone Clarence and get my orders. I mustn't be late."

She made one last effort to get her own way.

" I think you're just horrid," she said, and she turned her face into the pillow and drummed on the bed with her feet and hands in petulance that was not all acting.

But when she stole a glance at him she was quick to see that there was a danger that he might take her seriously, and that if he did his opinion of her would be gravely lowered. She could recognise the inevitable when she met it, and although she might resent the encounter she had too much sense to let him guess it.

" Darling," she said, all helpfulness and sympathy. " They'll tell you on the telephone what the time is. And if you want to you can telephone Clarence from here, before you dress or anything."

" I hadn't thought of that," said Randall.

His face lit up with a smile at his own stupidity, which would have been a reward for any woman who loved him and which would have wrung the heartstrings of any woman at all who could form a notion of the sort of hell to which he was striving to get back. It wrung Muriel's heartstrings, for that matter; she felt both sorrow and sympathy as she watching him walk over to the telephone on the wall. There was a good deal of maternal feeling in the love that she felt for him at that moment; it mingled with the exasperation she felt at having her wishes disregarded by this wilful child, and with the vague wonder about whether fate was planning to make her a second time a widow.

It was not difficult to be ordered back to France. That was the moment when England was pouring out the last blood from her veins, when grandfathers and their grandchildren were both being summoned to fill up the gaps in the ranks of her devoted armies. Randall went back to France that day, to land at the moment when the army was making its supreme effort to hold back the German offensive, when England and Germany, like two wrestlers, were both putting forth their last ounces of strength knowing well that a moment's weakening would lead to a fall. The Railway Transport Officer at the army base to whom Randall went for instructions looked at him doubtfully, for Randall was asking about a division regarding which nothing was known since yesterday. A few stragglers, a few motor transport drivers; that was all. As far as could be determined the division had obeyed its orders and had stood and fought it out to the last man, and the tide of the German advance was flowing over its grave.

Mr. Graham out of the kindness of his heart had pulled a string to gain for a young man a few days' relaxation and by doing that had saved his life. It was hardly likely that Randall would have been among the few survivors of that fight to the death—and most of those survivors were men who at the end of the war were found in German hospitals, limbless, or eyeless, or mad. Randall went up to find himself attached to another battalion of the Fusiliers, called upon to command a company of strangers fighting in another division. Until long after he had grown familiar with his new unit he never had time or strength to think about the strangeness of his surroundings. Those were the desperate months of battle; of wild rearguard actions; of night marches prolonged to the afternoon of the following day, when men stumbling along under pack and rifle would fall dead from sheer fatigue, when sleeplessness and weariness combined to muffle the brain into stupidity—and stupidity in a company commander meant death and defeat, when Lewis guns had to be sited to obtain the best field of fire, and inexperienced subalterns had to be supervised, and exhausted men coaxed and cajoled or forced into making one more effort, and one more effort after that.

Dig in and fight, fight and then retreat when a German advance elsewhere threatened the flank; fight to the limit of exhaustion to beat off the German assaults and finally save Armentières; stagger out of the line at last one night relieved and with a long rest promised, only to be roused at noon to march all the rest of the day, sleep until midnight in a muddy field in the pouring rain, and then march again until dawn and then go into action to plug a new gap that had appeared in the attenuated line. Some lieutenant-general probably received high praise and a K.C.B. for switching the division over so neatly across the tangled lines of communication and saving the day, while the filthy lousy infantry had the satisfaction (if they cared) of knowing they had tramped forty kilometres of *pavé* in twenty hours, out of one battle and into another.

For Randall came the news that he had been promoted, that he could mount his third star and was now a captain. It was a strange reminder for him that in all this whirling insanity of war he remained an individual known by name and record to the obscure gods of Whitehall. A group of English staff officers bent over a map-covered table in a French château could say, ' Which division shall we use ? ' and never know or care that their decision sent Captain Randall of the Royal Fusiliers into desperate action. A group of German staff officers bending over similar maps could decide, ' Let us attack here,' and Captain Randall would awake to the roar of the barrage and lead the fragments of his company in a counter-attack, bombing his way from traverse to traverse, as his share of undoing their work. It was as well to be reminded sometimes that he was an actual person and not just one fighting animal in a herd of fighting animals, a beast of the fields and trenches—or something even worse, even lower. Randall had kept white mice as a child and had forgotten about them during a couple of days of unexpected diversion; he had come back to them to find them dead of hunger and thirst. Was there a wayward god who owned Randall as Randall had owned those white mice and who now was pursuing other interests and leaving him to die in this cage of violence ?

Letters came to him sometimes. ' My Own Dearest, I love you and miss you.' ' My Dearest Son, Jimmy's report has just come and he is third this year and Father is pleased.' ' My Dear Charles, We had a visit from Muriel yesterday and I am glad to be able to tell you that she is looking well and happy.' Those letters, read by candlelight in a bombed-out billet, helped to keep him sane even though during those mad weeks he had not the strength to answer them save by field postcards with all the lines scratched out except ' I am quite well ' and ' I have received your letter '. And he, like thousands of other men, knew twinges of regret when he addressed those postcards because he had had to scratch out, and not leave untouched, the line that said ' I have been wounded and admitted into hospital '. A wound, almost any wound, would be better than these dregs of life.

Now at last came a period of rest, if rest it could be called, with the battalion filled up with drafts almost untrained who had to be taught their work, when the rest billets were bombed almost nightly, when paperwork had to be made up and conferences attended and new tactics studied. There was at least almost complete freedom from fear, a chance to take filthy clothes off, a chance to bathe and to sleep. There was at least the dubious knowledge that the various German offensives had ended, although that seemed too good to be true and the natural assumption was that Jerry was mounting some new surprise and would blast his way forward again shortly. There was the still more unsettling knowledge that a counter-offensive was being planned and was about to be launched—Randall had been in too many offensives not to be sceptical about them; victory (and not just the occupation of a few yards of blood-soaked trench) was also something too good to appear possible.

There was once again that sick feeling before a ' show ', waiting for dawn, waiting for the barrage to open, with one's wrist-watch ticking away the seconds, and fear (uncontrollable and despicable) consuming one's vitals. Fear not merely of dying but fear of dying in vain, even though while marching up yesterday they had passed hundreds of tanks hidden by the roadside, even though aeroplanes in scores were patrolling overhead, even though at the battalion conference a visiting staff officer had talked with supreme confidence about the results the new tactics were sure to bring. There was time during these seconds to put his hand in his pocket and touch Muriel's last letter, to think about her, just for a few moments to think about her lips and her hands, to feel comforted that someone at least was bound to him. Now the second-hand had completed its round, now hell was broken loose, now was the time to go forward at the head of his company, to remember in that appalling din what his orders were, and to keep a clear head and watch the barrage rolling ahead of him and the tanks out on the flank wallowing forward in sinister menace.

Randall lived through that day, and the next, and the

next, as incredibly they won their way forward, as incredibly
the machine-guns lashing out at them were silenced by the
tanks charging up from nowhere. Prisoners—not a shaking
shell-shocked half-dozen, but two hundred men with an
officer waving a white rag, cut off by a sudden surging
advance pushing through a weak point. Batteries of field
artillery, standing silent with their muzzles pointing towards
France but with their devoted crews lying in heaps of
shattered corpses. Jerry was fighting it out with all the
valour and discipline expected of him, staggering sometimes
under the frightful blows dealt out to him, but rallying again,
digging in, and fighting and dying where he stood. Randall
had heard the lie about German machine-gunners chained
to their guns, but the machine-gunners his company encountered were not chained and yet fought to the last to
hold back the tide of the resurgent British might.

A company commander had to use cunning and self-
control, however weary and sick he might be, sweeping
the area ahead with his field-glasses, holding back his line,
and sending a platoon creeping forward up a fold of ground
so slight that only a practised soldier with a clear head
could see that there a man inching forward on his belly
could just lie beneath the arch of the bullets' trajectory.
When rifle or bomb had killed the gunners a company commander then had to get his men forward again, watching
his flanks, keeping in touch to the right and the left, holding
a reserve in hand, however tiny, for the unforeseen emergency,
and at nightfall collecting his last strength to post sentries
and send out patrols, site his guns and see that there was
food and water for hungry and thirsty men, cartridges and
bombs for fighting men, and a note in the records for dead
men. Sleep for a little while, rouse himself to go out and
see that all was well, report to battalion headquarters, study
orders and maps, and then, having fallen asleep with his
face on his crossed forearms, struggle back to consciousness an hour before dawn ready for another day like the
preceding—but alike only in its weariness and anxiety, for
each day brought entirely different tactical problems that
had to be solved by cunning or valour, with death as the
price of failure.

They reached the outskirts of a village only half shattered, whose rubble heaps and cellars made it a dangerous place for tanks, and with a brickyard beside it where the clay pits and the piles of bricks constituted a strong point for a determined enemy to make a stand. The surge of the advance halted here as the hidden machine-guns sliced up the unwary. Randall, on his belly behind a low bank, studying the brickyard through his glasses, found the colonel crouching beside him.

" You must get forward, Randall," he said. " The Jocks on the right are held up. Get forward at all costs."

" Yes, sir," said Randall.

One fighting man could use that hideous expression ' at all costs ' to another without rousing rancour, and the colonel was as haggard, as weary, and as dirty as Randall, without even the vigour and flexibility of youth.

" I'll be over with Cox on the left," said the colonel. " I know I can trust you, Randall."

" Yes, sir."

The colonel crawled stiffly away while Randall sought with his glasses for dead ground by which entrance might be won to the brickfield.

A word to a runner, and then Randall corrected himself, halted the runner, and repeated the message at greater length and made sure it was understood; Randall had learned by now that there were men—even runners selected for their quick wits—who could not grasp the essentials of a tactical situation in the way he could, and a misunderstood message meant failure and bloody ruin. He got his Lewis guns into action and sent his reserve bombers crawling up the ditch at the edge of the brickfield. He made his way over to Lieutenant Clough's platoon and watched the preparations, whistle in hand. A ragged volley of bombs detonated down in the village.

" Now ! " said Randall, pealing on his whistle.

Shell-shocked madmen screaming in padded cells were haunted in their paroxysms by scenes and sounds like this. Bombs crashing everywhere; machine-guns raving; the bared teeth of a burly German skewered through the stomach with a bayonet; a little group of defenders blown apart by a well-flung bomb; the sudden meeting round the corner of a brick-pile with a German officer leading the supports forward;

shots and shouts, and the German officer down on his hands and knees with a torrent of blood pouring from his neck; and then, when it was all over, to know that it was not all over, but the position must be consolidated, guns posted and everything made ready for the counter-attack.

" Go and tell Sergeant Holly——" began Randall to his runner, but the runner fell dead as he spoke to him.

The company sergeant-major came round the corner of the brick-pile at that moment and was thrown against the bricks by a bullet which shattered his right arm. Randall went to help him, and another bullet screamed past his ear and knocked a chip from a brick and ricocheted off. For the moment there was no time to ascertain whence came those bullets which raked the passageway between the brick-piles, but as soon as Randall had finished giving his orders his attention was recalled to the matter when another man was hit there. These were grave losses, and it was equally serious that the marksman, whoever he was, overlooked the easiest route of communication through the brickfield.

" Keep back from there, sir," pleaded a runner; " 'e shoots as quick as lightnin'."

Flattened against the brick-pile, Randall worked a brick loose at the corner; taking off his helmet he could apply his eye to the notch and look for the sniper. The number of possible places was limited; already with the quick-wittedness of war Randall had taken note of the general direction from which the bullets came, and it was plunging fire, too—the sniper must be perched high up. Up the bank above the brickyard was something that looked like the foundations of a cottage. It could only be from there that the marksman was firing, although the closest inspection by Randall, at the range of nearly two hundred yards, showed him nothing.

" Try him with a greatcoat," he ordered over his shoulder.

The old, old stratagem—the greatcoat on a rifle muzzle thrust round the corner to draw fire. A bullet whacked against the bricks and screamed off again. Could there have been the smallest, almost invisible movement up there —there, between those bits of wall?

" Let's have that rifle," said Randall.

" Please, sir; please, sir," begged the runner.

" Shut up. Be ready with that greatcoat when I tell you."

The rifle could be laid in a gap in the edge of the brick-pile, pointing up at the bank. Would the sniper—a desperate man with his life at stake—notice it? It drew no shot. Slowly, so as to expose no single inch of himself, Randall changed position against the wall. Now was the time to put his shoulder to the butt of the rifle, his cheek to the stock. Would a bullet come flying through the gap, along the barrel of the rifle, to strike him between the eyes as he looked along the sights? Randall had to force himself to move the last few inches; in his imagination he could feel the impact of that bullet. The impact did not come; moving a quarter of an inch at a time, Randall trained the rifle on the gap between the fragments of wall. It was necessary that his aim should be good, and his pressure on the trigger steady. He would not be granted more than one shot. He settled himself as best he could.

" Greatcoat," he said; no more than that, so as not to disturb his breathing.

" I'm shovin' it out, sir," said the runner.

Something moved over there again. Randall pressed the trigger just before the sniper's bullet whacked against the wall through the greatcoat.

" D'yer get 'im, sir ? "

Randall put his eye to the notch; through the sights of the rifle, just as he ducked, he had seen something move violently, and he did not think it was the dust thrown up by the bullet. Now he saw a head in a German helmet show up there; he saw it turn and sink down. A man was writhing there in agony.

" Yes," said Randall.

ELEVEN

THE LINE MOVED ON over the maps that civilians in England and France and America studied in their newspapers; the soldiers in France were aware of the same thing, but less acutely because of their exhaustion and because four years of vain striving had inculcated into the lower ranks a cynical unbelief in the possibility of victory in the field. But the line moved on, and marvellously the division remained stationary in support as another division was moved up through it to take up the attack. A week of rest, bringing letters from home as a reminder that somewhere the lunatic turmoil of the guns could not be heard, that somewhere human beings still slept in beds and in the complete assurance that to-morrow night they would be alive and sleeping in beds again.

For Randall, among other letters, there was one from Mr. Graham—'I hope you will be interested to hear that the P–R flare has been adopted by the American Army, and I have issued licences permitting its manufacture in the United States. We may well believe that this will result in a considerable money payment in course of time.' The letter ended with good wishes, conventionally worded and yet obviously sincere. Randall re-read the letter, making his mind throw off the military problems that encumbered it. 'A considerable money payment' would be welcome 'in course of time'. His increase of pay resulting from his promotion to captain's rank had not made up for the allotment he made to Muriel, especially with the increase in income-tax. Before this money had meant little to him, merely the counters handed about in the game of life which he played in the intervals of the business of death. Now he had to think for a moment before he fell in with the suggestion that they should visit an estaminet for eggs and chips and a bottle of wine.

And the flare was no longer the Phillips–Randall, but the P–R; Randall had been aware of that for some time—he had seen the abbreviation on indents and official forms, and yesterday he had actually seen a stationary railway waggon chock-full of P–R flares in boxes. The news that the American army was adopting it, he supposed, was good. He had had a few encounters with American troops

in France, and a friend returning from Paris had told him
that he had seen a couple of American divisions (' each as
big as a Corps ', the friend said) march through the city.
American troops had been in action on the Marne, he
understood, at the time when he was taking part in the
defence of Armentières. Presumably there was some sort
of American army in existence; maybe by next year it
would be a force worth reckoning with, but it could never
approach the British army in size, and so presumably
its consumption of the P–R flare would not be too great
either.

There was much more satisfaction to be got from Muriel's
letters, with their chit-chat about work at the bank and life
in London. It was interesting to hear that Massey (Dick
Massey, Muriel called him) was home with a Blighty wound,
discharged from the army and walking about with a wooden
leg ' so that I couldn't hardly guess it ' said Muriel. When
Randall had been a very little boy at school he had known
Massey by sight as a Sixth Former, a very great man indeed,
with his school colours for cricket and football and half a
dozen other games; and later as Randall rose up the school
Massey had come occasionally, moustached and grown up,
to take part in Old Boys' games and to be regarded with
all the awe due to a man who had played in county cricket.
With a wooden leg he would never play cricket again, but
Randall still felt that feeling of awe when he thought of
the great Massey, and it was strange to read Muriel's casual
words about him—' Dick Massey, who was at the school
a few years before you '. Randall could even remember
that while he was still at school the headmaster had proudly
announced that Captain Richard Massey had been awarded
the Military Cross. That was more than two years ago now,
and in those two years he had become a captain himself,
and he was married, and his wife could write familiarly
about Dick Massey, and he had made some contribution
to the perfection of the P–R flare.

Muriel's letters were full of passion and affection, and
said how she was longing to see him again, and wondered
if he would get another leave (' not a hope ', wrote Randall
back in reply to this), and had some business comment
regarding paying off the mortgage on the house—Muriel

was apparently set on doing this, and as she was so anxious about it Randall felt no regrets about the allotment of his pay to her. It was curiously gratifying, for that matter, to think that he would soon be the owner of a house—it almost made him believe, in optimistic moments, that there was a future when he would live at peace in that house, and Muriel with him, when he would earn a civilian living, when death would not be waiting for him to-morrow. The thought inspired a tender, passionate letter. He sealed it in a ' green envelope ' with the declaration that it contained no military information; thereby it escaped the censorship of a brother officer—although still having to run the gauntlet of possible censorship at the Base—so that he could be sure that no one who knew him would read how he called Muriel ' My very dearest ' and signed himself ' Your adoring husband.' Even though he had served two years in the army he still had a sense of shame.

The letter finished, he wrote a polite reply to Mr. Graham, and a letter to his father and mother; he put his signature to a series of returns, gave some orders to the officer second in command of his company, and went along to the conference which had been called for the company and field officers of the brigade. The inevitable staff officer was there, with the brigadier and the deputy-assistant-quartermaster-general, a tank corps colonel, an artillery colonel—an ominous assembly. And a glance at the maps hung on the wall made a more ominous impression still.

" Gentlemen," said the staff officer, standing by the maps with a pointer in his hand, " here is the Hindenburg Line, as you doubtless recognise. When this is broken we can consider the war won. To-day we have to discuss the part the brigade is to play in breaking it."

Randall listened to the plan of attack as it was outlined and industriously took notes. He could have wished that the staff officer had had the good taste to refrain from that silly remark about considering the war won. That was the sort of idiotic thing the staff could be expected to say. In the ears of a fighting man it rang false, like the sentiment in ' Poppies of Wipers '. Randall and the men under his command—the whole of that incomparable army, for that matter—would do their duty at the cost of their lives, would pour out their blood and their strength, without the clap-trap appeal of sentimental songs or nonsense about winning the war. If Randall had been pinned down to it, he would naturally have declared his belief in ultimate victory, but it was a nebulous belief in something immeasurably distant—something of the nature of Judgment Day. Equally, if he had been pinned down to it, Randall would have declared an unshakable belief that victory would not come in the lifetime of any of those present—except perhaps the glib staff officer's.

" Thank you, gentlemen," said the brigadier, and the meeting stood up with a scraping of chairs and began to file out of the room, colonels before majors, and majors before captains, so that the captains had to wait their turns and had time to exchange cynical smiles.

So Bedlam came again, beginning with the long weary rehearsals, continuing with a night march, a muddy bivouac, and another night march, and then a plunge into a raging cataract of war madder than anything any of them had ever known. Tanks roared beside them and aeroplanes roared overhead. Tanks blazed in masses of evil-smelling smoke; aeroplanes plunged their noses into the earth ahead of them in plumes of smoke that might almost have been beacons to guide them. Even the infantry fought under the double arch of the shells' trajectory, under barrage and counter-barrage, in a battle that would seem to have no ending, over a landscape seamed with trenches and drenched in mustard gas.

Here was the Canal; Randall took his company across it on a suspension bridge a foot wide which swayed and bucked as he pounded over it, running with his last gasp of breath and his last ounce of strength—but it must not be his last, for there was a strong-point beyond that which must be stormed, trenches to be cleared, contact to be made to the right and the left, and the line carried forward—forward—forward, although heart and sinew seemed to have nothing left to give, as if arms were too heavy to throw another bomb, legs too weary to take another step, brains too weary to think another thought. Forward, over abandoned trench systems, along rutted lanes, along *pavé* roads, sleeping where they halted, waking and staggering forward again. A lane jammed with wrecked German transport—lorries and carts and dead horses all flung together where the planes had caught them. Something grimmer still here —a wooden T-shaped post on the edge of a field and a corpse bound to it; a corpse in a German uniform; the corpse of a coward or a spy who had died before a firing-squad with the division's advance allowing no time for burial. Here there were tents still standing, a camp abandoned with no time even to set it on fire. Here by the road-side was a dead horse, nose to the ground. Someone had stripped back the hide from the rounded hindquarters as they pointed to the sky, and someone had cut great steaks of horseflesh from them—here were the embers of the fire where they had been cooked. Even men utterly worn out could smile through parched lips at the sight of that, and could make jests about Jerry being hungry.

Here was the battle being renewed, shrapnel bursting overhead, a crossroads under the unremitting pounding of high explosive, a sudden deployment of the battalion, a rapid march for the company across a newly ploughed field in which one sank almost knee-deep at every step. On the far side of the field the ground fell away down to a little valley, at the bottom of which meandered a rivulet between stunted willows. And on the far side of the rivulet, struggling painfully through difficult ground, was a German field battery, guns, limbers and all, the horses labouring hock-deep under the urging of their drivers as they strove to gain the safety that lay beyond the further skyline. The battery commander must have badly misjudged his moment of retreat to present such a magnificent target at nine hundred yards—had he moved five minutes earlier he would have been safe, but an error of five minutes meant a vast misjudgment in a hotly contested rearguard action.

This was open warfare in very truth, and the old soldiers in the company had only had experience in trench warfare and the young drafts had had no experience at all. Randall tried to remember the old open-order signals—harder still, he had to get them obeyed by men at once excited and exhausted. The company straggled out into open order, platoon officers and sergeants manfully trying to maintain control.

" Nine hundred ! "

" Five rounds rapid ! "

Excited men, tired men, untrained men paid little attention to the orders; falling on their stomachs, they opened fire without adjusting their sights and emptied their magazines as fast as they could work bolt and trigger. Even the Lewis guns, with better-trained crews, were carried away with excitement, while the conditions for taking aim, with the valley dropping away below them, were difficult. All the lead that went winging across the valley seemed to be mis-directed. The battery struggled on while from the willows by the stream came the slower beat of German machine-guns and the air above Randall's head was filled with the shriek of bullets. The Lewis gun beside Randall jammed, and the cursing gunner, trying to clear the jam, fell forward, shot through the chest. Randall left it to run to where a dozen riflemen without an officer were lying firing wildly across the valley. He plumped down among them; the furrow in which they lay gave excellent cover.

" Cease fire, men ! " he said, twisting his neck to left and to right and repeating his words until he won obedience.

" Get your sights for nine hundred yards. Make sure of that, now. You, Winter—that's not nine hundred on your sights. That's better. Now reload, all of you. Now take careful aim at that battery. When I say ' Fire ! ' start shoot-ing, slowly. Make sure you take aim for every shot. Now, everyone ready ? Fire ! "

It was death that the rifles began to spit now across the valley—most of them at least. Randall saw that Private Jones was hopeless as a marksman.

" Give me your rifle, Jones."

Randall aimed carefully, squeezed the trigger, aimed and fired again. Men and horses across the valley were dropping; one gun, its team presumably disorganised by a wounded horse, swung clear round. A Lewis gun crew managed to steady themselves long enough to put in a long and accurate burst, so that horses and men fell like wheat under a scythe. Now everyone was paying stricter attention to his duty. Now the battery was wiped out. Every man and every horse was dead, and the guns stood helpless on the hillside. Now that that target had been satisfactorily

disposed of, attention could be paid to the covering rearguard down in the willows and plans made for rooting them
out. But over there on the left there were British troops
already across the stream; with their flank turned, those
fellows must retreat or die or surrender. There goes one
lot making a dash for it. Don't let them get away ! See
them all fall, caught in a machine-gun burst—that last one
lying on his belly with his short legs kicking. There's another
one ! Got 'im ! Hold your fire, here's one lot surrendering.
My God ! Did you see that ? The group that had made
its appearance, coming forward with its hands up, had been
caught in a blast from another German machine-gun, every
man falling dead, rightful victims of their fellow countrymen's
wrath. That meant that the other guns down there would
fight it out to the last.

" Sergeant Thwaites, see if you can get your section along
down that gully there. Hibberd ! They've got one gun in the
bend right ahead, one finger left of that white tree. Give
'em a long burst. Come on, man, we don't want to be here
all day."

With the annihilation of the rearguard they could push
forward again rapidly, marching across country under their
packs, pushing on, with their hearts bursting and their legs
aching, forward, forward, forward. At night they were the
outposts of the army, and the heavens opened and the rain
poured down on them, so heavily that it seemed, lying
shelterless where darkness had overtaken them, as if each
man were lying under a tap fully turned on. Short of sleep
and worn out as they were, they could still only sleep for
a few seconds at a time before the wet and the cold awoke
them again, so that it was a relief when dawn came and
enabled them to move their stiff limbs and call in the dazed
sentries who had been able to see nothing, hear nothing,
and move forward again.

It was they who were the black line that the civilians saw
moving daily farther forward on the maps in the newspapers,
but little they cared, in their fatigue and misery. It was
nothing to them that the American army had revealed itself
at St. Mihiel as a fighting force able to conduct its own
battles; it was nothing that Chancellors were changing in the
German Empire. Randall was lying by the road trying to

ease his aching legs when the battalion's second in command came by.

"Bulgaria's surrendered, Randall," said the major.

"Has it, sir?" said Randall with all the politeness at his command.

Bulgaria was to him no more than he was to Bulgaria, as long as his legs ached in this fashion, as long as every cell in his body complained of fatigue, as long as he was caught up in this war. There had been a time, ages ago, when the fall of Baghdad had been announced to the army with considerable solemnity, but no one had given Baghdad another thought, and apparently rightly, for the war was still going on and Baghdad was a city in which were laid the scenes of musical comedies. Baghdad—Bulgaria—who cared about either when he had to go over the top again to-morrow? Who could even believe that anything would end this war? Even with all the signs of military victory round him Randall could not believe in victory : he had been disillusioned too often. The Germans had retreated in 1917, only to fall back on a line against which the Allies had expended their best blood in vain; in reply they had broken through in 1918, and had been eventually held and beaten back. History was bound to repeat itself; soon they would reach a line—possibly even as far back as the German frontier—where Jerry would be thoroughly dug in and where the bloody see-saw would continue. No wonder Randall thought more about his aching legs than about the prospect of victory.

And now the nights were turning cold, and the rain was lashing at them. The billets where they rested at night had been stripped by the Germans; there was no fuel, there was no food—the gaunt civilians had to be supplied from the rations that came straggling up over the rebuilt bridges and along the ruined roads, and rations were scanty. But the ragged children would kneel by the road and sing 'l'amour sacré de la Patrie' as the weary columns marched by. And there was a terrified woman, her clothes in strips that failed to conceal her nakedness, and with her hair cut off short all over her head so that her skull was strangely bare and masculine, who burst in among them once; she had been guilty of being too kind to Jerry and had not fled when he retreated. This was what her sister women had done to her.

The battalion could only hand her over to the French authorities and march on; most of the men were indignant about
the treatment she had received, but a large minority grinned
broadly and decided that it was exactly what she deserved—
most of these were the newest drafts. Randall could bear the
cruelty he had seen when a group of Germans were cornered
in a trench during a desperate attack, or even the cruelty that
forced a coward into action at the cost of his sanity, but this
was something new to him in his ignorance of the world. He
thought of Muriel, and of the tender breasts against which he
had laid his cheek, and that night he wrote to her with more
than his usual vehemence.

The guns rolled and roared under the lowering autumn
skies. To the south there was an American army deeply
committed to action—not even the most incredulous British
soldier could doubt that now—and to the north it seemed as
if Belgium must soon be liberated. In this convulsive battle
it seemed to Randall as if the world was ending with the
dying year. He listened to a hot debate which sprang up
among his brother officers at the news that first Turkey and
then Austria had surrendered.

" The armistice terms permit of the free passage of allied
troops across Austria," said the colonel.

' Armistice ' was a strange technical word; Randall had
seen it written during his brief studies of military law, and
he had read it several times lately, but this was the first time
he had ever heard it spoken.

" They can bring back Allenby from Palestine and turn
him loose, then," said the second in command.

" Isn't it all mountains there ? " asked someone.

" In Austria ? I've never heard of any. Are there, sir ? "

The colonel thought there were mountains on the German-
Austrian frontier.

" But they can open another front there, at any rate, in
the spring," said the second in command. " Jerry'll feel a
squeeze then."

" And if they bomb Berlin to hell as well——" speculated
Captain Cooke.

It was almost as if they were beginning to hope for victory,
as if in the measurable future, in 1919, even, or in 1920,
Germany would be forced to admit defeat. They could even

begin to dare to hope that they would live to see it. No, it must be too good to be true.

" Jerry'll still have the interior lines," said the colonel sadly. " He'll be able to switch his reserves back and forward between here and Bavaria. He knocked out Rumania that way, and Russia, too."

Randall raked back in his memory, trying to dredge up the schoolboy geography he had once learned, and trying to recall his patchy newspaper reading since that time. He was a little vague about Vienna and the Danube and the Bavarian Alps, but he could visualise a besieged Germany against which the allied armies would fling themselves with a great outpouring of blood—some of it his blood, probably. And Muriel's last letter to him had told how she had been invited to a seat in a window to see the Lord Mayor's procession and she wondered if she would be able to wangle an hour away from the bank. There was another world than this, then; the doubt was how much longer it would survive this cataclysm—and the guns roared and the aeroplanes droned while he wondered.

The battalion was in action when it was announced in orders that German delegates were on their way through the line to ask for terms. It was on the march along a muddy lane when the guns fell silent with the armistice. They were inexpressibly weary, they were cold and wet, and they were hungry, actually hungry, having outmarched the supplies which were labouring up behind them. So, despite the uncanny silence which had fallen on the world, they could not yet believe the unbelievable, especially when the orders came through laying stress on the fact that this was an armistice and not peace, and that all military precautions must be taken —and more especially still when the orders each day were to the effect that they must march, and march, and march.

They had empty bellies. A single army biscuit each, a tin of bully between ten, a tin of jam between twenty; that was dinner, and no breakfast next morning. Parade and march, march while the rain soaked down upon them from the grey sky, while their nailed boots slipped on the *pavé*, while their stomachs were full of a gnawing pain. March, and tighten up discipline as the weary men grumbled.

" Sergeant, take that man's name. Here, corporal, I'll take

his pack; come on, man, pull yourself together. Sergeant-major, keep the men closed up. Who gave that man permission to fall out ? "

Hunger and cold and exhaustion, while they followed up Jerry across liberated France and into liberated Belgium; clear-thinking staff officers at general headquarters could see the necessity for an unrelenting pursuit and could frame their orders accordingly, sending Randall to tramp on blistered feet over endless kilometres of dreary road just ahead of the field kitchens trailing after him.

They marched into the Belgian village long after dark, silent and stupid, like five hundred mental defectives.

" This 'ere's your billet, sir."

The village smithy, of all places, its anvil long silent, its forge long cold. The night before the village had been in German occupation—there were German notices still affixed to walls and doors; in the stable at the back of the smithy where a platoon of Randall's company were now settling down a platoon of German soldiers had slept; in the bed to which the smith's wife (a grave, madonna-like woman) conducted him a German captain had lain last night. Not that anyone cared, although if the troops had been a trifle less weary there would have been plenty of jests about those German notices. As it was, all that anyone wanted to do was to gulp down the mouthful of food that was issued to each man and then to sleep and sleep and sleep, and to try not to think at the moment of to-morrow morning's parade and to-morrow's march.

It was only just daylight when the battalion formed up, hobbling on stiff legs and sore feet—it would take an hour or two of marching to get those parts of them painless again—to take their places in line, while a trio of old men with violins accompanied the village children in a couple of choruses. The first one was vaguely recognisable as ' Tipperary '; the second could be guessed at as ' La Brabançonne '. The three cheers which the battalion gave in reply were hardly more vigorous. Then as the first order was about to be given to march off, the sound of a motor bicycle was heard, and the machine came roaring in, ridden by a messenger with the blue-and-white brassard. Stolidly the battalion stood at attention as the message was read. A gleam of watery sunshine broke through the clouds and lit the colonel's face. He was actually grinning.

" The battalion will dismiss ! " he bellowed, forgetful of all military etiquette. He even waved the message form over his head. " No march to-day ! "

That was a peak of happiness, to stumble back again to billets, to cast the pack from off the galled shoulders, to unlace the boots from the chafed feet, and to sink down and rest in sloth. And before midday came another peak, when the bugle blew and the wondering men saw the travelling kitchens in the village square and realised that their lost transport had at last caught up with them. Here was hot food in quantity, ample rations, double rations. Everyone could eat and eat, with an appetite all the keener for the morning's rest, eat until waistbands were tight, and still have food left over for the villagers. And a ration of rum ! The world was a marvellous place—even the heavens made their contribution, for the sun went on shining, dispensing warmth and cheer to men who for long had known neither. Cigarettes —who cared if they were unheard-of brands with strange flavours ? It was possible to sit in the sun with legs stretched out that did not ache, with distended bellies warmed by that issue of rum, and lungs filled with tobacco smoke, and there could be very little more that hearts could desire.

Brains had ceased to be numb, too; now was the time at last to know that the war was over, that never again would the world rock as one crouched in a crack on its surface under a bombardment, never again would machine-gun bullets whine overhead; there was no chance of being torn into bloody fragments by a shell or of being gassed into a choking wreck. It was even possible to believe—although this was harder—that soon one would be out of the army, free of discipline, free to choose one's clothes and one's hour of rising, free to call one's soul one's own.

The battalion was in the highest physical condition after its months of toil in the open air, and the men's powers of recuperation were astonishing. Last night they had staggered into the village, exhausted automata; now, after sixteen hours' rest and a full meal they were lively young men again. The colonel used his discretion—infinitely wise discretion, thought the battalion—in ordering an issue of pay, and soon

the sight of those notes in the hands of ignorant British soldiers
began to work on the minds of the canny Walloon villagers.
Tiny hidden stores of beer and of wine made their appearance;
five hundred thirsty British soldiers drank every drop and
clamoured for more.

For the village, too, this was a great day, the day when
they had been liberated from the hated Boche. Six months
ago the Germans had swept away every able-bodied man
in the village for forced labour, leaving only cripples and
children and old men. Now the women could hope to see
their men again any day—and in the meantime here were
these lighthearted Tommies with their strange jokes and
their neat uniforms and their pockets full of money. Lightheartedness was infectious; before very long the whole
village was *en fête*, as much so as even on its saint's day.
Five hundred Tommies made the natural approaches to a
hundred Belgian housewives, and the housewives had no
husbands to raise protests; if they had fathers-in-law they
chose to ignore them; if they had mothers-in-law the mothers-
in-law were themselves too preoccupied to notice what the
daughters-in-law were doing. It was an uproarious celebra-
tion—the rest of the world had gone mad with joy on Armistice
Day, but in this one little corner the Armistice was celebrated
with delayed action and with the added vigour to be expected
of delayed action.

Randall came back to his billet by no means drunk. He
was elevated; a little by alcohol and a great deal by the
certainty that the war was over. Presumably the last week,
when his life had not been in danger, had eased his nerves,
although he had not been aware of it until now, while good
food and twenty-four hours' complete rest naturally played
their part, for he was in the hardest physical condition with
all the resilience of a youth of twenty. He went in through
the door from the dark smithy; beyond was the typical
Belgian kitchen, almost equally dark, for the tiny oil lamp
was turned low—oil was something terribly precious. The
two women stood up as he entered; one the dark maternal
wife of the absent smith, the other the usual old crone,
exactly like a hundred other old crones whom Randall had
seen in a hundred other billets, of varying stages of decrepitude,
but all apparently receiving food and a corner of the fire in

return for whatever little labour they were capable of giving. Randall had heard laughter before he entered; now he saw smiles as they greeted him in the dim light.

" So now the war is over at last, M. le Capitaine," said the young woman.

" Yes, the war is finished," said Randall.

He had discovered, when he first arrived in France, that Matriculation French, spoken with care, would serve as a medium of communication with French people, and that he could actually understand what was said to him in return as long as it was not said too fast and did not pursue unusual channels. His less gifted or less well-educated brother officers had often listened to his conversations with unconcealed envy and surprise.

" And we are liberated," said the young woman.

" Yes, certainly," said Randall.

The old crone broke in with something Randall could not understand, but as she laughed uproariously Randall smiled politely in reply.

" The dirty Boches," said the young woman.

" Ah yes, the dirty Boches."

Again the old crone said something to which he was clearly expected to reply.

" My aunt says that M. le Capitaine is very young," said the young woman in explanation.

" Ah yes. No. Perhaps," said Randall, throwing his small change of conversational French freely about in embarrassed profusion.

The next sentence was not so readily understood, but when his hostess made the gesture of raising a glass to her lips and further produced a bottle and glasses there could be no doubt as to what she meant. She poured a little into each glass and they looked at each other. The woman said something, but she had to repeat it twice before Randall grasped that she was offering a toast to King George V.

" Ah yes. *Vivent les Alliés*," said Randall. He had said that before, to patriotic Frenchmen.

He drank; it was brandy whose strength took him by surprise so that he coughed. By a miracle of memory he recalled the name of the King of the Belgians and returned the toast.

" *Vive Albert Premier*," he said, and they drank.

Then they drank the healths of President Wilson, and of M. Poincaré, and of King Victor Emmanuel, with his hostess filling the glasses when necessary. The old lady was laughing quite hilariously. She held out her glass for it to be refilled.

"That is all. It is finished," said the young woman, upending the empty bottle over the glass to prove her words.

Now the old lady was patting Randall's arm, and now she was plucking at the younger woman's hand to draw her within Randall's grasp. She came with almost no reluctance and with a smile on her lips.

" *Vivent les Alliés*," said the old lady.

Those lips were very close to Randall's, ripe and full and lovely. The eyes under the level brows were infinitely kind. And the war was over. Even with the old woman looking on there was only one thing to do, to kiss those lips. But the old woman was not there. They heard the door shut behind her. And here were the lips again. She was leaning against him, melting against him, saying words that Randall only half understood.

He heard her murmur, "So young!" but with his lips against hers what she said was not important, although the tone was vastly so. And in that shadowy kitchen where the tiny oil flame flickered in the draught care and weariness had no place—they dropped away at her touch. Instead the world was full of longing and desire. The smith's wife swept back the hair from her high forehead and looked at him; the trace of bewilderment in her expression was instantly submerged in tenderness. She stretched out her hand for the lamp, and led him through the other door, to the bed where he had lain last night in utter weariness.

TWELVE

SOLDIERS COME AND SOLDIERS GO. Next morning the battalion formed up and marched away, and some of the women who watched them go raised their aprons furtively to their eyes as the men went swinging by. Randall was there at the head of his company, but he did not see the smith's wife; he had only a faint recollection of her rising up beside him before dawn and leaving him—he had slept again after that, satiated, so heavily that the events of the night before were still blurred.

"March at ease," he ordered when they emerged from the village and set out on the long straight road that led towards Germany.

There was no trouble with discipline this morning, for the men were in the highest spirits, even those with headaches. Rest and food and relaxation had worked wonders, and every man in the ranks was exuberant. The war was over and they had won it. Discipline and tenacity and self-sacrifice had met with their reward at last. England was victorious, and they, the poor bloody infantry, having borne the burden of the day, were marching forward as conquerors, conscious of their merit and proud of their achievement.

Even Randall felt all this, although the feeling of triumph and relief had to conflict with a vague agitation of conscience. He had been untrue to the wife he dearly loved and who loved him just as dearly; the sweet confiding woman who had given him so much out of her infinite generosity. At the end of half an hour's march a horrible word suddenly rose up in his consciousness, like Banquo's ghost confronting Macbeth. 'Adultery' was the word; he had seen it written although he could not remember ever saying it. He had been guilty of adultery—double adultery, he presumed, if there was such a thing, seeing that the smith's wife was married, too. Giving the thing a name—that name—made it seem much worse. A shocking offence against his loving wife; he wondered how ever he would be able to write to her next.

"Rare time we 'ad last night, sir," said the platoon sergeant at Randall's side.

"I'm glad you did," said Randall.

"Corporal Dixon, 'e was sayin' to me, sir, 'e didn't want

to press no charges after all against Private 'Ughes. You remember, sir. Dumb insolence. Dixon said if it could be dropped, quietly-like, 'e'd be glad."

" Yes, I suppose that'll be all right."

" Dixon was a bit 'asty—'e's a 'asty kind of chap—and 'Ughes is a bit of a fool but there ain't no 'arm in 'im."

" Very well, sergeant."

" And about young Sykes, sir, 'im 'oo 'as applied for compassionate leave——"

It was not easy to go on worrying about adultery, or to be troubled with memories of a high forehead and tender eyes, when company business had to be attended to, when a long march had to be made—especially when in the course of a very few days he was overwhelmed by the new and singularly urgent business of attending to demobilisation, with ninety-nine out of every hundred soldiers clamouring for discharge, producing the most convincing arguments in favour of immediate release, and tending to sulk when their petitions met with no favour. And he himself was just as anxious to be demobilised, to be free again, with his two and a half years of service balanced against the fact that he was not yet twenty-one years of age, and his priority as a student of science balanced against his usefulness in the battalion.

Mr. Graham cut the knot, as he had cut knots before.

" The American Government," he wrote—the battalion had just reached the Rhine—" has admitted, of course, that we have grounds for a claim against them in respect to their manufacture and use of the P–R flare. The details will be settled by negotiation, no doubt in a manner satisfactory to us. Meanwhile, for your private information, I have prevailed upon the American military mission here to make application through the American military attaché for you to attend a conference in London on the subject. You may be glad of a chance of leave, and I understand that this may accelerate your demobilisation should you wish it."

Mr. Graham had indeed pulled some very important strings. Randall was made immediately conscious of this when he was summoned to divisional headquarters and was interviewed by a red-tabbed colonel on the staff.

" This comes to us with the endorsement of the Foreign Office," said the colonel, tapping his desk with a document.

" I wouldn't be surprised, sir," said Randall—he made himself say it; he made himself try to act like someone who took it for granted that government departments, and the Foreign Office above all government departments, should be interested in him.

" I didn't realise until now," went on the colonel, " that you were with the division."

" No ? " said Randall, nonplussed for the moment but doing his best to be nonchalant.

" You hear these names—the Lewis gun, say, or even Tickler's Jam, although that's not in quite the same category, is it ?—and don't stop to think there must have been a Lewis or a Tickler in the first place. I've talked about P–R flares a hundred times, of course, and didn't even know that it stood for Phillips–Randall, and as for knowing that the Randall was a captain in the division——"

Randall laughed at the incongruity of all this, and was surprised to see the colonel join in the laugh in a manner which could only be described as deferential. It was as if, unbelievable though it might be, Captain Randall was a much more important person because his name was attached to a standard weapon of war.

" The Foreign Office mention a request from the American military attaché," said the colonel.

It was as well that it was the Foreign Office—the name carried weight with the army. Randall had a moment of insight and knew that if the Board of Trade or the Ministry of Agriculture and Fisheries had been interested in him the colonel would not have been nearly as impressed.

" Naturally we must accede to the request of an allied government," went on the colonel. " This endorsement practically makes it obligatory."

" Yes, sir," said Randall.

" And I see," went on the colonel, " that you have applied for demobilisation for the purpose of continuing your scientific studies."

" Yes, sir."

That was verbally entirely correct, but the colonel's tone misrepresented the truth. Nobody would have guessed who heard the colonel speaking that Randall wanted merely to take a degree at the University of London; the colonel made it sound as if Randall intended to solve all the most recondite problems in science.

"We shouldn't keep a man like you cooling his heels here when you have important work to do," said the colonel. "I think the general will approve this application if I send it in to him."

"Thank you," replied Randall, trying to keep the eagerness out of his voice and as a result being condescending in a way that scared him until he saw that the colonel, nearly three times his age and vastly his superior in rank, did not resent being condescended to.

"Glad to do it," said the colonel

And so on a spring afternoon in 1919 Randall came walking out of the Crystal Palace, a civilian in unaccustomed civilian clothes. There was a watery sun shining, and the trees were budding and life was good. He could not help stealing glances down to assure himself that he had a white shirt on instead of a khaki one, and a black necktie with spots (he had to squint awkwardly to see this), and a blue serge suit, and black shoes. The felt hat on his head seemed strangely different from a service cap, but he still had his old walking-stick, which he swung light-heartedly as he strode along. The demobilisation machinery was quick-working; it was like a sausage machine in a butcher's shop—a bit of meat lying on the counter stood no chance of becoming sausage, but a bit of meat picked up and put into the maw of the machine was seized by it and hurried through a series of processes until it emerged at the other end completely transformed. The colonel had placed him in the machine's grasp, and here he was, transformed, newly cased, and free in a world that was to be entirely different from the wicked old pre-1914 world that Randall knew almost nothing about. Surely it was a sign of a changed world that he should have been demobilised in thirty-six hectic hours, and at a place within only a short walk of his home, his *own* house in Calmady Road. He had written to Muriel to say that to-morrow would be the earliest she could expect him—he very much doubted if she even had received the letter as yet.

He swung his stick and stepped out, drinking in the air of liberty. There was pride in the past and hope for the future. He and his comrades had emerged victorious from the most frightful war in history, and no one would ever again have to endure experiences like his. Jimmy—Jimmy must be twelve now, or was it thirteen?—would go through life and never hear a shell burst, never see a gutted corpse. The idiocy that had plunged the world into war would never be repeated; a well-organised civilisation would see to that, and now mankind, freed from the burden of armaments, and no longer fettered by old ideas, would advance rapidly to a spiritual and material freedom greater than that of the Garden of Eden, for not even the Tree of Knowledge would be forbidden.

He came out into the top end of Calmady Road; he could go through the passage to Harbord Road and his father's house, but he turned to his left and walked down the street to his own house. It was shut and silent, but he had expected it to be, for it was too early for Muriel to be home from the bank. He had no key, and he was philosophic about that, too—no one but a fool would have carried a latchkey through the experiences he had gone through during the last year. He left his kit in the porch and walked down the road to Little's; needing coppers for the telephone, he bought cigarettes and was a trifle surprised when Mrs. Little completed the purchase without recognising him. He looked up the number and telephoned the bank—idiotic that he had to check himself and ask for Mrs. Randall; always before he had asked for Mrs. Speake. Mrs. Randall had just left. Well, that was only to be expected. He walked down towards the station and waited at the tram stop; Muriel would be along in time.

There were still soldiers in uniform about, and it was momentarily surprising when they passed him by without saluting him. Things were different—if he had been waiting like this on a French roadside, for a lift in a lorry, say, he would have lain down beside the road in a comfortable attitude, without a thought. Here he had to stand up, or at best lean back against his walking-stick, while he waited for the trams to come up, drop their passengers, and go on again—was it a hundred years ago that he had last waited for her here?

And here she came, in the very last of the daylight, stepping neatly down from the tram, and standing in the road waiting for it to go on so that she could pass behind it. She wore a

trim grey suit and a black hat, and she looked round as
Randall started out from the kerb towards her. She saw a
young man, hardly more than a boy, in a badly fitting blue
suit and an appalling hat. She saw him take his hat off with
an outlandish flourish. It was the first time Randall had ever
taken off his hat to a lady; until he had joined the army he
had worn a schoolboy cap, and after he had joined the army
he had always saluted. It was only when he stepped off the
kerb that he remembered his hat and the need to take it off
when he addressed his wife, and he had had to find the brim
and drag the thing off, with his hands encumbered with
walking-stick and gloves. To Muriel it seemed as if some very
callow and highly undesirable young man was trying to scrape
acquaintance with her, and because of his undesirability she
flashed a scornful glance at him and turned away with uptilted
nose as the tram moved on and cleared the path for her.

" Muriel ! " said Randall, appalled, and she halted at her
name.

There was still a momentary hesitation, even though she
had heard his voice. It was a year since she had seen him,
and much had happened in that year. But now she realised
that this was her husband, revealed in civilian clothes, and
her ready tact told her the only thing to do. There was
nothing to gain and certainly something to lose by letting
him see that this was a shock to her. She must not let him
guess it, at least at present.

" Darling ! " she said, running back to him where he
stood petrified with shock. " I didn't know you in those
clothes ! "

She threw herself into his arms, kissed him, patted his
shoulder.

" It's really you ! " she said. " I wasn't expecting you so
soon. You're demobbed, of course. Your last letter said
you hadn't a hope. Wonderful ! "

They kissed again and again; perhaps the best possible
proof of the shock Randall had suffered and his recovery
from it was that he should kiss and embrace his wife like this
where all the world could see.

" Sweetheart ! " was all he could say, as the frightful
doubts died away within him.

" Let me look at you," she said, holding back from him

and smiling. " How nice you look. I suppose I always knew
what a nice husband I had, but I like to be sure."

Her lips were very full and ripe, and she could throw
herself so wholeheartedly into a mood that her eyes danced
with pleasure and excitement. She was not going to be the
one who should suggest the end of these embraces, public
though they were. She pressed her soft breast to him, so
that in the end it was he that said it.

" Let's go home," he said.

" Let's," she answered.

She took his arm and pressed it and they crossed the road.

" Grace and Marjorie are still with me, you know," she
said. " They get in a bit later than me, generally. Now that
you've come home they won't be able to stay, of course.
But to-night you'll be in my room—oh, darling—and it
won't matter about them. Grace's job's going to end quite
soon, anyway."

So here they were in his home; she was opening the
door, and she was throwing herself into his arms in the dark
hall.

" God, this is marvellous ! " he said; yet as he said it, even
while his arms were round her, a tide of memories surged
up in his mind. Memories of piled-up dead, memories of
catastrophic bombardments; and earlier memories, somehow,
of walking to school, of his mother's arms round him when he
was a little boy. These memories broke round him like the
gentle surf breaking round the waist of a man wading out at
last from the sea. They did not submerge him, and he was
only half conscious of them. His feet were on shore and he
was leaving the memories behind, while he faced the new
sunny land with no need to look back on the undertows and
currents through which he had fought his way.

Her hand had found the light switch, and she pressed it, to
reveal herself again to him.

" Darling," she said, " I'm going to fly round upstairs.
Everything's untidy up there and I don't want you to see
it—you know how we run off to work in the morning, and
we can't get a woman we can trust to come in. I'll only be
a minute. You know we weren't expecting you."

He released her and went into the sitting-room and switched
on the light—he had found this room hard to remember after

6

the little he had seen of it. Here it was—piano, chintz-covered chairs and all. And here was a silver photograph frame. Service dress, three stars, a clipped moustache; a heavy jaw and melancholy eyes. The late unknown Captain Henry Speake, who had died of wounds seventeen months ago. Randall felt a moment of distaste. On the opposite table was another silver frame with a photograph of himself, taken when he was an officer cadet; he had written to his mother asking her to give it to Muriel when she had pointed out in a letter to him that she had no photograph of him at all. It was odd to see what a smooth-faced boy he had been three years back; a mere child despite the uniform.

Photographs of women were dotted about the room, too, and over there was another photograph of a man. This was taken out of doors against a background of trees; the subject was a heavily built young man in tweeds, leaning on a walking-stick. There was something familiar about him, and it only took a second glance to tell that it was Massey —R. F. Massey—Captain Richard Massey, M.C.—Dick Massey, as Muriel had called him in her letters, the county cricketer. His features were just as Randall remembered them ten years back when Massey was a hirsute sixth former and he was a kid in the first form; the inevitable moustache was the only change. He was standing in an easy pose; as Muriel had written, there was no sign that one of his legs was artificial. Bad luck for Massey, to lose a leg that way—although Randall could make himself remember that there had been times when he would have gladly given a leg, too, in exchange for release from active service.

Muriel came bounding into the room and he turned gladly to her; as she came into his arms her eyes, over his shoulder, glanced quickly round the room, and she was a little sorry that she had left those photographs there. Then she raised her lips to his and Randall entered into Paradise; he was entering into Paradise for only a short stay, as he was due to emerge at the farther side in course of time—Paradise was just the threshold he crossed from war to peace, from a soldier's life to a civilian's.

THIRTEEN

" GOOD-BYE, DEAR," said Randall, calling up the stairs.

"Good-bye," said Muriel, leaning over the banisters as she stood on the upper landing in her dressing-gown. "Home to tea ? "

"I hope so," said Randall, "but I may be quite late. I've got to go and see Graham after my afternoon class."

"So you have; I was forgetting," said Muriel. "Give him my love. And be good."

"Yes, dear," said Randall. "Good-bye."

He stepped out into Calmady Road, notebooks and text-books under his arm, his old army trench coat to keep out the rain, his civilian felt hat jauntily cocked—he was thoroughly used to wearing the thing now. He climbed to the top of the tram and settled himself into a seat and opened his physics notebook; he could study his notes regardless of the swaying of the tram, of the tobacco smoke which eddied round him, of the coming and going of the passengers, of the stopping and starting of the tram at every corner. This was happiness, to abstract himself completely from the world, to lose himself in theoretical studies. There was pleasure in sharp physical exercise, in going out for a hard walk and striding along as fast as he could go, but there was an even greater pleasure in setting the mind to work as hard as it could, too, exercising it along new and interesting paths, remote from the details of living. He had made this trip often enough now, so that while not missing a symbol in the complicated mathematics of gases at low pressures he was quite well aware of how far the tram had progressed along its route; and when he reached his destination he was able to close his book and get up and run down the stairs without even looking out of the window for confirmation.

The class was a large one, like all the others, thanks to the post-war rush, with the students sharply divided into two groups, one composed of men from the armed services and the other of eighteen-year-olds, mere infants who had not seen bloodshed, with the youthful bloom on their cheeks and the carefree lightheartedness of their tender years. They had the mental elasticity of their youth, too; some of the old soldiers, with five years of war separating them from their last studies, found it hard to resume the students' habits of thought. Randal was fortunate in his being able to abstract himself and to achieve concentration in that way; he attended his lectures that morning, ate his lunch, and strolled over to the physics laboratory for his afternoon class all with the sublime indifference to outside distractions which is granted equally to the saint and the scholar. Indeed, it was with mild irritation that he looked at his watch and realised that it was time to put his apparatus away and go and keep his appointment with Mr. Graham.

"You had our last statement of account?" said Mr. Graham, when the formalities of greeting were completed and their cigarettes were alight and they were leaning back in their chairs contemplating each other with the readiness of understanding of old friends.

"Yes," said Randall, "I banked the cheque."

"You won't ever get another one that size," said Graham. "Not for the P–R flare, I mean. We might get some royalties from the pyrotechnic companies. And the armies and navies may need a few now and then—although they won't if they ever manage to agree on disarmament—but there won't be anything worth mentioning, I'm afraid. You haven't done badly, but it's all over."

"I haven't done badly," agreed Randall.

He had paid off the mortgage on the house, and there was a thousand pounds in his and Muriel's joint account. A generous Government was paying him an allowance to continue his studies; there was enough money to live comfortably while he took his degree—almost enough to enable him to go on to his doctorate—and he was free from worldly care. Moreover, he had the sense to appreciate his good fortune.

"There's no reason why we should be content with the P–R flare," said Graham. "There are other inventions only waiting to be made."

"Are there?" said Randall. He felt no urge to worry about them.

"Now here's something," said Graham. "Carnac—you

remember meeting him—my American colleague—wrote to me about it this week."

Graham's eyes were looking at him sharply from under his bushy brows, and Randall had to express a polite interest.

"What is it?" he asked.

"It's connected with the canning of green peas," said Graham. "Don't ask me for explanations, because what I don't know about the canning of peas is everything about the subject. But it appears that some peas are wrinkled and some peas are smooth—when they come out of the pod, I mean—and that's a matter of commercial importance."

"Is it?" said Randall.

Graham used the word 'canning' quite naturally; Randall would himself have said 'tinning,' and the other expression rang strange on his ear. It was as odd as that anyone should give a second thought to whether peas were wrinkled or smooth.

"Damn it," said Graham, "you must have noticed it. I've noticed it myself in the peas on my plate."

"I've noticed it, too," said Randall.

"Well, it doesn't do to sell wrinkled and smooth peas in the same tin. The public doesn't like it. If you could sort 'em out you could label your tin 'What's his name's All-Smooth Peas. Warranted not to wrinkle in the can.' Or you could say 'Highest Quality Wrinkled Peas. Superior to any smooth ones.' You see what I mean?"

"I suppose so," said Randall. "But——"

"But what?"

"Does anyone ever buy tinned peas?"

To the best of Randall's knowledge he had never seen a can of peas in his life.

"Of course they do. Not in England so much, perhaps, but it's a big industry in America. *And* it will be bigger. *And* it will spread over here."

"Maybe so," said Randall.

"You've got to believe me when I tell you it's important," said Graham patiently. "I wouldn't waste your time over it if it wasn't."

"But what's the problem?" asked Randall obtusely.

"God bless my soul, didn't I tell you what it was? It's a question of sorting out the wrinkled peas from the smooth

ones, once they're out of their pods. On a commercial
scale, of course."

" I see."

" In the canning industry," went on Graham patiently
" time's important—it's important everywhere, of course,
but especially in this, where the stuff's got to be canned
quick before it loses its freshness."

" Of course."

" And in the matter of food cost is a prime consideration.
People'll buy motor cars or gramophone records they can't
afford, but when it comes to food they'll eat something else
if it saves them money."

" I expect that's because it's the women that buy the
food," said Randall, and he felt a glow of achievement at
being able to make what he thought to be an original and
profound remark in the course of this alien conversation.

" Yes," said Graham. " So now you've got the whole
picture. How to sort out wrinkled peas from smooth ones;
how to do it quickly and cheaply, and as one link in the
chain of processes from the pea field to the can. See what
you can do about it. There's money in it if you can think
of the best way first."

" I don't think it's a bit of good asking me to think about
it," said Randall without mock-modesty. " I'm not an
inventor."

" Try, anyway," said Graham.

Randall was home just in time to drink tea with his wife.
It was rather a silent meal, as meals alone with Muriel had
tended to become lately. Randall did not exert himself to
provide small talk, and his mind had plenty to work on in
his scientific studies.

" A penny for your thoughts," said Muriel after a while,
keeping, with an effort, any sign of bitterness out of her
voice.

Randall drank tea to gain time. It would be no use telling
her exactly what he was thinking about. The word ' adiabatic '
meant nothing to her at all. The differential and the integral
calculus were to her things of entirely no use—Randall
once, with unwonted eloquence, had tried to explain to
her how the calculus had made man master of the universe
he lived in, and how its discovery had been more important

than that of gunpowder, and he had been hurt as well as surprised at her unbelief. Muriel was quite prepared to accept that in this ridiculous man-made world it might be necessary to juggle with x's and y's to obtain a science degree, but she could not conceive of the x's and y's having any real importance or even any intrinsic interest. A man might as well have to learn how to keep six balls in the air at once—for that matter it was a way of earning a living, too. It was no use talking about this morning's lecture to Muriel; but luckily there was something else he could talk about.

" Graham had a funny suggestion to make this afternoon," he said.

" Oh, I was going to ask what it was he wanted."

" He's got an invention in mind that he wants me to think about."

" Has he really ? " There was interest in Muriel's voice.

" Yes. It's all silly, of course."

" But what was it ? "

Randall told her.

" You're going to do it, of course ? " said Muriel; the sentence hardly needed the question mark at the end—it was more of a statement of fact.

" How can I, dear ? " said Randall. He realised that he had been apprehensive about just this very thing, the need to persuade Muriel that he was not an inventor.

" Of course you can," said Muriel. " You invented the flare, didn't you ? Yes, you did. And haven't you been studying science all these years ? What's the use of all your books and lectures and things if you can't invent something —not even when they actually come and ask you to ! You could make a lot of money that way—that is, if you don't let the Grahams and Phillipses and those people get it all."

" Dear——" said Randall. He tried to explain again the unpractical ideals of the pure scientist.

" But when you were talking to Dick about the flare and he called you a scientist you said you weren't one ! " said Muriel. That was so nearly like logic as to be excruciating; Randall could only open and shut his mouth in reply.

" And Mr. Graham said he thought you could, didn't

he ? " went on Muriel, still unanswerably. " I think you
ought to."

Randall had been married to Muriel for two years, and
he had lived with her for one year—one year and one night,
the night of the German offensive at St. Quentin; and as
a married man he was not very experienced. A year ago
he had become a man of peace instead of a man of war;
it was a tremendous change-over, like the metamorphosis
which some insects go through. There are insects which
spend a great part of their lives as predatory creatures
in ponds under the surface of the water, catching, killing
and devouring. Then comes a time when they emerge,
cast off their skins—their armour and weapons—and fly
away as decorative adults. Randall had gone through a
very similar metamorphosis, but he had not the advantage
of the insect's inherited instincts; he had been an efficient
predator, an efficient killer, but he had to learn to be an
efficient adult. He had learned—and it had been a difficult
lesson—that there were people (and Muriel the most important of them) who had no interest in the differential
calculus, but he had not yet learned to seek some common
interest to share with them. He might besides have laughed
at Muriel, or teased her, or even slapped her, but he did
none of these things. He was liable to fall silent, to withdraw into himself—as Muriel described it, he would ' get
into a mood ', and she resented the fact that it should always
be he who had the moods and she who had to make allowances
for them.

" I've got to work now, anyway," said Randall, with a
glance at the clock.

" Go and work then," said Muriel.

The back bedroom had been converted into a study for
Randall, and he had already grown fond of it; there was
something pleasant about entering it and switching on the
light and shutting the door, and lighting the gas fire, and
laying out his books and papers in order on his desk, whistling
quietly as he did so, and then, either at his desk or in his
easy chair, losing himself in his work. To-night he was vaguely
conscious of sounds down below, of a ring at the bell, of the
front door opening and shutting, and a murmur of voices
down below, but he paid no attention to them; they were

quite usual, as a good many of Muriel's friends had the habit of dropping in for the evening. He turned a page and thought no more about it.

Somebody was playing the piano, not very well, Probably Muriel; Randall could hear that noise and still not allow it to disturb his thoughts. And then there was a new sound, a metallic twanging, that he had not heard before; Randall's subconscious noted it as something new for some considerable time before he came to pay conscious attention to it. He had done nearly enough work for the evening, and he did not mind breaking off. To the sound of the music coming up from below he went through his reverse routine, putting his books and papers together, turning out the gas fire, and switching off the light before going down.

Downstairs in the sitting-room Muriel was at the piano, and, squatting on a pouffe beside her, craning his neck to read the music, was Massey.

" Hullo," said Randall.

" Hullo, ol' man," said Massey.

He was a big red-faced man with black hair already beginning to go thin on top ; across his knees was an instrument that looked like a small banjo.

" Dick's got a ukulele," said Muriel.

" And everybody's sorry but me," said Massey. " You just listen. Let's try that again, Mu."

The duet for piano and ukulele was certainly not very impressive, especially as the ukulele was not quite in tune with the piano.

" Pretty awful, eh ? " said Massey.

" It could be better, I suppose," said Randall politely.

" I'll get some supper," said Muriel, rising from the music stool.

As the door closed behind her Massey took hold of the piano and hauled himself to his feet. Standing up, he gave no sign that he had an artificial leg. He walked across to the fireplace and took his half-empty whisky glass from the mantelshelf and sipped from it as he stood by the fire.

" Can I get you a drink ? " he said.

" Well—no, I don't think I will, thanks," said Randall.

Massey was so frequent a visitor—and so frequent a drinker—that there was nothing out of the ordinary about

his offering to get a drink for his host; and Randall was
now again a sufficiently rare drinker for it to be nothing out
of the ordinary for him to refuse. He gave Massey a cigarette.

"How's the leg?" he asked politely.

"Pretty fair, thanks. It's still my sole means of support."

That was an old joke; Massey had been in and out of a
couple of jobs since the end of the war and usually eked out
a lean existence on his wound pension.

"You're a lucky bargee, you know, Randy," added Massey.

"I suppose I am," agreed Randall.

"I don't mean all this——" explained Massey, with a
gesture taking in the sitting-room with its piano and easy
chairs and the fire in the grate. "Of course you're lucky to
have it, but I mean—well, look at you. Work you seem to
enjoy doing. Sitting there saying, 'Well, I don't think I will'
when someone offers you a drink. Money in the bank—but
I don't really mean that, either. But looking forward to some
dam' degree or other in science, and quite happy looking forward after that to spending your life doing teaching or some
dam' thing."

"I don't know about the teaching," protested Randall.
He had vague ideas about being a research physicist.

"Anyway, you *want* to do *something*," said Massey. He
italicised the words by waving his nearly empty glass. "You
can take on where you left off. Yet you saw as much of the
war as I did. More, for that matter, I fancy."

"Yes, I'm lucky," said Randall.

He said nothing about the nightmares that still pursued
him, the dreams of rotting corpses and streaming blood.
He was lucky that he had been endowed with temperance
and self-control, that he was able to abstract himself from
his dreams by systematic thinking—during the war he had
learned that trick in order to abstract himself from the reality.

"Supper's ready," called Muriel.

"I was telling Randy he was a lucky bargee," said Massey,
while they ate.

"He doesn't deserve it," said Muriel, with some slight
bitterness.

That called for explanation, and Massey heard about
Randall's pigheadedness in refusing to tackle the problem
of sorting out wrinkled peas from smooth.

" That ought to be easy for a scientific bloke like you, ol' man," said Massey—always that same comment of the same eternal irrelevancy.

" It hasn't got a single thing to do with science," protested Randall. " It's something else——"

It was at that moment that the first step in the idea came to him. It was, of course, a matter of logic, of deciding upon what was the essence of the problem—what was there about wrinkledness in peas which could be used to effect the separation ? If the wrinkled peas were heavier, for instance, or lighter, it would be easy. If they were a different colour then perhaps with the aid of a photo-electric cell—Randall dallied for a second with the idea of differentiating by the aid of the shadowed surface of the wrinkled peas in a strong light as contrasted with the bright surface of the smooth ones. It was a possibility, of course, but far too slow and expensive and elaborate for things as numerous and as small as peas. What specific quality, what reaction had a wrinkled pea ? There was the point that it would roll differently from a smooth pea. That might be the key to the problem.

Randall came back to earth to find Muriel and Massey talking indifferently about Mr. Graham; his own absence from the conversation had passed unnoticed.

" He might give me a job," said Massey, with a roll of his eyes towards Randall.

" Yes, so he might," agreed Muriel brightly. " Do you think you could ask him, Charles ? "

" I *could*, I suppose," said Randall.

From what he knew of Graham's business he did not think that there was any chance of the request being granted.

" Maybe you'll get a chance next time you see him," said Massey.

" I'll remember about it."

There would be no reason at all for him to see Graham unless he had a sound suggestion to put forward on the wrinkled pea problem. There were a good many moments during the next two days when Randall's mental vision was haunted by pictures of peas—green peas and yellow peas, smooth peas and wrinkled peas, rolling or bouncing, gripped by pincers or spiked on pins, subjected to every manner of treatment and none satisfactory.

On the second afternoon he came home to receive a warmer welcome than usual from Muriel; sometimes Muriel was enthusiastically glad to see him, and sometimes she was a little indifferent. Randall was used to that by now; he was reconciled to the strange quirkiness of women, as something so ungovernable as to be beyond the laws of physics and perhaps even beyond those of physiology. To-day Muriel was glowing and tender. She was wearing a garnet-red velvet dress that set off her unusually high colour, and she was sprucer and better groomed than sometimes she was in the afternoons.

" Darling," said Muriel, and when she received his marital kiss she put her arms round him and held him to her. She kissed him with open mouth and pressed unreservedly against him.

" Darling," said Randall in return.

Her scent and her passion made his head swim a little.

" Do you love me ? " asked Muriel, pressing up against him.

For a month or more now Muriel had been going through a cold phase, rejecting Randall's advances a little pettishly, or submitting to them with something of a bad grace. That phase was over; now she was shameless, brazen, eager.

" I love you, darling," said Randall.

Under his hand he felt the stuff of her dress; something about its surface registered in his mind, and the impression began to react upon the half developed ideas there, even while Muriel gave him her mouth and throat to kiss, and as far as he knew he had no thought for anything else. When their embrace had worn itself out and he was standing a little apart from her the ideas deep down in his mind began to struggle to the surface although that surface was a whirlpool of passion.

" What's this stuff you're wearing ? " he asked, stroking the dress.

" Velvet," she said, and then, a little defensively, " Just velvet. You've seen this dress a hundred times."

" Yes, I know," he said, " but——"

" Why shouldn't I put a pretty dress on for you ? " she asked still defensively. " I wanted to show you how glad I was to see you."

" Yes, of course," said Randall. " I wasn't saying you

shouldn't. I like it. I only wanted to know what it was called."

The defensiveness faded out of Muriel's manner.

"That's all right, then, darling," she said. "Kiss me again."

The ideas struggling to the surface were submerged once more but not drowned; instead they grew in strength and vigour when Randall felt that velvet still under his hands.

That night in the big double bed Muriel was as receptive as she could be; it was almost as if she felt guilty about her previous coldness and was determined to make up for it; it was almost as if out of contrition she was driving herself by force of will to the last extremes of passion. Randall's heart went out to her; he had had momentary qualms of late—he had sensed a certain tiny condescension in Muriel's attitude towards him. He had been conscious of his own social inadequacy, of his immaturity, perhaps. When an older woman married a younger man (he had vaguely thought) the presumption is that she will be possessive and jealous. Muriel had never been either since his return from France— on the contrary, lately she had been to a certain extent offhand and even patronising, like an elder sister, say. He had been aware that he did not shine in company as Massey did, or Bill Bonnor, or the other young men who found his house a convenient rendezvous—he had not their social ease and he did not wear his clothes with their airy elegance. There might be good reason for Muriel's condescension. But his qualms disappeared under Muriel's caresses; she gave herself to him with utter abandon.

In the early morning he awoke with the grey light just beginning to show through the windows; Muriel was sleeping beside him, warm and tender, and he was relaxed and at his ease. He laid his hand on her bare shoulder, and she turned, emerging momentarily from sleep.

"Darling," she said, with a little moan, "how could I love anyone else?"

She was asleep again with the last word—she had said the one final thing to complete Randall's happiness. It may have been the touch of her shoulder that reminded Randall of the feel of her velvet dress; as he lay there in the faint light his drowsiness suddenly ended and he was wide awake—

not wide awake and sweating as he was when he woke from dreams of men buried under a pile of sandbags after a direct hit on a trench, but wide awake and breathing quietly and regularly, even smiling. The problem was solved. Practical tests would be necessary, he realised, but he need never worry again about smooth and wrinkled peas. He knew how to separate them; not only that, but as he turned his idea over in his mind and looked at it from varying angles he knew that it was the right idea, that it would fit economically and simply into any factory process that was likely to be used. It was delightful to lie there smiling in the half-dark, with Muriel's breathing to listen to, and her warmth and comfort beside him, while he knew that he had found the perfect solution, and that Graham would be pleased.

" I knew you would," said Muriel in the morning when he told her; that was an unusually tactless thing for Muriel to say, and Randall was a little piqued by it.

She might have been pleasantly surprised instead of taking it so much for granted, and she might have displayed an interest in the details, but Muriel was never at her best in the mornings —in fact this morning was something of an anticlimax after the ecstasies of the night before. Muriel was not markedly enthusiastic about kissing him, and her eyes were heavy-lidded and did not meet his frankly. Fortunately Randall was accustomed by now to an early morning lack of warmth. She was livelier when Randall spoke about going to tell Graham his idea.

" Are you sure he won't swindle you ? " she asked.

" Of course he won't, darling."

" He'll get his twenty per cent, all the same," sniffed Muriel. " Twenty per cent ! Just for sitting in an office doing nothing. Why don't you just go and patent it on your own ? You could leave him out and save money."

" Darling ! " said Randall, suppressing something of horror.

" Well, it does seem silly, doesn't it ? " said Muriel, quite unabashed.

Randall made a profound remark to himself, not for the first time, about the innate immorality of women, but outwardly he remained his usual self.

" Graham earns his commission all right," he said; in

business matters it was hopeless to try to appeal to Muriel's better feelings, but in this case there were good practical reasons that could be advanced. "He knows all about patents, and he fixes that up better than I could. I wouldn't know how to start. And he looks after the business side as well. I couldn't draw up a contract—I'd get swindled out of a lot more than twenty per cent by everyone else, wouldn't I?"

"I suppose so," said Muriel.

But Graham was much more cordial.

"Splendid!" he said, when Randall told him the news over the telephone. "What about lunch—no, damn it, I've got a lunch engagement to-day. Could you come in at three o'clock? I'm looking forward to seeing you."

And sitting across the desk from Graham, Randall outlined his idea.

"We need a conveyor belt with a surface offering plenty of friction," he said.

"In the factory," agreed Graham, "the food's carried everywhere by conveyor belt. So that ought to be easy to arrange."

"Yes," went on Randall. "But this would be a bit different. There's the surface I was speaking about. I think velvet ought to do the trick; or if not velvet I don't expect it would be hard to find a material with a suitable frictional coefficient. But the point about the belt would be that it wouldn't be horizontal."

"No? Most conveyor belts take their loads upwards or downwards—that's usual."

"I don't mean horizontal in that plane," said Randall patiently. "It wouldn't matter, I imagine, if the belt runs uphill or downhill, within limits. What I mean is that the belt would be inclined sideways—one edge higher than the other."

"Ah!" said Graham, light beginning to break.

"You dump the peas on the belt, and the belt would begin to carry them along. But at the same time they'd start rolling across the belt and falling off the edge. Maybe you'd have to have a cam to vibrate the belt a little to keep the peas rolling down — that'd be a matter for practical experiment."

" Yes, I understand."

" At any rate, we have the peas on the belt being carried along and at the same time rolling down to the edge and falling off."

" Yes."

" And the smooth peas would roll more readily than the wrinkled ones."

" Of course ! "

" That's a matter of finding the right surface for the belt, as I said. I've got velvet in my mind. But the smooth peas would roll down faster—or the wrinkled peas would roll down slower, which is really what I mean. If they roll down slower, they'll be carried farther along the belt before they fall off the edge."

" I get you," said Graham.

" So at the near end of the belt it'll be largely smooth peas that are falling off, and at the far end it'll be largely wrinkled ones. You can have a series of bins along under the edge of the belt. The near ones 'll collect the smooth peas, the far ones 'll collect the wrinkled ones. There may be some mixing in the centre bins, but those would be re-sorted, if necessary. That wouldn't be much trouble."

Graham was sitting quite still at his side of the desk, staring fixedly at his inkstand. After some seconds he allowed the fingertip of one hand to drum lightly on the desk, and then finally he looked across and met Randall's eyes.

" Perhaps this is it," he said; then he tapped on his desk again. " Now I don't want you to start building any hopes on it. We haven't tested the idea, and it may not work at all."

" That's quite possible," said Randall, taken a little by surprise at Graham's solemn aspect. From all appearance Graham might be talking about a funeral or something equally depressing.

" Then, if it works, it may not be patentable," said Graham. " Someone else may have used the notion long ago, or the Patent Office may not think there's enough originality about the idea. And there's the question of international patent, too. You've no idea how many pitfalls there are. Then after all that, supposing we have a patent granted us, and everything, the canning companies may not be interested even then. They may have thought of another idea, or they may find it doesn't fit in with their processes; or public demand may change so that they can sell mixed peas without sorting 'em. And even if everything were to go right, and the companies were to take it up, there might not be very much money in it. Not nearly as much as you might think."

" But I haven't thought there'd be much," said Randall; but Graham went on as gloomily as ever.

" They could use the idea and not admit our rights. I've known it happen. That means a long and expensive lawsuit, trips to America and God knows what. Perhaps a settlement in the end, with tuppence-ha'penny paid out, not enough to pay the expenses. You haven't had the experience I've had."

" You mean you don't want to go in for it after all ? " asked Randall a little blankly

" Well, I wouldn't go as far as that, quite," answered Graham. " I might as well handle the thing. But I don't want you to get too hopeful about it."

" I'm *not* hopeful," said Randall. It would have been hard for anyone to remain hopeful after hearing Graham's depressing remarks.

" I only thought about it because you asked me to," went on Randall, suddenly nettled. " I don't care——"

He broke off as Graham grinned at him across the desk.

" You'll have to forgive me," said Graham. " You don't know inventors like I do. I have to be cautious. The least sign of encouragement and they go right up in the air. They think they'll be millionaires next week. You've no idea what it's like. They're awful, most of them. They come in here disinterested idealists, and after ten minutes they are money-grabbing, suspicious, impatient—even the sensible ones are like that. I don't have to tell you what the freaks are like."

" I can guess," said Randall.

" Not quite all of them," went on Graham. " Lennie Phillips is all right—you remember him ? But that kind— you're another of 'em, I think—just give me a pain because they don't care about their own interests at all. One lot irritate me one way and the other lot irritates me the other."

"Sorry I irritate you," said Randall, happily conscious that the conversation was not serious.

"I'll live through it, I hope," conceded Graham; and then, becoming serious again, "Now what are we going to do about this? About the Randall new-model simplified pea-sorter, I mean? We've got to test the idea out. Have you got a workshop?"

"No," said Randall.

"What about your lab?"

Randall thought about the senior physics laboratory at the Central London College of Science. It *might* be done there, but——

"Not very easy," he said.

"The quicker the better, you know," said Graham. "Time's important. Carnac's letter's a fortnight old by now. Someone else may get the idea. Or a better one."

"Yes, I understand that."

"There are a good many workshops in London where I could get you bench-room," suggested Graham. "My knowledge of the mechanical back streets of the world is extensive."

His hand strayed to the telephone, and hesitated.

"There's always the damned difficulty of secrecy," he went on, half to himself. "Anyone will see you with a bucket full of peas and 'll guess what you're up to. I could ask Lennie Phillips if you could use his workshop. We can trust him, of course. And I don't think he's working on anything at present."

"I think I'd like that," said Randall. "Besides——"

"Besides——?"

Randall was thinking about making the tests. It was a side of the inventor's life which he had not really considered before this. In the only other invention with which he had been concerned his agent and his collaborator and a war-time Government had all taken a part, and that part had included the entire practical side. With his scientific training he was perfectly capable of making tests and deciding whether they were conclusive or not. And yet—and yet—— He felt a little out of his depth, moving in an alien world, as he had done when talking to a general on Salisbury Plain.

" I suppose I could ask Muriel to help me," he said at length.

" Your wife ?   I suppose you could," replied Graham.

There was an absence of cordiality in his tone which Randall attributed to a prejudice against the employment of completely unskilled assistants.

" You mean you'd rather I didn't ? "

" Why don't you get Phillips interested in it if you must have help ? " asked Graham in reply.

" I'd like that."

" He's a good practical man, although he's the last person you'd imagine to be that, from the looks of him.   We can telephone him.   Now what exactly are we to say ? "

" Well——" began Randall.

" Supposing he were to ask for an interest ?   If he does much work on it he'll be entitled to one.   Do you want to ask him for a favour—it's all right if you do, I suppose —or do you want to make a business proposition of it ? You'd better think it over carefully."

" Why not give him an interest ? "

" It's all one to me," said Graham with a shrug.   " I'll draw the same commission in either case.   It'll be money out of *your* pocket, though.   Yet it doesn't strike me as a bad idea, for all that.   The Randall–Phillips pea-sorter and the Phillips–Randall flare ; two moneymakers.   Last time it was his main idea, and he had two-thirds and you had one-third. Two-thirds to you this time and one-third to him ? "

" That sounds all right to me," said Randall.

" Miss Ebbisham could type a collaboration agreement in ten minutes," said Graham.   " I could find out whether Phillips is agreeable.   Shall I ? "

He put his hand to the telephone and looked across at Randall.

" Yes, please," said Randall.

He did not think then of that decision as being comparable with deciding to turn right-handed along a trench when a shell was about to fall into the left-hand trench.

FOURTEEN

MURIEL CAME DOWN into the kitchen in her dressing-gown and sat down opposite Randall as he was finishing his breakfast. Randall was shaved and dressed and looking absurdly young.

" Another cup of tea ? " he said. He noticed that Muriel had not brought down with her the cup he had taken up to her in bed, and he rose and turned to the dresser to get another.

" Thank you," said Muriel, trying to smile.

She drummed with her fingers on the kitchen table as he poured, and then she made herself meet his eyes. There was something strange about her expression, something almost secretive. She had to summon up all her will to bring herself to start the subject she wanted to speak about.

" Darling," she said, staring at him, and then hesitated.

" Yes, darling ? "

" Oh, can't you guess what I'm trying to say ? "

" No, darling, I can't. Really I can't. I'm sorry."

" I've missed this month," said Muriel harshly.

" Oh ! " said Randall.

That was all he was capable of saying for some seconds. He had always known that Muriel took the necessary birth control precautions, and he knew that such things were not absolutely certain. So Muriel might be going to have a child. To reach even that point in his thoughts took time, and beyond that point there were innumerable things to think about—the fact that now he would have to share Muriel with another was the first realisation. Then he had to think about money, and then (ashamed of himself that this should not have been the first thought) about the danger to Muriel, and then about the effect on their lives, and on his work, and——

" For God's sake don't look at me like that," said Muriel.

Randall shook himself out of his absorption. He had never seen Muriel as jumpy as this before, but that was understandable.

" Darling," he said, searching for words, " I hope you're not sorry."

" No, I'm not. I'm glad," said Muriel, still with that hint of harshness in her voice.

" It's made up our minds for us," said Randall. " I think I'm glad, too."

He was not very sure about being glad; some of his slowness was due to his conservative dislike of change, and some of it because of the tenseness of Muriel's manner.

" That's all right, then," said Muriel.

" After all," went on Randall, thinking up cheerful things to say, " we can afford it easily, I suppose. And if the pea-sorter works out all right, and it simply must, now, we'll have some more money. I'll get a job all right as soon as I get my degree."

" I wasn't thinking about those things," said Muriel.
" Yes I was. We won't have to worry about anything."

" When will it be ? Do you know, darling ? "

It was strange to be discussing Muriel's pregnancy; it was unusual and not quite natural—not as natural as, say, sitting on a court-martial on a trembling deserter.

" Some time next year. January, I suppose."

Randall counted on his fingers.

" Don't you mean February, dear ? " he asked.

" February, perhaps. But I'm not quite sure about the last time, either."

Neither was Randall, now that he came to think back.

" The doctor'll be able to tell, I suppose," he said.

" Oh yes. He'll give us plenty of notice."

Muriel was much calmer now, Randall noted with relief. She was smiling at him with one corner of her mouth, in a sort of motherly way. Motherly ? It might be in a sort of objective way, a sort of superior way. Randall understood after a second's debate; he was not privileged as she was to be a mother.

" Darling," he said, with surprise now making room for tenderness. " Do you feel all right ? Sick, or anything ? "

" Oh no," she answered, the lopsided smile more noticeable.
" No, of course not."

" I'll go and telephone Phillips," said Randall. " I won't go there to-day, of course."

" Oh, of course you will," said Muriel. " You're going to make the new tests to-day, aren't you? Of course you must go."

"Oh, damn the tests. Phillips can make 'em. I don't want to leave you, darling."

He was beside her now, his arms round her, but she put him aside.

"But I *want* you to leave me," she said. She was in the flurry and agitation to be expected of her condition. "Don't touch me just now. I—I want to think."

Her cheek was cold to his lips; he could feel her tremble a little, and he drew back from her, afraid of doing harm.

"Isn't there anything I can do?" he asked.

"No, nothing. You're very sweet, darling. You go off to Phillips's and make those tests. I'm sure they'll be all right. Don't miss your afternoon class if you can help it, but of course the tests come first. I'll see you at tea-time."

When he came down from upstairs, ready to start, he sought her again in the kitchen. In his few moments alone he had had time to think about this astonishing news and to find happiness in it as well as surprise.

"Darling," he said, "I think it's just top-hole, the whole thing. I hope you're glad, darling. It'll be nice to have a baby."

She was leaning against the kitchen wall, looking out of the window, and she turned slowly towards him.

"Of course it will be," she said.

She slipped her arm through his and walked with him to the front door. As she opened it she kissed him for the first time.

"Off you go and don't worry about me," she said, with a pat on his shoulder. "See you at tea-time."

This was happiness; this was one of the peaks of the graph of his life. He strode off towards the main road, swinging his walking-stick and stepping long and fast. More than a year of living with his wife had worked up to this climax. There had been moments of depression, naturally; Randall was sagely aware that married life had its moments of depression. When the novelty of living together and of having a house all to themselves had worn off they had come up rather desperately against reality once or twice. Randall had to make himself remember those moments, for already his memory was trying to slur them over. He knew now that that blankness he had faced had been unreal; it was incredible that he should have thought that a future with Muriel seemed featureless, when this lay in the future. Married people should all have children. Strange to think of those blank moments now; before even he had heard this news he had tended to forget them in Muriel's renewed passion and desire— in the last month or so (he could not date it exactly) she had been eager, she had made the advances. Randall grinned to himself as he walked along, thinking that it was not surprising that Muriel was going to have a baby, as the very best of birth-control precautions could hardly have stood up to the tests to which they had subjected them.

He ran up the steps of the tram and sat down, still bubbling with the joy of being alive. He had a couple of textbooks under his arm, but he never thought once about opening them. It was not only Muriel that he was thinking about; this was the day of the tests of the Randall–Phillips pea-sorter. He had almost no doubt that they would be successful. They had already made the preliminary experiments with hastily devised bits of apparatus, and there had been every indication that they were on the right track, that they had a quick and efficient means of sorting at their disposal as soon as they had decided upon the best surface for the moving belt and the best frequency of vibration. It could not fail, and Graham could not fail to sell the rights. There would be plenty of money with which to welcome the arrival into this world of Muriel's baby—their child.

When he rang the bell at the Phillips's front door Mrs. Phillips opened to him. She was smiling and young and motherly; behind her a toddling child stared up at Randall solemnly—Randall had seen the child a dozen times before without paying any special attention to it.

" Lennie's out in the workshop," said Mrs. Phillips. " You know your way."

Randall almost told her his news then and there, as they stood in the hall, but he was restrained not only by sudden shyness but by his eagerness to start the tests. He walked through the house and out into the garden where in a big skylit shed Phillips led the strange life of a professional inventor· He was standing by the long worktable as Randall entered.

" Hullo," he said. " All ready for the great day ? "

" All ready."

" I waited for you to come," went on Phillips. " I could

have made some test runs last night and I wouldn't. I had everything ready then."

" You've done the hell of a lot," said Randall, eyeing the preparations.

" You've got to thank Mary for a lot of it," said Phillips. " She spent most of yesterday shelling peas. You've no idea how much work it is getting two buckets of peas. And I had to rush out and buy another batch—one lot didn't have nearly enough wrinkled ones."

" Sorry you had all that trouble," said Randall.

" Oh, if Mary's not used to it by now she never will be," grinned Phillips. " Wives have a lot to put up with."

" They do," said Randall, and was going on to tell the news about his wife when Phillips interrupted him.

" Shoe-boxes," he said, pointing to an orderly row of cardboard boxes at the edge of the bench. " Mary had to go to the shop and beg a dozen boxes. I thought it might help if we could differentiate between the samples from various points along the belt. It would be better than a trough."

" I had the same idea," said Randall. He was looking at the broad loops of material hanging from a rail overhead. " And these are the belts ? "

" Yes. That one's velvet. And this repulsive purple one is plush—you remember how we thought we might try a longer nap. Mary had to go and buy remnants. I glued the surfaces on to canvas backing—Mary stitched 'em with her sewing machine. Well, here we are—these different velvets, a plush, a coarse canvas ; we can stick anything else we fancy on that. What about it ? "

" All right," said Randall.

Phillips began to move about the workshop with the quiet efficiency of the skilled worker. The hollow chest and drooping shoulders were not so much apparent as the beautiful long white hands went to work. The dark aquiline face was actually handsome as Phillips concentrated his whole attention on his task.

" What slope shall we try first ? " he asked, glancing over at Randall.

" Better try a slight one and then gradually increase it. Five degrees ? "

" Right-o. Here's the purple horror."

Phillips slipped the plush-covered belt over drums at either end of the bench and clamped first one drum and then the other downwards, with a quick reading of the pointers emerging from the drums against the protractors on the uprights.

"Gear ratio ten to one," he explained, slipping a driving band over a pulley. "We may as well run it slowly. Theoretically at least the speed of the belt shouldn't affect the results. Here goes."

He pressed a switch, the electric motor began to revolve, and the belt began slowly moving round the drums. Randall picked up one of the enamel buckets of peas. He climbed upon a chair and began to dribble a stream of peas down upon the belt.

"Umph," said Phillips.

The belt bore the peas steadily along to the farther drum; only a few, badly poured, ran down off the edge of the belt. The infinite majority completed the journey without hesitation and disappeared over the other drum; Randall heard them cascading into the waiting box.

"Umph, as you so rightly said," said Randall.

"Half and half. No differentiation at all," said Phillips, looking at the peas in the boxes along the side.

"It wouldn't be indicative, anyway, with such a small number," said Randall.

"All right, we'll try ten degrees," said Phillips. "But my guess is that that idea of yours for vibrating the belt is the only way to get anything definite."

"We'll try that later on. Let's test the various surfaces and slopes first."

This was recreation, an absorbing pastime; they had both of them forgotten that there might be financial reward. They were seeking a solution of a mechanical puzzle; compared with the labour and anxious concentration Randall gave to his work for his degree this was only child's play. There was a challenge about this work, but not the desperate sort of challenge offered by a scientific problem. The methodical approach and logical steps of the scientific method would be a help and to both of them the scientific method was natural. They were pleasantly conscious of mutual compatibility, of a common outlook and language and interest.

" That sets 'em rolling all right," said Randall.

But the run was unsatisfactory, and so were later ones.

" We'd better see what the velvet does," said Phillips. " This is long pile and this is short pile. The short pile might give us a quicker indication."

The peas ran much more freely on the velvet, as they soon discovered.

" You'd better come and look at this," said Phillips. He was trying to speak lightly, but there was an undertone of excitement in his voice.

Randall came beside him and looked down into the boxes. The left-hand one held the peas which had first run off. They were mostly smooth peas, although he could see a good many wrinkled ones. The next box—no different perhaps. The next one; maybe—maybe—there were more wrinkled ones and fewer smooth ones. The next one—maybe the same proportion. And in the end box, which held the peas that had been carried over the second roller, there was not a smooth pea to be seen. There were not very many, but they were all wrinkled.

" That's beginning to look like something," said Randall, elaborately casual.

" We'd better try it again with the same angle," said Phillips.

They tried it again, and they varied the conditions and tried again, and changed to the belt with the longer pile and tried once more. The best results were promising; the worst results were bad. There was a certain amount of differentiation with the good runs.

" It's *something*, of course," said Randall, " but I'll bet no commercial firm would look at it."

" We're on the track," said Phillips. " But it's queer about these surfaces. There isn't a regular gradation of effectiveness. Do you think there's an optimum point ? "

" Wait a minute," said Randall. " There's another question, too. Where's the vibrator ? I was watching the peas rolling and I'd like to try something. It's about time we started on the next series of possibilities, anyway."

The vibrator was a simple enough device—a mere bar clamped to the surface of the farther roller. At every revolution it gave a jerk to the belt.

" There's a bigger bar to give a bigger jerk if we want it,"
said Phillips.

" Perhaps we'll need it," agreed Randall.   " This'll give us
an indication."

" The slope had better be less than five degrees," suggested
Phillips.

They made the test; they watched the belt twitch rhyth-
mically, and at every twitch a few peas rolled a little way
sideways down the slope as the belt bore the ribbon of peas
along. Peas rattled down into the shoe-boxes, and then
the first ones of the ribbon reached the farther roller and
began to cascade into the box waiting for them. Randall
had poured the last of the peas from the bucket, and they
stood in silence as they travelled along the belt, some rolling
sideways, some travelling forward, until the last ones rolled
over the roller.

" Look at this," said Phillips.   " Look here."

In the shoe-boxes at the side there were only smooth peas.

" Not a wrinkled one among them," said Phillips;   there
was an edge of excitement noticeable again in his voice.

" Let's see here," said Randall, taking up the end box.
" Plenty of smooth ones here."

" I think that's just because the distance travelled isn't great
enough," said Phillips.   " Try again just with that batch."

Randall poured the contents of the box smoothly onto
the belt, and they watched again. At each twitch of the
belt a few peas rolled sideways as before and over the edge.

" All smooth," announced Phillips, looking at those which
had fallen over the edge.

" All wrinkled. Yes. Not a smooth one here," said
Randall, looking at those which had completed the journey
over the roller.

Their eyes met over the twitching belt.

" That seems to have done it," said Randall.

" Yes," said Phillips.

Then they grinned at each other.

" Let's try again with the other bucket," suggested Phillips.
" And I want to watch more closely. I've got an idea."

" So have I," said Randall.

The second test was as conclusive as the first.

" I think we've been lucky," said Phillips, straightening

himself up; he had been crouching to bring his eye to the level of the belt. "There's a necessary relationship between the size of the ridges in the wrinkled peas and the length and strength of the nap they lie on."

"I was going to say the same thing," said Randall. "You're right about our being lucky. By God you are. The vibration has to be just enough to overcome the static friction of the smooth peas without lifting the ridges on the others clear of the nap; we could have tried a lot of combinations before we hit on the right one."

"There's probably a pretty wide margin, all the same," said Phillips. "The mathematics of it ought to be interesting."

"There's an optimum point, of course, as you said," said Randall. "But there wouldn't be a steep peak in the curve all the same. The summit would be almost flat."

"Just as well," said Phillips. "That'll take care of the other variables, let's hope. Come on, I'll clamp the other bar on and halve the period of vibration. Then we can see."

They went on working rapidly and systematically, ascertaining the limiting factors first in one direction and then in the other. It was growing more and more obvious that the smooth peas could be shaken clear of the right surface while the wrinkled peas adhered. Some of the runs were perfect.

The laboratory door opened and Mary Phillips appeared, carrying a tray.

"Elevenses," she explained to Randall with a smile, and then she turned to her husband. "Do I get to hell out of here this morning or not?"

"Shall we let her stay?" asked Phillips of Randall.

"Of course!"

"I'm never sure of the reception I'm going to have," explained Mary. "Sometimes I'm invited in, almost as if I were a lady, and offered a chair. Lennie'll even tell me sometimes about what he thinks of Lloyd George. At other times I'm greeted by the bellowing of bulls and I have to put the tray down and run without even filling a cup for myself. Sugar? Hot milk? Cream?"

Phillips took a swing at Mary's attractive rear end as she stood pouring coffee and landed on it with his open hand with a resounding smack.

"Some husbands kiss their wives," said Mary to Randall

without a tremor. " But if mine had kissed me I should probably have spilled the coffee."

" I was merely informing you," said Phillips, " that the problem before us seems to have a solution."

" You might even call it the problem behind us," said Randall.

Mary looked first at one of them and then at the other.

" You're not teasing ? " she asked.

" No," said Phillips. He put his arm round her shoulders and kissed her cheek. " Does that prove the sincerity of my statement ? "

" That would prove pretty nearly anything," said Mary. " But have you really done it ? As quickly as this ? "

" It's done. All over bar the cheering." Phillips looked at his pencilled notes. " Run number eighteen was hopeful. Run number thirty-two was satisfactory."

" Satisfactory ? "

" Well, perhaps you might not think so. It was only a hundred per cent. Not ninety-nine point nine, but just one hundred. I suppose in course of time we might improve on that, but I'm satisfied. Let's show her, Randall."

They mixed the smooth peas with the wrinkled and demonstrated the test; not a single wrinkled pea escaped over the side, while two runs eliminated every smooth pea.

" You know," said Phillips, frowning over the belt, " I can see the practical troubles looming up already. This is where we come back to sanity. I'll bet that on a long run the nap of the belt gets clogged—there'll be some sort of deposit from the surface of the peas as sure as death. And in a dry climate there'll be static electricity to take into account— that'd upset all our nice calculations about friction. Or there'll be a variety of peas with the wrong size wrinkles. You don't know what miserable things can happen between a lab test and a factory trial."

" But those things can all be dealt with," protested Randall. " It wouldn't be difficult to change the belt, even with the factory going at full blast. And the static electricity——"

Mary looked at the two men plunging afresh into their work and began an unobtrusive withdrawal, but Phillips shot out a long thin hand and seized her wrist.

" I want another cup of coffee, woman," he said. " We're not really preoccupied, even if we appear to be."

" I'm glad of that," said Mary. " I've been waiting to offer you my congratulations."

" They are accepted," said Phillips. " We *do* accept them, don't we, Randall ? "

" Yes," said Randall.

He was mazed with the pleasure of success, and the obvious doting affection that existed between Phillips and Mary inspired him to loquacity.

" As a matter of fact," he began, sipping at his second cup of coffee, " there's something more for me to be congratulated about. This is a great day for me."

" I'm glad," said Mary. " What's the other good news ? "

Randall stumbled for a moment over the unaccustomed phrasing.

" My wife," he said. " She's going to have a baby."

" Splendid ! " said Phillips.

" I'm so glad," said Mary.

" The breaking point," said Phillips, " with the average man is about the three hundred and seventh napkin. Up to then the father changes them with equanimity. The graph of paternal equanimity plotted against napkin-incidence presents some curious cusps and nodes."

" That's very interesting," said Randall.

" It would be much more interesting," said Mary, " if he knew what he was talking about. But don't bother about him. When's it going to be ? "

" Muriel's not quite sure. It may be January or it may be February."

" In either case it's an early announcement," said Phillips counting on his fingers. " The proud father."

" People say that you went round boasting the very next morning," said Mary ; and then to Randall again, " But to-day was the first you knew of it ? "

" Muriel only told me this morning." This was friendly and delightful intimacy.

" Is she feeling all right ? Sick ? "

" No, not at all. I was surprised because of that. I thought every woman——"

" You don't *have* to be sick," said Mary. " What's she doing to-day ? "

" Just staying at home," said Randall. " I wanted to stay

with her—said I'd telephone you and postpone these tests, but she wouldn't hear of it."

"Why don't you telephone and ask her here?" asked Phillips. "Mary can give her lunch and discuss napkins with her. And we can show her the pea-sorter in action—a supreme felicity. The cream of motherhood, so to speak."

"There's some sense in what he says," said Mary. "Hidden among a lot of nonsense, of course. Why don't you telephone?"

"We haven't got a telephone," said Randall. It was not a remarkable avowal for that date and that social class, although in a few years' time the Post Office would begin to make England telephone-conscious.

"Oh," said Mary with such obvious disappointment that Randall hastened to reassure her.

"She didn't seem to mind being left alone at all," he said. "For that matter I might even say she was glad to be rid of me."

"I know that feeling," said Mary. "It doesn't last. She probably started regretting it as soon as she heard the door shut."

"Go and fetch her," said Phillips to Randall. "Why not?"

"Well——" began Randall doubtfully.

"It's eleven-thirty now," said Phillips. "You can be back with her by twelve forty-five. We've still got this corduroy stuff to try—there ought to be some interesting results associating vibration frequency with those grooves and ridges—and it'll take me some time to glue it on. You go along and fetch her. Otherwise she'll make her lunch off a tomato. Probably with a tear or two because her negligent husband took her at her word."

"Yes, do," said Mary.

"Well——" said Randall more doubtfully than ever. His mother had taught him that it was good manners not to be too eager to accept an invitation; and an invitation to lunch on a weekday was something rather out of the ordinary, in any case.

"Make him go, Mary," said Phillips. "I'll start on this belt."

That, of course, was the end of the argument.

FIFTEEN

RANDALL DROPPED NEATLY, left foot first, off the tram before it stopped and hurried across the street. This was a pleasant day, a delightful day, on which anything might happen. Some time ago Muriel had met Phillips and liked him; she could hardly help but like Mary. And she would be interested in their house and their furniture. She might feel, even as he did, a little self-conscious about accepting an invitation to lunch on a weekday, but that could hardly last in face of the Phillips's frank hospitality. He could not doubt that Muriel would be pleased—although she would probably spend some anxious thought over the question of what to wear to encounter the inspection of a strange woman in a big house. He turned the corner into Calmady Road and strode rapidly up to the gate; with a habit a year old he had his latchkey in his hand as he approached the front door. He stepped into the hall, and a rapid glance round assured him that Muriel was not downstairs. It was possible, of course, that she was out—that would be a nuisance. But she might be upstairs; she probably was. Randall ran lightly up the stairs and burst into the bedroom. Muriel screamed.

Randall stood by the bedroom door and Muriel went on screaming. This was frightful. This was more dreadful than anything he had ever known. The word ' adultery ' came up into his mind and filled it. Adultery was the word that had come up into his mind on that other occasion, marching through Belgium after the armistice. It had seemed a horrible word then. It seemed a horrible word now. The memories of that big feather bed and the smith's wife flooded into his mind in a series of horrible pictures—that was what the smith's wife had done with him, and was it what Muriel had just been doing this very minute ? Revive those memories and find horror in them—tear open a bridal veil and see a gaping skull. Muriel was screaming still as she lay there naked. God, and she had said she was going to have a child. God—and it was in this last month or so that her manner had changed, that she had been so passionate towards him. God—and he knew now that had been a pose; she had been forcing herself to seem like that. God—what an obscene horror all this was; Massey, rolling from the bed and leaping, one-legged and naked, to the far side of the room, and standing there, balancing on his single leg beside the window, holding on to the end of the dressing-table and staring at him.

" Keep back ! " said Massey through his teeth. " Keep back, damn you ! "

Randall took a step forward, like a machine. Muriel was still screaming, her breasts bare. And she had said she was pregnant. God, she said she was pregnant !

" Keep back ! " snarled Massey, his voice rising in volume and pitch. " Keep back ! "

He reached for the cut-glass powder jar on the dressing-table and swung it in one hand while he still held on with the other. Randall saw it swing, took another step forward. He dodged the flashing missile, which flew over his shoulder and crashed against the wall behind him; Muriel's screams soared up into a shriek at the echoing smash.

" Go forward ! " said Randall's fighting instinct within him. " Forward ! "

Was Jerry throwing bombs over the traverse ? Come on ! He charged as Massey reached for the hand-mirror which might have proved a dangerous weapon. Randall's arms were outstretched; his hands thrust Massey back from the dressing-table, one hand on his face and one hand on his chest. Massey reeled back. He crashed against the window-pane behind him, and the glass shattered with the impact. He tried to save himself, but on his one leg he had no chance. Head and shoulders and body through the glass; over he went, his one leg swinging up over the sill. Out through the window; an empty second, and then a crunching impact on the tiles below.

Randall did not step forward to look. The enemy was gone; he stared round him to take stock of the situation. Muriel saw his eyes, leaped from the bed and ran screaming from the room clothed in white flesh. He heard her run down the stairs; at the same time he heard cries in the street outside, women's voices. He stood there regaining his self-possession, emerging from his fighting madness, and reckoning up the facts. This was the day when he found out that his wife was unfaithful to him. This was the day when he knew

7

she was going to have a child and when he knew the child was the fruit of her unfaithfulness. With penetrating clairvoyance he knew what Massey had said to her, and what she had said to Massey; he knew of the carelessness and passion which had made her pregnant; he could guess at the frantic conference between them, and Massey, penniless and rootless, persuading Muriel to pretend to a new passion for her husband.

" Darling, how could I love anyone else ? "

Muriel had said that, nearly asleep, and moaning with passion; he thought she was speaking to Massey then, not to him, her husband. Why had she done it ? He knew. . . .

The cries and voices below the window were growing louder, and he stepped forward and looked out.

" There he is ! " said a woman's voice.

Bareheaded women, women with aprons, all the housewives from the houses round about, just as they had come running from their kitchens, and their toddling children with them thrust back out of the inner circle—semi-circle—which had formed round the strange white object lying on the low coping that divided the front garden from the pavement. There were other women running up—he could see them far down the street—and an old man or two. It was like a wartime civilian population, but here the children were in school and the men in the city. The faces were all turned up towards him.

" Did you do this ? " asked a voice of him.

" I'll come down," said Randall, and at his voice and at his words there was a flurry in the semi-circle.

There was no reason why he should not go down; he walked across the room, the shattered glass from the powder jar crunching under his shoes, and down the stairs. As he went down he heard the street door open and a new series of cries from the street. He reached the open street door and looked out. Muriel was by the gate, dressed fantastically in his old trench coat. She must have seized it to cover herself when she fled at his approach—she must have been cowering in the hall while he was standing in the bedroom coming back to himself. Women were gathering round her in protective poses. He stepped out and the circle shrank away a little. That strange object resting against the coping was a naked dead body; Randall had seen dead bodies in all sorts of frantic grotesquerie, but never one as grotesque as this, quite naked and doubled up so that the single leg protruded almost inexplicably from the shapeless mass. It was Massey, of course; when they should come to pull him out straight they would see the big face and the military moustache.

After this everything must have happened with torrential rapidity, but to Randall it seemed as if each petty event followed the one before with the slowness of a man toiling knee-deep across a wet ploughed field. Here came the milkman, hurrying along so that he was out of breath. Some-one must have told him what had happened. He took one look at the dead man, another look at the frightened women.

"Hullo, old chap," he said to Randall.

"Hullo."

"You've 'ad a bit of trouble," said the milkman. "But it's all over now."

"Yes," said Randall.

The milkman was looking nervously about him and spoke feverishly.

"There ain't no reason for you to get excited," he said. "No reason at all."

"Of course not," said Randall.

"Where the 'ell's that copper?" said the milkman softly to himself, and then aloud. "Supposin' you an' me was to sit down together, quietly-like. Let's sit down 'ere an' look down the street."

"What the hell should I sit down for?" asked Randall, genuinely puzzled.

"Nah, nah," said the milkman. "I told you there wasn't no reason for you to get excited."

"I'm not excited," said Randall. "For God's sake stop acting like a fool."

Randall was back in the world of reality; the nightmare world, where he knew perfectly well that everything round him was real and that events were proceeding logically, but with a logic so grim and far-fetched as to outdo any nightmare—like plodding through the mud at Passchendaele with men being killed all round him and a din so intense going on that it was stupefying. It had not seemed possible then that such horror could exist, but he had known that it did; in the same way it did not seem possible for this present situation to be real, but he knew that it was. The sooner this present horror should end, the better; he wondered if anyone had taken any action.

" Has anyone sent for the police ? " he asked.

" Yes," said the milkman. " Don't you worry your 'ead about that—oh, thank God."

The domed blue helmet was visible down the street; here came the policeman, immense, solid, walking fast, and silent on his rubber soles so that he moved like a well-oiled machine. On his dark-blue chest were his gaily coloured medal ribbons.

" Here it is, officer," said a woman.

The semi-circle made way for the policeman; he stood and looked down at the dead man; round at the women— Muriel still bundled in the trench coat, her bare feet and legs showing under it, and some woman's arms round her.

" Take her away," said the policeman, and his gaze travelled on and met Randall's.

" Good morning, sir," he said.

" Good morning," said Randall.

" He did it," said a woman's voice. " Look ! See the broken window up there."

Now everyone began to speak, everyone began to jostle. The crowd was growing momentarily.

" Stand clear, there ! " said the policeman; and then to the milkman, " You, find a telephone and tell the station."

" Mrs. Harris has done that," said a woman.

Someone else was putting something into the policeman's hands.

" It's a blanket," she said, pointing, with her eyes half-averted. " For—him."

Randall still had no feeling regarding Massey, who had been alive and was now dead. There was no room for any feeling for him, because Randall's emotional capacity was already overtaxed by his reactions to his discoveries regarding Muriel. The impact had left him numb at first, and now the mental bruising was growing painful. The deepest possible sorrow, the deepest possible unhappiness, was overwhelming him. How could Muriel have done that ? And how could she have done that in that way ? Randall felt weak, as if his sorrow was dissolving him, and then he stiffened. It was alien to all his training and beliefs that he should show

emotion in public—it was even alien that he should admit
emotion to himself. Whatever should happen he would
meet it as he knew he ought to, with a wooden indifference if
a smile were in bad taste or beyond his power. His face
hardened and he set his shoulders back; automatically his
hands clasped each other behind his back and he stood in the
' at ease ' position, as he had stood at a thousand parades,
ready for whatever should come, and with the pain stoically
ignored.

Ting-ting ! Ting-ting ! This was an ambulance making
its way through the crowd, the sweet note of its bell carrying
with it a sense of urgency. And at the same moment there
came a police car, sweeping up to the front gate, and men
in uniform, men in plain clothes, bundled out of it. A man
in a grey suit was obviously in charge; a sweeping look
round, an interchange of glances with the policeman, were
enough to give him a complete grasp of the situation.

" Move that crowd away, sergeant," he said.

Men were kneeling now beside Massey's dead body. Then
the man in the grey suit turned to Randall.

" This is your house ? " he asked.

" Yes."

" So you are Mr.—Randall ? "

" Yes."

" Would you mind telling me your full name ? "

" Charles Lewis Randall."

" And your profession ? "

" I'm a science student at the University of London."

" Thank you. Ex-service man, I suppose ? "

" Yes."

" What was your rank and unit ? "

" Captain. Royal Fusiliers."

" Thank you. Perhaps I could come inside ? I am a
detective-inspector of the Metropolitan Police."

" Come in," said Randall.

In the hall the detective looked rapidly round him.

" It was upstairs, I gather, that whatever happened took
place ? "

" Yes."

" Will you come up with me ? You might help me in my
investigation."

"Of course," said Randall.

The detective stood on the threshold of the bedroom, his feet together, like a man on the edge of a swimming bath, and leaned forward to look in. There was the bed gaping open, the bedclothes hanging, a pillow on the floor. Beyond the bed was the broken window, the jagged points of glass surrounding the empty space. The lace mat on the dressing-table had been dragged along so that half its length dangled over the end. The toilet articles were in confusion, a hair-brush on the floor, and, also on the floor but over below the broken window, was the hand mirror which Massey had seized in that last second. On the floor beside the door lay the scattered fragments of the powder jar which Massey had thrown. There were chips of glass everywhere, and on the flowered wallpaper at shoulder height, close to the door, was the mark where the powder bowl had struck—clear proof of the frantic violence with which it had been hurled. All this the detective's eye took in in one single moment, apparently. He nodded to himself and glanced at Randall again. Randall met his glance, and then the eyes of both of them, as if with a single thought, strayed back into the room. On one chair lay Muriel's clothes, her skirt and jumper and underclothing, the skirt folded neatly, shoes side by side below the chair. On the other chair lay a man's clothing in confusion, shirt and coat and trousers lying anyhow; a single shoe beside the chair, and, against the wall, grotesque, hideous, an artificial leg.

"Were you wounded?" asked the detective. "Is that your leg?"

"No," said Randall.

"I see," said the detective, nodding to himself again.

Then he heard a footstep on the doorstep down below.

"I'm up here," he called.

A heavy step mounted up the stairs to them; it was the police sergeant.

"I left Constable Ellis at the door, sir," he said; in his hand was his notebook with an elastic band on it.

"Right. What else?"

"The man's dead, sir. The doctor's there. He must have gone out backwards through that window, sir, and fallen straight down on his head."

"A one-legged man?"

" Yes, sir. I've got the name. Massey. Richard Fanning Massey, sir. Captain Massey."

" Yes ? " said the detective.

" And I have a statement from the wife, sir—Muriel Randall." The sergeant's glance flickered towards Randall and back again.

The detective turned to Randall.

" I did it," said Randall, but the detective gave no sign of having heard him.

" I shall have to take you into custody," he said. " You will be charged with being concerned in the death of—of Richard Fanning Massey. I must caution you that anything you say will be taken down in writing and may be given in evidence."

" I did it," said Randall.

Outside the house there was a bigger crowd than ever now, but its personnel had changed, and the police had cleared the whole section of the street outside the house, so that the crowd was packed thick at two lines, one twenty yards up the street and the other twenty yards down it.

" There 'e is ! " said a masculine cockney voice—the crowd before had been almost entirely of local women; now it was made up largely of men. But the women's heads were at the upper windows of the houses.

The police motor-car still stood at the gate. It was to this gate that he had come, walking by Muriel's side, when she was Mrs. Speake and he was on leave from France; it might have been another man and another woman, walking in another world, so different and distant was that past of less than three years ago. Randall had a penetrating insight for a few moments into the long and complex series of coincidences which had led him from a trench in the Salient to a police car outside the gate of a house in Calmady Road. Two young men were hurrying up the street; the sergeant opened the car door and ushered Randall in, and the young men appeared to be disconcerted and disappointed.

" Reporters," said the sergeant getting in beside Randall. " Drive on, Snow."

SIXTEEN

IT WAS HIS MOTHER who first came to Randall at the police station; the police were most kind and attentive and had asked him who it was whom he wished to be informed.

"Oh, Charles!" she said. "Oh, Charles! However did it happen?"

She was in a state bordering on hysteria as she threw herself into his arms, and Randall had to soothe her. He had to pat her shoulder and sit her down beside him and talk about indifferent subjects; the police helped by bringing them mugs of strong tea, so that Mrs. Randall had to say whether she needed sugar or not, and she had to smile over the thickness of the china, and these commonplaces brought her back to something like normal.

"That woman!" she said, and clenched her teeth and her hands.

"Gently, Mother," said Randall.

"I'd like to—I'd like to—oh, there isn't anything I wouldn't do to her!"

"It's all over now," said Randall—a fatuous remark, as he was aware, but he could think of nothing better to say.

"I knew she was a bad lot the moment I set eyes on her," said Mrs. Randall. "To think that she's been in my house and eaten my food!"

His mother's desperate animosity had one good result; Randall could not agree with her for fear of setting her off again into hysteria, so that he was compelled to speak about Muriel with moderation—he had to speak about her objectively, and when he did that he could hardly feel active anger. But the mention of her brought back the pain and the unhappiness even while he disguised his resentment, and then for his mother's sake he had to conceal the pain as well. It was a relief when his father arrived, hurrying in from the school where he had been sent for in haste.

"Hullo, son."

"Hullo, Father."

"Sorry to hear about your bad luck."

"Sorry to cause all this trouble."

It was almost a casual meeting, a looker-on would have

thought who was not in the secret. The artificial smiles were almost convincing; the tones of the voices were impressively indifferent. Mr. Randall took the chair his son offered; the constable might as well not have been there at all for all the attention bestowed upon him.

" No trouble to me," said Mr. Randall. " Old Hudson's the one to be sorry for. You ought to have seen his face when he heard he had to take my classes ! All his free periods gone and he's got a lot of papers to mark."

It was only after two or three minutes, and after half a dozen indifferent remarks, that Mr. Randall broached the subject that they were both of them thinking about.

" The first thing we have to do," he said, " is to get legal advice. Have you got anyone in mind ? "

" No," said Randall, " I don't know any lawyers. Do you ? "

" There's old Burdon," said Mr. Randall. " He's the solicitor for the school. I've met him a few times. Would he do ? "

" I suppose so," said Randall with a shrug.

This was not an assumed indifference; although Randall was playing a part—a part for which he had been so long trained that he assumed it automatically—when he concealed his sorrow over Muriel. But he was genuinely indifferent to his own fate; his world, his life, had come to an end, and it was too much of an effort to master his pain just to pretend to an interest in his own obsequies.

" I suppose I'd better go along to him now," said Mr Randall doubtfully.

" I should ring him up and save time," suggested Randall. " They'll let you use the telephone here, I expect."

Even though he had no interest in his future, Randall could not idly sit by and see this business executed inefficiently.

" That's not a bad idea," said Mr. Randall.

He returned five minutes later with something of the air of a man who has carried out a difficult mission successfully.

" Mr. Burdon's coming down himself," he said. " He sounded very concerned to hear the news. He—he told me to tell you not to volunteer any statement until he arrives."

" All right," said Randall.

His father had uttered the last sentence with noticeable

embarrassment, as touching on those realities of life which a gentleman would prefer to ignore in conversation. That speech involved recognition of the fact that Randall was under arrest—that he might have to stand trial in a court of law. But there was almost equal embarrassment in his father's manner as he made his next speech.

" Son," he said, leaning forward so as not to have to speak too loud, " how about money? I'll try to raise what's necessary."

" Oh, that's all right, Father, thank you," said Randall. " I've got lots."

With that awkward point safely negotiated, conversation tended to languish. Nobody wanted to discuss important issues, and even to those convention-bound people it seemed ridiculous to talk about trivialities in those particular circumstances.

" The children will be home any minute, dear," said Mr. Randall to his wife.

" Yes. I ought to be going, I suppose. They'll have heard——"

That was the worst moment of all, possibly. Mrs. Randall had not until then given full consideration to the effect of this catastrophe on the children, but now one possibility after another dawned upon her, and she looked at the two men with growing dismay which, too late, she tried to conceal. Finally she broke down.

" What are we going to *do*? " she asked, with the tears flowing freely.

The thoughts of the two men were paralleling hers. Jimmy and Doris at school—how could they face their schoolmates when their brother had killed a man, when the circumstances of scandal and horror in which it had happened must now be public property? Harriet had just started work in a city office—what would they think of her there? And the men who were beginning to pay her atten- tion—would any of them care to associate any more with a family where such things happened? Mr. Randall thought of his turbulent classes at school—would those adolescent fiends have any mercy on him? The Common-room; it would be hard to face his colleagues. And would the Board of Governors want to continue him in their employ? It was

not as if he was a popular member of the staff. It was only
last week that he had been studying the new pension scale
just issued and deciding that it would be six years before
he could possibly retire. To his eternal credit he disguised
his misgivings.

"Oh, nonsense, dear," he said. "Everything will be all
right. People will want to help us. You just see if they
don't."

"I hope so. I'm sure I hope so," sobbed Mrs. Randall.

Randall and his father exchanged glances; she was not
fit to be sent home alone.

"I'll come along with you, dear," said Mr. Randall bluffly;
and to his son, "I'll see you get all the things on this list,
old man. Burdon ought to be here any minute."

Mr. Burdon when he arrived proved to be a rather
cadaverous man of advanced middle age, dressed formally
in black coat and striped trousers, and with the hair that
grew on the left side of his head carefully trained over the
bald summit down to his right ear. He looked fixedly, with
piercing brown eyes, at Randall as he introduced himself.

"We can dispense with any formalities, I think," he said.
"I am your solicitor, and I need only remind you that all
communications between attorney and client are privileged.
I may not reveal to anyone what you say to me in connection with this case, and not only that, but I cannot be
compelled to reveal it, either, by any process of law."

"I understand that," said Randall.

"Now tell me what happened."

That was not easy. Randall felt mortally tired, he suddenly
discovered, and memory was blurred. It was strange that
he could not make his brain produce a logically connected
story. He could not even begin.

"Tell me," said Burdon, as though to a child.

"My wife——" began Randall, and stopped.

"There was trouble between you and your wife?"

"Oh no," said Randall with considerable irritation.
"Nothing like that."

"You had never quarrelled with her?"

"Nothing to speak of."

"Not lately?"

"Not at all lately."

" You were on good terms with her, in other words ? "

" Yes—oh yes."

" Then this Captain Massey. How did you come to know him ? "

Bit by bit the miserable story came out, each question from Burdon eliciting some part of it. It was impossible for Randall to tell the story in chronological order; this morning—a year ago—yesterday; Burdon listened patiently. Randall found himself opening his mouth to tell of Muriel's recent pretence at warmth in bed, but he shut it again and left the words unspoken.

" Mr. Randall," said Burdon, " it is only fools who do not tell their lawyer everything. There is no object whatever in concealment—no object whatever—and it may cause serious trouble. What were you going to say about your wife ? "

The pitiful story went on; the brown eyes were fixed upon Randall's grey ones, and Burdon's face never altered in expression—it was like a pale mask.

" Nearly all of what you are telling me," said Burdon to fill a gap, " will not be used in any way in evidence, but the more I know the better, all the same. Now tell me about these people, the Phillips. You told them your wife had said she was pregnant ? "

" Yes."

" Now this is particularly important, Mr. Randall. Please be quite certain about what you are saying. They—the Phillips—they urged you to go home and bring your wife back to lunch ? "

" Oh yes."

" Of course I'll be discussing the matter with them, but to save time I'll ask you now—you are quite sure that it was they, and not you, who first made the suggestion about your returning home unexpectedly ? "

" I think so," said Randall.

Burdon's face was not quite so mask-like. There was a change of expression, a flicker in the eye of something like relief. The change was apparent even to Randall's weary brain.

" What's so important about that ? " he asked pettishly.

Burdon's expression changed again, hardening. This was

the moment to bring home to his client the seriousness of his position.

"Now, Mr. Randall," he said, "you don't appear to understand. A man has met his death by violence. That is something very serious indeed. There may even be a charge of murder. *Murder*, Mr. Randall."

"My God!" said Randall.

That was a grim word. The pain and disgust and sorrow which the thought of Muriel caused him could not occupy so large a share of his thoughts now. Burdon saw the change in his expression and took special note of it. Here was a wronged husband who had killed his wife's lover—it was a situation in which the possibility of long-premeditated murder could not be overlooked. An educated man, a man of some inventive ability; he might easily have planned to-day's tragedy so as to give it an appearance of spontaneity. But that startled expression, that change of attitude, unless the man was a consummate actor (and Burdon, lawyer-like, kept that possibility in mind), seemed to show that he had never thought of murder. Burdon was perfectly prepared as part of his legal duties to prepare a murderer's defence; what he did not want to happen was that he should be left ignorant of important facts on account of a silly prejudice of his client to be thought innocent by his legal adviser.

"Murder," said Mr. Burdon reassuringly, "calls for premeditation; the smallest amount of premeditation will suffice. But you assure me, Mr. Randall, that there was no premeditation at all?"

"Of course not," said Randall.

"You had no idea that your wife was being unfaithful to you?"

A hot iron pushed into an open wound; the question made Randall writhe, as Burdon saw. Randall could have no doubt that Muriel's infidelity had been of some considerable duration. He had been deceived for two months at least, possibly for much longer. He could remember now a hundred little incidents to which he had not given a second thought when they happened; variations of mood and temper which he had believed to be beyond explanation but which he could now see were easy to explain. Those

cold fits, those warm fits—had Massey been kind to her
or unkind to her to produce them? And his own reactions
to them—had Muriel told Massey about them, lying warmly
in his arms? Laughing together perhaps? That thought
was actually nauseating. And he had no doubt at all that
it was Massey who had made Muriel pregnant, that it was
Massey who had persuaded Muriel to show a new affection
for her husband as one step in a well-constructed plan to
make him think the child was his. That was more frightful
than anything else.

" You had no idea," repeated Mr. Burdon.

The play of expression over Randall's face had been
almost convincing in itself, besides being intrinsically interesting, but jealous husbands, as Burdon knew, were unpredictable persons. The question might possibly have
caused the same pain if Randall had known about his wife
for months.

" No, I had no idea," snapped Randall. " For God's sake,
do you think I'd have let it go on ? "

" Gently, gently, Mr. Randall. Please remember that I
am asking these questions without personal animus, simply
in the course of my duty to you. So it was not until you
entered the room that the true state of affairs dawned upon
you ? "

" Yes."

" What exactly did you see ? "

The look on Randall's face caused even Burdon to let
pity temper his professional interest.

" Very well, Mr. Randall, I don't think we need to elaborate
on that. And what happened next ? "

Randall tried to tell him.

" I understand," said Burdon; that was not strictly the
truth. For someone as scrupulously accurate in his diction
as Burdon it was a misstatement. What Burdon meant was
that he could follow the course of events, as described by
Randall, but he was far from understanding them.

" Now, once again, Mr. Randall," he said, " this is very
important. You were still standing by the door when the
deceased threw this—this dressing-table ornament at you ? "

" I suppose so. I think so."

" You aren't really in doubt about it ? "

" No."

" So there was no question of your being forced into a brawl against your will ? To use a military metaphor, your retreat was not cut off ? "

" No, of course not."

" Now you must understand this, Mr. Randall. You could have turned round and gone out of that door and no one would have stopped you ? You could have gone to a civil court and obtained a remedy for your injuries, a satisfactory and exemplary remedy ? "

Randall merely looked blank, and Burdon had to explain.

" I mean you could have applied for a divorce from your wife, and obtained one, and at the same time you could have sued Massey for substantial damages."

" I suppose I could," said Randall.

" And instead you attacked the man, even though you could have gone away safe and sound."

" Oh, for God's sake——"

" Mr. Randall, these are the points which in course of time will be presented to a judge and jury. Your liberty—maybe even your life—will depend upon their correct presentation. I have already explained to you that you may be charged with a crime for which the penalty is death. Alternatively I have no doubt at all that you will at least be charged with a crime for which the maximum punishment is penal servitude for life. Prison is a terrible place, Mr. Randall. You must understand that there is a chance that you may be in prison for the rest of your days."

Around them the life of the police station was going on; more than once they had heard cell doors opening and shutting, gruff voices, keys jangling. Burdon's gesture reminded Randall of all this. But Randall was so tired; even Burdon could see that.

" Perhaps I had better not press you for further information just at present," he said. " It must be pretty nearly suppertime here now. Except for one thing. You did not make any statement to the police after your arrest ? "

" No."

" That is excellent," said Burdon.

The station sergeant told them that the restaurant at the corner would send in whatever supper Captain Randall chose to order from its limited menu, provided, of course, that he was prepared to pay for it. If not, then His Majesty would feed his guest on a somewhat less royal scale of hospitality.

" I don't care," said Randall. " I'm not hungry."

" You'd better eat something, all the same," said Burdon. " This is a difficult time for you."

So not much later Randall found himself rather gloomily contemplating a congealing chop flanked by potatoes and cabbage.

" Here's the evening paper if you'd care to look at it, sir," said the sergeant—he could not keep that ' sir ' out of his speech when addressing a captain.

Randall picked the paper up idly. The tone of the sergeant's voice should have warned him, but Randall was too stupid after all the events of the day to notice the warning. Once before he had picked up an evening paper and glanced at it idly, to find the world crashing round him. That had been on his wedding day, with Muriel's bath water roaring in the next room while the headlines shouted the first news of the battle of St. Quentin. The headlines to-night would not rock the world, but they rocked Randall's world.

' R. F. Massey Dead,' he read. ' Mysterious Incident.' Below the headlines there was an excited column :

' To-day the unclothed body of Captain R. F. Massey, who played cricket for Sussex during the seasons 1913 and 1914, was discovered lying in the front garden of a house in Calmady Road, Upper Oak. Captain Massey had presumably fallen through a window in an upper bedroom, receiving injuries which apparently were immediately fatal. The owner of the house where the unfortunate incident took place is Captain Charles Randall, well known as the inventor of the Phillips–Randall flare so extensively employed during the war. A neighbour said . . .'

Two-thirds of the front page did not suffice for the story; the back pages held column after column as well. It was months since the evening papers had had such an opportunity. There was everything an evening paper could possibly hope for in a story. A first-class cricketer was mysteriously dead, and the fact that he had not played cricket for six years was amply compensated for by the intriguing, suggestive fact that he had only one leg. His body was ' unclothed ', too—that word was the journalistic first choice, although farther on the word ' nude ' seemed to find favour as well. He had fallen out of a window, but he had fallen through it, smashing the glass—here was a picture, not at all clear, taken from Mrs. Tomlinson's bedroom window across the street to show the shattered pane, and an X down below to show where the body was found.

Randall read on with growing consternation. The newspaper knew — none better — the law regarding libel and regarding contempt of court. Yet the story gained in power as a result of the limitations imposed; not that Randall appreciated the point. He was only aware of the innuendoes and suggestions. He read that ' when inquiries were made for Mrs. Randall it was understood that she was too unwell to be interviewed '. That followed Mrs. Tomlinson's account of the screams she had heard issuing from the house at midday. There was as much about himself as the newspaper could scrape together from scanty sources—his war service, a few facts (mostly wrong) about the P–R flare, a mention of his father as mathematics master at the school (was nobody spared ?) and a line or two about his present status as a student of science receiving a government maintenance grant. Then the paper ' understood ' that an arrest had been made.

The paper was not like Randall's mind; it did not admit the existence of the word ' adultery ', but the whole story bellowed hints about adultery, about a jealous husband and a guilty wife and a slain paramour, hints that this was the old but ever fresh story of the returning soldier and the erring wife. An old story but spiced in this case with the most stimulating details about nudity and artificial legs, first-class cricketers and prominent inventors; the very restrictions imposed by the law gave an additional spice to the whole thing, a flavour of suspense, a promise of ' to be continued in our next '. No one could reasonably doubt that the man who read this story to-day would gladly pay his penny to-morrow to read the next instalment.

Nor could there be any doubt that everyone in England was reading this account or similar ones. Men who had gone through the war with him, men whose names and faces he had forgotten, would be reading his name and calling up his face in their memory. The colonel who had accelerated his demobilisation, the general who had supervised the tests of the P–R flare; to-night they would be telling in the mess, or at home, or in the club, how they had met him and what they thought of him. His fellow students at the College of Science would know about it. Graham—Phillips—Mrs. Phillips; and the friends of his sisters, the friends of his brother, the thousands who had shirked their way through mathematics at the school under 'Toffee' Randall; they would all know about it. Randall was not a man of exuberant imagination, but it seemed to him, in his distraught condition, as he held the newspaper on his knee, that he could hear the roar of voices saying 'Randall, Randall, Randall' as everyone in England talked about him, voices like a deafening surf on a stormy beach.

The chop which had arrived half-congealed was now wholly congealed, a mass of white fat with fatty potatoes on one side and cold cabbage on the other. Randall ate the piece of bread, forcing himself to do so, going through the motions of eating as though for the first time and as if he was following written instructions on how to do so—putting a piece in his mouth, moving that piece so that it lay between his jaws, working his lower jaw up and down on it, and then conveying the chewed result to the back of his mouth and swallowing down into a dry throat. And now Burdon was returning, anxious and agitated as he had not been before.

" Mr. Randall, you misinformed me."

" No ! "

" But you did. You said you had made no statement to the police."

" And I didn't—I haven't."

" The detective inspector showed me his notes. And the sergeant was there as a witness. Mr. Randall, don't you understand that by misinforming your legal adviser you are gravely prejudicing your position ? "

" But I haven't made any statement."

" Mr. Randall, you were cautioned by the detective inspector after he took you into custody, and then——"

" Well ? "

" And then, after that caution, you said ' I did it '."

" Did I ? I wouldn't be surprised."

" But that's a statement, Mr. Randall. A statement of the very gravest importance."

" I'm sorry," said Randall, " I didn't think of that as a statement. Very likely I said it. And it was true."

Mr. Burdon almost wrung his hands over the unlawyer-like behaviour of the people among whom he was forced to move. But he showed relief at the same time.

" At least," he said, " you will not contest the detective inspector's evidence on the point, or ask me to."

" Of course not. No doubt I said it—in fact I think I remember saying it. I'm sorry I told you I didn't make a statement—I thought you meant some long speech or something."

Burdon gave up discussion of the point.

" Very well then. We had better get on with the rest of our business. But I implore you, Mr. Randall, to be as careful as you can be."

" I will, if you think it matters."

" It matters more than I can tell you. For instance, to-morrow you will appear in the magistrate's court—that's the reason why we must settle everything to-night as far as possible. In a way it will be only a formality; under the law you must appear in a court as soon as possible as a precaution against illegal detention. Only evidence of your arrest will be given, the police will ask for a remand, I shall agree, and the magistrate will grant it."

" Well ? "

" When the detective inspector gives his evidence of arrest he will tell what you said in reply. That statement of yours is bound to have the profoundest influence both upon the prosecution and on the defence. It will affect our arrangements right from the start—we should have been at a serious disadvantage if I had not known about it."

" But I haven't any defence, anyway."

Burdon had to restrain himself from wringing his hands.

" Mr. Randall, your liberty—perhaps your life—depend on the decisions we make and the action we take. Please understand that—I've said it before, and you seem to pay me no attention. I have no doubt—although of course I make no

promises—from what you have already told me, that you
have a very good defence. Now, could you please go on with
the facts? Let us start again with the moment when Massey
threw the ornament at you, and recapitulate from there?"

Burdon's eyes rested for a moment on the frozen chop
and the full plate. His client had eaten nothing, or almost
nothing, but time was pressing.

"What do you want to know?" asked Randall wearily.

"The motives that actuated you when you attacked him."

Randall peered through the fog of fatigue at the pale bony
face. What could he tell this man that he could understand?
Randall had a mental picture of himself leading a counter
attack; the snarling bayonet-men beside him, the bombs
hurled from traverse to traverse, the confusion, the din, the
excitement, the knowledge that if it was probable death to
push on it was certain death to hesitate. Burdon could know
nothing of this; no one could, except his fellow soldiers, and
yet it had its bearing on the subject under discussion. Then
in memory he transferred himself back again to that bedroom.

"Muriel was screaming," he said.

That, too, was something very closely related to the subject,
even if at first sight it did not appear to be.

"Muriel was screaming," repeated Burdon, prompting him,
with unexpected gentleness in his voice.

"He said 'Keep back!' So I ran at him."

There was a logical connection there, of cause and effect,
as Burdon noted, even though it seemed illogical to him.

"Did Massey have any other weapon—anything that could
serve as a weapon?" he asked.

"Yes," said Randall, memory returning to him. "There
was the mirror."

"The mirror? Oh, you mean a hand-mirror?"

"Yes."

Burdon kept his voice studiously gentle so as not to break
the thread.

"That could be a dangerous implement. He could use it
like a hatchet or he could throw it. Did he pick it up?"

"I—don't—remember. I pushed him back. There was
the window. He went backwards through it."

"Did you mean to push him through it?"

"Yes. No. Yes. I think so."

An enemy pushed out through a window is an enemy safely disposed of. The fighting instincts could make that decision before the thinking brain could make the logical deduction.

" Did you intend to kill him ? "

" No." A pause. " No. Not particularly."

Burdon's brown eyes, like polished stones, studied the weary face. This was a man doing his best to tell the truth, and finding, as others before him, that the truth is hard to distinguish. The law was more plain. If someone, sane enough to know that a fall from a window could cause death, should push someone else through a window with the intent to cause him harm, and death resulted, that was murder, although death was not intended. That was murder; but the law also recognised manslaughter as a lesser offence, and then there was excusable homicide and justifiable homicide. The distinctions were clear; there was the question of intent, and the question of provocation; the question of a premeditated design or of the heat of passion; the question of self-defence, and the question as to whether self-defence had been kept within the bounds of the necessity to save the defender's life. Judicial rulings for a dozen generations past had drawn these distinctions. It was irritating that the case under consideration should be so vague in comparison. The only man in a position to know actually did not know if he had any intent to cause bodily harm; he was not sure if he had been defending himself or attacking, apparently.

Burdon tried to reconcile himself to his client's muddled state of mind. People's minds were more generally muddled than not, as he had found during a lifetime of legal practice; their lives were muddled, too—they were always finding themselves unable to pay their debts, or being careless while driving, or committing adultery, or having wives who committed adultery. They made statements to the police and forgot they had done so. There was no limit to human foolishness, and as an inscrutable fate had condemned him to live out his life in the midst of this foolishness there was nothing to do but to try and make the best of things. This man (thought Burdon, looking into the future) would be an unpredictable witness if called in his own defence—but that was true of nearly everybody. Properly coached and rehearsed, he might give a reasonable account of himself in his examination-in-chief, but under cross-examination he would be led into damaging admissions. But of whom among mere mortals could that not be said?

And there was still much more to be known.

" What did you do then, after he fell through the window? "

At least, decided Burdon, listening to Randall's replies to his further questions, the man had behaved with reasonable sanity after the first absurd folly. He had not tried to run away, he had not tried to attack his wife; he had suggested calling the police; he had not resisted arrest. It was hard to be patient with a man who did not think that ' I did it ' constituted a statement to the police, and the most vital statement imaginable at that, but patience was necessary with these people with untidy minds and lives. And, touching that same confession, he had been quite right when he had said that it would have the profoundest influence on the prosecution and on the defence. A jury would have to consider the state of mind of the man who said it; in the magistrate's court to-morrow it would be the point on which everything else would hinge. With that confession in evidence, and with the prisoner's plea of not guilty, it would be obvious to the whole world, including the prosecution, that the defence must be confined along the lines of self-defence and provocation.

And that led to other considerations; since the end of the war there had been a ' crime wave ' of alarming proportions, and especially had there been an increase in the frequency of crimes of violence. Many notable judicial figures had called attention to this from the bench; there would be an undoubted tendency to be severe with a man who had allowed his rage to lead him into killing a fellow man. From that point of view any reference to the ' unwritten law ', any attempt at justification along those lines, would be quite fatal. Self-defence would be the safest argument to advance, but the prosecution would be able to point out the weaknesses in the argument at once—no man with an open door to run away through (as he himself had said) need kill to save his life. The defence must be careful not to fall between the two stools of provocation and self-defence; it might be better to concentrate every effort to prove provocation—the throwing of the dressing-table ornament would then be one more provocation added to the tremendous provocation already offered.

But then it was manslaughter to kill even after provocation, and the punishment would be in the discretion of the court, with the only maximum penal servitude for life. A judge determined to put an end to crimes of violence might award a sentence that he considered exemplary; Burdon began to wonder whether, as Randall's legal adviser, he could in conscience recommend a defence that involved such a possibility. For self-defence is something quite different; it makes homicide excusable, and if it can be proved the prisoner is not guilty. A life sentence on the one hand, ' not guilty ' on the other; the defence would have to gamble, in any case, on the state of mind of the jury, on the attitude of the judge—Burdon pursed his thin lips in distaste as he thought of the word ' gamble ', but he had to admit to himself that sometimes even in lawsuits the gambling element was noticeable. And, from the point of view of the defence it would be better, far better, if the victim had not been a man with only one leg. There was no need to cross rivers before he came to them; counsel would make these decisions—in consultation with him, of course—and the decisions need not, indeed should not, be made until the last possible moment, possibly not even until in court judge, jury, and prosecution had all borne the inspection of defending counsel. Counsel had better be the best available. And that raised another point, which should be settled at once.

" Are you in the possession of any funds ? " asked Mr. Burdon—if he had said ' Have you any money ? ' he would have saved Randall the effort of a moment's wondering about what he meant, but such wording would have seemed brutal and indelicate.

" Oh yes, I've lots," said Randall when at last he understood what he was being asked.

" Lots ? " repeated Burdon, a little reluctant not only to pursue the subject but also to use a word both vulgar and vague.

" I've a thousand pounds in the bank," said Randall. " I

had a large cheque two months ago and I haven't decided
what to do with it."

" Indeed ? " said Burdon, pleasantly surprised that a young
undergraduate, the son of a schoolmaster, should own such
a substantial sum.

" There are some savings certificates as well," went on
Randall, " and the house—the mortgage is fully paid off."

" There's no need for any anxiety regarding money, then,"
said Burdon. He would have been greatly offended if a
cynic had suggested to him that his tone had altered with
the news, but there would have been a little truth in the
suggestion.

" Do you want some now ? " asked Randall.

" Not at this moment. I'll see that you are given a cheque-
book and then I'll ask you for the funds necessary."

The police sergeant came into the detention room. His
expression was grave, and he carried himself with a certain
solemnity.

" Will you come with me now ? " he said.

His tone was flat and wooden, and he used neither ' sir '
nor ' please '.

" They are going to charge you," explained Burdon.

The detective inspector was sitting at a desk down the
short corridor. He looked up from the registers in front of
him ; his eyes and face were without expression.

" You are about to be charged with the manslaughter of
Richard Fanning Massey," he said.

" Ah ! " said Burdon.

The charge was manslaughter and not murder, then.
The police must have made their inquiries rapidly, and
presumably the inspector must have been in telephone
communication with the Director of Public Prosecutions.
It was a measure of the infinite importance of the decision
that hearing of it should call forth this interjection from
Burdon. The inspector acknowledged it by a momentary
transference of his expressionless gaze from Randall to
Burdon and back again, and then he went on speaking.

" I must repeat the caution that anything you say will be
taken down in writing and may be used in evidence."

Randall opened his mouth to say ' all right ' but Burdon
extended a bony hand and Randall shut it again.

" You, Charles Lewis Randall," said the inspector, " are now charged with having unlawfully killed Richard Fanning Massey to-day, at 53 Calmady Road in the County of London."

Again Randall opened his mouth, and again the bony hand caused him to shut it again.

" You will appear before the Stipendiary Magistrate on this charge to-morrow," went on the inspector. " And you will be kept in custody until then."

A hand was laid on Randall's shoulder; it was only the lightest touch, but it was pregnant with the warning of infinite compulsion.

" I'll leave you now," said Burdon. " It's late already and I've a great deal more to do."

Randall turned politely; he was pale, almost haggard, with the stresses of the day.

" Now please remember," added Burdon, leaning forward to give weight to his words, " on no account are you to discuss this case with anyone at all, and especially not with the police. Should you feel obliged, for instance, to make a supplementary statement, do not do so until I have been informed and can be present. Have I impressed this sufficiently on you now ? "

" Yes," said Randall. " I won't."

" Good night, then. I'll be in court in plenty of time to see you to-morrow."

Now Burdon was gone, and now he was in a cell, and now he was alone with the door locked behind him, and now, with night closing down upon him, it was acutely borne in upon him that he was a prisoner. That he could not walk out and take a breath of the night air. That he could not go to the bookshelves and get himself a book. That it was hopeless to look forward to lectures and practical work to-morrow, hopeless to think of further pleasant sessions with Phillips watching peas rolling on vibrating belts. He was confined, he was a prisoner, he was under lock and key within four narrow walls, with fifty burly policemen just outside to keep him there. He was under restraint, and that was suddenly very bad. He began to walk the narrow cell; he looked through the grating in the door, walked back, returned to the grating again, looked at the harsh light outside, turned away again. This was restraint, imprisonment, something far different from the discipline of his army life and the pleasant self-discipline of the last year. He felt a raging surge of emotion; his hands clenched and his jaw set and his eyes opened wide, and he suddenly found himself on the verge of violence. The discovery was a shock, and he was instantly ashamed of himself, and instantly reached out for his self-control. It was sobering to think that he had almost begun to kick the furniture about, that he might have turned hysterical, like some drunken lout or unbalanced criminal, like some undisciplined recruit in the guardhouse. It was better to unclench and walk, up and down, up and down, until his feet dragged with exhaustion, until his legs ached, until his brain swam. Hours and hours of walking, until his thoughts began to move more slowly, until his emotions died away to a flat level like the inspector's voice, until he could feel nothing, think about nothing, so that when he thought of rest and turned towards the bed his knees gave way under him and he fell face forward, to lie half kneeling with his face on the coarse blanket, semi-conscious. Later he came back somewhat to his senses, cramped and cold, and drew his knees up on the bed, his face still buried in the blanket. And then tumultuous nightmare dreams assailed him. Along with the old horrors that thronged at the bedside there were now new ones—a mental picture of something obscene, and another of something else equally obscene, something one-legged and naked hopping on its one leg, grotesquely, unlike anything in the sane world, across a room to a window. That memory brought him back to stupefied wakefulness, crying out, sweating. He fought his way back to complete consciousness, and from there to complete self-control again, mastering himself so that he no longer shook although he sweated; that was an exhausting struggle, leaving him more weary than ever. He knew that if he gave way to his weariness those horrors would press round him again, and he struggled against it. That was a bad night.

SEVENTEEN

THE CURRENT WAS HURRYING Randall along; and now he could do nothing to change the direction in which he was being hurried. He was in the grip of the law. He could not escape, he could not protest. When a police constable said ' Come this way ' he had to obey; when the agelong routine of English criminal procedure dictated that he should appear before a magistrate he appeared before one, and it would have been of no avail to oppose his will to that of the law. If he should try to refuse he would be compelled to obey. The omnipotence of the law is a magnificent conception; what it meant in Randall's case was that if he had attempted to resist he would have been dragged, or carried, perhaps bound into a strait-jacket, to make his appearance in court —the law's omnipotence hinging ultimately on the undignified physical compulsion of the individual.

Not that it occurred to Randall (save for that first wild moment in the cell) to oppose his puny physical force to the might of the law; the absurdity and the lack of dignity of such a course were too apparent, even to one as stunned and stupefied as he. But even in his stupefaction he was conscious of the faintest dull resentment when the constable said ' Come this way ' or ' Go in there '. That dull resentment was almost the last sensation left to him after the upheavals of the day and the night. He took almost no note of his surroundings; few memories remained of those days.

It was raining in the police station yard; he felt the cold drops on his face as he heard the orders of the constables. A police van was filling with the drunks and disorderlies of the night before, but for him there was a motor-car. There was a dreary room, and Burdon was waiting for him in it.

" After the evidence has been given," said Burdon, " you will be asked if you plead Guilty or Not Guilty. I shall reply for you, pleading Not Guilty."

" Not guilty," said Randall stupidly.

" Yes, of course."

" But——" Randall was too weary to say what he vaguely thought.

" Not Guilty," said Burdon, " of course."

There was more animation in the bony face than Randall

had ever seen before. There was anxiety there, and it was the anxiety which weighed with Randall.

" All right," he said.

" Come this way," said a constable at the door.

Emerging into the court was like coming into the sunlight from a tunnel. More than that; it was like one of those silly dreams about entering a crowded bus and discovering oneself to be without clothes. Randall knew there were hundreds of eyes turned upon him, he knew there was a sudden buzz at his appearance, yet it seemed to him as if there was a screen in front of him and he could see nothing. A cultured voice was saying something. Now there was a hole in the screen and Burdon was bobbing up into it, his hair plastered thinly over the top of his head.

" I represent the prisoner," he was saying.

The screen was growing transparent. That was the inspector over there, holding up a book in his right hand. Now he was speaking, addressing his words to the man there with the neat winged collar—the magistrate ?

" I cautioned him, and told him I would take him into custody," said the inspector, " and he said, ' I did it '."

Randall heard a buzz in the court again.

" He said that after hearing the charge and the caution, inspector ? " asked the magistrate leaning forward.

" Yes, Your Honour. Later at the police station I again cautioned him and charged him with manslaughter. He made no reply."

There were hundreds of people in here, all crowded together, staring first at him and then at the inspector. Now Burdon was on his feet and everyone was looking at him; now the inspector was speaking again. Now the magistrate was saying something.

" Come this way," said the constable at Randall's side.

Here was the dreary room again, and Burdon almost bustling, almost smiling, infected, presumably, by the excitement of the court. Only a few words, and then——

" Come this way."

This time there was a black prison van waiting for them; at the sight of it Randall faltered in his steps, but there was a constable on each side of him, and with the faltering there came the slightest pressure at either elbow, the merest hint

of the might of the law. Randall stepped up into the dark
partitioned interior and sat with a policeman opposite and a
policeman at his side; the door slammed and they lurched
away through the streets. Outside the buses rumbled and
the tramcars clanked; outside there was light and activity
and freedom; inside sat the silent policemen, saying nothing
lest the law should construe any conversation as an attempt
to obtain a statement. Prison gates; men in uniform; rain
on his face for one grateful second. Paper work, a writing in
registers, a listing of his property.

" Come this way."

The isolation ward of the prison hospital; narrow iron
beds, all empty, with sheets whose coarseness was apparent
to the eye; the rules explained to him by somebody whose
geniality was almost genuine. He could have books, cigarettes,
letters, visitors; meals from outside if he cared to pay for
them; he could have everything except his liberty.

The magistrate had remanded him for a week; a strange
week, strange like the fact that he should be ' remanded '—
he had read that word almost without comprehension in his
other life, glancing through the evening paper on his way
home with never a thought, never the slightest suspicion,
that one day he would be ' remanded '. It was strange that
he should be a pariah, that he should be kept studiously
out of sight of the other prisoners, that when he walked
round and round the prison square he should walk there
alone save for the warders. He had killed a man; he was
defendant in a case which filled the headlines of the newspapers, and about him there was an aura—a miasma; his
presence would excite gossip among the other prisoners,
would have an unsettling effect, and the prison authorities,
sensitive to changes in the naturally unnatural atmosphere
of the prison, were somewhat resentful of his presence;
there is always danger of hysteria in a prison, even in one
like this, people with men awaiting trial, men confined for
not supporting their wives or families, first offenders. From
the point of view of the prison authorities it was better to
have no ripple disturbing the flat calm, the dreary sameness
of prison life, where no door opened and no door closed
without the turning of a key.

Prison was bad; loss of liberty was bad; the sensation of

being powerless in the grip of authority was bad. Maybe there was something to be said for the enforced idleness, as it gave Randall the chance to recover from his emotional exhaustion even while he chafed against confinement, but with his recovery came a renewed sensitivity to his surroundings, so that he became conscious of being a pariah, conscious that soon he would be on trial, that soon it would be decided whether, and for how long, he was to be confined behind locked doors and iron bars. That thought was frightening. It was always with him; less constant, but far more violent when it stirred, was the sorrow over Muriel—the thought of what she had given to Massey, the thought of the way she had deceived him, and the thought that he never would, never could, be with her again.

Burdon came to see him; in the visitors' room there was a long table, and across the table a glass partition, and Randall had to sit at one end of the table and his visitors—all except Burdon—at the other, and in the door was a glass panel through which a warder kept watch.

Burdon looked grave at this visit. It could even be thought that he was moved to pity.

" Bad news," he said.

" What is it ? " Randall had recovered so that he was ready for anything again now.

" Your account at the bank," said Burdon.

Randall guessed what was coming, although until that moment the possibility had not occurred to him.

" There's nothing in it ? "

" Not a penny. Nothing."

" Muriel took it out ? "

" Yes. I used my power of attorney to get a statement of account—Mrs. Randall even had the passbook in her possession. She drew out the whole balance on the morning of the twenty-fifth. Nine hundred and forty pounds odd."

" I might have guessed," said Randall.

It was one more thing for Burdon to try to understand, and to fail to understand—that a man should keep his money in a joint account so that his wife had as much power over it, and as much knowledge of how it was used, as her husband had. This was the best example Burdon had encountered so far of the folly of such a course.

appeared younger than his 22 years '. He had ' fair hair
and complexion ' and he ' seemed to be dazed by the turn
events had taken '. He was dressed in ' a brown tweed
jacket and grey flannel trousers considerably the worse for
wear '. The next paragraph described him, of course, as
' the inventor of the P–R flare, extensively used during the
war ' and mentioned that three months ago the Government had made a final grant of £1,000 to the inventors.
And the last line said that ' Mrs. Randall was not present
in court, and inquiry failed to discover her whereabouts '.
Randall felt a sick feeling when he thought of Muriel, something like the sickness men felt while waiting in the line
for the moment of attack. It was not hatred, it was nothing
violent; in fact the faint nausea was more noticeable than
any mental reaction.

On another page the newspaper commented editorially
on ' crimes of violence '. It avoided, through fear of the
penalties of contempt of court, any very direct allusion to
the Randall case, although it clearly was emboldened by
the ' I did it ' to which the detective inspector had sworn.
But that year of 1920 had already been distinguished by
some remarkable homicides inspired by lust or revenge.
The war, stirring up evil passions, and lessening the
sanctity of human life, was to blame; and morals were
at a low ebb, said the newspaper, with its tongue piously
in its cheek. Randall had learned much in these two days.
As he read those words he could picture newspapermen
thanking God for the Randall case, and rejoicing at the
quickening of their sales; making a profit out of his misery
and degradation, like those other people back in 1917 who
wrote ' Poppies of Wipers '. Randall crumpled the paper
and felt mad rage surging up in him. Not only his own
misery and degradation, either; his mother broken-hearted,
his brother and sisters unable to face their friends, his father
grey-faced and aged ten years in an hour.

Then there were the letters. They began to pour in from
the very first day, some addressed to Calmady Road and
some actually to the prison. Insane letters, dirty letters,
letters of sympathy and letters of vituperation. ' I'm glad
you socked the dirty little barstard.' ' If you pray to God
and then read the 13th Chapter of St. Matthew you will

find peace.' 'There is a place in Hell waiting for you. He had only one leg. It ought to be murder.' 'When you come out you will find me expecting you. I am only 35 and brunette and I know what trouble is.' 'Would you oblige me by signing and returning the enclosed card? I have the autographs of many notable people, including those of Hawley Harvey Crippen and William J. Locke.' 'May you be speedily acquitted.' 'I notice that you invented the P-R flare. I have an invention which I am anxious to put on the market——' 'The blood of thy brother crieth out from the ground.'

It was impossible not to be in a turmoil with those letters pouring in. It was impossible not to brood, and fret, and sometimes to rage; and as the days passed it was impossible not to feel fear. He was slowly recovering from his emotional exhaustion and able to think rationally about the future. This was prison life at its easiest and best, with visitors and a comparative absence of forced activity, but he could guess now at the sort of prison life a convict would lead. He was fretting over the loss of his liberty; a convict not only lost his liberty but was subjected every day to a hundred humiliations, a thousand petty reminders of his abject condition. And Randall realised that he might be forced to lead the life of a convict for months or for years, even for life.

That was the worst fate he had ever contemplated. There had been gloomy days in the Salient when he had thought about the imminence of his own violent death, of the huge shell fragment spinning through the air out of the volcano of the burst, which might leave him prostrate, disembowelled and shrieking; he had feared that kind of death, but no more than now he feared imprisonment. When the battalion had been out of the line in rest billets there had been the dark shadow of the inevitable return to the line, of the attack in which he might be killed. Now ahead of him was the inevitable trial, from which he could no more draw back than as a young subaltern he could draw back from going over the top; he would be a figure of public display—and he dreaded that as he had dreaded the dirt and sleeplessness and anxiety of the line—and then his destiny would be decided by forces over which he had no control; inscrutable fate would decide whether he was to spend months or years in hell, just as he had awaited before an attack for fate to decide whether he should be torn into a limbless, faceless idiot. This was fear; this was something to sweat about, lying wakeful through the night.

Mr. Ambrose Cane was a junior barrister, a fresh-faced youngish man with the inevitable winged collar. He was hardly more than thirty, but (so Burdon told Randall) he was already being talked about as a man with a great future ahead of him at the Bar. Cane had vigour and energy, and his outlook was one of reasoned optimism; when Burdon brought him to visit Randall in prison the interview was as good as a tonic. Cane had been instructed by Burdon to appear for Randall at the remand hearing in the magistrate's court; as he said with a smile, he was not a big enough gun to be entrusted with the defence when the trial should be called at the Central Criminal Court. When that time should come an eminent counsel would be retained, and Cane would be his junior; and until then it was Cane's duty to familiarise himself with the case, to know all about the evidence that was to be presented, to know the character and possible reactions of the witnesses, so as to save the eminent counsel's time—above all, it was his duty to know as much as might be known about the defendant.

Cane had a keen glance for Randall when he was introduced to him, but a ready smile. Randall met the glance with something of hostility, for he had grown cynical during even these few days in prison, and was aware that the glance was sizing him up, was estimating what effect his appearance would have on a jury, was trying to determine if he was an unstable type who could not be relied upon to stand up under cross-examination.

"I'm taking up your time somewhat unnecessarily to-day," said Cane. "There's not a great deal to discuss until after the hearing to-morrow."

"I've time to spare," said Randall, not knowing whether to be irritated or amused at this apology to a man kept in confinement.

"I shall reserve my cross-examination," went on Cane. "In view of the evidence that has already been presented there will not even be any need, in my opinion, to indicate the nature of the defence."

"Why?" snapped Randall. He had heard enough legal

phraseology from Burdon for the mere sound of it to annoy him.

" Because you said ' I did it ' after being cautioned," replied Cane.

That was speaking as man to man; that was leaving a naked fact unclothed in words. Cane was meeting Randall's unreasoning irritability with sound common sense, and after that the interview moved perfectly smoothly.

" We can be grateful that the coroner had the decency to adjourn the inquest," remarked Cane at one moment.

Randall had already discussed with Burdon the curious legal system—which he had never thought about until then —by which a man might be subjected to public trial three times, in the coroner's court, the magistrate's court, and at the assizes. He had not even known, until he was personally made acquainted with the fact, that an accused person had to appear in two courts at least. He could see the necessity for the magistrate's court, he grudgingly supposed.

" Hearsay evidence and wild verdicts," went on Cane, still with reference to coroner's inquests, " all reported in detail. They can do untold harm. A good thing we're saved from that."

And later he said something once more characterised by common sense, without flinching, without wrapping up his meaning in legal verbiage, and he met Randall's eyes unhesitatingly as he said it.

" There's only one disquieting feature in the case," he said. " And that is that Massey had only one leg. I'd feel a good deal happier if it wasn't for that. But a one-legged man is necessarily somewhat helpless. And I suppose, for what it's worth, we have to allow as well for the natural sympathy towards a disabled ex-service man with a good war record who was unable to get a job—but that's not nearly as important. It's the one leg that we shall have to discount as much as possible."

" I see," said Randall.

That was a disquieting thing to think about, something to make his midnight thoughts still more uneasy. Especially when one of the letters which had come to him was an anonymous one which said, among other things, ' I expect you will get fourteen years at least. Ha ! Ha ! Ha ! '

EIGHTEEN

" COME THIS WAY."

The same brief order, the same walk down through the prison, the same prison van, the same drive through the streets, with the gongs of the tramcars and the grinding of the gears of the buses to tantalise a man bereft of his freedom. A cell this time, below the court, the door locked and unlocked with a click of the bolt and a jangling of keys.

" Come this way."

Up into the dock, to face the stares and to be conscious of the excitement his presence caused. A brief formality. There were Burdon and Cane nodding at him. There was young Mrs. Tomlinson who lived across the road, pink with excitement, and wearing what was obviously a new hat, standing up taking the oath with a book in her hand. A grey-haired man in a winged collar was addressing her, asking her questions, and she was answering them breathlessly. Randall had not tried to catch her eye, but at this moment he became conscious that she was being careful not to look at him. Yes, soon after twelve o'clock midday on the twenty-third she had heard screams. She thought they came from Number 53 across the road. She was going out of the house to see what was the matter when she heard a crash of glass, and when she got outside there was a body lying under the window of Number 53. Mrs. Tomlinson closed her eyes and shook her head as though to shake off an unpleasant memory. Yes, the body was unclothed. Then Mr. Randall had appeared at the broken window. Oh yes, the upper bedroom window at Number 53 was broken, the one beneath which the body lay. He had said something. No, she was sorry but she could not remember what it was he said. It was something quite brief. Yes, soon afterwards Mrs. Randall had come running out of the house. She was wearing a man's trench coat. No, she did not appear to be wearing anything underneath it. Then Mr. Randall had come out of the front door. Then the police had come. And so on. There was Cane asking her something now. The screams seemed to go on for a long time ? A long time ? It only took two questions to reduce Mrs. Tomlinson's

estimate of the time between the first scream and the crash
of glass from five minutes to one. Yes, subsequently she
saw Mrs. Randall again. In Mrs. Norton's house. She was
wearing nothing at all under her trench coat. That will be
all, at present, Mrs. Tomlinson. Something was read out
to Mrs. Tomlinson. A pen was produced, and, a little
flustered, Mrs. Tomlinson signed.

A man now taking the oath.

" I am a registered medical practitioner and a police
surgeon." This, that, and the other. Deceased had been
dead for not more than half an hour at most. The cause
of death was an extensive fracture of the base of the skull.
It could be caused by a fall from a height, striking the
ground in an almost vertical position head downwards, so
that the spinal column was driven into the skull. Death
must have been very rapid. There was confirmation of this
from the amount of bleeding from the lacerations. Yes,
there were extensive lacerations. So many in the posterior
aspect of the shoulders, over the shoulder-blades, in other
words, so many in the posterior aspect of the right upper
arm, so many in the buttocks. The appearance of the
lacerations was entirely consistent with the deceased having
fallen backwards, through a window, in fact in one of the
wounds in the right arm he had found pieces of glass. No,
the lacerations could not have been at all a contributory
cause of death. They were hardly more than superficial.

Cane was asking a question.

No, he had not been able to observe any other injuries.
There was no mark of any blow. No sign of any struggle.
Thank you.

Other witnesses. Mary Elizabeth Norton. Policemen.
George William Lane, milk roundsman. Each witness signed
his deposition—that was the word Cane and Burdon had used.

Muriel Haythorpe Randall. Muriel walking across the
room. Muriel. This was unbearable. Randall stirred in his
uncomfortable chair, and on the instant the constable near
him stirred, too. The knowledge that the constable was
tensing himself, ready to restrain him if he should do anything violent, reminded Randall of the helplessness of his
position, reminded him of the eyes that watched him, so
that he made himself appear indifferent and relaxed. This

surge of excitement, this desperate increase in tension at
seeing Muriel and hearing her name, could not be analysed.
It was not hatred; it certainly was not love. It might be
anger, not anger at Muriel, but anger at the machinery of
justice which was subjecting him to such an ordeal and
which made use of such instruments. While Randall had
been struggling with his feelings there had been a louder
buzz round the room, a sharp remark from the magistrate,
a movement to and fro of officials repressing the disturbance.

Muriel was in black again, as she had been after Speake's
death, with a flower-pot-shaped hat pulled down low on her
forehead, and her dark eyes darting glances from beneath its
brim. She shot one glance at Randall, like a stab, like a
snake's bite so full was it of venom and so lightning quick.
Somebody was standing up in court and saying something,
distracting attention from Muriel. Apparently he was a
lawyer, here to look after Muriel's interests. Now Muriel
was holding up the book and taking the oath. Now she was
telling her story. She had been with Captain Massey in the
upper bedroom at No. 53 Calmady Road at midday on the
23rd. The prisoner had burst in upon them. He had said,
' Now I've got you.'

Randall started to get up out of his chair when he heard
that. He was more moved because it was an untruth than
because of the implications, which did not begin to impress
themselves on him until later. But Burdon had swung round
on the instant, to meet Randall's eye and to implore him
silently to stay calm. And there was the constable, ready for
anything. It was the menace of the law as much as Burdon's
glance which prevailed on Randall and led him to master
himself and force himself back into his chair, trembling with
the strain.

Muriel was going on with her testimony. She had not
seen what happened next. She had covered her eyes. But
she had heard the deceased cry, ' Keep back ! Keep back ! '
and then she had heard a crash of glass and when she looked
again the prisoner was rushing at her saying ' You next '
and she had managed to evade him and escape out of the room.
There was Cano saying he had no questions to ask. Muriel
was stepping out of the witness-box. Now the magistrate
was leaning forward, engaged in a triangular discussion with

Cane and with the grey-haired man. 'Reserve our defence.'
'Commit the prisoner for trial.' 'Bail.' 'Bail refused.' And
then—'Come this way,' said the constable.

Going downstairs, a sudden volume of sound from the
street outside the barred window came echoing in to them.
" Boo-oo. Boo-oo." And then a sudden rise in pitch and
volume, and the cries were charged with hatred and contempt
so that they sounded like " Yaa—yaa."

The police sergeant who was standing ready at the foot
of the stairs to receive Randall exchanged a significant glance
with the constable who was his escort, and at the sergeant's
gesture two other constables rose and hurried out, putting
on their helmets as they hurried.

" Yaa," shrieked the crowd outside.

The cell door was unlocked and held open by the sergeant.
Randall passed in and the door slammed and the lock clicked
behind him, and the cries died away. Later the door snapped
open and they took Randall out to the yard, to the prison van,
and drove him through the noisy streets back to the prison,
up to the prison hospital again.

'Randall committed for trial,' said the afternoon paper.
'Mrs. Randall gives evidence.' 'Hostile demonstration.'
Here was a smudgy picture. A taxicab at a kerb, and a
woman getting into it—she could be just recognised as
Muriel. Beyond could be seen policemen holding back a
frantic crowd. The paper said, 'When Mrs. Randall left the
court she was booed by a large crowd and had to be guarded
by a police escort as she entered her taxi:' Good God. So
those bloodthirsty cries had been directed at Muriel. She
had had to be guarded from a moral mob expressing its
disapproval of adultery. Good God ! More than anything
else—more even than the fact that he was confined in prison—
did this incident bring home to Randall the enormous and
relentless power of the forces which were hurrying him and
his little world along. A week ago could anyone have guessed
that Muriel—Muriel the housekeeper, Muriel the afternoon
window-shopper, Muriel who was not aware of the difference
between a Liberal and a National Liberal—could anyone have
guessed that Muriel would soon have to be guarded from a
mob howling for her blood ? Chance—a series of chances,
each apparently inconsiderable—had edged him and Muriel

into the power of the Press and the law, and now they could only submit to be whirled along by them.

Six years previously, in an ornate office room in Vienna, a little group of men in ornate uniforms had sat round a table and had reached a decision. By a narrow majority they had voted to send a bullying note to Belgrade and by that decision they had altered the course of a thousand million lives, and of a million million lives to come. That decision had killed Captain Henry Speake and left Muriel a widow; it had shot off R. F. Massey's leg; it had killed Lieutenant Cross of the Royal Fusiliers and had spared Captain C. L. Randall of the same regiment. For that matter it had profoundly affected the life of an undernourished house painter somewhere in that same city of Vienna. Randall had been a gangling schoolboy when that decision was made. While the war carried him along he had been vaguely aware of the forces that directed him. But he had known, too, that he was but one of four million fighting men, with whom he was proud to be associated. Everyone had been in the same situation. To-day it was different; the Press and the law had singled him out, and he was forced to struggle for his liberty, to battle against the tide alone, and under the eyes of the whole world.

There were so many ways in which things might have happened differently; Randall could think of some of them as he sat there in the prison hospital. Massey might never have been killed at all; he might have fallen through that window and suffered no more than scratches and bruises. In that case—Randall thought about this shrinkingly, as a man with a blistered foot steps forward tentatively when he has to begin walking—the business would have been only hateful and undignified; amusing to the outsider. (Amusing to the outsider! The naked paramour escaping the indignant husband by being flung through a window!) That was how it would have been, all the same, if Massey had not fallen in that particular way. It was one of a chain of tiny chances. Randall sitting in a prison thought of other links in the chain. If there had been a taxi available that day when he came home on leave, so that he was not compelled to travel home by tram. If he had sat in any other seat on that tram.

There was a new clarity about his thinking now. He knew now that if he had set out to have his way with Muriel without marriage he could have had it. Even that very first evening; Randall knew Muriel better, so much better, now, than then. He could remember how she had stood looking at him, her face a little uplifted, her bosom thrust a little forward. She would have melted if he had extended his arms to her and kissed her. He would have spent the night with her, and he would never have married her. And that other night, the night they heard Speake was killed; if that telegram had been delayed, had not been waiting for them when they reached home, he would certainly have had his way with her. He would have known her then for what she was. A German soldier had put out his hand and fired the shell that killed Speake. That hand was now probably fleshless and bony, buried in the Flanders mire, but it had held him back from Muriel's arms at that moment—and might be said to have thrust him into Muriel's arms later, and, continuing its pressure, it might be said to have thrust him now into prison, and in the future—Randall shuddered at the thought of the future.

He did not know of the absurd chance by which in the taxi his cap badge had caught in the trimming of Muriel's hat, causing her to withdraw from his advances, but he had a clear insight into many of the other incidents which had affected his life—the meeting with Graham, and Graham's kindly interference which had brought him back on leave the moment before the German offensive opened. Much more recently still: if Muriel had not chosen that particular morning (was it only a week ago? It seemed like a year!) to tell him that she was pregnant he would never have returned unexpectedly, and he would not now be in prison.

There was a moment of worse anguish then, when Randall remembered with unnatural clarity the pleasant life he had been leading, working for his degree, discussing methods of sorting peas with Graham and Phillips, returning home to Muriel, turning over in the little double bed to find Muriel beside him. That was extraordinarily painful; wishes sprang up suddenly in Randall's mind that nothing had happened during the past week, that his pleasant life had not been so rudely terminated. He found himself on the verge of wishing that he had not found out about Muriel, and he drew back shuddering again—could it be possible that he could have tolerated for a single moment the thought of being a deceived husband in exchange for a pleasant life ? That was hideous, utterly horrible. But that train of thought brought back all the pain and distress caused by Muriel's infidelity, all those vile, horrible thoughts that had passed through his mind when he had stood in the bedroom that morning. He had to stop himself from thinking about that. He simply had to.

The sound of keys and locks—the already well-known sequence of noises that heralded someone coming in—was desperately welcome.

" Come this way."

Burdon and Cane in the visitors' room saw him enter; they saw the distortion of his features and the misery in his eyes, and each of them noted, with some pity, that here was a man who endured imprisonment and uncertainty badly. They returned his pathetic smile of welcome, but Cane, his face above his winged collar clean-cut and handsome and healthy, was a busy man who could afford little time for polite verbiage. He opened the sheaf of notes in front of him.

" I have the depositions here," he said. " You heard the evidence your wife gave this morning ? "

" Yes." That was better; it was better to remember the malignant glance Muriel had darted at him.

" It's entirely at variance with the accounts you have given Mr. Burdon and me. What truth is there in what she said ? "

Limpingly, Randall told them all over again. He had not said a word from the time of his entrance into the room to the time of Muriel's flight from it. He had been too astonished, too surprised, to speak.

" Had you ever thought your wife was being unfaithful to you ? "

" No."

" But to your knowledge Massey had been a frequent visitor ? "

" Yes."

" It was absolutely by chance that you returned ? "

" Yes."

" The Phillipses offer complete confirmation of that," said Burdon, pointing to a passage in another batch of notes.

" And everything you have told us is absolutely true ? "
went on Cane, looking at Randall and only sparing a sideways nod for Burdon.

" Of course."

" Now, I don't want to press this, but you must understand
that as you were in a very agitated state of mind your memory
of those events may be at fault. You are sure that not only
are you telling us the truth as you remember it, but also that
your memory is correct ? "

" Oh yes."

Now Burdon and Cane could glance at each other; there
could be no doubting the complete sincerity of those words.
There was a softening of Cane's expression when he looked
back at Randall, and there was something less disinterested
in his tone as he asked the next question.

" Do you think your wife is capable of perjuring herself so
as to do you an injury ? "

" Oh ! " Muriel was unscrupulous. Randall could remember how she had suggested evading payment of Graham's
commission and how she had not seen the necessity for his
requesting return to his unit at the news of the German
offensive. And there was that glance she had given him.
" Yes. She would do that."

Cane turned back to Burdon.

" Coates'll make mincemeat of her," he said, and his smile
was grim now.

" The suggestion is," explained Burdon to Randall, " that
I instruct Sir Frederick Coates for the defence."

" Oh ! " said Randall; that was all he could say at the
moment.

Sir Frederick Coates was someone of whom even Randall
had heard—a great criminal barrister, briefed for the defence
in every celebrated cause. Randall thought about him for
some seconds before he came up with his comment.

" Won't he be rather expensive ? "

" Yes," replied Burdon. " Perhaps the most expensive
counsel at the Bar. But there's nobody quite like him.
Whether it's the jury or the bench, or handling witnesses
in cross-examination, he's worth every penny marked on
his brief. And his fee may not be quite as large as usual
in this case, having regard to the circumstances."

" I see," said Randall.

He was learning fast, both about the law and about Burdon. He could analyse Burdon's last sentence and glimpse the meaning behind it—Burdon would no more dream of expressing brutal truths in their naked verbiage than he would dream of exposing his own person in Piccadilly Circus. What Burdon meant was that Sir Frederick Coates would agree to a reduction in his fee (if he could be convinced that there was no chance of getting any more) because the case would be written up in the newspapers and so would keep him in the public eye.

" Is there enough money for him ? " asked Randall.

" I think so. Just enough."

When this case should be concluded Randall would be not merely penniless, but hopelessly in debt. Both to his father and to Phillips he would owe hundreds of pounds, more than he could hope to earn in two or three years of steady work. And what chance was there of his finding steady work, when he was still more than a year from obtaining his degree ? At that very moment there were in the streets of London officers in uniform, with medal ribbons on their breasts and masks on their faces, playing barrel organs as an appeal to charity. Nevertheless Randall's mind refused to think at all about the future as far as money or employment was concerned. In France on the eve of an attack no one thought about the problems of future civilian life—to-morrow's question of life or death was so urgent as to make any further speculation impossible. It was the same now, or very nearly.

In a month's time he would come up for trial, and his fate might be imprisonment for life. So much was at stake that Randall simply could not think beyond the trial. He knew something about prisons now, and he had had practical experience to supplement his previous vague knowledge. The shaven head, the degrading uniform, the monotonous tasks, the hectoring warders, the bad food and the severe conditions of living—these incidentals of imprisonment were bad, but they were the mere incidentals of imprisonment. It was imprisonment itself which was the frightful thing, the loss of liberty. When Randall thought about it he knew quite well why a captive bird would beat its life out against the wires of

its cage. He would beat his life out against the walls of his
cell. He was neither frantic nor panic-stricken, now that he
had mastered himself, but he was consumed with ugly fear.
In this discussion with Burdon, he had time to note cynically
Burdon's Olympian indifference to money, as long as it was
Randall's money that was under consideration and there was
enough of it. But he hardly resented that indifference; he
was indifferent himself to money while he was gripped with
this fear.

And there was a close resemblance between waiting to go
over the top and awaiting trial. He was willy-nilly having
to go through with this, having to submit himself to the
arbitrament of the court, just as willy-nilly he had had
to lead his company to the attack and submit himself to
the arbitrament of the bursting shells. The staff officer, the
divisional general, living at ease in his château, gave the
word that sent him forward, and every infantry soldier in
the army knew the fevered helplessness of wondering whether
his life was going to be thrown away as the result of a blunder,
as the result of ignorance, possibly even as a result of personal
pique. Now Randall was wondering whether his liberty
might be cast away in the same fashion, through a mistake,
through inefficiency, or through some personal peculiarity of
Sir Frederick Coates. There was the difference that he was
being consulted about who should direct the battle. He knew
that if he were to object strenuously to the briefing of Sir
Frederick, Burdon would shrug his shoulders and brief
someone else, but this difference was specious and plausible
and not real, for he knew far less about the comparative merits
of King's Counsel than he had done about divisional generals
—and that was almost nothing. His destiny was really in the
hands of the unknown, of strange gods, just as it had been
in the army.

Yet in France there had been things he could do that
might prolong his life. He could be ready for the first whistle
of a shell, so that he could fling himself down and let the
fragments scream over him. He could crawl low under the
trajectory of machine-gun bullets and freeze into immobility
when a flare lit the night while he was out on patrol between
the lines; he could whip his gas-mask on speedily at the first
sign of gas, and he could scan the terrain ahead of him and

try to plan a route through dead ground when he went forward
to stalk a machine-gun. So now he might supplement the
efforts of the strange gods with feeble efforts of his own. He
could try and think of points about which they might be
ignorant; without his help they would know far less about
Massey's character, or about Muriel's, than he did—and far
less about his own, too. He could try and tell them everything
without reserve, and when the time came, that dread time,
when he should be in the witness-box, he could stand up
sturdily and meet his fate eye to eye, refusing to be shaken,
refusing to go into a panic, displaying no weakness that might
entrap him.

But there was a long month ahead of him before he should
be brought to trial; four long weeks and two long days. It
was long enough for a young and healthy man, even deprived
of his liberty and under the shadow of fear, to regain his
mental poise and his objectivity, to emerge from the hurt and
stupefied condition into which the affair had plunged him, so
that the mist which had blurred his vision faded away; he
was a thinking man again now, conscious of his surroundings,
instead of being a dazed creature that suffered and endured
with no reactions save automatic ones.

He could look keenly at Sir Frederick Coates when Burdon
and Cane brought that eminent counsel to see him. Sir
Frederick was a man in his fifties, even possibly in his early
sixties, for his still-plentiful hair was quite white; but his
lean face was almost unwrinkled, and in repose it wore the
untroubled placidity of the saint or the ascetic who has found
peace. So Randall saw him at the moment of introduction.

" Good morning," said Sir Frederick.

The whole face underwent a transformation; the thin
sensitive lips smiled, a twinkle came into the dark eyes, one
eyebrow rose a sixteenth of an inch higher than the other.
This was the face of a man of quick wit and of an impish
sense of humour, soft-spoken and sure of himself.

" Sir Frederick's a busy man," said Burdon. " We must
not waste his time."

No one present at that interview could have ever thought
that Sir Frederick was capable of wasting time, or of allowing
others to waste it. He asked much the same questions that
Burdon and Cane asked, but each question followed its

predecessor without any perceptible gap, a steady flow of questions in that soft voice. It would be hard to lie in reply, harder still—impossible—to lie consistently and repeatedly, when there was hardly time to take breath, let alone think, in face of that ceaseless and insidious pressure. The questions would work along one flank of the subject, moving in steady progression, and then suddenly, without a moment's hesitation, they would be on the other flank; there would be no time to change front to meet them, and the questions were pertinent and penetrating—no disordered defence could keep them out. Fortunately Randall was not on the defensive. He could answer easily and usually readily; when he hesitated it was because he was really in doubt as to what was the truth of the matter he was being asked about.

" Now what was in your mind when you rushed at him ? "

" I don't think there was anything."

" You're not sure ? "

" I felt—I felt that he was dangerous."

" You had no desire to hurt him ? "

" No." A pause. " No. I hadn't got that far."

" You would swear, then, that you were defending yourself?"

" I suppose I would. Yes."

" You only suppose ? "

" I mean I think I was. Yes."

It was startling to find how much clarity Sir Frederick imparted to that hazy situation. There was humanity in his bearing, a sympathy towards human vagueness that Burdon had never shown or felt; Sir Frederick straightened out the tangles where Burdon's legal mind and Cane's keen-witted logic had failed. When the questioning ended the twinkle was still in Sir Frederick's eye.

" I'm prepared to undertake your defence, Mr. Randall," he said.

" Thank you," said Randall, and Burdon and Cane chorused their thanks in the background.

" There's another excellent piece of news," said Burdon, emerging from the background. " We have identified Massey's fingerprints on the handle of the mirror."

" Really ? " said Randall; it took a moment to appreciate the importance of this fact.

" Yes," said Cane. " Thank God for that postponed

coroner's inquest. The body wasn't buried yet and we were able to get examples for comparison."

"Some time to-day," went on Burdon, " the police will come and ask for permission to take your fingerprints. My advice is that you should agree."

"All right."

"I suppose it's too much to hope for," said Cane, " that you never touched that mirror, at least not for a long time ? "

Randall went back through his memory.

"I can't remember touching it," he announced. "Of course I must have touched it at some time or other, but I can't remember doing so. I kept my brush and comb and things in the bathroom."

"We'll soon know, anyway," said Cane.

These interviews were breaks in the dreary monotony of those long weeks in prison; they were the least trying of the interviews, too. It was bad when his mother and his father came to see him; sitting separated from them by the glass screen it was difficult to find subjects to talk about, and his mother was always inclined to shed a tear when the conversation came round, as it inevitably did, to the approaching trial, or to the conditions in which Randall was kept confined, or to the impact of the scandal on the members of the family. It actually called for a certain amount of self-sacrifice on Randall's part to continue to see his parents. There was a definite temptation to withdraw into himself, to forget about the world, to try to keep his mind inactive during those weary, dreary walks round the prison yard, to flinch away from reality now that he had grown conscious of it again. It might have been possible to do it thanks to that unvarying routine—breakfast, exercise, governor's inspection, doctor's visit, change of warders, nightfall. He might have done it, even while fear overshadowed him, even as the time for the trial marched steadily nearer.

But luckily he found an alternative; his father had brought him his physics textbooks and at a fortunate moment he opened one and, piqued when he found his eye running over the printed arguments without his mind reacting to them at all, he set himself seriously to pick up the threads. He was standing when he began; soon he was sitting down, and then he had books and notebooks open before him, his elbows on the table and his forehead resting on his hands, quite lost to his surroundings as he followed along the tortuous mathematical paths of scientific deduction. " The specific heat per unit mass must then vary as $p\frac{1}{n-1}$." Was he sure that it must ? He had better go back through the argument again. There was no need to withdraw into a world of his own making; he could withdraw into the world of mathematics, brightly and coldly lit, armoured against the exterior, like the turret of a battleship and in the same way full of purposeful and functional apparatus. There he could be oblivious, most of the time, of the black cloud of the approaching trial extending up from the horizon until it covered the whole sky.

It was actually Burdon, the apparently cold-blooded, who brought panic back the night before the trial. For Burdon was nervous and tense, as was obvious at a glance, while he was giving Randall last-minute advice. Burdon could discuss points of law and procedure with an interest quite devoid of emotion—one might almost think he had never experienced emotion in his life, but now that his work was actually to be put to the test he was worried. Perhaps he did not like the possibility of a professional failure. It is even possible that he had grown fond of Randall and dreaded the thought of his being sentenced to prison. In any case it was his strained manner and his incompletely concealed nervousness which were the cause of Randall going sleepless the night before the trial. Up and down his cell, walking until he was worn out, and then lying wakeful on the bed, thinking often of that anonymous letter, ' Fourteen years at least. Ha ! Ha ! Ha ! ' Fourteen years of prison; fourteen years of loss of liberty, with other horrors added. He sweated at the thought. And on the other hand he longed for freedom as a thirsty man longs for water. To-morrow or the next day would see fate cast the dice—liberty or prison. One or the other. And there was no means of foretelling which it would be—one could only speculate, endlessly and fruitlessly, and think about the evidence that was going to be presented, beginning at the beginning and working round in a circle back to the beginning again, with a jolt and a start when some temporarily forgotten point recurred to the mind again. It was horrible.

NINETEEN

THE FRONT PAGE OF the newspaper said ' Randall Manslaughter Trial Opens To-day.' The warder said, as always, ' Come this way.' Down the staircase with the wire-netting provision against suicide, wait while registers were marked, into the yard, into the van, a lurch, a sounding of the horn, and out into the streets. This was a longer journey, from Brixton to the Central Criminal Court, through the inner ring of southern suburbs and over the river. In other circumstances Randall could have been interested, as a connoisseur of South London side streets, in the route they took, avoiding main roads as far as possible, but he could not think about that now. Fourteen years at least. Fourteen years at least. For one horrible moment he thought about the route the prison van was following, but that was when it occurred to him that the driver must know every possible variation of the route, seeing that practically every morning of his life he must drive prisoners up to the Old Bailey for trial. Every day a vanload of prisoners, and most of them on their way from Brixton Prison to penal servitude. Fourteen years at least.

The street pattern of South London caused the van to pass through various plexuses of traffic, Kennington, the Elephant and Castle. Then over the bridge and into the roar of central London traffic. A rounding of corners at a slow speed. A lurch and then a stop. The door opened for the daylight to pour in, dazzling. ' Come this way.' Stone-flagged corridors; keys jangling; a cell door locked behind him. An eye at the peephole in the door, frequently returning, so that he knew, whether he stood or sat, that he was being observed under the harsh glare of the electric bulb. What else was there to do ? Think of something else, as he had tried to do under bombardment in France. Could he build up that equation again ?

$$\frac{C^a R\upsilon(1+a\theta)}{1} = hp\theta + \frac{qcd\theta}{dt} + \frac{sCd\theta}{dx} - \frac{\dfrac{(qkd\theta)}{d\,dx}}{dx}$$

No, he could only think about fourteen years at least. He
clenched his hands, and turned to see the eye at the peephole again. Waiting was bad; it was a strange relief for
the door to be unlocked and a voice to say, ' Come this
way.' Up the stairs, like and yet not like the stairs at the
police court, with a constable padding beside him on rubber
soles. And now out into the court, conscious of every eye
directed on him. This was all different; loftier, more imposing.
The royal coat of arms. Robes and wigs—it was strange to
see such things being actually worn. The constable had
edged him into position so that he stood with a rail before him
on which his hands rested. A well-modulated voice was
speaking—was saying his name.

' Charles Lewis Randall.' He looked round. ' You stand
charged upon the indictment with manslaughter, and the
particulars state that——'

He failed to hear the particulars, even when spoken in
that well-modulated voice. It went on and on, and then
ceased at last. The court fell silent, and everyone seemed
to be waiting. Then the well-modulated voice spoke again,
with a patient note that Randall recognised with a start as
indicating that something was being repeated for his benefit.

' To that charge do you plead guilty or not guilty ? '

He had to answer; he gripped the rail and tried to speak
up audibly.

' Not guilty.'

Was that his voice ? It did not sound like it at all. The
judge had said something, and now no one was paying him
attention, except the constable, who was nudging him and
indicating that he could sit down. He released his grip
on the rail, and it occurred to him that a thousand pairs of
hands before his had gripped that rail in the same way;
the hands of criminals, of murderers. The thought that he
was in the same situation as those men made him feel slightly
sick, and it was some time before he paid attention to his
new surroundings again. When he did so, he found it was
easy to identify them; the jury, the judge; at those tables
were the lawyers and their assistants. There were Coates
and Cane, and that man there must be counsel for the prosecution; strange that those wigs, which anyone would consider
grotesque from a mere description, should actually improve

a man's looks. And there were the reporters; one or two of them were looking at him very hard. And over there was the public gallery. People there were looking at him, too, looking at the man who had killed, looking at the man who had found his wife in bed with another, looking at the man who faced penal servitude, looking at the man whose name appeared in the newspaper headlines. There was need for self-control again.

Whatever formalities had been necessary were completed now, as he came out of his black mood. Here was counsel for the prosecution, standing up, one hand resting on the table and one clasping his gown, with his back almost turned to Randall.

" May it please you, my lord. Members of the jury——"

The dice were rolling. Fourteen years at least. Randall tried to make himself listen with the attention he would have given to a lecture on thermodynamics. But it was a question of making himself listen. He did not want to, strangely enough. Counsel for the prosecution was telling the jury about the law regarding homicide. He was speaking in a calm voice, almost as if disinterested. He only seemed to be moved by human motives on those occasions when he turned to the judge with a half-bow; for while he spoke about the law to the jury he was careful to say, with an appearance of the utmost deference, that whatever he said in the matter was ' subject to what my lord may say'. Now the dispassionate voice was speaking with a certain increase of intensity. Something he had just said had caused a flicker of interest through the court.

" Members of the jury, you must free your minds altogether of anything you may have heard or read about this so-called ' unwritten law'. My lord will tell you——"

The jury was listening to him with at least an appearance of rapt attention. Two women with hats over their eyes. An old man with a trim white beard. One more with a heavy black moustache.

"—a Mrs. Tomlinson, living at 46 Calmady Road, heard a woman's voice screaming in number 53, the house opposite. She——"

Two quite young men, seemingly out of place among the others who were elderly.

"—the deceased was a one-legged man. He had been wounded during the war and his right leg had been amputated just below the hip. This may help you to judge——"

In the back row there was a woman with a bright red scarf, a spot of colour in the sombre black.

"—you will hear the evidence of——"

The dispassionate voice was steadily continuing; despite its monotone it was a forceful voice. There was not another sound in the huge room.

"—I am sure you will have no hesitation in doing your duty——"

That clock was of the type whose minute hand moved in jumps. A minute at a time, or perhaps half a minute.

"—now, with the assistance of my learned friends, I will call the evidence before you."

With the end of the speech there was another ripple through the court, a ripple of anticipation, as if a prologue had been finished and the curtain was about to rise.

" Call Ann Helen Tomlinson."

Mrs. Tomlinson was pink and nervous and flustered. She dropped her handbag, and then, in picking it up, dropped the gospel which was being handed her. She looked once at Randall and looked away, and then she clearly made herself look again and force something of a smile. Someone else, not the bewigged lawyer whose speech had just ended, was standing up and asking questions, gently, so that Mrs. Tomlinson was led to reply. She said the same things that she said before, in the magistrates' court. Screams—crash of glass—body—Mrs. Randall. Thank you.

Sir Frederick Coates was standing up now, and there was another ripple through the court. One of the stars of the performance had come on to the stage. But Sir Frederick's manner was deferential, unobtrusive, almost as if he was apologising for the necessity to ask questions. Clearly he had no wish to frighten or to bully Mrs. Tomlinson.

" Can you tell us, Mrs. Tomlinson, what you were doing when you heard the first scream ? "

" Well—I was cooking."

" Can you tell us what you were cooking ? "

" Well, I was boiling some eggs."

What was there amusing about boiling eggs ? Why should

people smile ? Yet there was something incongruous about Mrs. Tomlinson speaking of her little domestic tasks while he waited to know if he would be sentenced to penal servitude.

" And when you heard the first scream did you leave the eggs ? "

" Well, no. You see, they were nearly done. The hourglass thing was just running out. So you see—you see——"

" Please go on, Mrs. Tomlinson. There is nothing to be ashamed of about doing your domestic duties properly."

" The eggs were for my dinner and the children's, so I didn't want them to get hard-boiled. So I turned the gas out and turned the eggs out of the water."

" How many eggs, Mrs. Tomlinson ? "

" Three."

" And you began to do this when you heard the first scream ? "

" Yes."

" And having turned out the gas and taken three eggs out of the water, what did you do then ? "

" I ran to the front door."

" And what did you hear ? "

" I heard a crash."

" A crash ? "

" A crash of glass."

" Was that after you opened the front door ? "

" No, before. Just before."

" And can you tell us about the screams at that time ? "

" They stopped."

" Altogether ? "

" They stopped when I heard the crash."

" And there were no more screams ? "

" Yes. There was one. That was after I'd opened the front door and seen—and seen——"

" Thank you, Mrs. Tomlinson. We know what you saw. You have given your evidence as a member of the public with a public duty should do."

Mrs. Tomlinson stepped down. Now came Inspector John Fowler. He gave his evidence just as before, in a flat tone without any stress at any point. He showed in his manner that he looked upon himself as part of the machinery of the

law, a cogwheel that turned; he had a duty to do in the
enforcement of the law, and that duty he did without animus,
and in accordance with the instructions regarding procedure
with which he had been familiar since he became a probationary
constable. Once again in his flat tone he repeated, " The
prisoner said, ' I did it ' " and " The prisoner made no
reply."

Sir Frederick was asking questions again.

" This mark on the wall where the dressing-table ornament
struck. How deep was it ? "

" Between three-quarters of an inch and one inch deep.
The wallpaper was broken."

" So the ornament must have been thrown with considerable
force ? "

" Yes."

" As hard as a man could possibly throw it ? "

" Certainly very hard."

" You found fragments of glass all over the room ? "

" I found a fragment in the far corner, and another under
the wardrobe."

There was the same flat tone. The inspector spoke as a
man interested only in the administration of justice, perfectly
ready to give testimony on the one side as on the other.
But—but—should he be anxious to obtain a conviction, that
attitude would be very effective with a jury.

" Now as regards the rest of the room. What appearances
did it present ? "

The inspector told the court in his toneless way. Presumably
it was the incongruity between that tone and the content of
his words that raised the titter that went round the court
when he said, ' The bed was in disorder '. The judge looked
up sharply and the titter was cut off in the middle. The
inspector spoke about the hand-mirror on the floor.

" The mirror will be mentioned in evidence again. What
about the dressing-table ? "

The inspector described how the long lace mat was dangling
over the end.

" The appearance was consistent with someone standing
by the window trying to pick up the mirror and being pushed
away as he did so ? "

" It could be. Either that or——"

" Yes, Inspector. Now tell us what you saw beside the bed."

The inspector told about the folded clothes, the artificial leg. Another titter began and was cut off.

" These appearances left you in no doubt about what had been going on in the room ? "

" Not in any doubt."

" Thank you."

The police sergeant confirming his inspector's evidence. No questions were asked him. Now the police surgeon describing the fracture of the base of the skull and the lacerations.

" I am a Member of the Royal College of Surgeons and Licentiate of the Royal College of Physicians of London. I was called to 53 Calmady Road . . ."

His manner was as passionless as the police officers'. Coates was asking the same question as Cane had asked in the magistrate's court. No, there was no sign of any other injuries. No marks of blows.

" Now as regards the lacerations. You said at the preliminary hearing they were consistent with the deceased having fallen through the window ? "

" Yes."

" The lacerations were confined to the back of the body ? "

" To the posterior surface of the body and limbs."

" Any in the front ? "

" No."

" If the deceased had gone head first through the window would you expect to find lacerations in the front of his body ? "

" Yes. Very likely."

" And the lacerations on the buttocks ? Could you describe them more closely ? "

" They were five in number, three on the left buttock and two on the right. They were made from above downwards, and were considerably deeper at the lower ends than at the upper ends."

" So, assuming the deceased fell backwards through the window, it appears that he dragged his buttocks over the points of glass in the lower edge of the frame ? "

" Yes."

" That is more consistent with a man staggering back against the window and overbalancing through it than with a man violently hurled against the window ? "

" I would not like to swear to that."

" But otherwise would you not expect to find lacerations in the upper part of the trunk and not in the lower part ? "

" I suppose that might be the case."

" Thank you. Now just one more point. You heard the evidence given about the height of this window from the ground ? "

" I know it is a little over ten feet."

" Would you normally expect a fall from a height of ten feet to be fatal ? "

" No. Not unless——"

" Not unless the victim happened to fall in just this way, vertically onto the top of his head ? "

" I suppose so."

" Can you give us an idea of the chances against a fall in that one particular attitude ? "

" I think it would be unlikely. Of course the deceased——"

" And otherwise the deceased might have escaped with minor injuries ? "

" He might have concussion——"

" Minor injuries ? "

" Well, yes, you might call them minor injuries."

" Thank you."

Now the judge was speaking and everyone was standing up.

" Come this way."

Down the stairs again; a group of other prisoners from the other court rooms, guarded by warders, eyed him curiously, just as he had been eyed in Brixton Prison, as the man with human blood on his hands, the man who faced penal servitude for life. Somebody called out something to him, and a warder clucked with annoyance at this unsettling encounter and hustled Randall into a cell—the first time that Randall had been treated with anything other than mechanical correctness. They brought him dinner, some kind of anonymous minced meat spread with mashed potatoes, and a helping of cabbage whose wateriness was almost welcome as a help to the sawdust-like dryness of everything else. Randall ate two mouthfuls and pushed the tray aside, turned back to it, knowing that it was foolish not to eat, and forced down two more mouthfuls before he decided it was hopeless. The cell door opened.

" Mr. Burdon wants to see you."

The visitors' room here was much like the one at Brixton, with a glass panel in the door through which they were watched by an officer. It was interesting to see the change in Burdon; he was almost animated, there was an almost human gleam in his stony dark eyes.

" Coates made every point there was to be made," he said. " I thought he was good."

" I suppose he was," said Randall.

" There's only your wife still to give evidence for the prosecution."

Randall did not, could not, make any reply to that. It was still painful to hear those words ' your wife '; it was still disturbing to think about Muriel.

" Then Coates makes his opening speech for the defence," went on Burdon, " and then he calls his evidence. There'll only be time just to begin it. You will be called first, of course."

" Yes," said Randall.

There was no point in discussing that again. The question as to whether he should or should not give evidence on his own behalf had been settled weeks ago.

" You're feeling all right ? " asked Burdon.

Randall felt the usual dull resentment at being sized up —he could guess that Burdon had come for the express purpose of seeing how he was standing the strain—but he smothered it and answered truthfully.

" Yes, I'm all right."

" Good," said Burdon.

Back into court again, up the stairs and into the dock— the dock; he had not formulated that word in his mind before this. Stand up for the judge, sit down again.

" Muriel Heythorpe Randall."

That flutter in the court again. Muriel wearing black, as before, with another black hat down over her eyes, a red buckle in the front of it being the only spot of colour. She was walking slowly, giving the impression of sickness or fatigue. Just as before, Randall felt his heart beat quicker at the sight of her, and, just as before, it could not be explained. It was not hatred or love, it was not fear. It was a mere increase in tension, but it made him swallow several times, and made his hands, lying in his lap, sweat a little in the palms and intertwine nervously. Somebody was standing up making some sort of request on Muriel's part, and the judge, after a sharp question, granted it. A chair was brought for Muriel and she sat down in it, her manner still indicating weakness. This time she did not spare a glance for Randall. And it was strange that Randall could look on her without any conscious emotion, that he could be quite neutral in his feelings towards her, and yet feel this disturbing rise in his blood pressure. Now the prosecuting counsel was asking her questions, drawing her out. It was just the same evidence as before. She had screamed and closed her eyes. The deceased had shouted 'Keep back'. There had been a crash of glass, and she had uncovered her eyes in time to see the accused rushing at her saying 'You next'. Then she dodged him and ran from the room. Muriel said all this in a somewhat mechanical tone, and she dropped a little in her chair. Coates was rising to cross-examine her; from his point of vantage in the dock Randall could see the questioning, rather hostile look which Muriel directed at Coates as she waited.

" Your husband's return was quite unexpected ? "

" Of course it was."

" You mean ' yes ' ? "

" Yes."

" When he left you were under the impression that he would not be home again until late afternoon ? "

" Yes."

" Was it his suggestion that he should go out on that particular day ? "

" He went out every day, of course."

" And on this day ? "

" He had a date to go and see Mr. Phillips about his invention."

" Now, please. Will you answer my question ? Was it his suggestion that he should go out for the day ? "

" I don't know what you mean."

" Very well, let's put it another way. Did your husband suggest staying at home on this particular occasion ? "

" He may have done."

" You mean ' yes ' ? "

" I suppose so."

" You mean ' yes ' ? "

" Yes, then."

Randall sitting watching her could have warned her. He could see the danger she was in. She was rating her abilities too high; she stood no chance whatever of being able to withhold or conceal evidence when Coates was questioning her and all the power of the law was supporting him.

" But it would have been exceptional if he had not gone out ? "

" On a weekday, yes."

" So this was an exceptional occasion ? "

" I suppose so—yes."

Now Muriel was looking at Randall at last, searching his face. He could only look back at her, expressionless. He felt pity, but he could not let her guess it.

" Can you tell us why ? "

" No ! "

" You have no idea why the prisoner made this unusual suggestion that he should stay at home with you ? "

" He didn't."

Coates looked over at the shorthand clerk, and up at the judge, and then back to Muriel.

" Two minutes ago you said he did. Did he or did he not ? "

" Oh yes. He did. I suppose he did."

" Was there a telephone in your house, Mrs. Randall ? "

" A telephone ? No."

" So that if he wanted to telephone and break his appointment he would have to go out and do so ? "

" Yes. Of course."

Muriel's confidence was visibly returning with this digression.

" And when he suggested doing this you persuaded him not to ? "

" I didn't persuade him."

" But we know he did not carry out his suggestion of breaking his appointment, don't we ? "

" Yes.   Naturally."

" So you mean he just changed his mind again without
any prompting from you ? "

" Yes."

" You're quite sure of that ? "

" As far as I remember, yes."

" What was it that caused him in the first place to make
the suggestion ? "

Muriel looked at him pitifully; and when Coates repeated his question it was with a strange new gentleness
in his voice.

" What was it ? "

" I told him I was going to have a child."

There was a buzz in court at that, but it died instantly
because Coates asked his next question without waiting.

" When the prisoner came into the bedroom was he
armed ? "

" No—I don't know."

" At least you don't remember seeing any weapon ? "

" No."

" And you screamed ? "

" Yes."

" May we take it, then, that you were startled rather than
frightened ? "

" I was frightened."

" What did the deceased do ? "

" The deceased ?   He jumped up."

" And stood by the window ? "

" Yes.   I suppose so."

" Your eyes were shut, or you covered them, and so you
did not see what he was doing ? "

" Yes,   That's true."

" We don't doubt that it's true.   But of course you heard
what was going on ? "

" Yes."

" You heard the deceased say ' Keep back ', and then you
heard the window smash, and then nothing more, so you
opened your eyes ? "

" Yes."

" There is evidence that at this time a dressing-table
ornament was thrown with considerable force and smashed

against the wall. You have not mentioned this in your evidence. You did not hear it ? "

" I expect I did."

" But you can't remember just when it happened ? "

" No."

" It was a time of great confusion, of course, and when you opened your eyes the prisoner was standing close by the window ? "

" Yes."

" And you got up and ran out of the room ? "

" Yes. He said——"

" You could still see that he had no weapon ? "

" Yes."

" He had nothing in his hands ? "

" No. I suppose not."

" You took refuge downstairs. The prisoner did not come downstairs after you ? "

" Not then——"

" We know that you had time to put on his trench coat which hung in the hall downstairs, also that he spoke to someone through the window. Do you agree that he did not pursue you downstairs ? "

" I suppose so."

" Had you quarrelled much with your husband before this incident ? "

Muriel waited before she answered. Randall, looking at her, could see that she was wondering whether it would be better to answer ' no ' or ' yes '.

" A little," she said, as a compromise. Perhaps it was the truth ; Randall could remember the little flare-ups incidental to life together.

" Only a little. So there could never have been any quarrelling over your relationships with other men ? "

Prosecuting counsel rose to his feet at that, and there was a brief thrust-and-parry between him and Coates, in the form of protest and explanations offered to the judge.

" Answer the question," said the judge.

" I will repeat it." said Coates as Muriel looked bewildered. " You had never quarrelled with your husband about other men ? "

" No. Of course not," said Muriel. It was plain that in

a strange way her middle-class mind was shocked at the
suggestion.

"You were careful never to give him any cause for
suspicion ? "

" Yes."

" So are you quite sure he said, ' Now I've got you ', when
he came into the room ? "

" Well—well—yes."

" If he had no suspicion before he would not have said that?"

" He might."

" Don't you think that if he had laid a trap for you he
would have come into the room with a weapon ? "

" Oh, I don't know—I don't know."

" You were startled, or frightened, of course, at his entrance
at that particular moment. Perhaps you just thought he said,
' Now I've got you ' because that might be a natural thing for
him to say ? "

" Oh—perhaps."

" Thank you, Mrs. Randall."

Somebody helped Muriel out of the witness-box, and
Randall was so preoccupied in following her with his eyes
that the words, ' That is the case for the prosecution,' cut
across his thoughts and he only looked round in time to see
prosecuting counsel sit down and Coates stand up.

" May it please your lordship. Members of the jury . . ."

Coates, too, was telling the jury about the law regarding
homicide. Just as prosecuting counsel had done, he was
turning to the judge every now and then with the utmost
deference, but in addition he was alluding sometimes to
' his learned friend here ' and indicating prosecuting counsel
as he did so with a wave of his hand. He was speaking gravely,
composedly and forcefully.

" But the evidence you will hear, ladies and gentlemen of
the jury, indicates something far different. . . ."

There was that word ' adultery '. Randall remembered how
he had thought of it when he was marching out of the Belgian
village after the armistice, after that night with the smith's
wife. It had flared up into his mind again when he stood at
the foot of the bed. Maybe if that other incident had never
taken place he would not have thought of that word then and
all its implications. Maybe . . .

" My learned friend here warned you against giving any weight to anything you may have heard of the ' unwritten law '. I add my warning to his: cast anything of that sort out of your mind completely while the evidence is being presented to you."

As Coates finished speaking, there was a small debate in the court. The judge looked at the clock before giving his decision.

" Come this way," said the constable.

Randall found himself being directed across the court and into the witness-box. The testament was being put into his hand and the oath was being recited to him. There was movement and excitement in the court; he could feel it all round him. The man who had been kept as a pariah in prison, the man who had killed, was going to be questioned. People would soon hear the sound of his voice. There was Cane, handsome and efficient, and yet looking as if he were a long way away, standing up and speaking to him.

" How old are you, Mr. Randall ? "

" Twenty-two."

" And your occupation ? "

" I am a science student. An undergraduate of the University of London."

These were the questions and answers Cane had gone through with him before.

" On the morning of the twenty-third you had an appointment with Mr. Leonard Phillips ? "

" Yes."

" An appointment made two days previously ? "

" Yes."

" You kept that appointment ? "

" Yes."

" But you came home unexpectedly ? "

" Yes."

" Would you tell us how that came about ? "

It was going on. Randall told his story. He told the story of his own shame. More than a month ago Cane had seen his tortured face as he discussed it, had heard his protests with sympathy and yet without relenting.

" You'll have to say it sooner or later to the prosecution if you don't say it to me," Cane had said.

And now . . .

" Had you the least idea that your wife was being unfaithful to you ? "

" No."

" You were utterly surprised by what you saw ? "

" Yes."

" Too surprised to speak ? "

" Yes."

" You said nothing at all ? "

" No."

" What did the deceased do ? "

" He went across to the window."

He had hopped, on his one leg, an obscene and horrible sight, but Cane had tactfully recommended the use of the word ' went '. He had not said what was in his mind, but Randall had known that he felt there was no advantage in reminding the jury that Massey was a one-legged man. And Randall had agreed, and remembered to say it now; as he said it he remembered that letter—' fourteen years at least '.

" And this ornament only just missed you ? "

" Yes."

" What did the deceased do then ? "

Randall told the truth as far as he could remember it.

" Thank you, Mr. Randall."

Coates was looking at the judge, the judge was looking at the clock. Everyone who was seated stood as the judge rose and walked out through his private door. He had hardly passed through before the constable was at Randall's elbow with his ' Come this way '. In the absence of the judge everyone was free to move and to stare and to speak while Randall was being led through the body of the court—it seemed an endless journey—from the witness-box to the stairs down to the cells. Someone said ' Good luck, Randall ' and someone else said, ' Just wait till to-morrow ' in a spiteful tone. Burdon was already downstairs to speak to him.

" Are you feeling quite fit ? "

" Yes," said Randall.

" Unfortunate in some ways that the end of the day should come just now, between your examination and cross-examination. You never can guess how these things will affect a jury."

" I think it's a good thing," said Cane, appearing in time to hear this last comment. " The jury have all night to think about Randall's evidence under examination. It has time to sink in. The cross-examination won't."

" But it'll be fresh in their minds."

" We'll see," said Cane.

We'll see if Randall gets fourteen years, thought Randall bitterly.

The prison van, the crowded streets, the return to Brixton Prison, the notation in the registers of his re-entrance. Randall was conscious of glances darted at him betraying a keener interest in him even than usual—he was the man under trial, the man whose liberty was at stake, the man who to-morrow would have to stand in the box and submit to cross-examination, the man who to-morrow might be under a life sentence. Randall was sharply reminded of this again when the question of supper arose. There was a strange look on the warder's face. It might well be his last supper as a man awaiting trial. This warder, Randall realised, had seen hundreds of prisoners come and go. They had eaten their last suppers. They had paced the floor for their last night. Then they had gone, and had never returned, but had been borne away after sentence to imprisonment, to penal servitude—some of them doubtless to the condemned cell. The women in the estaminets in the rest areas in France had seen hearty young men in hundreds, eating their eggs and chips, drinking their beer and wine, on their last nights before going up the line again, to wounds or death. And at slaughter-houses one saw lines of sheep and cattle filing along to where the pole-axe awaited them.

But still in the morning it was necessary to shave very carefully, to brush the badly fitting blue suit and see that the dark necktie was straight; it was necessary to look tidy and respectable and in no way outlandish—that had been the word Cane had used when discussing this very point before the trial. Would properly parting his hair save him from fourteen years? It might, perhaps. That thought revived the cold nervousness which the simple routine of dressing and shaving had temporarily stilled.

The witness-box again; no formalities, no preliminaries this morning. Counsel for the prosecution standing up to ask him questions; robe and wig; off to one side of him Randall was aware of Burdon's white face, tense and anxious, but beyond these two he was aware of no one else in the court.

" You know that deceased had lost his leg in the war ? "

" Yes."

The question was asked in the same level tone as the prosecution had used in its opening speech. The facts, the truth, justice without any partisan spirit were what the prosecution sought, like a scientist testing the data on which might rest a new hypothesis.

" When he got up from the bed and went to the window was he wearing his artificial leg ? "

" No."

" Then how did he get to the window ? "

" He hopped."

He hopped, obscene and naked; Randall remembered it. Cane had advised against using that word, but the prosecution had forced it out of him.

" And he stood balancing on one leg ? "

The memory was piercingly clear. He had only to phrase it.

" He stood holding on to the end of the dressing-table, with his back against the window."

" He was some distance away from you ? "

" Two or three yards, I suppose. Three or four."

" Try to be exact, if you please."

" It must have been four yards."

" You said you rushed at him. Why did you ' rush ' at him ? "

Coates had cleared up that point for him, long ago, in Brixton Prison.

" I felt I was in danger from him."

" You felt you were in danger from a one-legged man four yards away ? "

" Yes."

It sounded different when the prosecution phrased it that way, but it was the truth.

" Do you agree that the deceased said ' Keep back ' ? "

" Yes."

" Doesn't that sound as if you were already attacking him ? "

" Yes."

That was the correct answer to that question, but the inference was incorrect.

" You said you had no intention of hurting him. You were not angry ? "

" No."

" Not angry at finding someone in bed with your wife ? "

This all sounded so different. The people in court saw the tortured figure in the witness-box, saw the white face, saw the anxious glance that he directed towards his solicitor. It could be guilt. Randall knew that he must keep his head and his dignity. He must cling to the truth.

" I was not angry at that moment," he said.

" You agree that you pushed the deceased out through the window ? "

" Yes."

" And that window was a considerable height from the ground ? "

" Yes."

" So that that action might cause serious injury ? "

" Yes."

" Was it by accident that he went through the window? "

" Hardly."

" You mean you intended him to go through the window ? "

" Not in the way you mean."

" There can only be one way of going through a window. You did not care if the deceased should be injured in his fall, or even by the broken glass ? "

" No." That was the truth again, but so different.

" The door was behind you, the deceased was in front of you. Was there anything to prevent you from turning round and walking out of the room ? "

" No."

Question and answer, question and answer, while Randall knew that every question and every answer misrepresented the truth. The dispassionate tone of the voice that seemed to be seeking the truth and only the truth was calculated to mislead. Unless—standing there in the witness-box, looking at the counsel for the prosecution far away as though through the wrong end of a telescope, Randall felt a new and strange wave of misgiving. Perhaps prosecuting counsel was right and he was wrong. Perhaps he had really intended to kill Massey. He floundered at his next answer.

" Could you speak up a little ? When you came downstairs you made no attempt to assist the deceased or to examine his injuries ? "

" No."

" Thank you." ·

It was over. At any rate it was over. He might be facing a sentence of penal servitude, but at any rate the cross-examination was finished. Randall stood for a moment and turned to leave the witness-box. But here was someone checking him, saying something. Randall caught the word ' re-examination '. He looked round him a little bewildered, and there was Coates on his feet again, one eyebrow a little raised, a smile on his lips.

" Just a little longer, Mr. Randall. You can give us a great deal more help. My learned friend suggested that you could have turned round and gone out of the room. The deceased was standing facing you ? "

" Yes."

" Expecting a fight ? "

" Yes."

" With close to his hand the powder bowl which he threw at you ? "

" Yes."

" And other objects within reach ? "

" Yes."

" So that if you left the room it meant ducking and running out in fear ? "

" Yes."

" Now, another point. When you came downstairs and into the street you found a group of people there ? "

" Yes."

" Standing by the body of the deceased ? "

" Yes."

" So they could have administered aid ? "

" Yes."

" You asked if anyone had sent for the police ? "

" Yes."

" Now that is all, Mr. Randall."

It seemed a long journey back to the chair in the dock.

Randall sat down, feeling very weary. Another witness was already being sworn.

"I am a detective constable in the Fingerprint Department of the Metropolitan Police. I received from Detective-Inspector Fowler an ebony hand-mirror, exhibit 1. I examined it for fingerprints. I also took prints from the hands of the deceased and from the hands of the prisoner. On the handle of the mirror I identified fingerprints and a palm print of the deceased. I did not identify any fingerprints of the prisoner."

"Thank you."

Here was Phillips walking up to the witness-box, handsome and yet frail. He looked across at Randall with a nod and a smile.

Yes, he had worked all the morning in question with the accused. It was an appointment made two days before. They had worked extremely hard and with great concentration. Accused had often worked with him before in the same way. He had been most helpful and ingenious. In the course of a break in the work accused had mentioned to him and to his wife that Mrs. Randall was expecting a child. Yes, accused had appeared very gratified.

"Whose suggestion was it that Mrs. Randall should be invited to lunch?"

"Mine."

"Had the accused said anything to put that idea in your mind?"

"No. Definitely not."

"Had Mrs. Randall ever lunched at your house before?"

"No."

"Had she ever been invited?"

"No."

"So this was an exceptional occasion?"

"Yes."

"Did the accused immediately fall in with the suggestion?"

"No."

"It seemed to call for some little persuasion before he agreed?"

"Yes."

"Were there any reasons advanced for this hesitation?"

"Mr. Randall seemed unwilling to cause my wife trouble."

" Any other reason ? "

" There was no telephone at Mr. Randall's house."

" And so—— ? "

" If Mrs. Randall were to come Mr. Randall would have to go and fetch her."

" And what was finally decided ? "

" It was decided that Mr. Randall should go and fetch her."

" You were under that impression when the prisoner left your house ? "

" Yes. I did not know what had happened until the police called at my house in the afternoon."

" Thank you, Mr. Phillips."

Mary Phillips now, lovely and calm and maternal, with a smile for Randall, too. She was only questioned briefly, but everything she said confirmed the evidence her husband had given.

" Thank you, Mrs. Phillips."

Another smile for Randall before she left the witness-box.

" That is the evidence for the defence, my lord."

The judge was looking at the clock. Apparently it was his job to decide on the intervals in the trial, to adjourn for lunch at a time when it did not break too seriously into the course of the trial, just as at a cricket match they might have lunch a few minutes early if an innings should end just at that time. He rose, and everyone rose respectfully.

" Come this way," said the constable when he had disappeared.

This was early. Down below things were quiet, as none of the other courts had as yet adjourned. The warder there clucked with annoyance again at seeing Randall enter with his escort. There was no food ready for him.

" And Partington's quick over his lunch, too. Digestion like an ostrich. You may be out o' luck to-day, mate."

Out of luck; he might be sentenced this afternoon to fourteen years. The cell door clicked behind him. But he had his lunch, after all. A slice of bully beef and boiled potatoes. He actually managed to raise a wan smile at that, for the last time he had eaten bully beef was at the Crystal Palace while undergoing demobilisation, and then, having eaten bully beef on a majority of the days of his three years in the army, he had sworn never to eat it again. He had told Muriel so, and Muriel had respected his wishes and had never offered it to him. Muriel; he wished he had not thought of her at that moment. And to-day, with the evidence all given, with nothing left depending upon him, no one came near him during the lunch-time. Coates and Burdon and Cane were presumably discussing the speech Coates was to make. Or they might just be lunching well. The door was unlocked.

" Come this way. Better hurry."

Those last two words were at least a variation; the warder breathed heavily as he led Randall up the stairs. Apparently Mr. Justice Partington had taken even less time than expected over his lunch. Up the stairs and into the dock, where he was to hear his fate. Everyone stood while the judge entered. He sat down, wasting no time, and glanced across at Coates, who stood up.

" Members of the jury, the time is approaching when you will have to give your verdict——"

Coates was speaking quietly, but there was power and force in his tone. There was none of the coldness of the prosecuting counsel.

" The prisoner had just been dealt the worst blow a man may receive in his life. He had just encountered, without warning, the clearest and most shocking proof that his wife was unfaithful to him. Members of the jury, I must ask you to bear that fact in mind while you weigh the evidence. I am not reminding you of it, be quite sure of this, in order that you may think the deceased met with the fate that he deserved. My learned friend here and myself have both told you that there is no unwritten law, and if my lord should consider it necessary I expect he will tell you the same. But you must remember that the prisoner at that moment had been subjected to a terrible shock. He stood in a daze. The deceased was quicker-witted. There was no doubt in the deceased's mind as to what might happen. . . ."

The court was utterly silent. Every eye save the judge's was upon Coates; the judge was making rapid notes.

" . . . the prisoner was unarmed. He had not stopped and

bought a weapon on his way home, he had not picked up
the poker before he came upstairs, he did not even pick up
a chair to defend himself. . . ."

Coates was holding a little pack of white cards in his
hand. At this point he slipped off the top card and put it at
the bottom, and went on after a glance at the next.

" The deceased had thrown the powder jar. He now
seized the hand-mirror. The fingerprints prove that, just as
they prove the prisoner never touched it. An ebony hand-
mirror can be a dangerous weapon in the hands of a powerful
and desperate man. . . ."

Another change of cards.

" You will have noticed a direct contradiction between
the evidence given by the prisoner and that given by his
wife. I need not emphasise to intelligent people the importance of the point. Where evidence conflicts, it is well to
remember the other evidence. You heard what Mr. and
Mrs. Phillips had to say. They offer the clearest proof that
the prisoner's return was quite accidental. You heard Mrs.
Randall herself say that her husband had never suspected
her. But she swore that he said ' Now I've got you '. He
swears he said nothing at all. Think of the conditions under
which he had returned, think of the shock he had just
received, and decide for yourselves who is speaking the
truth."

Another change of cards.

" We are fortunate in being able to measure almost exactly
the time that elapsed between the prisoner's entrance into
the bedroom and the deceased meeting his death. You
will remember Mrs. Tomlinson's evidence. She heard the
first scream, the scream that greeted the prisoner when he
opened the door upon the guilty couple. . . ."

Horror. Horror. To stand at that door and see what
he saw.

" . . . and before she reached the front door she heard
the crash of the window. No time for a long quarrel. . . ."

Coates's voice was more gentle still. He took one final
glance at the top card in his hand before transferring it to
the bottom.

" The prisoner, just arrested by a police officer, says ' I
did it '. Is this what a man would say who had just planned

a cunning surprise? Members of the jury, you must
apply . . ."

Point by point Coates was proceeding with his argument,
carrying the jury along with him. He had a beautiful speaking voice, Randall suddenly realised, but he was not calling
attention to its beauty; the reasoning was close, but it was
on a level where it could be easily understood; there was
an appeal to passion and to sentiment, but it was hidden
beneath the quiet tone and the logical argument. A phrase
suddenly came up into Randall's mind; ' the art that con-
ceals art '. Coates was concealing his art. The jury must be
under the impression that he was presenting a case about
which there could only be one decision, a decision which
they could reach by the mere exertion of common sense,
and yet Coates was actually doing nothing of the kind.
Along with the carefully marshalled arguments he was
creating a state of mind. Even that quick change of the
white cards was effective; the first two or three changes had
occurred when Coates had scored a definite and simple
point. Now he had only to change cards to leave the jury
under the impression that the next point had been adequately
dealt with.

" . . . if you believe this you must acquit him, and that is
what I ask you to do in this case."

Coates had finished, on a quiet note, a note of complete
conviction. Randall could even forget his own peril for a
moment in his admiration of the man. But here was counsel
for the prosecution getting to his feet; now began the calm
cold voice of accusation.

" . . . my learned friend has told you . . ."

The jury were paying full attention. Randall looked at
them anxiously. Surely if Coates's speech had been as
convincing as it seemed they would not listen quite so closely?

" . . . the point to be remembered is that the deceased
died by violence, and admittedly at the hands of the
accused. . . ."

This was like a douche of cold water. Was it fair to say
things like that ? Randall looked at Coates to defend his
interests, but Coates made no sign. Randall felt panic.
There had been a time in the Salient when Jerry had formed
a habit of shelling the battalion front methodically every

noon, starting at the right hand and continuing along to the
left; Randall had known fear as he waited while the explosions and the fountains of earth had drawn nearer and nearer.
He knew fear again now, the same kind of fear.

" . . . the deceased was a man with one leg. . . ."

Would they never omit that point?

" . . . if you consider the accused should have known . . ."

This must be the end of everything.

" . . . a verdict which is consistent with justice."

At any rate it was over. Randall found himself shivering
a little. Now the judge was laying aside his pen and
straightening his papers. He looked up and Randall met his
eyes. They were cold eyes under white eyebrows. Dispassionate eyes. Merciless eyes. This was a judge who could
have no pity. Randall remembered Burdon's peculiar
manner when he said that Mr. Justice Partington was trying
the case. This was a judge who would know no sympathy,
who would punish terribly, who would look upon an
accused person as someone to be dealt with sternly, who
thought of the whole world as criminal and of himself as
selected by destiny to punish it. Until this moment Randall
had gained no insight into the mentality of the judge; the
latter had sat above the trial, Olympian, seemingly dispassionate even indifferent, but now he was descending
to give the affairs of these mere mortals the necessary
straightening out which would set them moving in the
direction he desired. Inside that exterior of sublime superi-
ority there was something which would pulsate with a
strange pleasure when the time came to select a punishment, some hidden inner creature which would know obscure
gratification at uttering the words which would send a young
creature to fourteen years of prison, fourteen years of shaven
head and grotesque uniform and cold prison walls.

" Members of the jury, these proceedings have been
selected for unusual notice in the press. I am sure you will
allow nothing you have read to influence your minds, and
that you will remember that you took an oath, when you
entered that jury box, to determine the matter according to
the evidence. And it is not for me, but for you, to decide on
the guilt or innocence of the prisoner. . . ."

There was no appearance of animus, no hint of hatred in

those dispassionate words ; the jury was being reassured, thought Randall, that if by finding him guilty they left the amount of punishment to the discretion of the judge there was no danger of anything untoward happening. The jury would be surprised if a savage sentence were to be awarded.

" . . . there were two people present at the time the deceased met his death. They give different versions of what was said then, and you may think the point is important. It is for you to decide who is speaking the truth and who is not, whether as the result of an honest mistake or by deliberate lying. It may occur to you that one of those two people has a special motive in trying to influence your opinion, while the other . . ."

The warder beside Randall drew in his breath sharply and changed his position uncomfortably. As the result of long experience he was (Randall thought) even more sensitive to what was going on than Randall was. Another phrase came into Randall's mind, picked up somewhere in a crime novel or in newspaper reading—' summing up dead against the prisoner '. That was what the judge was doing.

" . . . only if the man who kills is in immediate danger of death, and furthermore if he has done everything in his power to avoid the assault . . ."

Randall shifted his glance to the jury. The man with the beard, his eyes fixed on the judge, was nodding a little as if in agreement.

" . . . it is my duty to tell you what the law is, and the law regarding homicide has been defined . . ."

The judge's gaze did not waver. He kept those cold grey eyes on the jury, but no malignance appeared in them. They were as expressionless as the blank eyes of a statue.

" . . . you may consider a hand-mirror a deadly weapon, and if you do—using the same careful judgment as you use in your daily affairs—you may decide . . ."

Randall realised that the judge was choosing his words with the greatest possible care, and it dawned upon him that this was not merely because of their possible effect on the jury, but so that they could be read by other people without conveying an impression of bias. The significant pause, the slight wave of the hand, would never appear in print.

" . . . eleven and a half feet. You must judge for yourselves whether . . ."

Could he stand up and shout a protest against being subjected to this treatment ? No. He must sit still and make no sign at all; sit still and let no one guess at the cold fear mounting inside him.

" . . . the repulsive features of this case . . ."

Coates was sitting there, his eyes fixed on the judge. Perhaps he was learning as well as listening. Hatred for the careless implacable world rose in Randall's breast along with fear. Could he bear this ?

" . . . Please consider your verdict."

Dead stillness for a moment. The judge rising, the people standing, a wild buzz round the court.

" Come this way."

It had not been easy to rise, it was not easy to walk. The constable put out a hand to his elbow, but Randall shook it off as soon as he realised he was giving an impression of weakness. He had to step slowly, he had to think what he was doing, but he could walk down those steps unassisted. The interchange of glances between the warders down there; a pause for a space while it was decided into which cell he should be put. And hardly had the lock clicked behind him than he heard it reopen and the same repeated order.

" Come this way."

More significant glances between the warders. If the jury had reached a verdict so quickly, immediately after hearing that summing up, and following upon that speech for the prosecution, it could only be a verdict of guilty. Randall stood at the cell door. It was not easy. Those rats that the men in the trenches caught upon blankets spread with glue; they had screamed and struggled as the men approached to club them to death with entrenching-tool handles. He would not scream or struggle. He tried to keep the fear out of his eyes as he met the warder's glance. Slowly round the corner. Slowly up the stairs. He braced himself to enter the body of the court. Stand for the judge, who sat down at his bench, his white hand tapping almost restlessly

on the desk before him. Another glance from those cold
eyes. The jury were already coming in.

"Members of the jury, are you all agreed upon your
verdict?"

"Yes."

"Do you find the prisoner at the bar, Charles Lewis
Randall, guilty or not guilty?"

"Not guilty."

Had he heard it right? The court was in a buzz again, and
the judge was speaking sharply. A moment's silence again.

"You find him not guilty, and that is the verdict of you all?"

"Yes."

The buzz again. The cold eyes looked at him and looked
away.

"The prisoner is discharged."

Now there was confusion in Randall's mind. The judge
was saying something else, apparently to the jury, but
Randall did not listen to what was being said. The judge
was leaving the court; there was a moment's perfunctory
deference paid to him, and then the confusion in Randall's
mind was equalled only by the confusion in the room.
There was the same pleasurable excitement as in a class-
room on the last day of term at the moment the master
left, the same buzz, the same ecstatic hurrying to and fro,
the same carefree clearing up.

More than one stranger came and spoke to Randall.
Here was his father, holding out his hand and smiling.

"Congratulations, son."

His father looked very old and worn, and the hand which
Randall took was cold.

"All's well that ends well," said Burdon, joining them.

Coates, hurrying by, threw him a nod and a smile and
did not wait for Randall's thanks—Randall guessed that
he had other appointments to keep. Cane sauntered up, a
file of papers under his arm.

"It was Coates's cross-examination of Mrs. Randall that
did it," he said. "I thought it would."

An eager young man with a card.

"Can you let me have a few words on how it feels to be
acquitted?" he said.

Now a constable rolling up to them.

" If you please, gentlemen, would you mind leaving now ?
We have instructions to clear the court."

" We'd better go," said Burdon; there were other people
pressing towards the little group they made.

" We don't want anything to go wrong at the last minute,"
said Cane with a laugh and a jerk of his head towards the
door through which Mr. Justice Partington had disappeared.

They began to move towards the door at the back of the
court, where another constable was herding the people out.
There was a corridor beyond; Randall knew nothing of this
public route from the court to the outside world. In the
corridor there was a crowd waiting, and a babble of noise
arose from it as Randall appeared. Burdon beside him
halted at the sight of it.

" We can't go through there," he said. " Officer, can you
take us out another way ? "

The constable sized up the situation.

" Come this way, please," he said.

Please ! It was a tiny monosyllable which marked the
enormous difference between the man under arrest and the
free citizen. A short colloquy between the two police officers,
and then—

" Down here, please."

Down those self-same stairs, down into the hidden hall
below; a glimpse of prisoners under the guard of warders—
even the sound of keys and the clicking of cell doors. Randall
steeled himself to make a joke.

" I know my way through here."

Burdon laughed shortly and politely and no one else
appeared to have heard.

" I'll leave you now," said Cane. " Good-bye."

A nod all round and he was gone.

" Come this way, please."

Down the next flight of stairs and out into the sunlight
beside that grim door through which he had entered this
morning—was it only this morning ?

" I suppose you want a taxi, sir ? " said the constable.

" Yes, please," said Burdon.

Randall's father had said nothing since his first greeting,
but had walked along with them, frail and shrunken, without
a word. He spoke up now.

" You'll be coming home to us, I suppose, son ? "

Those were the words that marked the end of one era and presumably the beginning of another, but Randall was only conscious of the end and not of the beginning. Until then he had been content to be free, to have the shadow of fourteen years of penal servitude lifted from him. Now he looked ahead and could see nothing. Homeless and penniless, friendless and without a future. Muriel was not waiting for him at Calmady Road. He would never be able to attend classes again at the University. There would be reproach in the eyes of his sisters and his brother. Was there anything left at all ? He did not believe there was. A taxi was drawing up in front of them and they all climbed in.

" Go over Waterloo Bridge," ordered Burdon. " We'll direct you from there."

Out into the traffic, out into the noise of the buses.

" Quick work," said Burdon, pointing. A newsboy was yelling the news; people were surging round him handing over their pennies in exchange for his papers. There were the three posters of the three London evening papers, side by side.

' Randall Verdict ', said one.

' Randall Trial Result ', said the second.

' Unwritten Law Verdict ', said the third.

TWENTY

" YES," SAID GRAHAM. " It'll take a year or two, I grant you."

The keen eyes under the heavy eyebrows were watching Randall anxiously and noting that he was still showing the strain of the trial.

" Only a year or two ? " asked Randall bitterly.

" People *do* forget," replied Graham with great earnestness. " In a couple of years you could ask anyone, practically, ' Does the name Randall mean anything to you ? ' and he'd say ' No '."

" It's hard to believe that, judging by the state of things at present," said Randall.

Graham resisted the temptation to say, ' You're very young '.

" One sensation's replaced by another," he said instead. " To-day it's the Randall Manslaughter Case. To-morrow it will be the Elephant Murder, or something, and the next day it will be the Cradle Divorce Case. Nobody bothers to remember about them afterwards."

" Yes ? " said Randall.

" Even with your friends it'll be like that—with your acquaintances, I mean. Perhaps somebody'll say, ' Wasn't Randall mixed up in some lawsuit or other ? ' and somebody else'll say, ' I did hear something about it once. Can't remember what it was.' And that'll be all. Later on there won't even be that. People even die, you know. You'll notice that, as the years go on."

" No doubt," said Randall.

People died; Massey was dead. There was (as Randall noted in himself with some surprise) a certain amount of satisfaction in that. Nothing can terminate an illicit love affair as thoroughly and as definitely as the death of one of the lovers. Never again, never, would Massey give Muriel pleasure; never again would she enjoy him. And Massey— wooden leg and unemployment notwithstanding—had enjoyed life, had most certainly not wanted to die. Massey had been most amply repaid; so for that matter had Muriel been.

Graham saw the grim smile hovering about Randall's lips and wondered whether it was a good sign or not.

" Are you taking any action about divorce ? " he asked.

" Oh, hell," said Randall, " I don't know."

There was nothing that would bring back those headlines into the papers as effectively as would a divorce suit. Randall had learned much in the last two months. He had no literary gift and no gift for parody, but he could write those headlines now if he wanted to. ' Charles Lewis Randall Sues for Divorce.' ' Randall Manslaughter Trial Echo.' And the explanatory paragraph—' It will be remembered that Mr. Randall was tried and acquitted last year on a charge of manslaughter, when Richard Fanning Massey, the Sussex cricketer, who is now named as co-respondent, met his death at Mr. Randall's house.'

" You might consider taking all your medicine at one gulp," said Graham, " or not take two bites at one cherry."

" Can't be done," said Randall. " Burdon says it'd take a year at least—you have to wait six months at present to get a hearing for divorce."

That was part of the aftermath of war; so many people wanted divorces that, as Burdon had said, the calendar was full for months to come. Application for a divorce meant headlines now, when the suit was filed; headlines in six months when the case should be heard (and what headlines !) and headlines again in a year's time when the decree should be made absolute. And the evidence proving adultery would be perfect for reproduction in the gutter press.

" That certainly makes a difference," said Graham.

" You don't suppose I should ever want to marry again ? " said Randall.

" People do, you know."

" Not me," said Randall.

Graham knew enough not to attempt to continue to argue with a man of twenty-two on the subject of marriage.

" Besides," went on Randall, " there are some hellish complications."

It had been Burdon who had pointed the complications out.

" That child will be *your* child," Burdon had said.

" Mine ? "

" Yes."

Burdon had gone on to explain those parts of the law

which laid it down, logically and inexorably, that the paternity of a child conceived in wedlock must be attributed to the wife's husband if there had been access at all.

"Nothing you can do, and nothing Mrs. Randall can do, can alter that," said Burdon. "It's fundamental."

"My God!"

"The court would undoubtedly award you custody of the child," Burdon had continued. "I do not know if you would care to undertake that, but——"

Burdon's stony eyes, fixed upon Randall, had conveyed a frightful suggestion. It would be revenge, if Randall sought further revenge, to take Muriel's child from her. Why that should be frightful when Randall had never felt a single twinge of remorse at Massey's death could not be explained, but Randall had recoiled from the cruelty implied.

A halting sentence from Randall hinted at all this to Graham.

"It's your business, of course," said the latter, philosophically. "And if you don't want to there's nothing more to be said. Are you back at the University yet?"

"No."

He could face his friends; he could meet perfect strangers, but he could not force himself to encounter that part of the world that only thought of him as Randall of the unwritten law manslaughter.

"A pity, but I suppose it can't be helped. So you have no definite plans for the future?"

"No."

The future was utterly blank and featureless. Despair was beginning to make itself felt. An empty future of failure, and then of privation. It seemed that only the gutter awaited him. Graham looked sharply at Randall again, hesitated, and then spoke.

"I could make a suggestion, but I'm afraid of butting into your affairs——"

"I'd like to hear *any* suggestion. You're not butting in."

It had been Graham's kindly intervention that had brought Randall home on leave, and put him into a position to marry Muriel, but that had been only one of the myriad chances that had finally brought Randall here to Graham's office, penniless and without a future.

" Well——" Graham still hesitated.

" Well ? "

" Has the idea of America ever crossed your mind ? "

" America ? Good God, no ! "

Not for one single moment had he ever thought about the possibility of going to America. It was as likely as his going to Central Africa—less likely. Rum-running. Barbarism. Unfeeling success.

" Have you ever known any Americans ? "

" No. I can't really say that I have."

There were the two young officers who had come up the line on a visit to the battalion in 1917. Eager young men, anxious to learn—as if there was any chance of America building up an army comparable with those at that moment deciding the destiny of the world. Eager young men with outlandish intonations and a strange vocabulary; not merely eager but too eager. Randall had been showing them round his sector.

" Keep low here," he said. " Jerry has a sniper over there watching this point."

" A sniper ? "

Before he could be prevented, one of those eager young officers had stepped forward to look, and on the instant had come the bullet, hitting him between the eyes; the other officer would have shared his fate if Randall had not held him back. He had mourned over his dead ' buddy ', and the battalion had displayed a decent regret, but there had been a covert smile or two over the not-unexpected fate of the raw young subaltern entering into a war waged by veterans.

Randall could just remember those two young Americans; they were the only ones with whom he had ever had anything to do.

" You'd like Americans if ever you came to know them," said Graham.

" Perhaps I would," said Randall in polite agreement, but not thinking it at all likely.

" Business is dull over there at present," went on Graham. " But they're heading for a boom. By Golly, what a boom it'll be ! As soon as their election's over things'll start to move."

" Yes ? " said Randall politely again.

England in the depths of the depression of 1920 and experiencing a violent post-war reaction was not the place to discuss booms. And presidential elections in the United States were of hardly more interest to a young Englishman then than a famine in China. Randall was hardly to blame for not knowing that the presidential campaign now being waged would affect profoundly the lives of every inhabitant of the world, from Eskimos to Hottentots, for the next two generations to come at least. No more than twenty years from that day the office next door to the one in which he was sitting was going to be destroyed by a bomb, which conceivably would never have been manufactured, far less dropped, if the electorate of that barbaric country three thousand miles away had voted differently. But Randall sincerely believed, at the moment when he was talking to Graham, that bombs would never be dropped again, and in consequence he was the less likely to be interested in the efforts of Warren G. Harding and James M. Cox, whose names he had never seen written or heard spoken.

" You'd get a job all right in America," went on Graham. " Carnac would help you, I'm sure. Those pea-packing people in California would be interested."

" A job in America ? "

The thought of a job in America was more disturbing still. Randall had been brought up in a world where a job was something a young man obtained on completing his education and stayed with until retirement; his father had taught the same mathematics in the same school for thirty years.

" And at present you can still get into America all right," went on Graham. " But soon they'll be restricting immigration the same as we are doing here, and there's no knowing what they'll decide—Carnac was telling me about the legislation that's being brought in in Washington. This is the time to go, if you're going at all, from every point of view."

" I suppose you're right," said Randall.

" Actually they've started already keeping an eye on who comes in," said Graham, " but you're all right. ' Moral turpitude ' is the thing they worry about. But you've never been divorced. And as for this other thing—you were acquitted, found not guilty, so you're in the clear. You're an able-bodied young man and can read and write and are not likely to become dependent on charity. They'll let you in if you decide to go."

There was a certain brutality about that speech—possibly deliberately injected into the conversation by Graham—which brought Randall back to reality. He had been postponing taking decisions, excusably during the first few days while he had been recovering from the nervous exhaustion caused by the trial, but inexcusably since then, he knew. It dawned upon him that he had been pampering himself a little; even—and this made him feel ashamed— that he had been indulging in self-pity. The choices ahead of him might all be undesirable, but that was no excuse for not making any choice whatever. And here was Graham pointing out another undreamed-of possibility, and the more he thought about it the more favourably it compared with the other distasteful ones.

" You know, there's something in that idea," said Randall, meditatively.

His world had come to an end with the trial. He did not want to face any of the old associations. He was going to have to start again, in any case, build up new associations, put out new roots. He might as well do that in a new world as in the old—better, perhaps.

" I think you can take it as absolutely certain," said Graham, " that not a soul in the United States has ever heard of the Randall case."

" Do you really mean that ? "

" Yes. They have their own scandals there. And it's a big place—it's quite possible for a real juicy murder in the East not to get a single line in the West. Nobody'll ever have heard of you, except the people that know of you as a promising young inventor."

That was wonderful, even putting aside this nonsense about the promising young inventor.

" You can drop the ' Charles ' and call yourself ' C. Lewis Randall ' if you wanted to," went on Graham. " But that's a matter of taste—not really necessary."

A clean break, a clean slate, a fresh start. That would compensate at least in some degree for having to adjust himself to new surroundings and a new vocabulary. And if he were going to be a failure, if he were going to starve.

it might be better to starve in the unfamiliar streets of America than in the familiar ones of London, and it might be better to starve unknown to the father and mother and sisters and brother on whom he might find himself a sponging dependant if he were weak.

" You think Carnac would help me find a job ? " he said.

" I'm sure," said Graham.

In Randall's pocket was a letter. There was no real reason for him to think about it now—or perhaps there was. He had shown it to no one. His mother had given it to him when the postman brought it, and had followed him with her eyes when he went away to read it privately, and had since then looked at him questioningly without venturing to ask what it was that Muriel had written to him. The letter was still in his pocket, like a cancer in his breast.

' You never were any good,' wrote Muriel. ' You were only just a kid always. That day you were demobbed and met me off the tram I thought so as soon as I saw you. I thought you looked awful. I was used to a real man like Harry and not a kid like you in cheap clothes. You didn't ever grow up either. You went to your classes and you read your books. You wouldn't have been any good as a husband to anybody. Dick was worth ten of you and I used to tell him so. You were always such a fool. You used to let anybody cheat you. I'm glad I'm free of you and I hope you'll be like Dick and never get a job after what has happened. I hope your damn mother likes it. You might just as well have gone to prison and I hope the time will soon come when you wish you had.'

It was the letter of a woman mad with rage. A woman, too, who had been booed in the streets by an indignant mob—a woman even who might be a little unbalanced because of her pregnancy; but that letter hurt. If he were going to be a failure he would much rather Muriel did not know about it.

Randall's reaction was a healthy one. Despite all he had learned during the last two months (and that was a great deal) he was not quite introspective enough to take note of these reactions, but he might have been gratified if he had. Mortifying flesh does not change colour when pinched or irritated, but healthy flesh flushes red. Randall was

sufficiently recovered by now to give a positive response
to the pin-pricks of Muriel's letter. He would confound her.
The simplest way would be to make a fortune, to become
a towering success. There seemed to be small enough chance
of that, but he could estimate the chances against its happening
in England better than he could the chances against it in
America. And, by George, Muriel had always wanted to
travel, to see foreign countries; he had laughed at her when
they had discussed it, and had said that his trips to the
Continent in 1917 and 1918 had cured him of any desire for
foreign travel. America—skyscrapers, wealth, luxury—had a
special appeal for Muriel. And Graham had mentioned
California. Sun-soaked beaches, the blue Pacific, Hollywood
and film stars; Muriel would give her front teeth to see those.
She would be green with envy if she heard he had gone to
California—and if he were to go she would hear all right, he
guessed, for they had enough mutual friends still to make that
possible. Five minutes ago the thought of ever going to
America had not occurred to him. Now it seemed perfectly
possible. Now it was even attractive.

" I don't think I'd mind going at all," he said, and he
meant that he would like very much to go.

The river of time was whirling him along. Chance eddies
had flung him here; chance eddies had flung him there. The
broad river had a myriad channels, and now an eddy was
parting him from the other flotsam with which he had been
circling and was pushing him far over into another channel
altogether. There he might circle, there he might come into
contact with other flotsam, but always he would be hurried
along, down the smooth reaches, over the cataracts until at
last he would be cast ashore and the river would hurry along
without him.